"I WANT YOU TO
I INSIST

Verity, Lady Talbot, Countess of Rushland, looked stunned, appalled. Miles hadn't expected her to be happy about his proposal. That was why he had planned everything so carefully, so she would have no way out.

Her chin came up, and she arched one fine, aristocratic brow. "You *insist* upon it?"

"That deed of yours isn't worth the paper it's printed on. If you refuse my offer, you won't have a farthing to your name."

"I concede such a marriage might help me, Miles. What do you hope to gain from it?"

"You," he said in a silky voice. "In my bed."

HIGH PRAISE FOR JOAN JOHNSTON
Winner of *Romantic Times* Best Western Author of the Year Award and Best Western Series Award
AND HER PREVIOUS BESTSELLING NOVELS

THE INHERITANCE

"With her usual expertise for finding just the right balance of poignancy and humor, Joan Johnston delivers a delightful romance peopled with engaging characters who will surely steal your heart."—*Romantic Times*

"WELL-WRITTEN . . . A TREMENDOUS TALE . . . THE CHARACTERS ARE ALL FIRST-RATE."—*Affaire de Coeur*

OUTLAW'S BRIDE

"Intrigue and passion, combined with a tender love story, make this one delicious, and the subplots promise us closer looks at her riveting characters in future books."—*Rendezvous*

"*OUTLAW'S BRIDE* is a very amusing and imaginative romp that has the Joan Johnston stamp of excellence all over it . . . A HIGHLY RECOMMENDED TREAT."—*Affaire de Coeur*

KID CALHOUN

"4+ Hearts! Powerful and moving . . . Joan Johnston has cleverly merged the aura of the Americana-style romance with the grittier Westerns she has written in the past, making *KID CALHOUN* into a feast for all her fans. This irresistible love story once again ensures Ms. Johnston a place in readers' hearts and on their 'keeper' shelves."—*Romantic Times*

"UNFORGETTABLE . . . A TOUCHING TAPESTRY."—*Affaire de Coeur*

"This most enjoyable Western is packed with spunky women, tough men, rotten bad guys and ornery kids . . . just the ingredients for a fine read."—*Heartland Critiques*

"This story has surprises at every turn . . . and it's all pulled together with Ms. Johnston's special blend of humor. Plenty of action and adventure to keep you entertained, this is a top-notch Western romance with sparkling characters and dynamic dialogue."—*Rendezvous*

Dell Books by Joan Johnston

After the Kiss
The Barefoot Bride
The Bodyguard
Captive
The Inheritance
Kid Calhoun
Maverick Heart
Outlaw's Bride
Sweetwater Seduction

JOAN JOHNSTON

A DELL BOOK

Published by
Dell Publishing
a division of
Bantam Doubleday Dell Publishing Group, Inc.
1540 Broadway
New York, New York 10036

ISBN: 0-440-21762-8

Printed in the United States of America

Published simultaneously in Canada

December 1995

10 9 8 7 6 5

OPM

MAVERICK
HEART

Prologue

LONDON, ENGLAND 1853

She could hear him pacing in the hall, the sound of his Wellington boots echoing off the high, second-story ceiling of the London town house. When he reached the end of the hall he slapped his riding whip against his buckskins, turned, and marched back the other direction. She opened her mouth to beg her maid, Jenny, to close the bedroom door, but her throat was so parched her voice cracked before coherent sound emerged. She gripped the bedsheets as another pain racked her belly.

Verity, Lady Talbot, Countess of Rushland, bit her lip until she tasted blood, writhing as she labored to expel the child, unwilling to scream because that would bring him back into the room.

She didn't want him here. She wanted another man, the child's father.

The pain passed, as many others had over the

previous afternoon and interminable night, leaving her exhausted, enervated, and on the verge of tears. Yesterday she had turned eighteen. Today she would become a mother.

Dawn's pinkened fingertips steadily crawled their way over the windowsill. The smell of burned wax assailed her nostrils as Jenny blew out the guttering candle beside her bed before hurrying down to the kitchen for more hot water.

Miles. Where are you? Why aren't you here? I'm so sorry. I made a mistake. If only I could undo it, I would.

Leah, the elderly, white-haired nurse who had watched over Verity since her mother had died giving birth to her, patted Verity's forehead with a cool, damp cloth, then pressed it against her cracked lips. "There, there, sweeting. Don't try to speak. Save your strength. The babe cannot be long now in coming."

"The earl—" she rasped.

"Your husband is pacing the hall, anxiously awaiting his heir," Leah said with a soothing smile. "I must say, his lordship is impatient to become a father. But, after all, when a man's heir is about to be born—"

"Please. Don't say any more."

Verity closed her eyes and forced her mind away from thoughts of her child's father. Miles Broderick—Viscount Linden since his elder brother's death nine months ago—was lost to her. She was married to Chester Talbot, Earl of Rushland. There was no turning back.

At least Chester had no inkling of the truth. She hadn't realized she was with child when she married the earl, believing, foolishly, that her lack of courses during the weeks before her marriage was merely the result of anxiety and unhappiness. Else she would have found some way out of the marriage, no matter what hardship it caused her badly dipped father to lose the generous settlement the earl had paid to have her.

Verity forced back the self-pity and summoned righteous anger. Because, when all was said and done, it was not her father's debts that had forced her into marriage, it was Chester's threats against Miles.

It was amazing to think a man as young as Miles—he had turned one and twenty over the past summer—could have earned such a deadly enemy. Verity knew the enmity was long-standing, dating to the days when both boys had attended Eton. When Chester had attempted to bully Miles, the smaller, slighter boy had beaten him in a bout of fisticuffs. Humbled and humiliated, Chester had proceeded to make Miles's life at Eton a living hell. He had continued his malicious behavior when the two boys attended Oxford and was still at it years later.

She had asked Miles if there was nothing he could do to cry friends with Lord Talbot. Miles had shaken his head and said, "He will not have it. He must beat me. It is not in him to give up."

"Could you not let him win once?" Verity had asked. "Perhaps if the challenge were gone . . ."

Miles had shaken his head. "He would only become more brutal. For such as he, it is the fear and pain of his victim that give joy, not the defeat itself."

Chester had told her, without a trace of guilt or remorse, that he was responsible for the carriage accident that had caused the death of Miles's elder brother, Gregory, and torn the flesh on the right side of Miles's face to the bone. Chester had promised he could end Miles's life just as easily as he had ended Gregory's if she continued in her refusal to marry him.

"Believe me," he had said. "I will arrange Miles's death so no suspicion will fall upon me. Do not think you can warn him. I will simply wait for a time when his guard is down and kill him."

The strange look in his yellow eyes, a sort of reptilian blankness, had made her shudder. Oh, yes, she had believed him.

And married a monster.

It was too late for regrets. What was done was done. Miles's child would bear another man's name. And she was condemned to be Countess of Rushland for as long as Chester Talbot lived.

Verity moaned and threw her head from side to side as a vise gripped her belly. She suddenly felt the urge to push. When she did, the pain was excruciating. "Leah! It hurts!"

"Yes, lovey," Leah crooned as she made preparations for the coming child. "There is pain before the joy. Soon you will have the babe safe in your arms."

Tears seeped from Verity's closed eyelids as she panted to catch her breath. There was no respite before her body was besieged again. She groaned in agony as rough fingers of pain clamped down on her belly to force the child out.

"It's coming. I have the head . . . and now the shoulders . . . Oh, lovey," Leah said excitedly. "It's a boy!"

Miles, we have a son!

"You've given the earl his heir!"

The sob of joy died in Verity's throat at Leah's pronouncement, and a knot of fear rose to take its place. God help her if Chester ever realized how she had cheated him. Her husband's heir did not bear a drop of Talbot blood. Tragic as that circumstance was, it was not nearly as heartbreaking to her as the knowledge that the man she loved would never be able to acknowledge his son. She sobbed again, but this time it was a wrenching sound of despair.

"Oh, lovey, don't cry," Leah said as she placed the swaddled babe in its mother's embrace. "Look here, what a fine boy he is!"

As Verity took her son in her arms, she felt such a swell of love that she thought her heart would burst. Here was the best part of herself, and of Miles.

I will make him a man worthy of his father, she vowed.

She hadn't realized Leah had left the room until she discovered Chester standing beside the bed. She looked up and saw nothing, no emotion at all, reflected back to her from his pale, golden eyes. That, in itself, was frightening.

"Let me see him."

She swallowed over the lump in her throat, lifted the birthing sheet away from the babe's head, and whispered, "Here is your son, my lord."

"Damn you to hell, woman!" he snarled. "Damn you to bloody, bloody hell!"

She shrank from the venom in his voice, clutching her son to her bosom.

He raked his whip across her shoulders once, twice.

She screamed in agony and terror, and Leah came running.

"My lord! My lord!" Leah cried. "What is wrong?"

Verity waited for the upraised whip to fall again, but her husband lowered it slowly until she could see his trembling hand, the whip clutched between his white-knuckled fingers.

"Get out," he said to Leah.

"But, my lord—"

"Get out and close the door."

Verity didn't dare make eye contact with Leah for fear Chester would turn his violence on the older woman, as well. "Go, Leah," she said.

Leah backed out of the room, closing the door with a quiet *snick* behind her.

Verity's heart leapt to her throat and pounded there, preventing her from begging for mercy.

How had he known the babe was not his? What had he seen?

She looked at the child again and gasped when she saw what had been hidden at first by the swaddling clothes.

The soft down on her newborn son's head was black.

She was blond, as was her husband. Miles had hair as black as night.

What had made Chester suspect the truth? She had said nothing, done nothing. Except she had not come virgin to his bed. She had wondered that he said nothing on their wedding night and been relieved when she believed her deceit had not been discovered.

He must have doubted all along. And waited, like the gambler he was, to see whether the child was undeniably his son. Or female, which would not have affected the succession. But he had lost his gamble.

She looked up at him, at the perfect features turned ugly by malice. "What will you do?" she asked.

"What would you have me do, my dear? Announce to the world that my enemy has cuckolded me? No thank you."

"But . . . How will you explain . . . ?"

"The dark hair on my son's head?" he said. "If anyone should be so rude as to ask, I shall blame it on my uncle, the Black Sheep of the family." He laughed, a harsh, unpleasant sound. "Now that I think of it, you will name the child Randal, after my uncle. Of course, I shall make certain there are no other blond-headed children with whom to compare my heir."

He used the butt of the whip to force her chin up. "I'll not take the chance of getting another son on you. I may have to acknowledge another man's brat as my heir, but I must draw the line at putting my own blood second to that of my enemy."

"But—"

"You need not worry that I will bother you further. I will find what comfort I may in other beds. Unless, of course, the boy should die . . ."

Verity clutched the babe close. "You wouldn't dare—" Her mind raced. What would she—could she—do if he tried to take the child from her?

"There is no need to resort to murder . . . in this case," he drawled. "I am quite sure there are other ways to make the son of Miles Broderick pay for the sins of his father."

Verity stared at her husband in horrified disbelief. "If you dare touch a hair on this child's head, I'll leave you. I'll run away—"

He grasped her hair and yanked until she cried out with pain. She grabbed at his wrist, but there was nothing she could do to save herself while protecting the child in her arms.

"You will stay exactly where I put you," he said. "Otherwise I will cry your perfidy to the heavens and make your precious son a bastard. Do not mistake me. I will betray your shame—and mine—if you force me to it.

"Enjoy your son, madam. At least I have the

satisfaction of knowing he is all you will ever have of Miles Broderick."

"Why did you insist on marrying me? Why won't you let me go?"

"I like to win," he said, releasing her hair and taking a step backward. "I think we must call this round a draw. I have robbed Miles of his firstborn son, as he has robbed me of my heir. However, I am still ahead in the game. So long as Miles is alive, I have the pleasure of knowing he dies a little every day at the thought of the woman he loves lying with her legs spread beneath me."

Verity gasped at his crudity, then remembered what Miles had told her about Chester. *It is the pain and fear of his victims he enjoys most.*

She forced the expression of revulsion from her face as Chester leaned close enough to whisper, "We will be the only ones who know the truth, won't we, my dear? Frankly, I don't care to have an icy fish like you in my bed. It is enough that I keep you from him."

Verity lowered her eyes. She would not give Chester the satisfaction of knowing how sick it made her feel to think she had coupled with such a beast.

She also saw no reason to inform Chester that he was wrong about the heartache Miles was enduring at the moment. Miles had suffered, to be sure. She had gone to see him the day the announcement she was breaking her engagement to him appeared in the *Times* and told him a string of lies to make him believe that she no longer loved him. She had explained how she was revolted by the horrible wound on his face and could never bear a lifetime of seeing him across the breakfast table. She had then announced that, since Chester had the most money and best title to offer her if Miles was no longer an eligible suitor, she had accepted the earl's proposal. In fact, they were to be married within the month, as soon as the banns were read.

She shivered as she remembered how the blood had drained from Miles's face, leaving the livid red scar outlined against his flesh. It hurt even now to think of the contempt in his voice as he ordered her to leave Linden's Folly, where he had gone to recuperate from his awful wound. He hadn't made a single argument to win her back that day. He hadn't once pleaded with her to change her mind before she turned and walked away. She didn't think she would ever forgive him for having so little faith in her love for him.

She knew it was foolishly unreasonable to have expected Miles to divine the terrible trouble she was in—that she was being coerced into a marriage she found abhorrent. If he had shown the least little bit of trust in her love, she knew she would have transferred her burden onto his shoulders that day at Linden's Folly and let him cope with Chester's threats in his own way. But in a moment of pique at his abrupt dismissal of her, she had turned and left him.

And sealed her own fate, and his, and that of their son.

She was certain Miles hated her now far more than he could ever despise his nemesis, Chester Talbot. It was very little comfort to know that because Miles believed she had betrayed him, Chester would be thwarted in his plan of lifelong revenge.

Verity focused once more on the handsome Talbot features before her but saw only evil. She spoke the first thoughts that came into her mind.

"I hate you. I find you an utterly revolting human being."

Chester slapped her hard with his open palm.

She resisted the urge to reach for her stinging cheek. She stared defiantly at her husband, blinking away the tears of pain that formed in her eyes.

I will not cry. I will not give him the satisfaction of seeing me cry.

"I cannot control what you think, my dear," he said in an acid voice. "But, by God, you will hold that shrew's tongue of yours when you are in my presence.

"Now I'm afraid I must bid you good-bye. I trust you will keep that brat of yours out of my way in the future."

Verity watched with relief and revulsion as the devil walked out her bedroom door, closing it with a *snick* behind him. She heard him speak briefly to Leah and listened to the muffled sounds of Leah's frantic reply. She waited, and when Leah did not come in, she knew her husband had forbidden her old nurse to attend her.

Miles, my love, I am so alone. How will I live the

long years chained by law to this animal? How will I live the rest of my life without your love?

It was a bitter bargain she had made to save Miles. And an even worse one she must endure to keep her son from being named a bastard. It was easy to hate Chester for his role in all of this. But she refused to let hate consume her.

Verity felt the babe nuzzling at her breast and looked down at the miracle in her arms. Here was a blessing among all her woes. Here was someone she could love wholeheartedly. She drew a forefinger across the babe's cheek. He turned instinctively toward her finger, rooting until she moved aside her gown and he found what he sought. She was surprised at how vigorously he took suck.

"You shall be strong, Randal Talbot, and clever and good. I shall not let the Earl of Rushland make of you a mean-spirited and bitter man. On my love for your father, I swear it."

She stared at the closed door. Chester's threats had worked. For her child's sake, she would stay. And because her child's future depended upon it, she would do nothing to reveal the secret of her son's birth to anyone.

Not even his father.

1

Wyoming Territory 1875

"Rand and I are going to ride ahead, Lady Talbot."

Verity, Lady Talbot, Countess of Rushland, shifted to a more comfortable position in her sidesaddle, wishing she could race across the vast Wyoming plains herself instead of plodding along beside a wagon pulled by oxen. Experience had stolen her freedom to do impulsive things. "Is it really wise to ride off without knowing what's ahead of you, Winnifred? You might get lost."

"How could we possibly get lost? You can see for miles and miles in every direction."

"Freddy is right, Mother," Rand said. "Besides, I promise to take good care of her."

"And I'll take good care of Rand," Freddy added with an impish grin.

Rand laughed. "Oh, I do hope so, minx. In every

way. And very soon. Our wedding isn't far off now."

Freddy, bless her heart, blushed a fiery red. She always did when Rand teased her about their wedding night.

It was easy to see why her son had chosen Lady Winnifred Worth as his bride. Freddy had stunning red hair, and her figure made an eloquent statement in a dark green habit trimmed in military braid. But Verity wasn't sure Rand knew what he was getting. Freddy—imagine a young Englishwoman preferring such a name—was as wild and brazen a young lady of seventeen as the Countess of Rushland had ever met.

Verity smiled inwardly. That was probably why she liked Freddy so much. The girl reminded her of herself at the same vulnerable age. Verity had grown up, grown staid, grown careful. Mistakes, she had learned to her regret, could be costly.

Verity dabbed at the perspiration on her forehead with a lace-trimmed handkerchief. It came away smudged with dirt. "I know the wagon is awfully slow—"

"And an utter dustbucket!" Rand said, brushing at kerseymere trousers that would have appalled his valet, if that man could have been persuaded to leave the hallowed shores of England and journey to the American West. The toes of his Hessians sported a layer of fine dust. "It's a good thing Robert can't see me now. He'd have apoplexy."

"You folks better stay close to the wagon," the teamster driving the wagon warned. "There's Injuns hereabouts. Sioux ain't all sittin' on the reservation eatin' agency beef, no sirree Bob. Chances are we'll butt heads with some hostiles."

"You've been threatening us with Indians ever since we left Cheyenne two days ago," Freddy said. "I haven't seen so much as an eagle feather, let alone a band of murdering savages. Just grass, grass, and more grass. I think you're making it all up!"

"Ain't no joke, lady. Usually don't see Injuns till it's too late," the teamster said. "Show 'em, Rufus."

The man riding shotgun for the teamster lifted his hat.

Freddy gasped. "What happened to your head?"

"Scalped," the man said flatly.

Freddy reached up to smooth the thick bun of auburn hair gathered into a net at her nape, then snugged the brim of her Spanish leghorn hat, brushing at the jaunty golden plume that skimmed her cheek. "They wouldn't dare touch one hair on a lady's head!"

"Ain't no ladies come this way much." The teamster spat a glob of tobacco juice onto the dusty trail that led north from Cheyenne to Fort Laramie. "You ain't safe just 'cause you're female, if that's what you're thinkin'. That red hair of yourn is sure to catch some Sioux buck's eye. He'd take your scalp same as ol' Rufus here."

"He'd have to catch me first!" Freddy kicked her Thoroughbred mare into a gallop, and with a shout of excitement, Rand spurred his stallion after her.

Verity barely managed to keep her dainty chestnut mare, the best of the three Thoroughbreds she had brought all the way from England as breeding stock, from bolting after them.

"Plumb crazy," the teamster said to no one in particular. "Giddyap there, Belle, you lazy good-for-nothing. Move it out, Henry, you dumb sonofabitch."

Verity winced at the bullwhacker's language, but forbore to correct him. Things were different in America. There was no social structure as she knew it. Even the lowliest bullwhacker considered himself the equal of an English lady. The fact that she was a countess, the widow of an earl, mattered not at all, only whether she had enough in her purse to pay the fare. Which, in her case, was becoming more and more questionable.

That was not to say that the men she had met in the West had not been deferential. She was given the same courtesy—and curious attention—as any other woman in this womanless land.

A bullwhip cracked over the team of oxen, accompanied by a plethora of expletives, but Verity couldn't see that the enormous, lumbering animals increased their pace even a little.

She looked worriedly toward the horizon where her son and his fiancée had disappeared over a rise in the grassy terrain. "How much chance is there, really, of their meeting up with Indians?" she asked the teamster.

"It's a gamble, lady." The bullwhacker spat into the dirt again. "Maybe they will, and maybe they won't. Out here, the stakes are high. Lose, and you lose your life."

Verity's hands tightened unconsciously on the reins, and her horse sidestepped. She didn't care much for gambling. She invariably lost.

Rand was an excellent shot, and so was Freddy, for that matter, but neither of them carried weapons. Surely they would stay close enough to reach the safety of the wagon if they were attacked.

She shivered. This was a frightening land, brutal and violent. She hadn't wanted to come to the Wyoming Territory, but once the decision had been made, there was no turning back. Every shilling she and Rand had was invested in this venture. The wagon held a year's worth of supplies, everything they would need to set up housekeeping when they reached their destination.

As for the land itself, she was forced to admit it was breathtaking. The grass grew tall and undulated like a green, wind-tossed sea. The vastness of this lonely place was overwhelming. They had ridden for two days without seeing another living soul except antelope and jackrabbits. It was difficult to believe there were murdering savages out there somewhere. And that this was going to be her home.

Verity shivered again.

Who would have thought that the only thing of value the Earl of Rushland would leave her at his death was a cattle ranch in the Wyoming Territory? Rand, who had inherited his father's title, but nothing else, had been persuaded to come along to help his mother run the ranch. Only days before they left their homeland, he had chosen an English bride and brought her along with him.

But really, this was the last place Verity wanted to be. Because *he* was here. Somewhere. The man she had once loved more than life. The father of her son.

Miles had left England twenty-two years ago and never returned. She had kept track of his travels through stories that circulated among the *ton*. She knew he had spent some time on a whaler out of Boston, and that he had owned a sugar plantation in New Orleans. He had headed for Texas just before the War Between the States, and she had held her breath for four years while he fought as a member of the Confederate army.

After the war, he had bought a cattle ranch in Texas. It was a year or so later that she learned through *ton* gossip that Miles had driven a herd of cattle north and settled in the Wyoming Territory. What she had never learned, what she had never dared to ask, was why he had never come home to England. She had lived all those years fearing that he would return, take one look at Rand—who had his father's black hair and gray eyes—and instantly surmise the truth.

That day had never come. She prayed it never would.

Fortunately, Wyoming was a big place, so their paths were unlikely to cross. Nevertheless, she would have felt better with an ocean still separating them.

When she crested the rise, the scene that greeted Verity made her stomach knot.

Rand and Freddy were laid low across their saddles, fleeing a band of savages on horseback. There had to be at least ten of them brandishing guns. Their wild, bloodcurdling yells echoed on the wind.

Her first instinct was to chase after them, but the teamster must have realized what she intended, because he reached out and grabbed her reins near the bit.

"Let me go!" she cried. "I have to—"

"There's nothin' you can do, lady. It'll all be over 'fore you get there."

She wanted to deny his words, but before her horrified eyes she saw the half-naked Indian brave in the lead aim his rifle and fire. Rand jerked in the saddle and nearly fell off, but somehow managed to hang on.

"He's been shot! My son's been shot!"

She watched Freddy slow her mount enough to catch Rand's reins and take off again. Before the Indians could catch up to the two of them, they had crossed a ridge and disappeared.

"We have to do something! We have to help them!"

The bullwhacker shook his head. "Sorry, ma'am. Ain't nothin' nobody can do for 'em now. We'd just git ourselves killed if we make a fuss."

She spurred her mount, intent on freeing herself. Her horse plunged and curveted, but the teamster's hold was inexorable.

"Hey, Slim," Rufus said. "Lookee there."

Verity's eyes followed where the man's shotgun pointed.

"I'll be hornswoggled," the teamster said. "If it ain't the damned cavalry to the rescue!"

Verity stared in disbelief as a double column of blue-coated cavalry appeared, riding at a gallop. A second look revealed that several of the pursuers weren't in uniform. They all disappeared over the same ridge that had swallowed everyone else.

The cavalry provided enough distraction to cause the teamster to loosen his hold. Verity saw her chance and viciously spurred her horse. The mare leapt forward, jerking the reins free. Verity leaned forward as the wind blurred her eyesight, heading her mount in the direction everyone else had gone.

The Thoroughbred she was riding was bred for speed over short distances. In a country like this, where the grass had no beginning and no end, Verity knew she had to catch up to the cavalry quickly, or she would find herself lost and alone in the wilderness. She willed one of the soldiers to look back and notice her. But no one did.

She fell steadily farther and farther behind.

Suddenly the cavalry whirled their horses and fled back in her direction as though the devil were on their heels. She heard a sort of rumbling, like thunder, but a glance upward revealed a cloudless August sky. Without warning, her horse plunged and reared. The sidesaddle didn't provide enough to hold on to, and she felt herself bouncing helplessly off the animal's back.

As the Thoroughbred bolted, she flew through the air, skidding to a stop on her face, shoulder, and hip. Her stylish beaver hat came loose and rolled away. She lay stunned, her scraped cheek nestled against the cool grass. Beneath her the earth trembled, as though giant feet trod upon it. She heard—felt—the cacophony of sound rolling toward her. Dear God, what could it be?

She shoved herself upward the length of her arms and stared, amazed and confused by what she saw.

Huge, shaggy, hump-backed creatures spread across the landscape like a raging muddy river as far as the eye could see. They had nearly caught up to the cavalry, which was galloping away to the east, away from the horde.

It took a moment for the reality of the situation to sink in. She searched quickly for her mount, but the Thoroughbred was long gone. There was no way she could escape the rising tide that threatened to overwhelm her.

Instinct made her scream, a primeval cry for survival.

The wind carried the high, keening sound over the rumble of thousands of hooves.

And someone heard it.

She stared with disbelieving, joyful eyes as one man separated himself from the others. He wasn't wearing cavalry blue, but the gold of buckskin. His horse was an odd shade of gray, and it was smaller, sturdier than her Thoroughbred. The animal was shiny with sweat, and a lather of salty foam showed along its shoulders and chest.

She struggled to her feet, not an easy job with the yards and yards of lavender velvet that surrounded her. She gathered as much of her skirt as she could in her hands to get it out of the way. She had expected her savior to slow his mount as he closed the short distance between them, but he continued at a full gallop, as though he had no intention of stopping.

She felt her heart sink.

A quick glance revealed that the river of animals was edging closer. He must have decided she wasn't worth the risk. She watched him come, bent low over his mount, his face lost in the horse's flying mane. She felt the copper taste of fear in her throat. She was going to die. In this wilderness. Crushed to death by thousands of thundering hooves.

Her long hair had come loose from its pins and flew like a ragged golden flag across her face. If this was the end, she wasn't going to watch it happen. She turned her back on death, on disaster. She curled her arms around herself, to keep her insides from flying apart. She resisted the urge to run, to grab at whatever chance she might have for a few more moments of life. That would only prolong the inevitable.

In what she believed to be the last moments of her life, the image of a once-beloved face rose before her. Miles, as he had looked before the accident that eventually left the right side of his face with a slashing scar from temple to throat—handsome, youthful, insouciant. Miles, holding her in his arms, smiling tenderly down at her, one eye blackened by a grown-up bout of fisticuffs with his nemesis, Chester Talbot. Miles, gray eyes icy with rage as he confronted her in the vestry of St. George's, the day she had married his enemy.

In vivid scenes, she relived it all, the joy and the laughter . . . the disillusion and the anguish. The secret she had kept from Miles all these years would die with her at last.

One moment she was standing there certain her life was over, the next she was scooped up by a powerful arm and pulled across the saddle into the buckskin-clad man's lap.

"Hang on!" he shouted over the encroaching beasts.

He spurred his mount, and she felt the gray horse respond with what had to be more heart than strength. The horde was gaining. They didn't have a chance, but neither man nor horse seemed aware of that.

The ground dropped out from under them, and she realized the horse had skidded down on its haunches into a deep, narrow gully. The man headed the gray toward an overhanging lip of earth. He yanked his mount to a stop in the shallow refuge and slid off the winded animal, bringing her with him, his arm clutched under her breasts. He half dragged, half carried her, until his back was against a wall of dirt and stone.

"This is the best chance we have," he said in a curt voice. "If we're lucky, the buffalo will turn at the ravine or jump over it. If we're not . . ."

He didn't have to say it. She knew what their fate would be. She angled her head and looked up at him for the first time.

As their eyes met, she heard him gasp.

She turned to face him, eyes wide, mouth slack. "Miles?"

There was no more time for talk, for apologies, for regrets. The buffalo were upon them.

He pulled her into his arms, holding her tightly. She clung to him, terrified, holding on to him as to a strong oak in a windstorm. Oh, how familiar this felt. Miles. Her bastion of strength.

He smelled strange, of woodsmoke and leather and sweaty horse, not at all like a cultured English gentleman. His shoulders were broader, his body harder, but she fit against him the same perfect way. She felt his lips pressed hard against her temple and moaned deep in her throat.

It was a sound of yearning. For what had been. For what might have been.

His arms tightened around her, and she heard him make a guttural sound in his throat. A desperate sound. A hungry sound.

Then the earth shuddered and shattered as the buffalo leapt the narrow ravine and thundered over them. Dirt and stones sprayed around them. The air filled with dust. It was impossible to breathe. The end couldn't be far away. Their moments were numbered.

His mouth found hers, and she tasted the bittersweetness of lost love. His kiss wasn't gentle. It wasn't tender. It had all the raw, aching passion of what had once been between them. His hands tangled in her hair and held her captive as his mouth plundered hers. She arched against him helplessly, surrendering to the inevitability of his power over her.

She loved him. Had always loved him. Would always love him.

He never trusted you. He never believed in your love.

The pain was like an arrow in her flesh, the wound as excruciating now as it had been all those years ago. She clung to the remnants of the dream that had been shattered, let her fingers sift through his dark hair, arched her body into the strength of his. But it was as though her mind were detached from the rest of her, watching, judging the man who was making passionate love to her.

He broke the kiss and looked into her eyes.

And she knew. He had not forgiven her any more than she had forgiven him.

His eyes were drawn away by a voice at the top of the ravine.

The buffalo were gone, and she could see through the settling dust that the cavalry had found them.

"You okay, Mr. Broderick?"

"I'm fine, Captain Bennett."

So he wasn't called Viscount Linden here. In the very short time she had spent in America, she had already learned that a man was judged strictly on who he was, rather than who his forebears had been.

"You all right, ma'am?" the soldier asked.

"I'm fine." Verity took a step back from Miles. It felt like more.

"I'll get my horse," Miles said.

The captain reached down a hand. "Let me help you up here, ma'am."

She allowed him to pull her out of the ravine, then stood, dusty and disheveled, in the center of what had to be two dozen mounted soldiers and—she counted four—civilians, who gawked at her like children ogling a freak at the fair.

The captain ordered one of his men to give up his horse and ride double with another soldier, and Verity quickly found herself mounted astride. It took some time to straighten her skirt to cover her legs. She had ridden astride as a very young child, but it felt strange to do so now.

"Did you find my son and his fiancée?" she asked.

The captain shook his head. "Sorry, ma'am. They're long gone, along with those Sioux. We won't catch up to them this side of the Platte."

"You have to go after them! You have to do something!" No fishwife had ever sounded so shrill, but she couldn't help the sharpness in her voice. Terror squeezed at her, stealing calm, stealing reason.

The soldiers parted as Miles climbed over the top of the ravine on horseback.

"Who is it you're looking for, Verity?" His gray eyes were wintry, his voice equally cold.

Captain Bennett turned to Miles with a questioning look. "You know this lady?"

"Captain Bennett, may I present Lady Talbot, Countess of Rushland."

She heard the sneer in Miles's voice, the virulent loathing. She would have given anything to go back and change the past. But it was too late. She stared at the man whose life she had saved at the expense of her own happiness. It was sadly ironic that he despised her so much.

The captain tipped his hat and nodded his head in lieu of a bow. "Ma'am."

"What are you doing out here alone?" Miles asked. "Where's the rest of your party?"

"You're a little late asking that question," Verity retorted.

"I was busy earlier."

She wasn't sure whether he meant rescuing her or kissing her, but the flush skating up her throat would have answered for either reason.

"Chester died a year ago," Verity said. "I was traveling with my son, Randal, Lord Talbot, his fiancée, Lady Winnifred Worth, and some men we hired in Cheyenne to drive our wagonload of supplies. I suppose the teamsters are back there somewhere." She gestured agitatedly over her shoulder. "My son—" She swallowed over the constriction in her throat. "The last time I saw my son and his fiancée, they were being chased by Indians. I think Rand has been shot."

Miles and Captain Bennett exchanged glances.

"You're going after them, aren't you?" she asked, her gaze skidding from one grim-lipped face to the other.

"We'll take a look around, ma'am," the captain assured her. "Only . . ."

"Only what?"

"What Captain Bennett is loath to say is that we probably won't find your son or Lady Winnifred alive. If we find them at all. The buffalo have likely wiped out all sign of their direction," Miles replied.

Verity reeled. Miles reached out to catch her, and she jerked herself free. "Don't touch me! Don't you dare come near me again!"

His shoulders squared, and his lips flattened.

"We'll take you to the fort, Lady Talbot," the captain said. "And arrange for an escort to ride with you back to Cheyenne."

"Why would I want an escort to Cheyenne?"

"This is no place for a lady."

"I have land here, a ranch. When my son is found—and he will be—we're going to settle there and raise cattle and Thoroughbred horses."

"Verity—"

"It's Lady Talbot," she snapped. "And I'll thank you not to forget it."

"I've lived with it for the past twenty-two years," Miles said in a low, fierce voice. "I'm not likely to forget it now."

He sounded hurt and angry. But she was the one who had suffered. She was the one who had been forced to marry against her will.

"It's dangerous for you to live out here alone," the captain said.

"That's my concern, Captain Bennett, not yours." She was every inch the countess she had learned to be, her voice imperious, her body ramrod straight in the saddle. The captain backed down, as others had before him.

"I want a half-dozen soldiers to find that wagon and make sure it arrives safely at the fort," the captain said.

Verity was surprised at the finagling that went on as the young men volunteered for what she thought could only be hazardous duty. Moments later the soldiers were on their way.

"Form them up, O'Malley," the captain instructed the top sergeant.

Sergeant O'Malley roared "Column of twos!" and the men lined up quickly behind him. Miles spoke for a moment to the four men besides himself dressed in civilian clothes, and they dropped to the back of the line.

Verity rode beside the captain. She bit back an objection when Miles rode up on her other side, boxing her in. She wouldn't give him the satisfaction of knowing his presence made her uncomfortable. He was doing his best to be irritating, and she was determined not to succumb to his provocation.

But the ride was long and dusty and boring. She hadn't seen Miles for more than twenty years. Curiosity forced her to speak.

"Why are you riding with the soldiers?" she asked.

"A bunch of Sioux raided my ranch, killed one of my cowhands, stole a bunch of my cattle. My men and I were out looking for the culprits when we ran into this cavalry patrol and decided to join forces."

"You have a ranch around here?" It was a disconcerting thought.

"A couple thousand acres along the Chugwater. Of course, I only have title to about five hundred acres of it, along with a house by the river. The rest of what I claim is government land. But my cattle are grazing there, so I guess that makes it mine." He raised a brow. "Where's that ranch of yours?"

She raised her eyes to his. "Along the Chugwater."

"Looks like we'll be neighbors."

She hesitated a moment, then said, "I look forward to meeting your wife."

"I never married."

Her glance shot to his. But he wasn't giving away anything. Oh, he had aged well. He was more handsome now at—forty-three?—than he had been at twenty-one, even considering the ragged, years-old scar that raked one side of his face. She supposed it was the lines that gave his face character—the furrows in his brow, the creases around his mouth, the tracks of crow's feet at the corners of his eyes. And, of course, the scar, a slashing white rift in skin burnished by the sun and weathered by the seasons.

She could see the years had hardened him, putting muscle on his lean frame. His hands had burned brown and were, she knew from his touch, callused. He looked as unforgiving as he obviously was.

The years of not knowing whether he was happy, whether he had found another woman to love, had been bad enough. Seeing Miles again, finding him hale and hearty, arrogant and unforgiving—oh, that was much, much worse.

He had abandoned her to Chester and gone on with his life. It was a hard truth to accept. Easier, of course, when it was staring her in the face. Maybe now she would be able to let go of the past. Maybe now she would be able to forget Miles Broderick, Viscount Linden, second son of the Earl of Vare, and go on with her life, without the regret, without the painful memories that had plagued her.

She wanted to ask, needed to ask, why he had stayed away from England for so long. But she couldn't. Because he was liable to start asking questions of his own. Her secret had been too deeply buried for too long to be exhumed now.

Pique and pride had kept her from telling Miles the truth about Chester the one time, years ago, when the opportunity had presented itself. Now she was afraid of what he would do if he knew.

"It's not over," he said in a voice too soft to be heard except by her.

"What?"

"Between us," he said.

She met his eyes and felt a shiver roll through her. "What do you want from me, Miles?" she asked in a voice equally soft, equally urgent.

"Revenge, Verity. I want revenge."

2

"Hang on, Rand! Oh, please, hang on!" Freddy pulled Rand's horse after her as she spurred her mount to greater speed. But she was losing the race for freedom. The savages were gaining and would soon capture them—if they were lucky enough to be captured rather than killed outright. Except, when she remembered the sorry state of Rufus's head, she thought perhaps she would rather be dead when the Indians performed their surgery. If she weren't so close to tears, she would be laughing, the whole situation was so ridiculous. She had only come to this godforsaken land on a dare. A dare!

Of course she liked Randal Talbot a great deal. Of all her suitors, the young Earl of Rushland was the one most willing to join in some outrageous escapade she forwarded. And he was handsome, with aristocratic features, a lean body that showed to advantage in the latest fashions, unruly black hair, and devilish gray eyes.

But he hadn't any money, not a jot. Which made him totally unsuitable in her parents' eyes. Naturally, that unsuitability made him all the more attractive to her. If her mother hadn't objected so strenuously to Lord Talbot, maybe she would not have felt the need to rebel in the way she had. "I absolutely forbid it!" her mother, the Duchess of Worth, had said when Freddy casually mentioned Lord Talbot's marriage proposal over breakfast one morning.

She hadn't intended to say yes to Rushland, she was just making polite conversation. After all, he was only twenty-one, and besides, when he kissed her—which she had let him do twice—it was very pleasant, but that was all. Her married friend, Isobel, Lady Osborne, had assured her that she would know the right man when she found him, because when she kissed him, he would make her toes curl.

Lord Talbot was not the right man.

But her mother's response had set up her hackles, and she had risen to Rushland's defense. "Is it because he didn't come to you and Father first?" she demanded. "That's old-fashioned, Mother. Young men seek permission from a lady for her hand these days. I'm sure Rushland will be around to visit Father soon."

"The duke will not see him," her mother snapped.

"Father wouldn't dare deny him!"

"Wouldn't deny whom?" her father asked as he took his place at the head of the breakfast table.

She waited for the footman, Frith, to pour her father's coffee, and for him to take the first sip before she answered. The duke was a bear before he had his first drink of coffee in the morning. "Wouldn't deny Randal Talbot an audience. You see, Father, Lord Talbot has proposed."

"Proposed what?"

"Marriage, Father," she replied, barely keeping the exasperation from her voice. Really, for all his shrewdness in politics, he could be obtuse about personal matters.

"Who is this Randal Talbot?" The duke leaned back as Frith placed a plate filled with delicacies from the sideboard, his favorite kidneys and shirred eggs and some toast, in front of him.

"The Earl of Rushland, Father." She watched him relish a bite of eggs.

The Duke of Worth loved food, and it showed. Despite his short height, he managed to look substantial rather than fat. Freddy had inherited her petite stature from him and from her mother, both of whom would have done well on Lilliput—as much for their narrow attitudes as for their size. Which brought her back to Rushland.

"I think you may have known Lord Talbot's father, the fifth Earl of Rushland," she said.

"Eh? Thought he died," the duke said absently, now well into the kidneys.

"He did," Freddy said patiently. "Last year."

"And didn't leave a thing to his heir but debts," her mother interjected.

"Money isn't everything, Mother," Freddy retorted.

"It is something to consider, pet," her father said, dabbing at his mustache with his napkin. His mustache was his pride and joy, and he kept it neatly trimmed and waxed. He had eschewed the popular side whiskers worn by most of his friends. "You like nice things. Nice clothes, nice horses, nice parties. Nice things cost money."

"I know that, Father. But you have money."

He chuckled. "Yes, pet, but when you marry, you'll be depending on your husband to support you."

"I have trust funds—"

"That come to you at thirty," he said. "And not a day before. I'm sure your husband will appreciate your fortune when the time comes. You're only seventeen, pet. There are a few years to be lived in between. I have faith in your mother's judgment about these matters, and so should you."

The butler, Smythe, entered the dining room and announced, "You have a visitor, Lady Winnifred."

"Who could be calling so early?" the duchess asked, eyeing her daughter.

Freddy heard the unspoken message. *No gentleman would commit such a solecism.*

"The Earl of Rushland, Your Grace," Smythe replied to the duchess.

"Tell the young man we're having breakfast and to come back at a decent hour," the duchess said.

Freddy rose and tossed down her napkin. "I'll see him now."

The duchess rose, clutching her napkin in both hands. "I think not!"

"Sit down, both of you," the duke said. "I insist on a civil breakfast."

"I'll excuse myself then, Father, so I won't disturb you and Mother any further."

"Now, pet—"

"Winnifred, I insist—"

She was gone, shutting the door on the mouths of parental authority. She took a deep breath and let it out, a feat much easier to accomplish since she had left off wearing corsets. Her mother had said a word or two about that, as well, but it hadn't made any difference. Freddy refused to be bound up like a prisoner in the docks just because it was the fashion.

She hurried to the drawing room of their London town house, knowing that was where Smythe would have left Rushland waiting.

He looked particularly handsome this morning in a dark brown frock coat, white linen shirt, fawn breeches, and black boots. There was a glint of mischief in his eyes as he smiled at her and held out his hands. "Good morning, Lady Winnifred. Did I cause a problem coming so early?"

She placed her hands in his, because it would have been awkward not to, managed an equally brilliant smile, and said, "Nothing that I couldn't handle, Lord Talbot."

"I couldn't wait any longer for your answer." His face held a boyishly eager expression that made her feel guilty. She hadn't encouraged his suit, but she hadn't discouraged it, either. She knew he put more weight on the kisses she had allowed than she did. But how was she to find her Prince Charming if she didn't kiss a few frogs first?

"You haven't spoken to my father," she said, stalling for time.

He looked surprised. "I thought you were making this decision."

She felt a spurt of irritation because he was right, and because she had decided not to marry him and didn't want to hurt his feelings by telling him so.

"I must seem in a ramshackle rush to get this done," he confessed with a grin that she found entirely too charming, "but Mother and I have decided to emigrate to America, and I want to take my bride along with me."

"What?" His thumb was caressing her wrist and drawing a tingling response that she didn't understand, seeing as how he was *not* her Prince Charming. She freed her hands and tucked them behind her back in the folds of her blue India silk dress. She had been so distracted by what she was feeling that it took her a moment to absorb the essence of what Rand had said. Her green eyes shot wide with disbelief. "You're *emigrating?* To *America?*"

The grin flashed again. "I know it sounds unbelievable, but when the will was read, all Father left to Mother was a ranch somewhere in the American West. There's a condition in the will that makes it impossible for her to sell the property for five years, or some such nonsense, so she's decided to go there to live. I couldn't very well leave her to manage a ranch all by herself, could I?"

"No," she murmured. "I suppose you couldn't."

"Anyway, I think it's a marvelous opportunity. I shall go to America and make my fortune."

He reached for her hands again, and she found herself giving them into his keeping.

"I want very much to take you with me as my wife."

His voice, vibrant with feeling, made her stomach shift sideways. His heart was in his eyes, and Freddy wasn't proof against the entreaty there. She felt herself swaying toward him. At the last possible instant, she caught herself and took a step backward instead, agitatedly brushing back a single auburn curl that had slid forward onto her shoulder. "When did you decide all this?"

The grin was back, but his eyes were wary, conceding she had the power to devastate his hopes. "This morning, actually. At breakfast."

"That couldn't have been more than an hour ago."

"More like half an hour," he admitted.

Apparently Rushland didn't look before he leapt any more than she did. But crossing an ocean was a pretty big leap, even for her. "You expect me to go with you to America?"

He sobered. In fact, she had never seen him look more serious in his life. Her heart began thumping a little harder. She had always thought of herself as an adventuresome person, but it was slowly dawning on her that she had no desire to leave her family and go so far away.

"Lord Talbot, I—"

He caught her chin between his thumb and forefinger and lifted her face up to his. Her breath snagged in her throat.

"I love you very much. Please don't say no."

She swallowed, somehow, but had no idea where to go from there. She felt tears sting her nose as he tucked the persistently errant curl behind her shoulder.

"I can't promise much in the way of worldly goods," he admitted. "At least, not at first. I can and will promise to do my utmost to make you happy." His thumb caressed her cheek. "The only question is, do you love me?"

"Of c-course I l-love you," she replied quickly, stuttering a little at the misrepresentation of her feelings. She loved him as a friend, as a fellow mischiefmaker, as a rebel every bit as opposed to authority as she was. She didn't love him as a woman should love the man she was pledged to marry. "I—"

"Take your hands off my daughter."

The duke stood in the doorway, the duchess beside him, her hand curled through his arm, both of them looking terribly regal.

Rushland's hand came away quickly and

clenched into a fist at his side. He nodded to her father, but there was nothing deferential in the gesture. "Your Grace."

"This interview is at an end," the duke said.

"But Father—"

"Winnifred, this matter is best left between the gentleman and me."

Freddy took the single step necessary to put her at Rushland's side and slipped her arm through his in an imitation of her mother's pose. "Since the gentleman has asked me to become his wife, I think this concerns both of us, Father."

"Winnifred," her mother warned. "The Duke of Worth's only daughter wouldn't dare do something so stupidly impulsive as to engage herself to this . . . this *nothing!*"

Maybe if her mother hadn't used that precise word, maybe if Freddy hadn't glanced at Rushland at that precise moment and seen the flash of wounded pride, maybe things would have turned out differently.

"Oh, I would dare, Mother," she said in a brittle voice. "I'd dare a great deal more. Lord Talbot and I intend to be married as soon as possible and sail for America, where we shall live on a ranch in the wilderness."

"I won't allow it." The duke was agitated enough to twist at the perfect curl of his mustache. "You're only seventeen. There's not a clergyman in England who'll perform the nuptials without my consent."

"Then we'll be married in America," Freddy replied.

Her mother faltered, leaning heavily against her father, and Freddy saw the tic in her father's right eyelid that appeared whenever he was truly angry.

"I forbid it," the duke said. "Rushland, you will leave this house immediately."

"If he goes, Father, I go," Freddy threatened.

She waited for her mother to plead with her father for reason. But the duchess's face remained as unsympathetic as the duke's. *And they wondered where she got her stubborn, independent streak.*

"You'll be locked in your room, young lady, if that's what it takes, until you come to your senses," her father warned in a dire voice.

"You can keep me locked up, but as soon as I can manage it, I'll escape." She turned to Rushland. "Don't leave without me. I'll join you as soon as I can."

Rushland took one look at the duke's choleric color, gave her a quick nod, and made as dignified an exit as any thwarted suitor could.

Her father had locked her up, and she had proven as good as her word. That was how she had come to America as the fiancée of a man she didn't love and had never intended to marry. At least she had managed to put off the wedding.

Freddy had been meaning to tell Rushland for weeks that she couldn't marry him, that she had only been proving to her parents that they couldn't control her life. Somehow the right moment had never presented itself. Now they were both likely to die without her ever having said anything. She glanced over her shoulder to see how Rushland was faring. He was still holding on. Barely. "Don't let go, Rand!"

"Leave me," he shouted. "Save yourself."

"Shut up and hang on," she snapped back.

Freddy was unprepared for the lasso that settled around her shoulders, equally startled when a quick jerk tore her out of the sidesaddle. She was falling before she could extend a hand to save herself.

"Rand!" she cried in terror. "Raaaand!"

"Oh, God! Fredd—"

His voice ended abruptly, as though someone had clamped a hand over his mouth. Or clubbed him. Or cut his throat.

All those thoughts raced through Freddy's head in the seconds it took her to land—rather painfully—flat on her back. For a moment she lay stunned, aware of her fate, but unwilling to accept it.

Her eyes widened as she spied the crowd of painted faces that quickly surrounded her on horseback. She would have gasped, but when she tried to breathe, breath wouldn't come.

The Indians seemed intent on terrifying her—and they were doing an exceedingly good job of it—screeching and whooping and waving their rifles. The noise was deafening, and though her mind filtered the sounds, she couldn't make out a word of their guttural gibberish.

Freddy searched for Rushland, but kept lowering her eyes because what she found was so . . .

foreign. She had never seen so much naked male flesh. Actually, being gently raised, she had never seen *any* naked male flesh. The scene before her was rather overwhelming. She was aware of vivid impressions rather than individual men.

Burnished copper skin. Flat male nipples. Broad, muscled chests. Good Lord! She could even see thighs and knees! Of course one knew men had them, but it was rather a revelation seeing them exposed—bony and slim, stout and thick. In other circumstances, she would have been fascinated. Unfortunately, she was too terrified to indulge her curiosity.

Abruptly the noose around her shoulders tightened, and she was dragged to her feet.

Despite the pain, she came up fighting, teeth bared, fingers curled into claws. "You'll have to kill me before I'll let you touch one hair on my head!"

The Indians laughed and pointed.

Her eyes narrowed. She didn't think the situation was the least bit amusing. When a space opened between two horses, she darted toward it.

The noose jerked her backward, and she landed hard on her bottom. She was on her feet in an instant, lunging for another space. Again the noose jerked, and she went tumbling. She rose again, and again a space miraculously appeared between the shoulders of two horses. But she knew their game now and didn't choose to play.

She halted where she was, panting, trembling like a wild animal that knows it is trapped. Her hat was long gone, but someone grabbed at the net that still covered her hair. As she lurched sideways, it tore free, and her hair spilled in silken waves down her back all the way to her waist.

She heard the hissed-in breaths, the utter silence that followed as they stared at her auburn hair. She swallowed over the knot in her throat. She could see her fate written on their fascinated faces.

She groaned, remembering what the teamster had said. Being female wouldn't save her. They would take her scalp all the same. She waited stoically for the final blow to fall. She wouldn't scream or beg them for mercy. They would see how an English gentlewoman, daughter of a duke and descended from the blood of kings, chose to die with her head up and her chin held high.

"What are you called?"

Freddy was startled to hear English spoken by a strange voice and whirled to find the source of it. She stared, confused by what she saw.

Her captor's eyes were black and inscrutable, but his nose was less flat, his lips less thin, and his forehead less high than those of the others. His skin was lighter, too, more golden than copper. *He's not Indian,* she thought, and felt a thrill of relief run through her.

Another look made her question that conclusion. His black hair was long and straight to his shoulders, held at his brow by a narrow strip of rawhide, and his face was painted in yellow stripes like that of the others. His chest and arms—virile sinew and bone—were bare. Her eyes skimmed down a wall of rippling muscle to the buckskin leggings that covered the rest of him. And saw his hand fisted around the rope that held her captive.

Her glance flashed back to his face. "I'm Lady Winnifred Worth," she answered him at last. And with all the dignity she could muster, demanded, "Who are you?"

"I am called Hawk."

"Are you a white man?" she asked.

His features hardened. "I am Sioux."

That wasn't the answer she had been hoping for. "Then how did you learn to speak English?"

"I went to the white man's school."

But didn't care much for the experience, she concluded from the disdainful look on his face. "What are you going to do with me?"

"You are my prisoner."

She swallowed, unwilling to speculate on what that meant. "What about Rushland?" When the English-speaking Sioux frowned in confusion, she rephrased her question. "What happened to the man who was with me?"

"He is dead."

She let out a howl and attacked.

Freddy had the satisfaction of feeling her nails tear into Hawk's skin before her wrists were gripped by iron hands and forced away. "You beast! You animal! Rushland never did a thing to harm you. Why did you have to kill him?"

The Sioux held her at arm's length until she was too exhausted to struggle any more. "You are strong. You will make a good wife."

"Wife?" she shrieked. She struggled frantically against his hold, but she felt like a butterfly whose wings were pinned by giant hands.

"You belong to me now," he told her. "You cannot escape."

Her chin snapped up defiantly. "This is ridiculous! You can't own me! I insist you let me go." She tried to free her wrists, and when she couldn't, resorted to kicking at him with her calfskin half-boots. Her enormous riding skirt got in the way, telegraphing what she intended, so he was able to shift easily out of her reach.

He snatched a handful of her hair and held on when she tried to jerk free. She yelped in pain and froze, panting with fright as she stared into his dark, fathomless eyes.

"You will bear many fierce sons for me," he said.

She stared at him, disbelieving. Her heart thumped wildly as he began speaking to the others in Sioux. She tried to brace for whatever was coming, but her head was spinning, and she thought there was a very good chance she might faint. She ducked her head instinctively when one of the Indians loosened the rope and lifted it over her head. It took her a second to realize what was happening, but before she could run, Hawk grabbed her wrists and held them together while a second Indian twined a piece of rawhide around them several times.

Then Hawk let her go.

She waged a futile struggle against her bonds.

"You will only hurt yourself," he said, laying a hand on her wrists. "To fight now is useless. There is no escape."

She pulled free of his touch and glared at him. Tears threatened, but she gritted her teeth and forced them back. Somehow she was certain these Indians wouldn't appreciate a fit of hysterics.

Freddy wasn't sure which feelings to acknowledge, there were so many bombarding her at once. *You belong to me.* She fought back the terror, the anger, the frustration at what those words implied. Imagine coming all the way to America to escape her parents' restrictions, only to become the slave of some white savage!

At least she was alive. Rushland was dead. And it was all her fault. She was the one who had urged Rand to leave the safety of the wagon and ride off across the prairie with her. Her chest ached unbearably with the weight of guilt and shame and grief.

Freddy tried not to imagine how Rand's mother would feel when she heard that her only son had been murdered by savages. Assuming Lady Talbot ever found out what had happened. Freddy couldn't help wondering whether both her fate and Rand's would remain a mystery never to be solved.

An Indian spoke behind her, and Hawk answered in the same guttural tongue.

"It seems your friend is not dead after all," Hawk said in English.

"What?" She blinked to clear the film of tears from her eyes. "Rushland's alive?"

"Two Bears only knocked him from the saddle. He has lost a lot of blood from the wound in his shoulder, but he is alive."

"You have to help him!" Without conscious thought she reached out to touch Hawk's arm with her bound hands. She realized what she was doing too late. He recoiled as her fingers touched his skin.

He stared at her with narrowed eyes but didn't speak.

She threaded her fingers into a knot in front of her. "Please, won't you let me help my friend?"

"Two Bears will care for him."

Without another word he settled her into the sidesaddle on her Thoroughbred, while one of the Indians stood nearby holding the reins.

"Do not try to escape," Hawk warned. "Or your friend will die."

"Where are you taking me?" she asked.

He ignored her, as though she were an animal on a leash to be tugged and pulled where he willed. She watched him mount a horse that wore a bridle but no saddle, by simply leaping onto the animal's back. She had never seen anything so graceful. The Indian on the ground handed her reins to Hawk, and he led her away at the head of the small band of Sioux.

She saw two Indian braves tying Rushland on his belly across his horse's back. There was blood all over his saddle.

She kneed her horse to draw even with Hawk.

"You have to stop the bleeding, or Rushland will die."

Hawk spoke to the Indians in their foreign tongue, and one of them riffled through Rushland's saddlebags until he found a linen shirt. He lifted the unconscious man slightly and stuffed the wadded up garment against his shoulder before tightening the ropes around him.

"How can you be so cruel?" she demanded of Hawk. "He needs a doctor."

"We brought no medicine man with us. His wound will be tended when we reach our camp."

"Are we going to the reservation?"

"Why would you think that?"

"Isn't that where the Sioux live?"

"There are many who would rather hunt buffalo than take the cattle and corn the white man offers."

Freddy eyed the twenty or so Longhorn cattle the Indians were herding before them. "Those look like cattle to me."

"Ah, but those were stolen from our enemies, not given as charity to the poor," he said.

"Is that why the soldiers were chasing you?"

"Among other reasons."

"They'll come hunting for us. I'm certain Rushland's mother will demand it."

"The buffalo wiped out all sign of our passing. They will never find us. They will give up and go home, as others have before them."

"You don't know Lady Talbot," Freddy said.

"She's like one of those terriers that grabs hold with its teeth and won't let go no matter what you do." Freddy eyed Hawk defiantly. "She'll never give up till she finds us."

3

Verity stared at Lieutenant Colonel William Travis Peters with an unrelenting gaze. "I insist you go after them."

The commandant of Fort Laramie rearranged the papers on his Georgian desk—the only piece of furniture in the room not constructed from pine logs—one more time. "I'm afraid it's impossible, Lady Talbot. If we had some idea which way they were headed, it would be different. The Wyoming Territory is a big place, and I don't have the men to spare for a wild-goose chase."

Verity rose from the uncomfortable ladderback chair in front of the colonel's desk. "Very well. I shall have to go hunting for them on my own."

The colonel had risen the instant she did and folded his hands behind his back, leaving her staring across his immense girth at a double row of brass buttons. "I'd have to advise against that, Lady Talbot. You have no idea what you're dealing with here. The hostiles—excuse me—the non-treaty Sioux, that is, those Indians who didn't sign the Treaty of 1868 agreeing to stay on a reservation, have no respect for human life. They'd as soon shoot a man as look at him. They'd do worse to a lady, believe me, ma'am."

"All the more reason why I need to begin searching for my son and his fiancée as soon as possible," Verity said firmly. "I would appreciate it, Colonel Peters, if you would suggest someone who could lead my expedition."

The colonel sputtered. "But Lady Talbot, don't you see how foolish—"

"Very well, I'll find someone myself."

A voice from the rear said, "I'll do it."

Verity turned and saw Miles slouched in a chair at the back of the room, one ankle crossed over the opposite knee. How long had he been there? She hadn't heard him enter, hadn't heard him walk the short distance from the door to the pine-and-rawhide chair in the corner. She glanced at the foot he had angled across his knee and realized why. He wasn't wearing sturdy Wellingtons or Hussars or Hessians, but knee-high Indian moccasins.

It dawned on her suddenly that this man, with whom she had once shared the intimate secrets of her body, was a stranger to her.

She had immediately noticed the difference in Miles's pattern of speech, how his crisp English accent had broadened and flattened over the years spent away from England. His dialogue was equally foreign, being dotted with quaint Western provincialisms. His manner of dress was no less influenced by the land he had apparently adopted as his own. His fringed buckskins were worn shiny smooth in spots and looked like they might have served more than once as a table napkin. But he didn't seem to mind being seen by a lady in all his dirt.

He had also lost the delicacy of manners common to English noblemen of his rank. He was sitting—if his deplorable posture could be called that—in the presence of a lady, and showed no intention of rising to his feet. She felt a flare of anger at the insult but bit her tongue. She needed Miles's help. Castigating him for his lack of courtesy would not help the situation.

When he spoke, he ignored her as if she weren't there and addressed his comments to the colonel.

"I plan to take the four men I brought with me and keep looking for that band of Sioux until we catch up to them. I'll take the responsibility for keeping an eye on Lady Talbot if she comes along with us."

"Are you sure you want to take a woman on such a dangerous journey?" the colonel asked.

Miles shrugged. "It's up to her. She's the one who wants to find her son."

Miles was the last person Verity would have chosen for the job. Because he was going to know, the instant he laid eyes on Rand, the secret she had kept from him all these years. She dreaded what vengeance he might feel he had to exact for that wrong. Verity couldn't worry about that now. She would simply have to deal with that problem if—when—it arose.

She searched Miles's face, suspicious of his motives. Why had he offered to help? What did he want from her in exchange? They hadn't spoken since he had threatened vengeance on her. He had ridden back to the tail end of the column and joined the four men in civilian clothes who had turned out to be cowhands on his ranch.

Unfortunately, she was in no position to haggle. It didn't matter what price he asked. She would pay it. She wasn't about to deny herself the assistance he offered. She had to find her son. Rand might be lying hurt somewhere. He might be dying . . . And Freddy . . . It didn't bear thinking what horrors she might be forced to endure. Every moment mattered.

"I'll gladly accept whatever help you're willing to offer, Lord Lind—Mr. Broderick," she corrected herself. "When do we leave?"

Miles made a sound that might have been a snort of amusement. "It isn't quite that simple."

"Why not? My son is wounded. Lady Winnifred may be— The situation is urgent. We must leave as soon as possible." Thanks to years of hiding what she felt from Chester, she managed to keep her voice calm, even though she felt frantic inside.

But Miles had always been more perceptive of her feelings than Chester, because he had cared what she felt. From the narrowing of his eyes, from the way his hands closed on the arms of the rawhide chair, she realized she hadn't fooled him with her act of bravado. He knew just how scared she was.

But he didn't offer words of comfort, as a man who cared might have done. His voice was hard, uncompromising, unrelenting. No, this was not the Miles Broderick she had known.

"Rushing out of here isn't going to help if we end up having to turn right around to come back for supplies. You'll be another mouth to feed, and I sure as hell didn't pack anything for a lady first time around. I need to spend a little time with the sutler here at the fort.

"Meanwhile, you better get yourself rigged out in some clothes that let you ride astride. I don't have a sidesaddle, and even if I did, you'll need a better seat if we have to make a run for it.

"And you might want to wash up a bit before we go. It'll be the last chance you'll have for a while. There's not much in the way of amenities out on the range. You look like you could use a rag and some soap."

She flushed as he gave her a rude examination that was nothing short of insolent. For the first time Verity became aware of her rumpled and torn velvet riding habit. She had forgotten entirely about her appearance in the desperation of the moment. She reached up to smooth her hair and realized that blond strands had fallen down where pins were missing from the bun she had secured at her nape that morning.

Her thin leather gloves were torn, revealing scratches on her palms, and she could only imagine the condition her face was in. She reached up and winced when her fingertips came in contact with the bloody scratches on her cheek.

"My things are all with the wagon," she said. "Has it arrived at the fort?"

"Uh . . . that's another problem," the colonel said. "I'm afraid your wagon was a total loss. The buffalo didn't leave much but splinters. Everything was trampled beyond recognition."

"What?" Verity stared at him, goggle-eyed. Her jaw worked, but she found herself momentarily speechless. She closed her eyes to keep the two men from seeing the depth of her despair. She gritted her teeth to still the quiver in her chin.

She felt a hand at her elbow, and her eyes snapped open. Miles stood beside her, ready to assist her.

"I'm fine," she said, stiffening her knees to keep them from collapsing under her. "Only . . ." She took a shuddery breath and said, "Everything I brought with me from England was on that wagon. Everything we needed . . ." Verity sank onto a wooden chair Miles shoved behind her knees.

She looked up at him, letting him see the desolation she felt. She searched in vain for a spark of sympathy, an offer of comfort in his remote gray eyes.

Then she remembered Rufus and Slim. She turned to the colonel. "The two men—"

"I'm afraid they're dead, ma'am."

"My God." She held herself rigidly upright in the chair, clenching her hands together in her lap to still their trembling.

She had been grateful—and amazed—to discover when Chester's will was read that he had left her anything at all. It had seemed like a miracle that she would be able to offer her destitute son a way to redeem his fortune. She had convinced herself that they would enjoy their new life in the Wyoming Territory.

So far everything had gone dreadfully awry.

Rand and Freddy had been captured by Indians. Everything she had brought with her to start a new life had been trampled by buffalo. And the one man she had ever loved had turned up demanding vengeance for a wrong she had done him more than two decades ago.

She lifted her eyes and sought out Miles, who had leaned back against the planked wall, his arms crossed over his chest.

"Do you still want to come with me?" he said. "Or would you rather wait here until I get back?"

Verity looked—really looked—at Miles. The coiled tension in his shoulders betrayed him. He wanted her to say she would go with him. Because she would be completely at his mercy if she did.

She eyed the slashing scar running through the shadow of beard, his shaggy black hair, the filthy buckskins. She tried to remember the handsome youth who had courted her, but found nothing in the steely gray eyes staring back at her from beneath dark brows that remotely resembled the English gentleman she had loved.

There was nothing gentle about this man.

She stared out the colonel's window onto the immense parade ground at the center of the fort and considered her choices.

Fort Laramie, located at the junction of the Laramie and North Platte rivers, wasn't much of a refuge from marauding Indians, to Verity's way of thinking. There were no stout walls, no walls of any kind, just wooden buildings arranged around a central quadrangle with the river curving around one end of it.

There were blue-coated soldiers aplenty, several two-story barracks' worth, and maybe that was all that was needed to hold off the savages. She had to be out of her mind to consider leaving what safety the fort offered to travel into the wilderness with a man who despised her.

But she couldn't bear to stay behind, to wait and wonder what had happened to Rand and Freddy. She had to know.

"I'll go with you," she told Miles. "However, since my wagon was lost, I don't have anything to wear besides—"

"I'm sure my wife will have something to fit you, ma'am," the colonel offered.

Verity wanted to refuse, but realized it would only be foolish pride speaking. "Thank you, Colonel Peters. I would be much obliged."

"I'll meet you at the colonel's quarters in an

hour," Miles said. He turned without another word or look and left the colonel's office.

Verity took a deep, calming breath. In an hour they would be on their way to find Rand and Freddy. She could last another hour without going to pieces. She knew she would be all right once they were on the trail.

Help is on the way, my dear ones. Be strong. We shall soon have you safe.

"Lady Talbot?"

She turned to the colonel and forced a smile onto her lips. "I'm ready, Colonel Peters."

The colonel walked her to his home, a white clapboard house shaded by a deep railed veranda on each floor, one of several structures that he explained were officers' quarters, all set along the southwest side of the parade ground, at the bend in the river. As they entered the house she saw that the stairs took up half of a long central hallway with rooms branching out to either side.

"This is my wife, Mrs. Peters," the colonel said, as he introduced the two of them in what turned out to be the parlor. "This is Lady Talbot, dear, the Countess of Rushland."

"It's a pleasure to meet you, Lady Talbot," Mrs. Peters said with a welcoming smile. The woman dipped a slight curtsy which Verity would have considered her due in England, but which seemed out of place here.

Verity put a hand under Mrs. Peters's arm to assist her out of the curtsy. "I'm the one imposing on you. I hope we can be friends."

She could see Mrs. Peters was pleased by her overture. "I'd like that very much," Mrs. Peters said. "We don't get many white women out here. I'm glad to meet you."

"I thought you might help Lady Talbot freshen up and find something for her to wear," the colonel said. "She has a long ride ahead of her."

"Of course, darling," Mrs. Peters said to her husband. "I'll take care of everything. Now shoo, go back to work."

Verity watched, entranced, as the colonel leaned down to give his wife a quick buss on the cheek, which raised roses among the wrinkles. Familiarity in public between spouses was another difference from the world she had left behind. Most upper-class English gentlemen confined contact with their wives to the dance floor and the bedroom.

The endearments between husband and wife, the *dear* and the *darling,* were stranger still. She fought back a rush of envy, a wistful longing for what might have been. Surely if she had married Miles all those years ago, they would have used such expressions for each other. She forced such thoughts away. She had learned to make the best of what life offered rather than sink into melancholy over what she couldn't have. It was the only way she had survived the past twenty-two years.

"Let's see what we can do to get you cleaned up," Mrs. Peters said as she led Verity toward the kitchen that was appended to the back of the house. "Although," the elderly woman said, her brown eyes sparkling with laughter, "I don't know what the colonel was thinking of to imagine anything of mine would fit you."

Verity could see why the colonel had believed his wife might find something for her to wear. They were both unusually tall women. The resemblance ended there. Mrs. Peters was broad-shouldered, small-bosomed, and stout. Perhaps the colonel remembered her as she once had been.

The older lady pursed her lips. "Perhaps I can take something in. At least the length will be right," she mused.

"Sit here," she ordered Verity, pulling out a chair at a small wooden table in the kitchen. The lever squealed as she primed the pump and filled a bowl with water. She found a clean cloth and some carbolic in a brown bottle and sat down beside Verity.

"That's a nasty scratch," she said as she surveyed the damage to Verity's cheek.

"My horse threw me." Verity inspected her hands. "Thank goodness I was wearing gloves. There isn't much damage to my hands." She pulled off the torn gloves, gritting her teeth as the leather rubbed against the bloody scratches on her palms.

"This might sting a little." Mrs. Peters daubed the cloth with carbolic and applied it to Verity's cheek.

Verity hissed in a breath. The antiseptic acid burned like fire.

"Sorry, dear. It's the only thing I know to do." Mrs. Peters repeated the process with Verity's palms. "Shouldn't leave any scars after you heal," she said. "Lucky for you. Your hands are quite beautiful, and so soft."

The contrast was apparent. Mrs. Peters's hands were rough and reddened from whatever harsh soap she used and callused from hard work. Verity looked at her own hands, soft and smooth except for the new scratches. She had never done any physical labor in her life. The butler, the footman, the cook, the housekeeper, the groom, the gardener, and the maids had done everything, and Leah had kept her company. But the servants were all in England, and Leah had died two years ago from an infection of the lungs.

Now she had to rely on her own ingenuity and willingness to work. She was willing. She just wasn't sure how she would ever be able to learn everything there was to know. Verity wondered—not for the first time, and she suspected not for the last—whether she had made a mistake leaving England, whether she would be able to survive in this new land. But she didn't have much choice. The ranch was the only home she had left.

Mrs. Peters kept up a steady stream of chatter as she led Verity to her upstairs bedroom and began rummaging through her wardrobe. Verity kept waiting for the questions. *Why are you here? What happened to your own clothes?* But the colonel's wife managed to keep a dialogue going without once indulging her curiosity.

"I suppose you're wondering what I'm doing out here," Verity volunteered. She held herself still while Mrs. Peters measured and pinned the waist of a brown corduroy skirt that was split into two legs to enable her to ride astride.

Mrs. Peters eyed her keenly. "I figured you'd tell me if you wanted me to know."

"I came here with my son and his fiancée—" She was surprised when her throat constricted. She had to swallow to clear a path for speech. "They were captured by Indians," she said evenly.

"I'm so sorry. So very, very sorry."

Verity took one look at the sympathy on Mrs. Peters's face, registered the tone of her voice, and realized the woman was offering her consolation on her loss. "They're not dead," she said sharply.

Mrs. Peters didn't contradict her, but it was plain she didn't believe her, either.

Rand couldn't be dead. She had given up too much for her son, had changed her life forever because of him. Her happiness had revolved around him, and his happiness had always ensured her own. God couldn't let him die. She would do anything to get Rand back, promise anything. Only, please, God, he couldn't be dead!

"Mr. Broderick is going to help me search for my son and his fiancée," she explained to the older woman.

"Miles Broderick is a good man. If anyone can find them, he can."

Verity felt reassured as much by Mrs. Peters's assessment of Miles's character as by her confidence in his tracking ability.

"What brought you here, if I may ask?" Mrs. Peters said.

"My son and I plan to settle on a ranch my late husband purchased as an investment."

"Oh? Whereabouts?"

"As I understand it, the ranch house is situated where the Chugwater runs into the Laramie River."

"Oh?" She frowned. "Who sold your husband that place?"

"A man named Loomis, I think."

Mrs. Peters's lips pursed, and she made a sound in her throat.

"Is something wrong?"

"Wouldn't be Ben Loomis sold you that ranch, would it? The Muleshoe Ranch?"

"Yes, it was. I believe it is called the Muleshoe."

"Oh, dear."

"What?" Verity asked, alarmed by the look on Mrs. Peters's face.

"I knew that Ben Loomis was no account, but I never thought he would do anything as low-down as this."

"As what?" Verity said.

"That ranch of yours, the one Ben sold you, well, I think he also sold it to somebody else."

"What are you talking about?" Verity felt her heart skittering around in her chest. She had never counted on this, never counted on fraud. Although she shouldn't be surprised, not really. That was how Chester had lost his very large fortune, investing in every harebrained scheme presented to him.

This was disaster on a scale she hadn't imagined. The loss of the wagonload of supplies was a minor setback in comparison. It simply wasn't possible that the ranch she had counted on becoming her son's heritage, the only home they had, belonged to someone else.

"Are you telling me that someone is living on the Muleshoe Ranch right now?"

"That's exactly what I'm saying," Mrs. Peters replied.

"Who?" Verity asked.

"Why, Mr. Broderick bought the place near two years ago."

Verity breathed out a shaky sigh and put a hand to her head where the pulse was pounding at her temple.

Of course it would be Miles. How had he done it? Was he a part of the swindle? Was that what he had meant when he said he would have his revenge? Had he known all along that both of them laid claim to the same piece of property?

The echoing knock at the front door made Verity jump. Oh, God, that was probably Miles now! What should she do? What should she say?

"I'll be finished here in a moment," Mrs. Peters said, knotting a thread in the hem and cutting it with her teeth. "Why don't you go downstairs and make Mr. Broderick comfortable in the parlor?"

Verity hastily put back on her lavender velvet riding skirt. She gripped the banister with her fingertips to spare her scraped palm as she headed down the steep stairs. Her mind was scurrying to make heads or tails of the information she had just gleaned from the colonel's wife. What did it all mean? Was it sheer coincidence? She couldn't believe that. How had she been so neatly manipulated into such a trap? What further revenge did Miles have in mind for her?

She would demand that he tell her his intentions. But she was afraid, so very afraid, to hear what they were.

4

"Is it true you're living on the Muleshoe Ranch?" Verity asked the instant she opened the door.

Miles hadn't planned to keep his possession of the ranch a secret. He just hadn't expected Verity to find out about it so soon. Perhaps it was better this way. She might as well know going in that she had no choices, that they had all been taken away from her.

"Yes," he said. "I'm living at the ranch."

She made an agonized sound in her throat. Her eyes slid closed, and she clasped her lower lip with her teeth. He was afraid she was going to faint.

"You never were very good at handling the little misfortunes in life," he taunted. "That hasn't changed." He had kept the good side of his face turned toward her more because of habit than anything else. But he realized he didn't want to make it easier for her. He wanted to remind her of what she had done.

Her eyes snapped open, and she glared at him —until he turned fully to face her. Then her glance skipped away. But she didn't bother refuting the accusation. It was true, and she knew it.

"Are you going to let me in?" he asked.

She stepped back and clutched the doorknob as he walked by her. She gestured—what an elegantly polished move it was—toward the parlor. "Mrs. Peters said to make yourself comfortable."

He stepped into the meagerly furnished room, which had a couple of maple tables covered with doilies, a horsehair sofa, and a wing chair arranged around a Turkish rug in front of the fireplace. He stood by the mantel and gestured to the pale rose sofa. "Come join me."

It was an order, but he was surprised when she obeyed it. He watched her walk toward him, a vision of dignity even in her disheveled state. She settled herself on the sofa and played with her velvet skirt, straightening it around her, avoiding his eyes, avoiding him. Only he wasn't going anywhere. Sooner or later she would have to look at him. She would have to confront the mutilated features that had so revolted her that she had repudiated her engagement to him and married another man.

He hadn't looked at a mirror in over twenty years. He shaved by feel, so he knew the course of the jagged line by heart. But he had never forgotten what he looked like when the doctor had removed the bandages at Linden's Folly and held up a mirror so he could see himself. The ragged red streak had run past his right eye and across the edge of his mouth, sending his attempts at a careless smile askew. He hadn't considered himself a vain man, but the image looking back at him had been terrible to see.

"The scar will fade," the doctor assured him.

"How long will that take?" he had asked.

"A few months, a year at the most."

He had faltered. A full year before he could face Verity and know that she would not shrink from him? It had seemed a lifetime. It was certainly too long to wait to see the woman he loved.

He had convinced himself Verity wouldn't care. She loved him too much to be put off by external appearances. He had been confident of her support because she had spoken to him once of the plight of an English soldier who had returned missing a limb after fighting the natives in India. She had told him how any woman must be saddened by such a loss but would cherish the return of her beloved above all else.

It had been a staggering blow when she rejected him.

Twenty-two years had passed since that day, and the pain was as fresh as if her betrayal had happened only hours ago. He stood, staring down at her, waiting for her to look at him again, preparing himself for her revulsion, feeling angry all over again at the devastation she had wrought on his heart and mind and soul with a few callous words.

At last she raised her eyes to his. She was troubled. Frightened. Annoyed. He recognized all those emotions as easily as if she had spoken her feelings aloud. But there was no disgust. Or loathing. Not even distaste.

He supposed it was true then, what the whores had told him. His face must not look as frightening as it once had. He had believed they told him only what they thought he wanted to hear, because he paid them so well for the use of their bodies. Verity's unwavering gaze convinced him they had not lied.

He knew his stare made her uncomfortable, but he was fascinated by her eyes. They were a marvelous blue that he had, at various moments in his foolish youth, compared to a summer sky, the sea on white sand, and the sparkle of a sapphire. He hadn't noticed earlier, but he saw now they were edged by tiny webbed lines. She was no longer the fresh, innocent girl of seventeen he had fallen in love with at first sight. She was a woman of thirty-nine.

And he still wanted her as much as he ever had.

The thought shocked him. He had told himself for years that he hated her. Confronted by her presence, he was startled to discover that what he felt foremost was not dislike but desire.

He focused his gaze on her mouth and remembered how it had once been ripe and red beneath his, her lips plump and full from his kisses. As he stared, she slicked her tongue across her lips. He wanted to taste her, to feel the dampness on her lips. He reminded himself that this woman had betrayed him. She had cruelly rejected him and married his enemy. He wondered if she knew he intended to have her. He realized she still had no idea of the utter hopelessness of her situation.

"I'm quite sure I'm in possession of a deed to the Muleshoe Ranch," she said.

He smiled pleasantly. "I have a deed to the same property."

"That's not possible."

"Of course it is."

"If we both have a deed, who owns the ranch?"

"I do." When she arched a demanding brow he explained, "My deed is dated, was recorded, a full six months before yours."

She made a soft, mourning sound in her throat. "You planned this."

He nodded.

"What do you want from me, Miles?" Her voice was quiet, outwardly calm. Her nervousness showed in the way she picked at a piece of nonexistent lint on her skirt, the way she threaded her fingers, then spread her hands flat on the brocade sofa on either side of her, then knotted them again. Oh, she was worried, all right. And she ought to be.

"I told you, Verity. I want revenge."

He watched her swallow hard.

"Why?" she asked.

"I found out the truth, Verity."

She blanched. She opened her mouth, but no sound came out.

"Chester murdered my brother."

She exhaled explosively. What flashed in her eyes was not the shock he had expected but relief. Which made no sense. He must have mistaken her expression.

"I found the man who cut the traces on my carriage," he said. "With the proper incentive, he admitted who had paid him. I followed that man to another, who led me to another."

"The trail led back to Chester." She stated it as a fact.

Had Chester confessed his guilt to her? If so, how could she have taken such a blackguard to her bed? Shaken at such a possibility, he continued, "Unfortunately, the trail didn't lead all the way back to Chester. There wasn't enough evidence to convict him of the crime in court. But I know he was responsible for my brother's death."

She lifted her chin. "You've waited too long if you want revenge against Chester for killing Gregory. Chester is beyond any judgment but God's."

"I've had my revenge on Chester."

Her smooth brow furrowed. "You have?"

"It took a very long time to ruin him financially, but persistence—and his own inability to resist a gamble—finally did him in."

She gaped at him, disbelieving. "*You* ruined Chester?"

His lips twisted. "Who do you think suggested all those risky business ventures?"

She shook her head. "It isn't possible. You haven't been in England for over twenty years!"

He took great relish in revealing to her the

depth of his involvement in her husband's ruin. "I hired an adept English solicitor who fed information to Chester. Talbot's destruction was accomplished very methodically over a period of years. Rather like a very slow, very deadly poison."

"Was having the Muleshoe come to me some part of the plan?"

"I bought the Muleshoe Ranch, then suggested to Ben Loomis that he might find an easy mark in Chester Talbot. Then I simply made sure Chester had no other assets remaining except the ranch and that it couldn't be disposed of easily."

"So, you maneuvered me into coming here."

"I made sure you had no other choice except to come," he conceded. "But the circumstances of our actual meeting were accidental. Even I couldn't arrange for such a timely buffalo stampede."

He watched her eyes narrow, the blue turning dark as a sea at midnight when she realized the enormity of the control he had exercised over her life. She had been the queen in a very nasty game of chess. And he had captured her at last.

"It seems you've thought of everything."

"I like to be thorough. Now it's your turn."

He watched the pulse beat frantically beneath her ear.

"I don't understand," she said.

"Don't you, Verity?" He reached up and let his fingers trail down his right cheek, following the path of the scar that ran from his temple to his throat.

"I'm sorry, Miles," she said in a whisper. "I never meant to hurt you."

"I've waited a great many years to hear you say that. At one time I thought it would help. It doesn't matter to me now how sorry you are. I have no use for your apology, since I have no intention of granting you forgiveness."

"If you would let me explain—"

"It's a little late for explanations. You married my enemy. What excuse is there for that? You married the man who murdered my brother, a fiend who—"

"Miles, if you would only let me explain—"

"Don't say anything, Verity. I haven't finished telling you the extent of your husband's iniquity."

"I know what he was, Miles."

"Then how could you have married him? How could you have stayed with him all those years?" Miles was appalled at his vehement outburst. He turned his back on her and stared out the front window of the colonel's house onto the parade ground, where soldiers marched in rigid formation. His stance was equally rigid. "Did you know Chester had me shanghaied?"

"What?"

"You must have wondered why I left England."

"Of course I wondered when you disappeared. No one knew where you had gone. I asked Chester—" She cut herself off.

He turned and saw the flush on her face. "Asked him what?"

"If he had killed you," she said. "I knew there was no love lost between you."

Miles snorted.

"He swore he didn't know where you were."

"Chester stood by on the docks while I was beaten to within an inch of my life by a couple of thugs. He watched as they threw what was left of me on board a smuggler's vessel. I suppose I should be grateful he didn't have me killed.

"Over the next two years, I had reason to wish otherwise. I didn't think there was a more sadistic man than Chester Talbot, until I met the captain of that ship."

"I'm so sorry, Miles."

"You don't have to apologize for him," he said in a harsh voice.

She winced before she lowered her eyes. "He was my husband."

"I know that. Thinking of you—imagining you—with him has been a painful thorn in my side for a very long time."

"I didn't think you would care what happened to me after . . ."

He shoved a hand through his hair in agitation. "God knows I tried not to."

"I thought you hated me."

He had wanted to hate her. But his feelings for this woman weren't nearly as simple as he would have liked them to be. And he didn't choose to examine them right now. "I've waited a great many years for you to become a widow, so I could have you for myself."

Her gaze shot to his, and her lip curled cynically. "You could have rid the world of Chester Talbot long ago if that had truly been your wish."

"I'm no murderer. As you'll no doubt recall, Chester killed himself."

"It's a fine line you've drawn, Miles," she said. "He killed himself because you ruined him."

He shrugged. "He held the gun."

"You cocked the trigger."

"He pulled it."

She held out her hands to him, palms up, her expression sober. "I'm yours, Miles. What do you want from me?"

"I want you to marry me. In fact, I insist upon it."

She looked stunned, appalled. He hadn't expected her to be happy about it. That was why he had planned everything so carefully, so she would have no way out.

The second half of what he had said must have registered, because her chin came up, and she arched one fine, aristocratic brow. "You *insist* upon it?"

"Think a moment before you refuse my generous offer. You're welcome to consult a lawyer, of course, but that deed of yours isn't worth the paper it's printed on. If you refuse my offer, you and your son won't have a farthing to your names. What will you do to survive? Assuming, of course, that Rand isn't already dead and that we can find him."

She surged to her feet. "Rand is alive!"

"I won't argue the point," he said.

"I concede such a marriage might help me, Miles. What do you hope to gain from it?"

"You," he said in a silky voice. "In my bed."

She caught her lower lip with her teeth. Her chin quivered, and he watched her struggle not to cry.

It was a cruel way of reminding her what they had been to each other all those years ago. *Lovers.* It was hard to remember how much in love with her he had been. She had only used him and thrown him away when a wealthier—and better-looking—catch came along. "I want back what Chester Talbot stole from me," he said.

At last, she raised her eyes to his. "Chester won't know you have me back. He's dead, Miles."

A muscle jerked in his cheek. "I'll know."

"Do you love me? Do you have any feelings at all for me?"

"I despise you for your faithlessness," he said.

"I was forced to marry him."

He barked a laugh. "Forced to marry a rich and handsome earl? How gullible do you think I am?"

"He threatened to kill you if I didn't marry him."

He felt an explosive shock of joy at her revelation before a clamp tightened around his chest, making it difficult to breathe. He didn't dare believe her. She was making it up to save herself from his vengeance. Because it was the one excuse that could possibly make him forgive her for what she had done. It had to be a lie.

"If I thought that were true—" He shook his

head. "I saw how you looked at me that day at Linden's Folly. At my face . . ."

"I swear—"

He held up a hand. "Don't bother swearing anything to me. I don't trust you to speak the truth."

Her eyes pooled with tears. "Oh, Miles, if only you would listen to me. If only you would believe me. I *had* to marry him. He told me he had caused the carriage accident that killed Gregory. He threatened to kill you, too, if I didn't marry him."

"If you married him to keep me safe, you made a bad bargain."

"You're alive, aren't you?" she snapped back. "He only promised he wouldn't kill you. And he didn't. I didn't know he had arranged for you to be shanghaied. I should have realized . . . He knew how much I loved you."

He snorted in disgust. "There's no need to lie. Lies won't help you now."

"I'm not lying, Miles. I love you. I've never stopped loving you."

"You have a damned strange way of showing it. You married a man I hated, a man who tried to destroy me."

"I married him to *save* you!" she cried.

"I don't believe you."

They stood across from each other, breathless, angry, hurting. It was Verity who retreated.

She took a step back from him and said, "A marriage between us wouldn't work, Miles. We can never get back what we lost."

"I don't need you to love me. I sure as hell don't

love you. I want you in my bed. And that's all I want."

"What about what I want, Miles?"

"You'll have food and clothing and a roof over your head." He paused and added the inducement he was sure would make the difference. "And your son will inherit my land and my fortune."

She sank onto the sofa. And laughed. It was a husky sound that sent a shiver up his spine. "Oh, Miles. Oh." She circled her aching ribs as her laughter grew. "If you only knew! My son will inherit your land. Oh, please don't make me laugh. It hurts!"

He was confused by her reaction. She should have leapt at his offer of marriage. He had reasoned it all out. It was the only rational choice she had. She was caught in the iron jaws of a trap from which there was no escape.

But he had heard of animals so desperate to be free that they chewed off their own limbs. Was Verity like that? Would she destroy herself and her son rather than surrender to him? Could he let her go if it came to that?

He had tried to stop loving her. Tried desperately. But he would have had to destroy a part of himself to completely eradicate her. So he had built a protective wall around the heart she had broken and kept it safe from assault for over twenty years.

But the mere sight of her took his breath away. The feel of her skin beneath his fingertips had made his heart pound erratically. His loins ached with wanting her.

He should have left well enough alone. He should have been satisfied with destroying Chester. That should have been vengeance enough for the death of his brother and the theft of the woman he loved. He had gone a step farther and manipulated things in an attempt to recapture a fleeting instant in time when he had been happy as he never had been before or since.

She was right. It was impossible. But he still felt too much resentment, too much rage, too much pain to forgive and forget. There was too much of her locked up inside of him, and he didn't know how to free himself from that bondage. So, in a moment of madness, he had decided to take her captive, as well.

He reached out a hand to her. "You're mine, Verity. At long last, you're mine."

She rose abruptly and backed along the edge of the sofa out of his reach. "Don't do this, Miles. We'll both be sorry for it."

"Marry me, Verity."

She sobbed, a desperate, hopeless sound. "If I thought you loved me . . ."

He could feel her resistance. He was afraid, suddenly, that she was going to refuse him. He said the one thing he could think of that might force her acceptance. "Marry me, or you can get somebody else to help you find your son."

"What?"

"You heard me."

He watched the stupendous effort it took for her to control her temper. In the end, she lost the battle.

"That's blackmail!" she said between gritted teeth. "You know I don't have the money to hire someone else!"

"What's your answer, Verity?"

"Damn you, Miles!"

"Is that a yes?"

"Yes," she hissed. "Yes, I'll marry you. I don't know what pleasure you'll get from having me in your bed when you obviously despise me. Just remember that every time you force yourself on me, I'll be cringing."

His hand started up toward the scar on his face. He caught himself and dropped it to his side, where it curled into a determined fist. "You can close your eyes if you find the sight of me offensive. But I will have you."

"Even if I'm unwilling?"

"You wanted me once. You were on fire for me," he reminded her. He had never forgotten how she had clung to him, how she had cried out in pain when he took her virginity, her fingernails digging into his skin and leaving bloodred crescents on his shoulders, how he had kissed away her tears, how she had given him fevered kisses and forgiven him for leaving her unsatisfied. He had promised her the next time he would show her what ecstasy was.

But there had been no next time.

"What happened between us happened a long time ago," she said.

"It seems like yesterday to me." He could have bitten off his tongue for revealing so much. "There's an army chaplain here at the fort. I've made arrangements for him to marry us before we leave."

Her eyes widened. "You mean right now?"

"The longer we delay, the longer it will be until we can start hunting for your son."

"But . . . right now?"

"I can send for the chaplain as soon as you've combed your hair. But personally, I find that tousled look quite delectable."

He saw the anger and disbelief in her eyes. He thought for a moment she would make some retort, or at least reach up and tuck at a few wayward strands of hair. She did neither. Instead, her eyes narrowed, and her lips flattened mutinously.

"You must have been awfully sure of yourself to make plans with the chaplain in advance," she said.

"I know you very well."

"You don't know me at all," she replied. "I'm not as gullible or yielding as I used to be, Miles. You'll get no more from me than you're willing to give in return."

His eyes grew cold, and a muscle jerked in his scarred cheek. "That, of course, remains to be seen."

5

She should have told him Rand was his son. Several times a confession had been on the tip of her tongue. But if Miles couldn't accept the possibility that she had married Chester to save him, why would he have believed Randal Talbot was his son? It was more likely he would have accused her of lying to get his cooperation in the search for Rand.

And if Miles wanted vengeance for her supposed betrayal in marrying Chester, what revenge might he feel compelled to take if he discovered she had kept the knowledge of his son's existence from him all these years?

It was better to keep her secret a little while longer.

If they found Rand, Miles would be able to see the truth for himself. She shuddered at the thought.

Meanwhile, she didn't at all appreciate being manipulated into marriage. It was never what she had dreamed would happen if she ever saw Miles again. In her fantasy, he had taken her into his arms and made love to her as he had that one stolen afternoon they had shared together. That precious memory was all that had sustained her over the long years she had spent sleeping alone.

Verity stood with her jaw clenched. It seemed her whole life had been lived waiting for happily ever after. But it never seemed to arrive. Here she was, a bride for the second time, and this wedding was no more joyful than her first. Except that she had once been very much in love with the man standing beside her now.

She had borrowed some pins from Mrs. Peters and styled her hair, but she wasn't as adept at it as the maid she had left behind in London. She could feel several curls slipping free at her nape. She was wearing the lawn basque-waist and frog-trimmed lavender jacket from her riding habit—both a little the worse for wear—together with the brown corduroy riding skirt Mrs. Peters had altered for her. It was not an outfit designed to give a bride confidence in her appearance. Except, Miles hadn't taken his eyes off her since the ceremony had begun. Everywhere his eyes touched her she felt warmed by his gaze. Or was it only the August heat? A trickle of sweat stole its way down between her shoulder blades.

She listened to the words being spoken by the military chaplain in the parlor of Colonel Peters's home, but she was hearing Miles's voice in the vestry of St. George's in London on the day of her first wedding, hurt, confused, begging her not to marry Chester.

She had been standing with her father, waiting to make the journey down the aisle a mere three weeks after her betrothal to Chester had been announced. Miles had not been invited to the wedding, for obvious reasons, so she had no expectation of seeing him again before she was bound forever to Chester Talbot. She had felt like Joan of Arc at the stake, with the fire already lit, hoping for a last-minute reprieve. She didn't want to give up her chance for love and happiness with Miles, but she knew the sacrifice was necessary.

Then Miles had appeared at the church door, a silhouette in the morning sunlight.

Her heart had soared with gladness. Here was her knight in shining armor, come to rescue her. Only there could be no deliverance, not without condemning Miles to death. It sounded melodramatic to think in such terms, but she knew Chester was in deadly earnest. She was literally buying Miles's life with her own.

Miles had turned toward her, and she had seen for only the second time the livid scar that ran from his temple to the corner of his eye downward through his mouth all the way to his throat. She had gasped, horrified anew at the disfigurement. Oh, not for her own sake—which was what the foolish man believed because of the lies she had told him—but for his.

Before the accident, Miles had been an extremely handsome man. It was hard to look at him now without flinching. She felt sorry that his beauty had been spoiled, but it didn't make her love him any less.

From the anguish in his gray eyes as they stared at each other across the small distance separating them, she knew he had misunderstood her reaction to the sight of him.

She left her father's side and crossed to speak privately with him. As she approached, he angled his body so she saw only the uninjured side of his face. "Miles—"

"Don't say anything, just listen," he said in a hard-edged voice. "I'm asking you to wait for me, Verity. I . . . the doctor tells me I won't always look like this. The scar will fade in a year or less and . . . and now that my brother is dead I am Viscount Linden. I have the fortune your father needs to pay his debts. I—"

She raised a hand to his lips to silence his desperate words. She wanted to tell him she loved him despite the barely healed tear in his flesh. That he was more than flesh and bone to her, he was life itself. But it was too late for them both.

Neither could she bring herself to wound him further by repeating the lies she had told him about his repugnance to her. So she simply said, "No, Miles."

"If you would only wait—"

Tears sprang to her eyes. It felt as though a weight were crushing her chest. "Miles, I can't. I—"

Just as her resolve was weakening, Chester appeared at her side.

"Is there some problem?"

It was impossible then to say anything. She couldn't repeat Chester's threats in Miles's presence, not without provoking a confrontation between the two men that might lead to death for the man she loved.

"I can't wait, Miles," she said, begging him with her eyes to understand what she couldn't speak in words. "Father needs the settlement . . ."

His eyes narrowed. He had told her he had the money. That excuse was no longer valid.

"It's because of this, isn't it?" He flung a hand toward the wound on his face. "I wanted to believe it didn't matter. I thought you loved me."

"Miles, try to understand—" She felt Chester's hand tighten painfully on her forearm. She looked up at him and saw the stern warning in his pale yellow eyes.

"I won't give you up, Verity," Miles said.

"Step aside, Linden. The lady has made her choice," Chester said.

"Verity?" Miles said, his voice urgent.

She kept her gaze lowered, unable to bear the accusation in his. She waited, praying for a miracle.

It didn't happen.

"Take her and welcome," Miles snarled at Chester.

Then he was gone. And she had burned in the fire for years and years afterward.

She had not seen Miles again until this morning, when she had stood awaiting her death on the grassy plains. She had thought of him often, especially after she learned she would bear his child, always wondering if she had made the right decision. Should she have told Miles of Chester's threats? Could he have found a way to protect himself? Had she needlessly sacrificed her happiness and his?

She would never know.

It now appeared that, over the years, he had been thinking of her, too. But his thoughts had not been in the least charitable. He had been working behind the scenes to have his revenge. He had induced Chester to waste his fortune. He had made her a pauper and stolen her son's—his own son's—inheritance. He had slowly and methodically destroyed all feelings of love he might have had for her in his heart.

The Miles she had known hadn't possessed a cruel or vindictive bone in his body. There was something hard, something callous, about the man standing beside her. Other young men recovered from a lost love and went on with their lives. Why had Miles nursed his anger for so many years?

The more important question now, perhaps, was whether there was any chance for them to find happiness together. It hardly seemed possible they could recapture the love they had once felt for each other. She had cherished another person entirely, a young and carefree English gentleman. She didn't know this embittered and vengeful man.

"Verity?"

"What?"

"Your turn to say 'I do,'" Miles said.

She had missed his vows altogether. She glanced around the colonel's parlor, at the amiable face of the colonel, the more concerned features of Mrs. Peters, the four other men who had been introduced to her as Miles's hired hands, and finally the chaplain, who, with his untrimmed hair and wrinkled blue wool uniform, bore little resemblance to the pristine clergy she had known in England.

She looked into Miles's somber gray eyes. His hand tightened on hers.

Don't do it, Verity, an inner voice warned her.

I have to.

You're being foolish.

So she was a fool. She had never been able to give up on happily ever after. There was only one answer she could give. In her heart, hope beat strong and steady.

"I do," she said.

She heard Miles exhale and realized he had been unsure whether she would say yes. Had his threats all been a bluff? Would he have let her go if she had refused to marry him? Would he have helped her find Rand anyway?

She had suspected he wasn't playing fair. Of course, he wasn't playing at all. He was deadly serious, and a great deal was at stake in the contest. He wanted to possess her, body and soul.

Well, two could play the same game. From now

on, she intended to fight for happiness. She would do whatever it took—scheming, conniving, conspiring—to win Miles's love back again. Thanks to Miles's insistence on marriage, they would be legally tied together while she worked toward her goal.

"Are we done?" Miles asked the chaplain.

"You may kiss the bride," the chaplain said.

"I don't think—" Miles began.

She turned to face Miles and put her arms around his neck. The boldness of even that small action took all the courage she had. She would get better at it, she was sure. For now, it appeared she had done enough. Miles lowered his head toward hers. She closed her eyes and held herself still, waiting for the touch of his lips.

They were soft and warm and a little damp.

He lifted his head, and she raised her eyes to seek his. He looked—oh, she hoped he was—a little bit confused.

Moments later Miles was being slapped heartily on the back by his hired hands, and Mrs. Peters was embracing her.

"Please say you'll stay here with us, at least for tonight," Mrs. Peters said.

"We have to get moving," Miles answered for Verity. "If we leave now, there's still a good chance we can catch up to those Sioux."

"Everything seems so sudden," Mrs. Peters said, concern etched on her brow.

"Miles and I were childhood sweethearts," Verity explained, telling a little, but not all, of the tale. "Please don't worry about me."

Too soon Verity found herself being ushered outside. Six saddled horses and a mule loaded down with supplies were tied to the hitching rail. Miles helped her mount astride, which was easier with the split skirt but felt no less awkward once she was in the saddle, then mounted himself, while his four cowhands stepped into their saddles.

Colonel and Mrs. Peters stood together on the veranda with their arms around each other and waved good-bye.

"Be careful with that bride of yours," the colonel admonished Miles.

"Good luck, Mrs. Broderick," Mrs. Peters said. "I hope you'll bring your son and his fiancée to visit once you find them."

"I will," she promised.

Mrs. Broderick. At least she was no longer the Countess of Rushland. In England, if she ever returned, she would be Lady Linden. Viscountess Linden. It was a step down in rank, but one she didn't in the least mind taking.

One of the men grabbed the lead attached to the mule's halter, and they all headed north across the length of the quadrangle. In a very short time the fort had disappeared behind them. Verity's eyes naturally strayed to the four men Miles had brought along.

Miles had told her he had eight hired hands in all, but half the cowboys had stayed behind at the ranch to tend to the stock. She wondered if they were anything like these four.

As Miles had introduced them one by one in the colonel's parlor before the wedding, the four men had removed their motley mixture of high-crowned, curly-brimmed Western hats.

"This is Shorty," Miles began.

She recognized right away that Western folk had a refined sense of humor. Shorty was the tallest, skinniest man she had ever seen in her life. She had smiled and said, "Hello, Shorty."

"Ma'am." He blushed pink as a boy caught stealing from the altar plate in church, stuffed his hat back on his head, got nudged hard with an elbow in the ribs by the man to his right, and snatched it back off again.

"This is Red," Miles said.

She supposed Red must once have had red hair, but he was bald as an egg. It wasn't just his head that was missing hair. He had no beard, no eyebrows, not even eyelashes. It gave him an odd, sinister appearance. "Good afternoon, Red."

"Nice to meet you, ma'am." He had a disconcerting way of looking at her that made her feel like he could see inside her. She was the one who lowered her gaze first.

"This older fellow here is Frog," Miles said.

Before he spoke, Verity thought Frog must have gotten his name from his badly bowed legs.

"Howdy, ma'am."

Two words out of his mouth, and she knew it was his voice that had labeled him. He croaked like a bullfrog. She managed to say "Nice to meet you, Frog," without succumbing to the urge to laugh.

"Finally, I'd like you to meet Tom Grimes."

Verity looked at Tom closely, wondering why he didn't have a nickname like the others. He had intense brown, almost black, eyes that were heavy-lidded, a sensual mouth and a beaked nose. His whole body seemed tense, as though at any moment he might spring into action. She noticed he was the only one besides Miles wearing a gun, a revolver in a fancy holster tied low on his hip. She wasn't really looking for what she found. Her eyes skittered away from the huge erection making his jeans bulge.

"Back off, Tom," Miles said in a soft voice. "This one's already taken."

Tom licked his lips like he was hungry, and she was a plate of rare roast beef and Yorkshire pudding. She had never met a man who was so rudely blatant about what he wanted from a woman. She saw the challenge in Tom's eyes and the tautness in Miles's body that eased only after Tom said, "Whatever you say, boss."

It appeared Tom was well named after all—Tom as in *tomcat.* She shivered at the lecherous look he gave her. Why on earth would Miles have hired such a man?

"Tom is deadly with a gun," Miles said. "He never misses what he aims at."

With the threat of Indians looming, she found herself feeling a little more tolerant of Tom's company than she might have been under other circumstances. Especially since it was clear Miles had no intention of allowing Tom to importune her.

"How far will we be traveling today?" she asked Miles.

"There's plenty of daylight left before we have to start looking for a place to lay down a bedroll."

"Isn't there somewhere we could spend the night with a roof over our heads?" Verity asked.

"Do you want to find your son, or spend a comfortable night inside?"

Her cheeks burned. "That's not fair. You know Rand and Freddy—Lady Winnifred—come first with me."

"There aren't many folks living around here. If there was a place I thought we could stay—"

"What about the Hanrahan place?" Tom suggested.

Miles grunted thoughtfully. "Maybe. We'd have to spend most of the night riding to get there. Hardly seems worth it. Verity?"

"I . . ." She was so very tired of riding. Her inner thighs already ached as a result of being spread unnaturally over the broad back of her mount. But a glance around at the wide open spaces gave a certain appeal to four walls and a roof. "I'd rather ride for the Hanrahan ranch," she said.

Miles shrugged. "Fine with me." He angled himself in the saddle so he could see the four men riding behind them. "You boys spread out and ride on ahead to see if you can find any sign of those Sioux. If we're lucky, they'll stay with the cattle.

They won't be able to drive them hard without losing some, and they won't want to do that. Their prisoners should also slow them down."

Red licked the edge of a cigarette paper, rolled the smoke one-handed to seal the tobacco inside, then stuck it in the corner of his mouth. "Injuns'll probably just kill them two if they make any trouble."

Verity stared straight ahead and struggled not to reveal the despair she felt at that bit of plain speaking.

"Damn it, Red. Keep your opinions to yourself," Miles said.

"Aw, hell, boss. I forgot— Sorry, ma'am."

"You boys get moving," Miles said. "If you run into trouble, fire a warning shot and the rest of us will come running. If you hit a trail, fire two shots and leave sign which way you're headed. If nothing turns up, we'll all meet at the Hanrahans', spend the rest of the night there, and move on tomorrow. Any questions?"

There were none.

"I'll head straight north with Mrs. Broderick. See you later, boys. And good hunting."

Verity watched the four men ride off in different directions. "Aren't they afraid they might run into the Indians when they're all alone?"

"A man learns to keep his eyes and ears open. If they see any sign at all, it'll be hours old. They'll be careful."

"How many hours before we catch up to the Indians?"

He eyed her askance. "I think you'd better prepare yourself for the possibility that we won't catch up to Rand at all."

Verity forced herself to remain calm. Ranting and raving wasn't going to change anything. "We have to find them, Miles."

"I hope we do" was all he said.

They rode for a long time without speaking. Verity watched the sun sliding down over the horizon with a feeling of panic. She had lived all of her married life in London, where there was a constant glow of light even at night. It had been years since she had experienced the utter blackness of night she had known as a girl growing up in the English countryside.

"How are we going to find our way in the dark?" she asked.

"Once the sun goes down, we'll have to stop for a while and wait for the moon to come up."

"It's frightening to be out here in the middle of nowhere with night coming."

"I'll light a fire. That'll keep the critters away."

"It's not the four-footed animals I was worrying about."

"The Sioux are long gone, Verity."

"It isn't the Sioux, either."

He eyed her quizzically. Then his features hardened. "I have no intention of forcing myself on you tonight."

She was grateful for the fading light that hid the flush staining her throat. Until Miles had brought it up, she hadn't considered what he might do to her when they stopped. She hurried to give him another reason for her distress. "I was thinking of how Rand and Freddy must feel. I can't bear to lose my son, Miles. He's everything to me."

"What is he like?"

Verity was surprised Miles had asked, but more than willing to talk about her—their—son. "You'd like him."

"A son of Chester Talbot's? I doubt it."

"He isn't—" The words of denial were out before she could stop them. She caught herself before she revealed everything and then wondered why she didn't just tell Miles the truth. He was bound to notice the resemblance to himself when he saw Rand. Her son reminded her a great deal of Miles at the same age, especially when he smiled.

But it would cause Miles needless pain if she told him he had a son and Rand was never found. Better to wait.

Lurking beneath her noble reason for hiding the truth was one a bit more selfish. If, God forbid, Rand was not found, she would never have to reveal to Miles the wrong she had done him. She would not have to live the rest of her life with whatever blame he would have heaped upon her for keeping his son from him. They would still have a chance at happiness together.

But she couldn't resist telling him about Rand. Because when the two men met—and despite the consequences she was sure to pay, she hoped they would—she wanted Miles to have the best possible impression of his son.

"You would like Rand," she repeated. "He's a fine man."

Miles snorted.

She ignored him and continued, "I've taught him to be considerate and thoughtful of other people's feelings. He rides like he was born on a horse, and he can drive to an inch. He's strong and courageous. He has no vices—"

"He sounds too perfect to be true," Miles interrupted.

Verity flared up in defense of her son. "He's a wonderful young man."

"I would expect a mother to say that about her son. You'll never convince me Chester Talbot could raise such a paragon."

"Chester had very little to do with Rand," she snapped. And then made a face because she had again revealed more than she had intended.

"Why not?" Miles asked. "The boy was his heir."

"He . . . they didn't get along."

"Why not?"

"I . . . They . . . Rand could never please Chester." Because he had been Miles's son.

"No, I suppose having a son like you describe wouldn't be at all pleasing to a man like Chester Talbot. But I'm surprised he didn't corrupt the boy with his own foulness."

"I wouldn't have allowed it."

"How could you have prevented it?"

"I sent Rand away to school as soon as it was possible to do so." It had been hard, heartbreaking really, to give up her son so young, but she had known it was the only way to save him. "Chester was with his cronies a great deal of the time when Rand was home on holiday. And there were ways to keep them separated." She had resorted to them all.

"What did the boy think of your machinations? Didn't he miss his father?"

"No. No, he did not." She didn't explain herself and, thank God, Miles didn't ask for an explanation.

She couldn't very well tell him that Chester had barely spoken to Rand over the years except to criticize him, that he had refused to have Rand in his presence except on occasions when it would have looked odd for his son and heir to be absent.

Nor could she reveal the times she had held Rand as a child while he cried wretched tears, wondering what he had done to so displease his father that he didn't want anything to do with him.

She had tried to explain to Rand that there was nothing wrong with him, that it was Chester's fault he was unable to love his son. Rand had never given up trying to earn his father's love, even though he had failed to the very end.

In the few hours before his self-inflicted gunshot wound in the chest had finally killed him, Chester had refused to see Rand. But Rand would not be denied. He had entered his father's room and stayed alone with him for some time. When he had come out at last, he had been white-faced.

When she had asked her son, "What's wrong? What did he say to you?" Rand had replied, "Only what he has said before. Leave be, Mother. I am only sick at heart."

Her horse stumbled, and Verity realized it was nearly impossible to see a foot in front of her. "Are we stopping soon?"

"I guess we'd better."

"How long before the moon comes up?"

"An hour or so." Miles halted his horse and dismounted. "I'll see if I can find some buffalo chips for the fire."

"Buffalo chips?"

"There's no wood out here, but dried buffalo dung—which is mostly undigested grass—burns pretty well."

"Oh."

Verity pulled her gelding to a stop, then realized there was no ladylike way to dismount. She would have to lift her leg over the horse's rump. Not that she could have urged her tired muscles into any display of grace and strength.

Miles solved the problem for her by grasping her waist with both hands and tugging her off the horse. She slid down the length of him. A frisson of awareness skittered down her spine. For a moment she thought he was going to let her go, but his arms closed around her, pulling her close. One hand cupped her buttocks, pressing her against him.

Nothing but a few layers of cloth separated them, and she was amazed and appalled to discover he was aroused. And frightened, despite his promise. She held herself rigid.

She felt the tension in him, realized the battle he waged for control. She would have given anything to be able to see his face, but it was too dark.

Abruptly he released her. "I'll be back. Don't wander off." Then he disappeared into the darkness.

She took advantage of the few moments of privacy Miles had given her to relieve herself, then stood by the horses and waited for him to return. Red had taken the mule with him, so as far as she knew, they had nothing with them to eat. Not that she could have forced anything down. But there was a canteen hanging from Miles's saddle, and she helped herself to a drink. The water wasn't fresh, but it was wet.

"Give me a minute to get a fire going, and I'll make us some coffee."

She whirled, and Miles was standing at her shoulder. "I didn't hear you coming."

"That's the general idea behind wearing moccasins," he said.

She watched him dig a shallow pit before breaking up the buffalo chips into smaller pieces and dropping them in. He used a few bits of dry grass and a sulfur match to start the fire.

"Come over here and make yourself comfortable," he said.

When she hesitated, he said, "I won't deny I want you, Verity. But I can wait."

That was small comfort, but apparently all she was going to get. The fire looked warm. She crossed the short distance between them, settled herself awkwardly on the ground, and held out her hands to the heat.

The supplies in Miles's saddlebags included a blue and white speckled coffeepot and a couple of tin cups. Before long the smell of coffee wafted to her on the night breeze. Miles poured her a cup of coffee and handed it to her.

"Careful, it's hot."

She had to hold the tin cup by the handle and the rim to avoid being burned. He joined her but sat outside the light from the fire, so his face remained in shadows.

Verity had nothing in her life with which to compare this experience. It was like a nighttime picnic, only there were no servants to set up tables and chairs and prepare the food and serve it. There was no furniture at all to sit on, not even a blanket, for that matter, between her and the ground.

She heard only the crackle and pop of the fire as grass seeds in the dung exploded, the occasional stomp of the horses' hooves, and the sound of grass being ripped from the earth as the animals grazed.

She and Miles were completely alone in the middle of nowhere. She should be terrified.

But it was obvious none of this was new to Miles, and his confidence in the situation communicated itself to her. He had already demonstrated that he had enough self-control not to ravish her. If the situation weren't what it was, she might even have enjoyed herself.

A wolf howled, and the horses lifted their heads

and stared alertly into the darkness. Verity held her breath until the animals lowered their heads to graze again. "Are you sure we aren't in any danger?"

"Wolves won't come near the fire," Miles reassured her.

"Of all the sites you could have chosen for your revenge, why did you pick this godforsaken wilderness?" she asked.

"Wyoming is where I live. It's my home."

She snorted, a totally unladylike sound. "You could have made a home anywhere. Why here?"

"I don't know exactly how to explain it to you, except to say there are places here where you know no other human being has ever set foot before you."

"It's desolate."

"I like the wide open spaces. And no one here minds the way I look."

She darted a glance in his direction. Of course not, when there were men like Rufus around who had been scalped.

And a thousand other souls like Miles who had run from their pasts to a place where only the present mattered.

"Why didn't you ever write to me?" she asked.

He took a swallow of coffee before he answered. "What was there to say?"

"You could have told me where you were, what you were doing. Didn't you think I would worry?"

"No," he said baldly. "Did you?"

She stared straight ahead. "Yes. At first. When I

thought you might have left England because I had hurt you. When you stayed away so long . . . I couldn't believe you would be gone so long just to punish me. I thought something must have happened to you."

"Something did."

"I know, you were shanghaied. But when you made it back to dry land, when you were free . . ." She turned to face him. "Not a word, Miles. Not a word to tell me you were alive. I had to find out from gossip what had happened to you."

"I didn't think you cared," he said, echoing her cruel words back to her.

Her cry of anguished protest spooked one of the horses. It whinnied and skittered sideways. Miles dropped his cup and was on his feet beside the animal in an instant, calming it. Verity used the time to regain her composure. She set down what was left of her coffee and folded her hands in her lap.

When Miles returned to the fire, he stood close enough behind her that she could feel his heat. "What was I supposed to think when you chose to marry a man I hated, a man who hated me?" he said. "I didn't know Talbot had threatened you."

She rose and turned to face him, putting a little more distance between them. "You should have known I loved you too much to marry another man. You should have trusted me!"

His eyes reflected the firelight. "Like you trusted me? You never even gave me a chance to confront Chester." He shook his head in disgust. "You made all the choices, Verity. If they were the wrong ones, you have no one to blame but yourself."

"I've paid for my mistakes."

"Not quite yet, you haven't. There's a little something owed to me."

"Miles, I—"

"Come here, Verity."

He didn't wait for her to respond, simply reached out and pulled her into his arms. She could have resisted him, could have spit and clawed and kicked. It would have been futile, because he was stronger than she was. And hypocritical, because she didn't want to resist him.

Her eyes closed as he lowered his mouth to hers. She had waited long, lonely years to be held in his arms, to be loved once more, to be exactly where she was.

She felt the anger in his kiss as he captured her lips, and she sought to soothe the savage beast. But her surrender only seemed to incite him. She gasped as he tore at the buttons of her basque-waist, thrusting his hand inside the layers of muslin beneath it to capture her naked breast. He made an animal sound in his throat as his hand teased her, caressed her, shaped her flesh.

Her heart pounded out of control as his lips sought her throat, the shell of her ear, then found her mouth once more. He seemed ravenous, as though he couldn't get enough of her.

He suddenly froze, then lifted his head, searching the darkness with his eyes much as the horses had done when the wolf howled.

She stared at him with dazed eyes. "What's wrong?"

"Be still." He let go of her abruptly and kicked out the fire. Then he grabbed her wrist and headed for the horses.

She struggled to repair her bodice one-handed, but before she could, Miles had hoisted her into the saddle. He tightened the cinch on her saddle, then on his, before mounting.

"Follow me. Be as quiet as you can," he murmured.

Then he headed off across the prairie. She was stunned to realize the moon had come up. It didn't seem possible so much time had passed.

What did you hear? she wanted to ask. *Where are we going?* But she had seen enough of the dangers in this land to realize it was no idle warning he had given her. She remained silent. And followed where he led.

6

Miles had lived long enough in the wilderness to trust his instincts. It wasn't what he had heard that had spooked him, it was what he hadn't heard. The night sounds had ceased. It was a sign that something predatory had invaded the area. Until he knew precisely what—or who—it was, he wasn't taking any chances on getting caught, literally, with his pants down.

What had possessed him to touch her? To kiss her? He had known there was no possibility he could have satisfaction before journey's end. So why had he tortured himself by reaching for her?

His body ached with unrequited desire.

He hungered. She was what he hungered for.

He thirsted. Only she could quench his thirst.

Miles had been denied for so long that the need was overwhelming. It was like laying a feast in front of a starving man. You could not expect him to ignore it, especially when he feared someone might snatch it out of his reach before he could devour it.

The hairs stood up on his arms in awareness as Verity rode up beside him. His body throbbed to life. He had every reason to hate her, but hate was not the spur that drove him. She had stolen his heart the first time he looked into her deep blue eyes, and it had felt as though he were torn in two the day he lost her. In twenty-two years he had not found another woman to replace her, and it would have been a lie to say he hadn't tried. No one else would do. Without her, he was not whole.

"What is it, Miles?" Verity whispered. "Is someone out there?"

"Shh," he warned. Then he heard what he had been listening for. Hoofbeats . . . one horse. He pulled his gun from the holster and said to her, "Stay behind me."

"Boss?"

Miles breathed a sigh of relief and holstered his gun. "What is it, Tom?"

"I found the Sioux. They're camped east of the Hanrahan place. I don't think they saw me. I hightailed it back here, hoping I could catch you."

"Any idea where the others are?"

"I found Shorty and left him watching the Sioux camp. Red and Frog are too far west to run into them."

"How many are there?" Miles asked.

"A half dozen or so."

"Not too many for the three of us to manage, then."

Verity laid a hand on Miles's arm. "You can't be thinking of attacking them! You might shoot Rand or Freddy by mistake."

"Sorry, ma'am," Tom said, "but I didn't see any sign of your kin."

"But . . . that's impossible. They have to be with them."

"Maybe it's a different band of Sioux," Miles suggested.

Tom shook his head. "It's Hawk, all right. The cattle aren't with him, so maybe he sent his prisoners and the cattle on ahead while he stopped with the rest. They're up to no good, hanging around the Hanrahan place like that."

"If Rand and Freddy aren't with this bunch of Indians, maybe we should just go around them and keep looking," Verity said.

"I have a personal score to settle with Hawk," Miles replied. "There's no telling when we'd run him to ground like this again. I don't intend to lose my chance at him."

"But—"

"The cattle will be bedded down somewhere for the night, which means Rand and Freddy won't be moving in the dark. We won't lose much time if we stay here long enough to take care of Hawk."

"What happens if you're killed confronting Hawk?" Verity asked. "How will I find Rand and Freddy if something happens to you?"

"I don't intend to give Hawk an easy target,"

Miles said. "The question is, what am I going to do with you while I'm busy with Hawk?" he mused aloud.

"You're not going to leave me behind," she answered certainly. "If you insist on this idiocy, give me a gun, and let me go with you."

"I didn't know you could shoot."

"There are lots of things you don't know about me."

Miles hesitated only another moment before he handed her his revolver, butt first. "Have you used a weapon like this?"

"Not exactly like this," she conceded.

"It's a Colt .45 Peacemaker. I've got five bullets in it. The first chamber is empty. Just chamber a bullet, cock it, and pull the trigger.

"When we get where we're going, I'll settle you somewhere out of the way. Fire only if you're attacked. And save the last bullet for yourself." He saw the incredulous look on her face. "I mean it," he said.

Her face looked pale in the moonlight. "All right, Miles."

He wondered if she would be able to do it. Probably not. He had better make sure she didn't have any need to turn the gun on herself.

It was nearing midnight by the time they reached the area where Tom had spotted the Sioux.

Tom slowed and raised a hand to halt the others. "Their camp is over that next rise," he said quietly. "The wind is coming this way, so their horses can't smell us. It also carries the sound away. Otherwise, I'd never have gotten close to them the first time." Tom pointed ahead. "I left Shorty concealed behind that ridge up ahead."

Miles dismounted and pulled Verity off her horse right where they were. "Wait here for us," he told her. "Don't stick your head up, or you're liable to get it shot off. Do you understand?"

"I want to see what's going on," she protested.

"It's too dangerous. I want you to promise me you'll stay here."

"No."

"Damn it, Verity—"

"Miles," Tom said, "we need to get moving."

"Stay here," Miles repeated. Then, because there was always the chance he wouldn't be coming back, he kissed her. His lips were hard on hers, angry because he might be deprived forever of more than this bare taste of her. It was hard to tear himself away. He turned his back on her and mounted his horse.

And heard her whisper, "Come back safe to me."

He put her from his mind as he rode away with Tom, focusing his entire being on the fight ahead of them. They met up with Shorty and crawled to the top of the rise on their bellies to reconnoiter. Despite the late hour, the Indians were still awake, talking around the campfire. The three cowboys retreated a little way to plan how best to attack the band of savages.

"I vote we wait till they're asleep," Shorty said, "and bushwhack 'em."

"It makes sense to wait until they settle down for the night before we make our move," Miles agreed. "But they'll leave a lookout for sure. I wouldn't count on our chances of sneaking up on them."

"If we wait long enough, whatever guard they set may get tired of watching for trouble, maybe even fall asleep," Tom suggested.

"We've got to make sure they can't get to their horses when we start shooting," Miles said. "Otherwise, they'll get away, and we'll play hell finding them again."

Their plan was simple. They would wait until nearly dawn. Shorty would stampede the ponies while Miles and Tom charged on horseback, firing into the Indian camp.

"Leave Hawk to me," Miles told Tom. "I want him alive so he can answer questions about his captives."

"What about your wife?" Tom asked. "Somebody has to tell her what's going on. She's expecting us to attack any minute."

"I'll go wait with her. If Hawk makes a move we don't expect, come get me. Otherwise, I'll join you just before dawn. And Tom . . . Make sure you give some warning if you come looking for me, or you're liable to get a bullet between the eyes."

Tom's grin flashed in the moonlight. "Sure, boss. Man's got a right to some privacy on his wedding night."

"I'm not—"

"No need to explain, boss," Tom said.

"Don't worry about us, boss," Shorty said.

"But—" Miles realized he was wasting his time. He had no intention of making love to his wife, despite what they thought. Or, he hadn't, until Tom had put the idea in his head. As he rode back toward Verity he thought, *Why not?* It was probably the only time they would be alone for days to come. Now that he knew where the Indians were, he didn't have to worry about them sneaking up on him when he wasn't paying attention.

While Miles had no intention of getting himself killed in the morning, he had learned things didn't always turn out the way one planned. This might be the last chance he would ever have to make love to his wife.

Verity was jumpy, frightened by every sound. She heard the hoofbeats before she saw anything and held the gun out in front of her with two shaking hands, ready to fire it.

"It's me," Miles called quietly into the darkness.

"Oh, thank God," she said, letting the heavy weapon drop in front of her. She hurried toward him as he dismounted. "What's going on? I thought you were going to attack them. I didn't hear any shots."

"We decided to wait until dawn."

"Why wait? Every minute counts. Rand and Freddy—"

Miles took the gun from her and slipped it back

into his holster. "A couple of hours isn't going to make any difference."

"How do you know that?" Verity demanded in a desperate, but necessarily hushed, voice. "It could make all the difference! There's no telling what might be happening to them this very minute. Why—"

He covered her mouth with his hand. "Enough. There's nothing we can do until dawn. The time until then is ours, yours and mine."

She made a muffled protest behind his hand.

"I've waited a long time for you, Verity. Too long. I don't intend to wait any longer."

She shook her head vehemently no.

"I'm going to take my hand away from your mouth. Keep your voice low," he warned, "or you'll bring those Sioux down on us."

"You're insane!" she hissed. "How can you think about coupling at a time like this?"

"What better time, when there may be no tomorrow."

She gasped. "You said there was no danger."

"I said I didn't intend to get myself killed. That doesn't mean something can't go wrong."

She stuck out a flattened palm to keep him at a distance. "Miles, let's talk about this."

"The time for talking is over, Verity. You're my wife. I'm your husband. It's our wedding night."

Verity was furious—because Miles was taking unfair advantage of the fact she didn't dare rage at him for fear of alerting the savages to their presence. And terrified—because he seemed a stranger, and the circumstances were so foreign to anything she had imagined. It was irrational to fight against something she wanted to happen, but reason had very little sway right now.

She tried to run, but Miles caught her before she had taken two steps. He thrust a hand into her hair, scattering pins and twisting a handful of silky curls around his fist, pulling her head back to expose her throat. The feel of his mouth against her flesh sent a chaotic wave of sensation rolling through her. She bit her lip to keep from crying out, remembering at the last instant the danger of making any sound. Instead, she grabbed a handful of his hair, yanking hard enough in her fear and anger to draw a grunt of pain from him.

"Don't fight me," he warned harshly. His hand circled her waist to hold her struggling body captive while his mouth strangled her cry of furious despair.

Not this way, Miles. Not in anger. Not with force.

He released her mouth abruptly and stood panting, his eyes glittering with desire in the moonlight. "Don't fight me. Don't. Because I intend to have you whether you will it or not. But . . ."

She knew what he couldn't say. They had been cheated of a lifetime together. They might have only one night. And he wanted it to be a night of joy, a night of unspoken love.

"All right, Miles."

His brows arrowed down, as though he didn't

believe she had surrendered so easily. He watched her with inscrutable eyes as he slid his hands down to her buttocks and held her pressed against his aroused body. There was too much cloth between them, and he seemed to realize it the same instant as she did.

Boldly, daring her to fight him, he shoved her velvet jacket off her shoulders, then unbuttoned the basque-waist enough to pull it up over her head. He released the buttons on her riding skirt and let it slide off over her hips to the ground, leaving her clothed only in her corset and thin muslin undergarments. She saw the tension in his shoulders, the tautness of his features, as he reached between her thighs. Her knees nearly buckled, and she grabbed his forearm to keep herself steady as his hand closed over her.

His eyes linked with hers as he staked his claim. "Mine, Verity. You're mine."

"I've always been yours, Miles."

He made a hoarse sound of denial in his throat, but he wasted no time in capturing her mouth with his.

There was a desperation in what they did that made Verity's throat swell with feeling. He finished undressing her and himself in a frenzied hurry. There was no time to feel ashamed of her nakedness, no time to express her admiration of his, before their bodies were aligned from chest to hip.

She was aware of the greater breadth of his shoulders as her arms closed around him. She gasped as her fingers met the ridged skin along his back where he had been whipped. Tears of pity and remorse stung her eyes and nose. But there was no time to indulge emotion. He lowered her to the cool grass and mounted her, smothering her cry of pain at his intrusion where no man had been since the birth of their son.

She had thought it would be over quickly. That had been her experience with Chester, and with Miles the one time they had been together. But once he was inside her, Miles paused and began a thorough exploration of her body with his mouth and hands that soon had her writhing beneath him.

She felt overwhelmed by her own needs, incapable of fulfilling his. "Miles, I can't—"

"You can," he countered. "You will."

He took what she would have given freely, if it had been asked of her, his hands and mouth urgent, impatient to have what they had both been denied for too many years.

He had done this with more than a few other women, she realized with a pang, because he knew exactly where to touch her, how to make her moan with pleasure. She worried that she wouldn't please him but was incapable of voicing that fear, incapable of thinking much, really, at all.

Her body, which had lain untouched night after night for years, was overpowered by sensations. She had thought she couldn't feel again, only to discover that she felt everything with a heightened awareness that made it all seem unreal. To finally be held in Miles's strong arms, to feel the play of muscle beneath warm flesh, to feel his moist breath against her throat, to taste him, to have his callused hands caress her skin, brought forth tides of regret for the years that had been stolen from them.

As best she could, she forced the regrets back, refusing to let them spoil what was happening between them now. She let herself glory in the animal sounds of satisfaction issuing from his throat. Her body arced beneath his, flesh mating with flesh. Her insides tightened in a way that frightened her, and she retreated from him.

He would not allow it. "Come with me, Verity," he urged. "Don't leave me now."

She didn't understand what he wanted from her, but her body no longer seemed under her control. Her insides clenched around him, and her thigh muscles locked in an agony of tension. She wanted to cry out, to beg for surcease, but she bit back the sound. She could do nothing to stop the waves of feeling that shuddered over her, through her, an ecstasy so powerful it was almost pain.

She had a fleeting glimpse of Miles before her eyes closed, his features rigid, his head and body arched back, the sinew and muscle defined in his shoulders and chest.

His pelvis pressed hard against hers, spreading her legs wider as he pushed himself deeper. She felt the flood of warm seed as his body pulsed inside her and heard a muffled cry of exultation. Then she felt his welcome weight as he lowered himself to mantle her nakedness. She wrapped her arms around his waist and held him close, not caring that he was too heavy, that it was hard to breathe, only grateful for what they had shared at long last.

He said nothing and the silence grew long and poignant between them.

She felt his body tense as her forefinger traced the scar on his face from temple . . . to eye . . . to mouth . . .

He grabbed her hand. "Don't," he said in a tight voice.

She felt a chill of fear that he would always and forever shut her out, that in the years to come they would have only the release of passion, but never the love that should go with it.

He misinterpreted her tremors of emotion and said, "You're cold." He rose and drew her to her feet. "We'd better get dressed."

He turned his back on her, leaving her to manage on her own while he dressed himself. She was surprised to realize how much time had passed. There was a faint ridge of gold and orange along the horizon.

Dawn had arrived.

She turned to him when she was completely dressed and discovered him watching her with hooded eyes.

"You're even more beautiful than I remembered you."

She felt a rush of pleasure at the compliment, which denied the dirt on her face and hands and the untidy golden curls falling on her shoulders. "I . . ." She looked into his eyes, searching for more than admiration of her physical form, searching for any hint of caring.

She didn't find it. If anything, his eyes were even more remote than they had been before they made love.

"I've got to go now," he said, handing her his .45 again. "Be careful. Be quiet. I'll get back here as quickly as I can."

He got on his horse and rode away.

For about two minutes, she stood there watching him. Then she had the most awful premonition that if she didn't follow him, she would never see him again.

She hurried to her horse, tightened the girth on the saddle, and made an awkward attempt at mounting. It wasn't pretty, but moments later she was in the saddle and headed after Miles at a walk, keeping her distance in the rolling terrain, praying he wouldn't look back and see her. She dismounted before she topped each rise and led her horse to the edge to be certain she didn't run into him. At last, she found what she sought.

Miles and his two cowhands were crouched down behind a ridge looking over the edge. She presumed the Indians were on the other side. The three men scooted back out of sight, mounted their horses and, at a signal from Miles, charged over the hill.

As she tried to mount, the sound of gunshots caused her horse to sidestep nervously, so her foot fell free of the stirrup. That made the gelding leap sideways, jerking the reins from her hands. She tried talking calmly to the frightened animal as she moved slowly toward him, but several more gunshots finished what they had started. The animal loped away, head high and reins dragging.

She could have screamed in vexation. She ran toward the fight she could hear in progress, stumbled at the top of the hill when she realized there was no one in the depression below her, then nearly fell in her haste to get down the slope. She gathered her feet under her and kept on running. It was hard going up the other side, and she was exhausted when she sank down to peer over the ridge at the battle going on below.

Miles was locked in hand-to-hand combat with one of the Indians. An Indian was lying sprawled in death by the campfire, along with one of Miles's men. The other cowhand was missing.

She had tucked the huge gun into her waistband, and tugged at it to get it out. She hadn't been entirely honest with Miles when she said she knew how to use the .45 revolver. She could aim it, and she could fire it. She was not at all sure she could hit anything with it.

Which meant that if she hoped to be any help at all to Miles, she was going to have to get closer. She started walking down the hill, the gun held in front of her with both hands, her eyes never leaving the two men. She realized with horror that the

Indian fighting with Miles held a knife, and that Miles was trying to avoid being stabbed with it.

"Miles!" she cried.

Too late she realized she shouldn't have screamed. Miles turned to look at her, and the Sioux took advantage of his inattention to jerk free of Miles's hold. The knife flashed in the first rays of sunlight as it sought Miles's heart.

Verity stood frozen, unable to believe her eyes. If she didn't shoot, Miles would die. If she did, she might hit him instead of the Indian. As the Sioux slashed downward with the knife, she aimed at the his naked chest and fired.

The hammer came down on an empty chamber.

She cried out in frustration, cocked the gun, which now had a bullet in the chamber, and fired again, this time not bothering to aim. The recoil sent Verity onto her backside. She kept her eyes on Miles as she fell, hoping against hope that her shot had hit its intended target.

The bullet didn't come anywhere close to hitting anyone, but it had distracted the Sioux and gave Miles time to throw up an arm to catch the arcing blade. In shock and dismay, she watched an ugly red blossom grow on his buckskin sleeve.

Verity lifted the gun to fire again from where she sat, but the Sioux had jerked himself free of Miles's grasp and was running toward a pony not far away. Miles leapt up and raced for his own horse, as though to pursue the Indian.

"Miles!" she screamed. "Miles!"

He hesitated.

The Indian was on his pony and riding away before Miles could even reach his horse. She could see Miles's mouth moving as though he were speaking to her, but because the roar of the gun had left her ears ringing, she had no idea what he was saying.

She came stumbling toward him as fast as her legs could carry her. He caught her as she threw herself into his one-armed embrace.

She quickly pulled herself free and winced when she caught sight of his bloody sleeve. "You're hurt. Oh, Miles, you're hurt!"

She didn't even realize she was crying until he said, "Don't waste your tears, Verity. It's nothing. I'm fine."

"Nothing? You've been stabbed. You're bleeding!"

"It's nothing. A flesh wound." Then, angrily, "Why the hell didn't you stay put? Because of you, Hawk got away."

"Because of me? Why, you pompous jackass! If I hadn't been here that savage would have killed you."

His eyes glittered. "I can take care of myself."

"Sure you can, that's why you're standing there bleeding all over the ground!"

He pulled his arm close against his chest in an attempt to slow down what was becoming an alarming flow of blood. "Verity—"

"Don't say another word to me, Miles. I'm liable to take this gun and shoot you myself!"

He carefully plucked the gun from her hand. His lips threatened to curl into a smile. "All right, spitfire. You saved the day. Now, see what you can do about fixing up this arm of mine before I bleed to death."

Her anger was instantly consumed by concern, and she moved aside the ruined buckskin to examine his wound.

"You don't seem very squeamish around all this blood," Miles said.

"I suppose I got used to it after all the times I bandaged Rand's childhood nicks and cuts."

Of course, this wound was considerably more severe. She tore away part of her muslin drawers to stanch the blood, while Miles's eyes constantly searched the rolling hills around them for danger.

"That will have to do until we can get back to the fort," she said.

"We're not going back to the fort."

"You need a doctor, Miles."

"We've got unfinished business. Or had you forgotten about your son and his fiancée?"

She had. Completely. She had been thinking only of Miles. She paled at the implications of that fact.

"We have to keep moving," Miles said. "Hawk will catch up to the rest of his band in a hurry, and he's not going to be in a good mood when he gets there."

"You think he'll hurt Rand and Freddy?"

"Let's just say I think we'd better move as quickly as we can. Where'd you leave your horse?"

Verity raised stricken eyes to Miles. "He . . . he bolted when the gunfire started. He ran away."

He didn't swear. He didn't have to. She could see exactly what he was thinking.

"We'll have to ride double until we can find him," he said. "Come on. Let's go."

Verity glanced at the bodies by the fire. "What about . . ."

"Shorty's dead. He won't mind if we bury him later."

Verity was appalled at the callousness of such a statement. But she also was aware that every moment they delayed now might mean the difference between life and death for Rand and Freddy.

"Where's Tom?" she asked.

"The rest of the Sioux took off in different directions. He lit out after a couple of them."

"Shouldn't he be back by now?"

Miles frowned. "Yeah. He should. As soon as we catch your horse, we'll follow his trail. It shouldn't take us long to find him."

Miles mounted his horse, then reached his good hand down to help her up behind his saddle. "Put your arms around me and hold on tight. We have some riding to do."

He was a sturdy bulwark to lean upon in this time of trouble. She laid her cheek against his back and knotted her hands around his stomach.

Miles hadn't been killed. One disaster had been averted. But where, oh where, were Rand and Freddy now?

7

Freddy fought back the panic she felt as she listened in pitch blackness for any sound of life. She might have been at the bottom of a well and the world far above her. Except she could feel a buffalo hide beneath her legs where her skirt was rucked up and smell scents that were foreign enough to make her nose twitch.

She tried to move but was quickly reminded that her hands and feet were tied achingly tight with rawhide. Incredible as it seemed, she must have fallen asleep. She had no other way to account for the lost hours. It had been broad daylight when Hawk shoved her inside the Indian tipi and left her tied hand and foot to ponder her fate.

They had galloped through the day, leaving behind the Indians who drove the cattle, arriving at this camp by late afternoon. She and Rand had been separated, and she had been left alone the rest of the day and into the dark—to wait and wonder when Hawk would return.

Freddy's heart began to pound when she realized she could hear someone breathing beside her in the darkness. This tipi surely belonged to one of the Indians, and he must be sleeping next to her. Because Hawk had been the one to put her there, she guessed it must be him.

Her heart was thudding so hard she was afraid he would hear it. She forced herself to continue breathing slowly and deeply while she decided what she should do. Every thought of escape ended with the realization that even if she could somehow free her hands and steal a horse, she had no idea which direction to go. And she couldn't leave without Rand.

She had no idea where they were keeping him. She didn't even know if he was still alive.

"You've really done it this time, Lady Winnifred," she whispered.

The body beside her responded with a grunt.

She froze, waiting for the attack on her person she was sure would come at any moment. A full minute later, when the body beside her remained still, she realized she had gotten a reprieve.

What she needed was a knife to free her hands. And to defend herself. Hawk had carried one tied at his waist. He might have it on him now. If she could just get it from him, she might be able to free herself, escape the tipi, and find Rand.

She reached stealthily in the direction of the

breathing body, lowering her hands to where she thought Hawk's waist might be.

Kerseymere!

The instant her fingers touched fine cloth she realized it couldn't possibly be an Indian lying beside her. Unless Rand had died, and Hawk had taken his clothes. She shuddered at the thought. It was too frightening to allow her imagination to go in that direction.

"Rand?"

There was no answer.

She reached over to nudge the body beside her lightly with her elbow—and came into contact with flesh instead of cloth. She froze. Whoever was lying beside her was naked from the waist up. And from the small movements she could hear now, she had woken him up!

Her pulse beat a rapid tattoo.

"Freddy? Is that you?"

"Thank God. Oh, thank God." Freddy blinked back the tears of relief that prickled her eyes. "Rand. Oh, Rand," she whispered. "You're alive!"

He rolled over into her, groaned, then lay still.

"Are you tied up?" she asked.

"Yeah. What about you?"

"Hand and foot."

"Is there any water in here?" he asked.

"I don't know. Let me look around." She said look, but what she meant was feel. When it was still light she had noticed an iron kettle and some gourds near the entrance to the tipi. She turned onto her stomach and inched her way across the buffalo robe that covered most of the dirt floor. The slight breeze had to be coming from the flapped opening in the tipi.

She recognized the shapes by feel in the dark, reached inside with her fingertips and felt the wetness. "There's water here. It might be better if you come get it. If you can. That way I won't take the chance of spilling it."

"Give me a minute," Rand said.

She heard his painful progress, punctuated with grunts and groans, as he wormed his way toward her.

"Remind me next time to watch out a little better for marauding Indians," he said when he was finally beside her.

"I will." *If there is a next time,* Freddy thought.

"Where's that water?"

"It should be right in front of you."

She felt him lean forward and heard him noisily slurping the liquid. When he was done, he sat slumped where he was.

"How are you, Rand?"

"Tired, mostly. Whatever that Indian woman packed on my shoulder after she cut out the bullet must have worked. It doesn't hurt as much now as it did earlier. Are you . . . I mean . . . they didn't . . ."

"They haven't hurt me." *Yet.* Freddy shivered at the thought of the interview she had endured with Hawk before he left her alone in the tipi. The insane man had told her again that he planned to make her his wife. She wasn't sure what, exactly, was involved in being a Sioux wife, but she was certain she was completely unsuited for the job.

Freddy scooted closer and pressed herself against Rand, surprised at how good it felt to lean on a strong, familiar shoulder. The warmth of his bare flesh was strangely comforting. "I'm afraid that if we don't get out of here soon . . ."

They both knew what it was she feared.

Rand's hands were tied in front, so he slipped them over her head—hissing as he pulled his torn shoulder muscles—and pulled her back against him. "I won't let that happen, Freddy."

It was a promise she wasn't sure he could keep, but she appreciated the fact he had made it.

"What are we going to do, Rand?"

"I don't know. I don't think they intend to kill us right away. Otherwise, they wouldn't have bothered removing the bullet from my shoulder."

"Do you think they might ransom us?" Freddy asked.

"There's a chance of that. I suggest we put our heads together and figure out a way to save ourselves. Who do you suppose owns this tipi?"

"Hawk."

"How do you know that?"

"He told me." She made an unladylike sound. "Believe it or not, he speaks English. He also seems to be the leader of this band of savages. He says he's Sioux, but I'd swear he's at least part white."

"I think I've seen the man you're talking about. He was in the tipi arguing with the woman who fixed me up. Maybe we could reason with him," Rand said.

"He didn't seem like the reasonable type to me. Where do you suppose he is now?" Freddy asked.

"When the Indians carted me from the tipi where they removed the bullet to this one, Hawk was riding out again with a half-dozen or so Indians."

"Do you think they know about your mother? Do you think they're going back to get her and the wagonload of supplies?" Freddy asked anxiously.

"I don't know. The buffalo cut us completely off from Mother. Maybe they never saw her."

Freddy felt the tenseness in Rand's arms and shoulders. "She's all right, Rand. Rufus and Slim would have known what to do to keep them all safe."

"You're probably right," he said. But he didn't relax. "Let's see how hard it would be to get out of here."

"You mean right now?"

"I mean right now."

He released her, inched his way over to the flap of hide that covered the entrance to the tipi, and nudged it open with his tied hands. A dog lying across the entrance instantly raised its head and growled. Rand stuck his head out, and the dog barked once.

Rand let the flap drop closed. "We're not going out that way without waking up the whole village."

"There isn't anything in here we could use to slit the tipi and go out the other side, either,"

Freddy said. "I looked when they first put me in here."

"At least we can untie each other," Rand said.

"I doubt it. This rawhide was wet when they tied me up. When it dried, it tightened. I don't think there's any way to get it off except to cut it." Freddy was unable to stifle a loud yawn.

"You're tired."

"I thought I was too terrified to be sleepy, but I guess not," Freddy conceded with a rueful laugh.

"We can talk just as well lying down," Rand said as he rejoined her and eased the two of them backward. He hissed in pain as his shoulder made contact with the ground.

"Are you all right?"

"It only hurts when I move," he said with a snort that ended in a hiss of pain as he slid his arms over her head.

Freddy turned on her side in Rand's embrace and snuggled her head against his good shoulder. The hair on his chest tickled her nose. She drew back, smoothed the hair flat with her hand, then laid her cheek on her hand. She could feel his heart thudding slowly and steadily. "I have a confession to make, Rand."

"Uh-oh. What have you done now? Made a bet with Hawk that we can get free before morning?"

"This is serious."

"I'm sorry. What is it?"

"Do you remember the day you proposed to me?"

"How could I forget it? My knees were knocking, my palms were sweaty, and I wasn't sure I would be able to get two words past the knot in my throat."

"I mean, do you remember how my parents were so opposed to our engagement?" She put an open palm against his cheek, so she could judge his reactions in the dark. She felt the spasm as his teeth clenched.

"I remember."

"When you first mentioned marriage, I had every intention of refusing you. But I don't like being told what to do by anybody, especially my parents. Naturally, when they said no to your proposal, I said yes."

"I see."

"Do you, Rand?" She traced his mouth and found his lips flattened. He understood enough to be angry.

"When were you planning to tell me all this?"

She made a feeble attempt to laugh. "Would you believe I tried a dozen times and couldn't get the words out? I never wanted to hurt you, Rand. Our engagement, this trip, was like a snowball that kept getting bigger and bigger and rolling faster and faster out of control. Before I knew it I was on a ship bound for America. Then I was on a train headed west. Then I found myself on a riverboat, then another train. Finally, I was on horseback headed for a ranch in the middle of nowhere. I just . . . never found the right moment to speak."

"But you always intended to return home to

your parents eventually, unbroached and unmarried?"

"Yes."

"You realize that's impossible now. You have no choice except to marry me as soon as we get back to civilization. If we get back," he muttered.

"How would anyone in England ever find out about us spending the night together unchaperoned?"

"Do you dislike me so much, Freddy, that you'd welcome a scandal rather than marry me?"

"Oh, Rand, I like you very much. In fact, I always liked you the best of all my suitors. I'm just not ready to get married yet."

"It's too late to back out now, Freddy."

"It's never too late to back out, Rand."

He laughed. "I can see the more insistent I become, the stronger your refusals will be. At least I know how your mind works. All right, Freddy. I won't force you to marry me—assuming, of course, that we both live through this.

"But I asked you to be my wife because I'm very much in love with you. Surely you won't mind if I use this time we have together to see if I can make you fall a little in love with me."

"Rand, I—"

She wasn't expecting the kiss. Even if she had suspected it was coming, she couldn't have imagined the effect it would have on her. After all, she had already kissed Rand twice, and nothing very momentous had happened.

This time, her toes curled right up in her half-boots.

When he released her mouth, she stared, wide-eyed, at the shadow where his face should be. She reached up to touch her lips. They still tingled. It had to be the dire situation . . . or pity . . . or something.

"Have I ever told you how beautiful you are?"

"Countless times," she retorted, still off-balance from the searing kiss.

His fingers threaded through her hair. "Your hair is incredibly soft and silky."

"Rand, I don't think—"

"Don't think," he said in a husky voice. "Just let yourself feel."

His hands tangled in her hair, and he used his hold to draw her mouth toward his. She opened her mouth in protest, and his lips captured hers. The feelings were as extraordinary as they were unfamiliar.

First the utter softness of his lips, the heat of his mouth on hers, the rough wetness of his tongue as it sought entry. She kept her lips pressed together, but oh, she was tempted to let him in.

He nibbled at her lips with teeth and tongue until they were soft and puffy and unbelievably sensitive. For the first time in her life she felt the hard length of an aroused male against her belly. His bound hands pressed against the small of her back, urging her against him.

"Feel how I want you, how I need you," he crooned.

Freddy panicked and shoved at Rand's bare chest with her bound hands. "Let me go! Please. Stop, Rand. This is wrong. This is crazy. This shouldn't be happening!"

He released the pressure on her spine immediately but did nothing to take his arms from around her. "Be still, Freddy. You're hurting my shoulder. Lie still."

She lay panting in his arms, frightened as a fox that can hear the hounds baying. "I don't understand," she said. "I don't understand."

"What is it you don't understand?" Rand asked in a quiet voice.

"This isn't supposed to happen. I don't love you. How can this be happening?"

"Shh. Be still. I won't kiss you again. Relax and go to sleep. You're safe with me."

Rand soothed her with quiet words until she settled in his arms. She was not really relaxed, but at least she was no longer trying to escape him.

Rand had enough sexual experience to know that an innocent could be seduced even when there were no emotional ties to bind them. It had happened to him the first time. He had no reason to doubt the same principle would apply to a woman. Perhaps it had been unfair to use his knowledge on Freddy. But he had no intention of playing fair if it meant there was the least chance he would lose her.

He had loved her for a long time, which was saying a lot when she was seventeen and he was twenty-one. Frankly, he had been amazed when she agreed to marry him. It hadn't taken him long to realize she had doubts.

He had seen her watching him during the long journey across the ocean with her lower lip caught in her teeth. He had listened to enough aborted "Rand, I need to . . ." and "Rand, I have to . . ." declarations to suspect what she was trying to say. He had always managed to divert her so she hadn't been able to make her awful confession.

Until tonight.

He had finally let her speak because he knew, even if she did not, that there was no turning back. He would be her husband. She would be his wife. But his work was cut out for him. Quite simply, he wanted her to love him before they stood in front of a vicar and said the vows that would bind them together for life.

They were both nearly asleep when a sound at the entrance to the tipi brought them wide awake. Rand lifted his arms from around Freddy and rose, prepared to defend her, if necessary.

"Who's there?" Freddy said.

"Do not be afraid," a woman's voice whispered in the darkness. "It is only Willow. I tended the wound of the white man."

When she entered the tipi, Willow carried a torch. She moved to the center of the tipi where a ring of stones held kindling. Moments later the fire was lit. She extinguished the torch and sat down across the fire from them.

At first, all the Sioux had looked the same to Freddy, with their straight black hair and dark brown eyes. As she stared at Willow, she noticed individual features that made her distinctive. An overlapping eyetooth. An especially wide mouth. A bump on the bridge of her nose. Eyes that were wide-set with short, straight brows. And she was even shorter than Freddy, who was of less than average height.

Rand and Freddy exchanged worried glances. *Why had she come? What did she want?*

"How is it you speak English?" Freddy asked.

"Hawk taught me the words."

Willow traced the beaded design on her moccasin. Silence descended again.

"Did you have something you wanted to say to us?" Freddy asked, unable to bear the building tension.

Rand frowned at Freddy's impatience.

Willow answered her question. "I wish to help you escape."

Freddy gasped and turned a hopeful look toward Rand.

"Why would you do that?" Rand asked, less willing to believe such good fortune could fall into their laps.

"Because Hawk chooses this woman to be his wife," she said with a scornful jerk of her head in Freddy's direction. "Once she is gone, he will see that I am the woman—the only woman—who was meant to share his pallet."

"You want to marry Hawk yourself?" Freddy asked.

"We are husband and wife already," Willow said.

"Then why does he want me? He can't have two wives," Freddy protested. "It's against the law."

"It is not against our law," Willow said.

"Cut us free, and we'll be on our way," Freddy said, holding out her bound hands.

"Wait a minute," Rand said. "Maybe this is some kind of trap."

"We can't be more trapped than we already are," Freddy pointed out.

"I guess you're right," Rand conceded. He turned to Willow and said, "What do you want us to do?"

"I have taken away the dog that guarded you. I will lead you through the camp to ponies I have waiting to carry you away from here."

"We don't know where we are," Freddy said. "How will we know which way to go?"

"The white man's fort is to the south. That is all I can tell you."

"Won't Hawk be angry with you when he finds out what you've done?" Rand asked.

Willow shrugged. "Perhaps. But the white woman will be gone."

"What if Hawk comes after us?" Freddy asked.

"You may be certain he will come after you, as soon as he discovers you are gone," Willow said. "That is why you must ride like the wind. Do not stop until you reach the safety of the fort."

"Are we that close to the fort?" Rand asked, surprised.

Willow smiled. "Hawk is very smart. And very brave. It pleases him to do what he does under the noses of the soldiers, who believe him to be far away in the hills to the north. Now, come with me."

Rand held out his bound hands. "You'll have to cut us free first. And I'll need a shirt to replace the one you took."

Willow crossed to a parfleche near the edge of the tipi and pulled out a beaded buckskin shirt. She thrust it at Rand, who grabbed it between numbed fingers. Then she pulled a knife from a sheath tied by a thong to the waist of her buckskin dress.

Rand felt the coolness of the metal against his flesh and felt the pressure of it against his leather boots. Moments later he experienced a series of excruciating pinpricks as blood flowed into his numbed hands and feet.

"Oh, Rand, it hurts!" Freddy said as she carefully opened and closed her hands after Willow cut her bonds. She reached down to rub her calves. "I'm not sure my legs will support me."

Rand gritted his teeth as he lifted his arms to slip the shirt down over his head. Fortunately the agony was over quickly. The buckskin was warm, and heavier than the fine lawn shirt he was used to wearing. He ran his fingers over the colorful beaded design. "Did you make this?" he asked Willow.

She nodded.

"It's beautiful." He shook his hands as painful

pinpricks gave warning that blood was circulating once more.

Willow reached for Rand's hands and began to massage them. "It will not take long before the feeling returns." She eyed Freddy and asked, "Is this your man?"

"Yes," Rand answered for her.

Freddy shot him an annoyed look, but she didn't contradict him. He wasn't sure why he hadn't let her answer for herself, except he didn't want to hear her deny again that she belonged to him. The matter was settled in his mind. The vows might as well have been said. As far as he was concerned, they were husband and wife.

He staggered to his feet and leaned on Willow until his wobbly legs would support him. When he was standing on his own, he turned and held out his hands to Freddy and pulled her onto her feet.

"Can you walk?" he asked her.

"I can try."

Rand winced at the pain when he took his first steps and saw from the pinched look around Freddy's mouth that she wasn't in much better shape. He admired her fortitude. Most English ladies he knew would already have collapsed. Not his Freddy.

"Follow me," Willow said. She left the tipi without waiting to see if they followed.

Holding each other upright, Freddy and Rand hobbled their way after her through the sleeping village, using the half moon and a star-filled sky for light. As Willow had promised, the dog that had slept in front of the tipi was absent, and they didn't encounter any more animals. Two Roman-nosed, sway-backed Indian ponies were waiting along the edge of a stream, not many yards from the nearest tipi. Neither pony was saddled, and each had only a halter arrangement instead of a bridle with a sturdy metal bit.

"Where are our horses?" Freddy asked.

"Hawk gave them to the bravest of the men who raided with him," she said.

Rand and Freddy exchanged an annoyed look before he boosted her onto the nearest sorry-looking pony and handed her the reins. She could feel the body heat of the animal through the thin layer of separation provided by her undergarments.

If Freddy had been any other properly bred English girl, it would have been a novel sensation. But she had ridden bareback in her rowdy youth and absolutely loved it. The feel of the power between her thighs was exhilarating, rather than terrifying. "Oh, Rand," she breathed. "I think we're actually going to get away."

"I've never been so glad in my life that you're a neck-or-nothing rider," Rand muttered as he mounted his own pony. His legs nearly reached the ground on either side of the animal.

Freddy *tsked* as she examined the halter that provided the only control she had over the Indian pony. "I suppose it doesn't matter that I probably can't stop this animal, because I don't want him to stop anytime soon."

"Thank you, Willow," Rand said. "We'll be forever in your debt. If there's ever any way I can repay you—"

"I want nothing from you, white man. One further warning I will give you. Do not lead the soldiers back to this place. We will be gone from here long before you can return. And Hawk will be watching and waiting with many braves to ambush and kill you. Now go."

Freddy didn't have to be told twice. She kicked the Indian pony hard and the animal jumped into a stiff-legged trot with Rand not far behind her.

Freddy felt like shouting. Once away from the village, they loped until the horses were winded, then slowed to a walk to allow them a rest. "We're free, Rand. We're free! All we have to do is keep riding south and—oh, my God. How do we know we're going in the right direction?"

"I thought she pointed us in the right direction."

"I assumed you knew which way to go."

"Why would you assume that?"

"You're a man. You're supposed to know these things."

"I'm afraid I don't."

Freddy halted her mount, and Rand pulled his pony to a stop beside her. She looked up at the sky. "Isn't there some way you can tell from the stars which direction is north?"

"I think so. But I never learned how."

"What now?"

"We could wait till daylight. I could figure it out

then. Assuming the sun comes up tomorrow, of course."

"That isn't funny."

"I wasn't joking. Look at those clouds scudding past the moon. If it rains we'll be out of luck."

"We can't stop. You heard what Willow said. Hawk will come after us as soon as he returns. We need to get to the fort before then."

"Then I suggest we keep riding in the same direction," Rand said. "And hope it's south."

"I guess we don't have much choice." Freddy kicked her horse into a mile-eating trot, and Rand followed after her.

Unfortunately, they were headed due north.

8

"I'm hungry, and I want to go home."

"You sound like a seven-year-old," Rand said, ruffling Freddy's hair as he would a pouting child's.

"Oh, surely ten or eleven at least," Freddy quipped.

She met Rand's heavy-lidded gaze and glanced quickly away from the tenderness—mixed with something not quite so benign—she found there.

Rand's arm circled her waist as they lay spooned together. The rising sun hadn't yet warmed the ground, and she snuggled close to share his warmth. She felt surprisingly safe and secure, even though they had no shelter over their heads, no weapons to defend themselves against predators, animal or human. She knew Rand would protect her with his life.

She had awakened to find him watching her, his gray eyes lambent, his lips full. Instinctively she had recognized the signs for what they were. She had stretched lazily, like a cat, letting her breasts brush against his chest and causing him to make a sound in his throat somewhere between a grunt and a groan.

She wouldn't have known what to do if he had taken advantage of her invitation. She was merely testing her sexual wings, making a little soaring trip and flying right back to the nest. She supposed the fact that she felt free to tease him meant that she trusted him. Which surprised her, because she was not normally a trusting sort of person. At least not where young men—the kind who might compromise an unwary female and force her into an unwanted marriage—were concerned.

"I know I'm used to being a little indulged," she said.

Rand snorted at the understatement.

"But I've always believed that if the circumstances ever arose when I needed to be strong, I could be." She swallowed over the surprising lump of feeling that clogged her throat. "I don't feel very brave at the moment, Rand. In fact, I'm feeling pretty scared."

Rand closed his arms tighter around the woman he loved, bracing for the pain that occurred when he strained the muscles in his wounded shoulder. He understood her fear. They had spent the night along the bank of an unknown river, hidden amid thickly overgrown cottonwoods and willow trees matted together with tough vines. Completely lost.

"I'll take care of you, Freddy," Rand murmured. "I'll be strong for both of us."

But his comment was more wishful thinking than fact. He had been so weakened by his wound that they had been forced to stop after only a few hours of riding. As soon as the sun began to rise he realized it was a good thing they had stopped, because they had been headed in the wrong direction. It was sheer luck they had stumbled upon this river in the dark and been able to quench their thirst. He planned to follow the river south today, in the hope it would lead them to civilization, preferably not of the Indian variety.

"I wish I knew how to make a trap," Rand said. "We've seen enough rabbits to fill both our stomachs. Of course, I have nothing with which to start a fire, so we'd have to eat our rabbit raw."

"I could never eat a rabbit," Freddy said, "cooked or raw."

"Why not? They're quite tasty, actually. Roasted, I mean. I've never had occasion to eat one raw myself."

Freddy made a face. "My father raised rabbits for food on his summer estate. I used to sneak in and play with them when they were babies. I could never eat one after that."

"You'd be surprised what you could eat when you're really hungry."

"Not rabbits. Please, Rand. How about a pheasant? We've seen plenty of those, too."

"Pheasant it is," Rand said. "Since I can't catch either one, you might as well wish for what you want. Raw pheasant. Sounds delightful." He smacked his lips.

Freddy chuckled. "That's what I like about you, Rand. You could always make me laugh."

"Is that all you like about me?" Rand knew he was taking a chance asking such a personal question. But if he was going to woo and win her, he had to know what she admired in a man.

"You're not afraid to take chances," she said. "Like coming all the way to America to seek your fortune."

"I didn't have much choice. My father left me nothing in England."

"A lot of men would simply have chosen a rich wife and—" Freddy cut herself off.

Rand smiled. "Has the difference in our circumstances finally occurred to you, love? Yes, you have a fortune, or will someday, but no, that isn't the reason I came courting."

"I never thought for a moment—"

He kissed her to shut her up, because of course the thought had occurred to her. A little late, perhaps, but she wasn't as grown up as she liked to think. He was barely four years her senior, yet he didn't think he had ever been as naive or innocent as he believed her to be even now. Yet it was that very innocence that drew him. He had always believed the greatest beauty was to be found in an unfolding bud.

The instant Rand's tongue touched her closed

lips, Freddy wrenched free. It was the same thing he had tried to do when he kissed her in the tipi, the first time her toes curled. Of course, they had been curling pretty regularly ever since. She stared at him, eyes cautious, a little anxious. Maybe it was a trick of some kind, something meant to make her believe he was *the one,* even though he wasn't her Prince Charming. She had to admit it was working.

"It definitely wasn't your fortune that attracted me to you, Freddy."

"What was it, then?"

"Fishing for compliments? If only you were fishing for fish. There are people in the Far East, I believe, who actually eat raw fish."

Freddy watched his lips curl into a mocking smile and smiled back at him, wondering all the while if he was going to kiss her again. An undercurrent of tension shimmered between them. Because she wanted it to happen again. And suspected he did, too.

She found it difficult to describe everything she was feeling. Agitated. Excited. Breathless. And curious about what would have happened if she had let him do with his tongue whatever it was he had been about to do.

"I fell in love with your eyes, Freddy," Rand murmured against her forehead.

"My eyes?"

"You have the eyes of a dreamer—open and trusting and full of possibilities. I want to share those dreams, Freddy. I want very much to be a part of them."

His lips caressed her temple, slid down to close the eyes he had professed to love, then kissed the tip of her nose, and finally, at long, long last, found her mouth. Her lips were waiting for him.

Rand held Freddy loosely, ready to release her if she made the slightest effort to be free. She had done nothing to protest his kisses, but her cheeks had grown roses, and her eyelids remained lowered. She was a picture of maidenly modesty. He wondered what would happen if he kissed her as he wanted to, with his tongue, and touched her breasts with his hands and mouth.

Their mouths met and clung. Her lips were softer than he had imagined lips could be, yielding, totally unFreddylike. He broke the kiss and watched as her tongue slid out to harvest the dampness left by his. Tasting him.

"I want to kiss you, Freddy. May I?"

"All right, Rand." She squeezed her eyes more tightly closed and pursed her lips into a bow.

He fought to keep from laughing, knowing that would be fatal to his cause. "Relax," he murmured in her ear.

Her eyes flashed open. "I can't re—"

He covered her mouth with his, letting his lips settle on hers, letting her feel the weight of them, the firmness, before he sent his tongue probing the seam of her lips, demanding the secrets of her mouth.

She jerked away once again and stared at him,

wide-eyed. "What was that . . . what were you doing, Rand?"

"It's part of kissing."

"Nobody except you ever kissed me like that!"

"I hope not! That kind of kissing is reserved for men and their—"

She narrowed her eyes suspiciously. "Mistresses?"

"A smart man will teach his wife how to please him in bed."

"What about her pleasure?" Freddy demanded.

"Pleasing her is a great part of what pleases him," he answered quietly.

"I see."

"Do you?"

Truthfully, Freddy conceded, it was all a bit confusing. But she didn't want to air her ignorance in front of Rand, not when he had already accused her of behaving like a child. She wanted him to see her as a woman. She didn't want to examine why that should matter when she had already told him she couldn't marry him. She settled back into his embrace and began idly tracing the line of his stubbled jaw. She was afraid to invite another kiss, uncertain whether she wanted to take any step leading to greater intimacy with him. Especially when she didn't love him.

"I've never felt a man's beard before," she said, subtly withdrawing from the subject of kisses. "It's odd how good it feels. Just now, when you kissed me, your beard scraped my cheek and . . . it made me shiver." She shivered again, remembering the experience. "Does it hurt when you shave?"

"No," he said with a strangled laugh.

"Why do you suppose hair grows on a man's face?"

"I have no idea."

"I like how the stubble looks on you. Sort of dark and dangerous. It makes you seem almost a stranger. Only, I know I'm safe with you."

Like a lamb with a very hungry lion, Rand thought as his genitals drew up tight. He was going to explode if she didn't stop speaking so provocatively, touching him so intimately.

They were completely off the subject he had originally wanted to pursue, but he was willing to let her mind wander where it would. It was akin to their fanciful conversation about rabbits and pheasants. Since there was little he could do to change himself overnight into her ideal man, he would simply have to be the man he was and hope she could learn to appreciate him.

His body responded poignantly to the feel of her fingers roaming the flesh at his throat. He inched himself away so she wouldn't be able to detect his arousal—not for her sake, but for his. He had spent a hellish night wanting to touch, wanting to taste the woman in his arms, yet bound by honor to keep his distance. Now she seemed willing, and he was having the devil of a time putting honor above other, more urgent, needs. That was despite the ache in his shoulder, which warned him he might well be biting off more than he could chew comfortably.

"Stop wiggling," Freddy chided. "You keep moving my pillow." She rearranged her head on his arm and sighed in contentment.

They lay in silence, watching the sun rise higher in a wide blue sky. Two jays chattered like an old married couple, while the wind rustled the cottonwoods, and the river tumbled noisily over its stony bed. They could have been lying beside a peaceful brook in England.

But they weren't.

"We have to get up soon, love. We can't stay here. It's too dangerous," Rand said.

"It can't be more dangerous than riding across the open prairie unarmed and lost." Freddy let her fingers walk down Rand's throat to the open neck of the buckskin shirt. She felt him shudder beneath her touch and marveled at her power over him.

She felt his hand squeeze her breast and froze. She lifted her gaze to meet his. "Rand . . ."

It wasn't necessary to complete her protest. He withdrew his hand.

She felt bereft. But also relieved. They weren't a married couple, and she wasn't sure they ever would be, despite Rand's insistence the previous evening that marriage to him was necessary to save her reputation.

He gave her a sharp nudge and began struggling to sit up. Her muscles were stiff, but she managed to get to her feet more easily than Rand, who needed her help to rise. She kept her shoulder under his arm, afraid he would fall if she left him on his own.

"Are you sure you can stand?"

"I'm going to do more than that. I'm going to spend the next several hours sitting upright on a horse."

"We could stay here, Rand. Maybe—"

"Hawk will be coming after us. We have to ride for the fort as hard and as fast as we can. I wouldn't stand a chance in a fight, not with this broken wing of mine." Not, Rand thought, that he would have much chance in a fair fight, either. He was a decent boxer, having indulged in the sport with other young men his age. But he doubted the Sioux would follow Marquis of Queensberry rules. And he had no skill with a knife, which he suspected Hawk might very well use against him.

"You're awfully brave to even think about fighting that dreadful Indian," Freddy said.

"If I were really courageous I'd have stayed in England and learned a trade," Rand replied. "I was too proud to want my friends to see I had to earn my living with my hands. This venture provided an escape from the ignominy of being a poor man in a privileged society where money matters only if you don't have it."

Freddy walked with Rand toward the thick bushes some distance away where they had left the horses tied overnight. "Plying a trade has always been the fate of second sons," she pointed out.

"It's not quite so honorable for heirs left without a fortune," he said, fighting the rancor he felt every time he thought of the profligate spending that had robbed him of his heritage.

Freddy paused long enough to reach up and put her fingers to Rand's lips. "It doesn't matter, Rand. In fact, it all seems pretty silly when you think of the two of us here without a change of clothing or a bite to eat, reduced to considering the bare necessities of survival. Because, I'm not quite sure, but I think—in spite of everything—I'm actually enjoying myself."

"You would," Rand said with a grin. He hugged her quickly, tightly, until she squeaked. "I think that's another reason why I fell in love with you, Freddy. You're irrepressible."

"Whatever that means," she said, uncomfortable with the mention of love, because she didn't love Rand in return.

"You take life's little jabs, and you bounce right back."

"Sort of like a boxer?"

His grin widened. "Oh, I'd like to see you in the ring, love, going a few rounds with adversity. You'd beat him every time."

"You think so?"

"I'd bet on it." Which was saying a lot because, frankly, Rand wasn't much of a gambler. He had seen what wagering—on cards, on dice, and on risky ventures—had done to his father. Or rather, the man who had been married to his mother and had given Rand his name, but very little else of himself.

"Rand!" Freddy whispered urgently.

Her tone of voice warned him something was wrong. And the whinnies of the frightened horses.

The Indian ponies yanked the reins free and raced away, stranding them on foot. Escape from the Sioux was unlikely now. Only that was no longer their immediate problem.

"Is that a . . . a bear, Rand?" Freddy rasped.

It was. A very large, very dangerous-looking bear. "Climb a tree, Freddy."

"What?"

"The tree closest to you. Shinny up it. You can do that, can't you?" Rand said in a calm, quiet voice.

"What good will that do? Bears can climb, too."

"Do it, Freddy," Rand said, losing patience as panic gained ground.

Rand had never seen a bear up close. He wasn't looking forward to getting a better look at this one. Luckily the wind was in Rand's face, which meant the animal wasn't aware of them. Yet. Its attention had been drawn by the fleeing horses.

He gave Freddy a boost that sent her a couple of feet higher up the tree. The cottonwoods didn't have comfortable branches for sitting on, but Freddy settled herself in a fork twelve or thirteen feet above the ground.

"Rand? What are you going to do?"

"I'm going to distract the bear and lead him away from you."

"That doesn't sound like a very good idea. Why don't you climb a tree, too?"

"I don't think I could manage it, Freddy. Not with the wound in my shoulder."

"Please, Rand, don't do anything to get yourself killed."

"Love me?" he asked with a cheeky smile.

"I just don't want to be left alone out here!" she shot back.

"If we're lucky, that monster will be so busy chasing me that he won't notice you. Whatever happens, stay where you are until you're sure the bear is gone and it's safe to come down. Then follow the river south. You won't forget?"

"I won't forget." Freddy realized what Rand was saying without saying it in so many words. *I might not survive. I might be killed.* In that case, she should do her best to reach the fort on her own.

Freddy felt a tightness in her chest that wasn't entirely fear for her own well-being. She looked into Rand's eyes and saw the willingness there to sacrifice himself for her. And it drew an unwanted response from her. "Please, be careful, Rand."

"I promise I'll do my best to stay alive. I'm looking forward to having a houseful of children with you and watching my grandchildren grow up around my knees."

The future he envisioned sounded idyllic, Freddy had to admit. It was unlikely either one of them was going to survive to see it. Rand might not outlive his encounter with the bear. If he was killed, her survival was very much in doubt. She wished fervently that she did love him, that she had made love to him when she had the chance, because her life might end without her ever knowing that emotion, that experience.

Wishing didn't make things so.

She started to speak again, but realized Rand was no longer aware of her. He seemed totally focused on the bear that was ambling in their direction, apparently still unaware of their presence.

Rand's heart was beating so hard he could actually hear it thudding against the wall of his chest. He took a deep breath and huffed it out in an attempt to calm himself. He looked up and down the river to see if there was any refuge he could seek once he drew the bear's attention. The underbrush seemed even thicker downstream. That was the direction he would run.

He shouted and waved his arms. With a clutch of alarm he watched the bear raise its nose to the wind, looking for a scent to match the sound. "Hey! This way!"

The bear saw him.

Rand wasn't certain the bear would chase him if he ran away, but it seemed likely. He took off, knowing he had to lead the bear away from Freddy. He didn't allow himself to think farther than that, because the grisly possibilities were too overwhelming to consider.

He held his wrist tight against his chest as he ran to protect his wounded shoulder. But he stumbled, and as he reached out to catch himself, the wound tore open and began to bleed again. Every jarring footfall after that brought excruciating pain. He fought the blackness that threatened behind his eyes. Fine end that would be for the Earl of Rushland, to faint dead away and be eaten by a bear!

The thought made him smile, which quickly became a wince as he tripped and jerked his shoulder painfully. He ran like he was sprinting for his team at Oxford, with a guinea bet that he could trounce Mortimer Fry in the dash.

He glanced over his shoulder. The lumbering beast was almost upon him, jaws slobbering, *huge* teeth revealed by his open mouth.

Rand looked for some means of escaping the inevitable and spied the remains of an immense rotted tree trunk ahead of him. An animal had recently been burrowing there, and Rand thought perhaps he could wedge himself in the hole beneath the trunk and escape the bear's reach.

Maybe.

He pressed a hand to the stitch in his side. If he could just run . . . a little bit . . . farther.

He threw himself onto the ground and scuttled under the rotted log very like a beetle hiding under a leaf. Oh, the beetle felt safe from harm, but one step by a heavy foot could easily crush it. Rand knew his situation was equally fragile.

The bear didn't hesitate. It immediately began digging with its claws in an attempt to dislodge him from his hiding place.

Rand grunted in surprise when the swipe of claws raked across his chest, shredding the buckskin as though it had been his lawn shirt. He was too stunned at first to feel the pain of his own torn flesh.

He pressed himself farther back into the hole. It was clear now, if it hadn't been before, that it was only a matter of time before the bear widened the narrow hole enough to reach him. His lungs filled with the smell of damp rot, of freshly turned earth. He felt oddly detached, as though he were observing this happening to someone else. He watched himself look methodically for some route of escape and, finding none, begin to face the prospect of death.

He didn't want Freddy's last memories of him to be of a screaming man. He was determined to die quietly. He tried to brace himself for the horror to come. His mind skittered around, refusing to focus on the unthinkable.

"Bear! Hey, you, Bear! Over here."

Holy Christ! Freddy was taunting the bear, trying to get its attention. "Freddy!" Rand shouted. "Freddy, go back!"

It was too late. The bear abruptly stopped digging, and the opening that had been blocked by its rancid body filled with blinding light.

The animal was gone.

Rand sucked in a breathful of fresh air as he wiggled himself free of his hidey-hole. The sight that greeted his eyes made his heart skip a beat.

The bear had covered half the distance to Freddy. She was running, and the bear was chasing her. He picked up the closest thing he could find, a fair-sized rock, and threw it as hard as he could.

It hit the bear square on the rump, but the lumbering beast didn't even slow down.

"Freddy!" Rand cried in agony. She was going to be mauled before his eyes. There was nothing he could do to prevent it. Nothing! He started running toward her, knowing his effort was futile.

His life flashed before him, along with all the questions he had been so sure he would find the answers to someday. He wished he had confronted his mother with the things his father had told him on his deathbed. Surely she would have told him the truth if he had asked her.

His lungs were bursting. His heart racketed in his bleeding chest. Too late! Too late! No more . . . time . . . for regrets. The bear had caught up to Freddy. It took a swipe at her with its paw, and he heard her shriek as her feet flew out from under her.

At the same time Rand cried her name, several shots rang out in the distance.

The bear turned to look in the direction of the gunshots.

Rand halted where he was, his breath caught in his chest. Hope flared. If only help came in time. If only . . .

The bear glanced back at Freddy's prone figure, then searched the wind with its snout. Another shot rang out, much closer this time, and the grizzly bounded away in the opposite direction from the noise.

They were saved!

Rand raced to where Freddy lay unmoving on the ground. As he turned her over, her eyelids fluttered open.

"Rand? The bear?"

"He's gone, Freddy. Are you all right?" he asked.

She exposed her sturdy leather boot, which bore the clear marks of the bear's claws. "I need a new pair of boots," she said with an attempt at a smile. "But I'm fine."

Rand pulled her tight against him, his mouth pressed to her temple. "God, Freddy! What made you do something so impossibly stupid? You could have been killed!"

"I . . . I don't know what came over me, Rand. I only know I wouldn't have wanted to live myself if anything had happened to you."

Rand looked into her green eyes and saw the confusion there. She might not know it yet, but she did care for him. And not just a little.

"Who fired those shots?" Freddy asked. "They saved our lives."

"I don't know," Rand said. "But I'm going to shake the hand of whoever it was."

Then he saw two Indians galloping directly toward them.

"Oh, hell," he muttered. "Bloody, bloody hell."

9

Miles had planned to take vengeance on Verity for her betrayal of him by using her body for his own pleasure. For years he had imagined having her under him, no matter what it took to get her there. When the moment came—to his surprise and consternation—he had drawn back from using force to have her.

Her behavior was even more confusing than his.

Despite what Verity had threatened, if she found his face frightening or awful, if she found his touch distasteful, she had given no sign of it. She had opened herself to him, responded wholeheartedly to him, and when he had found satisfaction, she had circled her arms around him and held him close.

Could she possibly have been telling the truth?

Could a naive and gullible Verity have been forced by Chester's threats into a marriage she hadn't wanted? Had she really loved him enough to make such a sacrifice for him? Still, she had shown very little trust in a man she supposedly loved. She had married Chester without even giving Miles a chance to help her out of her dilemma.

"Miles?"

He had been so deep in thought, her voice startled him. He glanced up from under the brim of his Stetson at the blinding sun and realized half the morning was gone. They had been riding steadily north along the Platte River on a line parallel to the trail they would have taken to the Hanrahan ranch. But they had not seen hide nor hair of Tom or the Indians.

"Shouldn't we have caught up to Tom by now?" Verity asked.

"We lost a lot of time tracking down your horse."

"I could have ridden pillion behind you."

"Riding double would have been dangerous if we ran into the Sioux and had to light out." He heard the anger in his voice and realized it wasn't caused by their delay in following Tom so much as by his confusion about their relationship. He sighed.

He might be willing to give her the benefit of the doubt regarding her marriage to Chester. But he wasn't going to apologize for ruining Talbot. And he wasn't going to let her out of the marriage to him.

"I'm sorry, Miles," she said.

"For what?"

"For everything."

His gaze met hers across the small distance that separated them on horseback. "That covers a lot of territory. Anything specific you have in mind?"

He watched her gnaw on her lower lip, leaving it pink and swollen. She opened her mouth to speak and closed it again. Finally she said, "I never meant the things I said about your face—the scar, I mean. It never mattered to me."

"That's not what you said twenty-two years ago," he reminded her.

"Twenty-two years ago I told you what I thought would make you hate me enough to let me go without an argument." She shook her head sadly. "I guess I was convincing."

"I believed you."

"Do you believe me now?"

He ran the reins through his hands in agitation. "Does it matter?"

"It does if we're going to have a life together."

"Is that what you want?"

She angled her body in the saddle to face him squarely. "I thought it was what you wanted."

He shook his head. "I wanted revenge."

"Chester is dead. You've gotten me back. I'd say you've accomplished what you set out to do."

"Not quite." He had planned to hurt and humiliate her the way he had been hurt and humiliated. He had not, he realized now, made any plans at all beyond that. He eyed her coolly.

"You have some further vengeance planned?" she asked. When he didn't answer she prodded, "What's stopping you?"

"Let's just say I'm reconsidering the situation."

She met his gaze warily. "Then you've forgiven me for what happened?"

He reined his horse around a fallen log and noted absently where a bear had been digging there recently.

"I'm not sure that's possible."

"Then how can we hope to have any sort of life together?"

He brushed his fingers over the worn design tooled in the saddle leather. "I need some time, Verity. I'm going to have to learn to trust you all over again. You can understand why I might have some trouble doing that."

He saw the worry in her eyes. She opened her mouth to say something, then closed it again without speaking. Suddenly, she pointed to a spot behind him, over his left shoulder.

"Miles, look!"

He swiveled his horse around to see what had caught her attention. Black smoke billowed to the west.

"What is it?" she asked.

Miles felt the bile come up from his stomach to burn his throat as he realized what he was seeing. "The Hanrahan place," he said. "The Sioux must have circled around and gone back to do what they had planned in the first place. Come on. Let's go."

"Wait! What about Rand and Freddy?"

"Sophie and Earl Hanrahan have a new baby. That's also where Frog and Red were headed. There may be a chance I can get there in time to help."

Five years ago Miles had seen smoke and followed it to a poor dirt farm. When he got there, he could hear the screams of several victims trapped inside a burning line shack. The single door to the windowless shack had been blocked from the outside. Apparently some cattleman had decided to rid himself of a nester family squatting on his government rangeland by burning them out.

Miles had dragged away the heavy iron plow blocking the door, but by then the screams had stopped. Once he got the door open, he could see that, between the raging fire and the dense smoke, he probably wasn't going to find anyone alive inside. But he couldn't stand there doing nothing, so he had wrapped himself in a sopping wet blanket, taken a deep breath, and crawled inside.

Just inside the door he had encountered a body in flames. He had grabbed a thick-soled workingman's shoe and dragged the body out of the fire. He had covered the burning body with the wet blanket he had been using to protect himself, then picked up the thin, charred body of the gangly farm boy in his arms and stumbled outside with it.

He would never forget the sickly sweet odor of burned flesh, or his horror as the boy's skin sloughed off on his hands when he lowered the kid to the ground.

The smoke was too thick, the fire too hot, for

him to go back inside. Or that was what he told himself on the nights when he awoke trembling with nausea and fear, his body bathed in sweat, his hands pressed to his ears to quiet the screams of the man and woman—the boy's parents—who had burned to death that day. He would always wonder whether a second effort by him could have saved them.

He had stayed at the ramshackle farm and nursed the boy, protecting him from the rancher who had come to see the results of his handiwork, then holding vigil while he waited for the fourteen-year-old to die of his horrible burns. Somehow, the kid had survived.

Sully had been with him ever since. He was a constant reminder to Miles of the damage fire could do to the human body.

If the Hanrahans had stayed in the house after it had caught fire . . . He gagged as the remembered odor of burning flesh rose in his nostrils but managed to swallow down his gorge.

He was stunned by the fear that rose within him. *I can't help anyone who's caught in that fire. I can't.*

He spurred his horse hard in the direction of the fire, anyway, hoping to hell there was something he could do to help, short of running into a burning building.

"Miles—" Verity cried to stop him. She had something important to tell him, only she was still searching for the right words.

But he was already gone.

She kicked her exhausted horse into as close to a gallop as it could manage, terrified of being left behind.

When Miles had admitted he was reconsidering his vengeance and started talking about learning to trust her again, Verity had realized the predicament she was in.

On the one hand, confessing to Miles that Rand was his son would clear the slate and allow them to go on with their lives together with honesty between them.

On the other hand, she had no doubt Miles was going to be livid with anger when he learned he had a son she had kept secret from him all these years.

On the other, other hand, she had very little hope he would believe she hadn't known she was pregnant when she married Chester.

She had to figure out a way to tell him the truth —before they found Rand—that didn't paint her as a villainess. Or he was going to forget all about learning to trust again and return to his plan of vengeance.

Long before he reached the ranch house Miles realized whatever had happened there was over and done. Nothing was left of the house but a smoking ruin of blackened timbers. He felt an intense sense of relief.

Giant flames still licked at the barn, devouring the wood and spitting out billows of smoke that partially obliterated the figures moving around the barnyard.

He watched two men frantically racing back and forth dumping buckets of water on the chicken house and a tool storage shed, trying to keep them from catching fire as well. A third man pulled furiously on a pump handle. A constant stream of water splashed onto the muddy ground between bucket refills.

Miles was glad to see that Earl Hanrahan was the man at the pump and breathed a sigh of relief when he recognized Red and Frog as the two men carrying buckets. His breath caught in his throat when a quick search revealed no sign of Mrs. Hanrahan or the baby.

He rode as close as he could to the fire without spooking his horse—or himself—then dismounted and ran the rest of the way to Hanrahan on foot. "Everybody all right?" he called out when he was close enough to be heard over the roar of the fire and the crash of burning timbers.

Earl Hanrahan paused for a moment with the pump lever upraised and stared at him. His red-rimmed eyes looked ghastly in a face blackened by smoke. "Sophie's dead," he said flatly. He glanced over his shoulder at the blackened ashes. "She was in the house when they attacked." Earl turned back to stare blankly at Miles. "She never got out."

Earl started pumping again, yanking on the iron handle so hard it squealed in rebellion before water began gushing out.

Miles didn't ask about the baby. Earl would

have said if the baby was all right. Which he hadn't. So probably the little girl was gone, too. Miles breathed through his mouth, afraid of what his nose might detect in the devastation. A second look at the house convinced him there was nothing more left of Earl's wife and baby than charred bones. Flesh had burned, but he would no longer be able to smell it. He pressed his lips flat and let himself breathe normally again.

He clapped a hand on Earl's shoulder, which was all the comfort he could offer. "What can I do? How can I help?"

Earl stopped pumping abruptly to survey the damage. The roof of the henhouse was on fire, and one side of the tool shed was engulfed. His hands fell away from the pump and hung at his sides. "Nothing," he said, his voice raw from breathing smoke. "There's nothing to be done now."

When Frog arrived with his bucket, there was no water to fill it. He looked at Earl, then back toward the burning roof of the chicken house. "Can't stop it now," Frog said.

A moment later Red joined Frog at the pump. "You quittin', Earl?"

Earl took a step back from the pump. "Let 'em burn."

Miles had forgotten about Verity and was surprised when she clasped her hand in his. He turned and saw she was staring aghast at the remains of the house.

"Was it Indians?" she asked.

"What else?" Earl replied bitterly.

"We made them pay," Red said, gesturing toward a body crumpled near the corral and another near the house.

"Was it Hawk?" Miles asked.

"Don't know," Red said. "Where's Shorty and Tom?"

"We found Hawk and a few of his braves camped not far from here and attacked them just before dawn. Shorty didn't make it. Tom chased off after a couple of bucks who escaped. I was hunting him when Verity spotted the smoke."

"Where's your wife?" Verity asked Earl.

Miles squeezed Verity's hand to cut her off, but he was too late. Earl had heard her.

"Sophie's dead," he said. "And the baby. They got trapped in the house."

"I'm so sorry," Verity said.

Miles saw the tears well in her eyes and wondered if she was crying because of the senseless deaths, or because it was so obvious Earl couldn't.

"Why don't you come back to my place with me?" Miles said to Earl. "Red and Frog can stay here and—"

"Thanks, Miles. I'd rather bury them myself. And I won't be leaving. I'm staying here with them."

"But—"

Earl raised his head from slumped shoulders. Tears glittered in his eyes. "I can't leave them here all alone. You understand, don't you, Miles?"

Miles put a hand on the other man's shoulder

and felt his body trembling. "Sure, Earl. We'll stay and help, if that's all right."

Earl nodded, then turned and headed for the ruins of the house.

Verity pressed herself against Miles, and his arms closed around her, as much to comfort himself as to comfort her.

"Oh, Miles," she murmured. "That poor, poor man."

He felt her trembling, too, and realized she was imagining her son dead, and Freddy. And not without good reason.

"Hey, boss. I think you better come here and look at this . . . without the lady," Red said.

He felt Verity quiver in his embrace. "Wait here," he ordered. He freed himself and started toward where Red knelt by one of the dead Sioux.

Verity quickly caught up to him.

He stopped and took her shoulders in his hands. "You should wait here."

She looked up at him with pleading eyes. "Whatever it is, Miles, I have to know."

"All right. But hold on to my hand. I don't want you landing on the ground if you faint."

"I won't faint," she promised him.

He had his doubts. But he took her hand and dragged her after him toward where Red waited.

Red had turned the Indian onto his back.

Miles saw right away what had garnered Red's attention. The Indian was wearing a signet ring. And he had a pocket watch tied on a rawhide string around his neck.

"Recognize these?" Miles said to Verity as Red handed him the two pieces of jewelry.

Verity's face felt stiff. She nodded jerkily. "They belong to Rand." She glanced up at Miles, whose solemn features frightened her. "It doesn't mean he's dead."

"There's something else I didn't mention, because I didn't want to worry you," Miles said.

"What?" Verity asked.

"Rand's and Freddy's horses . . . They were Thoroughbreds, weren't they?"

She nodded, because she couldn't get any sound past the thickness in her throat.

"Two Thoroughbreds were picketed at the Indian camp we attacked."

Verity made a sound of denial in her throat.

"I never had the chance to ask Hawk whether his captives were alive or dead, but the odds are overwhelmingly against their being alive. They should have been with those Sioux we saw camped back there . . . but they weren't. I think you have to face the fact that Rand may be dead. And Freddy . . . Freddy may not survive even a brief captivity."

"There's something else here I think you ought to see," Red said. He pulled back a beaded buckskin vest to reveal a white lawn shirt. There was a hole in the shoulder, and a stain where blood had obviously been rinsed from the garment.

Miles felt a shiver run down his spine. He glanced at Verity.

She took the two steps to close the distance between her and the dead Indian, then knelt beside him. She fingered the seams, the cuffs, the buttons she had sewn with her own hand. She rose and turned to Miles.

"That shirt belongs . . . belonged . . . to Rand," she said. "I made it for him myself."

Miles caught her as she swayed.

"It's time to go home, Verity. It's time to give up the search."

"No, Miles, please!"

"There's no use in going any farther. We aren't going to find them alive."

"Oh, God." *Rand is not dead. I won't believe he's dead. If I don't grieve, he can't be dead.*

As Verity's knees buckled, Miles's good arm slipped around her, and he pulled her close against his chest.

Verity heard the blood thudding beneath her ears, heard the breath rasp in and out of her open mouth, heard Miles and Red exchange words but understood nothing of what they said. Her head lolled back across Miles's arm, and she saw sky—blue, cloudless, immense.

Tell him Rand is his son. That will make him keep looking.

It would also make him hate her forever, if Rand was never found.

But if they continued searching, they might find Rand's body. Then she would have to accept his death. If they stopped looking now, she could continue to believe Rand would turn up alive.

What should she do?

She knew what she ought to do. She ought to tell Miles the truth. Let *him* make the decision whether to continue searching with the knowledge it was his son who was lost. But she couldn't do it. She was too afraid of losing everything. She had to hold on to her hope.

"I'm going to take my wife home, Red," Miles said. "You and Frog follow after me as soon as you help bury Mrs. Hanrahan and the baby." He gave Red directions how to find Shorty, so he could be brought back to the Muleshoe and buried in the small cemetery behind the house.

"What about Tom?" Red asked.

"If Tom hasn't gotten himself killed chasing off after those Sioux, he knows the way back home."

"Will the two of you be safe by yourselves?" Red asked.

"It's only a half day's ride. Hawk should be hidden away somewhere licking his wounds for as long as it takes us to get where we're going."

"So long, boss," Red said. "We'll see you back at the ranch.

Verity never remembered much about the ride to the Muleshoe Ranch. It was late afternoon when she caught her first glimpse of her new home.

"There it is."

Verity looked where Miles pointed. The one-story log ranch house sat on the crest of a barren hillside that sloped downward to a verdant valley. The Chugwater River curled into the distance. Leafy cottonwoods and lush green laurel bushes rimmed the river. Another long, low rectangular log building not far from the house appeared to be a bunkhouse. The unpainted two-story wooden barn was made of planked wood and stood downhill—and downwind—of the house.

Near the barn were corrals that contained a dozen or more sturdy mustangs. Ahead of her, scattered across the prairie, were what had to be thousands of Longhorn cattle. Miles must be very rich. It was hard to believe he had freely chosen to remain in such primitive surroundings rather than return to England.

She began to pick out people—men—moving among the buildings. Someone forking hay into the corral. Someone in the doorway to the barn shoeing a horse. Someone sitting in a rocker on the shaded porch of the house. Someone crouched down scratching the belly of a short-haired yellow dog whose leg was thumping in response.

Rather than dismounting immediately when he reached the front of the house, Miles called to the men, "Gather 'round, boys."

He didn't have to say it twice. The men, who had been staring ever since Miles and Verity rode into the yard, abandoned what they were doing and circled the two of them. All except the man in the rocker on the porch. He stayed where he was.

"I'd like to introduce my wife, Mrs. Broderick," Miles said.

Grins appeared on the faces of the three men standing before them. Verity noticed one hung back a little from the other two. It was hard for her to look at the third man, because he didn't seem to have any ears.

"That was quick work, boss," one of the men said. "I didn't even know you was lookin' for a wife."

"Could've given a little warning," another grumbled. "Would've cleaned up a little."

"Come meet Mrs. Broderick, Sully," Miles said.

The young man Miles had spoken to—the man without ears—held back a moment, then stepped close enough that she could see the awful scars on his neck and head and hands. He had been badly burned once upon a time, which explained how he had lost his ears. She felt Miles watching her, waiting for her reaction. She hid her revulsion and held out her hand. "It's a pleasure to meet you, Sully."

Sully grasped her hand with his scarred fingers. His chin nodded jerkily as he acknowledged her. "Ma'am."

"I'm Chip," another of the men said. "Pleased to meet you, ma'am."

His grin widened, his mouth came open, and she realized that though he was only middle-aged, he had no front teeth. "Nice to meet you," she said faintly.

"Pickles, you're next," Miles said.

Verity had never seen such a sour face on a man. He was the only one of Miles's cowhands even the least bit overweight. His face was jowly, his chin doubled, his stomach paunchy. His face was bewhiskered and spittle from tobacco had collected in his gray beard.

"Consarn it, Miles. Ain't no place for a woman. You'd be better off goin' back where you came from, ma'am."

Apparently Pickles had a sour disposition to match his face.

"She's here to stay, Pickles. I don't want to hear another word about it," Miles said.

The old man pulled an oversized hat down around his ears and walked off muttering, "Consarn it. Ain't no place for a woman."

Sully and Chip tipped their hats and headed back to work. Miles turned his horse around to face the old man sitting in the rocker on the porch. Now that he had been acknowledged, the elderly cowboy rose and walked—limped—down the two front steps and crossed to Verity. He was wearing a none-too-clean apron around his waist.

"Last, but certainly not least, I'd like you to meet Cookie—he's the cook."

Cookie nodded. "Ma'am. 'Bout time Miles found hisself a woman and settled down."

She could see Cookie was limping, but she thought it was age more than anything else that gave him his hitching gait. At least age was a normal infirmity, she thought. Then Cookie reached up to tip his hat, and she saw his hand. She was mortified when he caught her staring. He held his hand out so she could see several fingers were only stumps.

"Lassoed an old mossyhorn when I was kid and dallied the rope 'round the horn without payin' attention. He took off, rope jerked taut, cut my fingers clean off."

"I'm sorry."

"Sorry don't do much out here. Learned my lesson and lived to tell about it. That's about all a man can hope for."

Verity sat there wondering what she had gotten herself into. How would she survive here, in this place, with these men, the only woman around for miles?

Miles had surrounded himself with misfits. She wondered if he had done it consciously, or whether he had recognized some inner torment, some sense of isolation, in the other men that he felt himself.

"Left some vittles on the stove, boss," Cookie said, "Didn't know you was comin', ma'am, but there's always extra. Never know who'll show up at the door. I'll be headin' over to the bunkhouse. Gotta serve up grub for the boys."

Verity was sore and tired. Her inner thighs were rubbed raw, and the ache in her muscles was bone deep. She was past worrying about how graceful she looked dismounting. She simply wasn't sure she had the strength left to lift her leg over the horse's rump.

She felt Miles's hands at her waist. He gave a tug, and she fell off the horse toward him. He kept her at arm's distance and set her on her feet in front of him. His hands stayed where they were long enough to be sure she had her legs steady under her before he let her go.

She half expected him to say "Welcome home,

Verity." What he actually said was far more revealing. "There aren't any servants here. I'll expect you to pull your share of the weight."

"I know absolutely nothing about ranch life," she said.

"Then I guess you'd better learn."

"Who's going to teach me?"

"Cookie can help you find your way around the kitchen. You can ask me whatever else you need to know."

"Fine," she snapped. "Is there anything else?"

"Come on inside. There's something I want to show you."

"A broom? A mop? A dustrag?"

"The bedroom."

10

To describe the inside of her new home as Spartan would have been to overestimate its comforts. A wooden trestle table with four mismatched chairs took up the center of the front room. A cast-iron four-hole stove stood against one wall, with a sideboard next to it and a sink with an iron pump beyond that. A stone fireplace took up most of the other wall.

What looked like a door settled on two wooden flour barrels appeared, from the amount of paper and the several books scattered on it, to be a desk. It sat under the four-paned window facing the front of the house. A willow rocker and a rat-bitten stuffed chair sat before the fireplace atop the skin of some immense wild animal with paws and claws.

When she turned wide-eyed to Miles, he said, "Grizzly."

The log walls were chinked with a concoction of mud and newspaper. The wall decorations consisted of steel traps hung from nails, tanning hoops with the skins attached, and the antlers of a deer that she realized, as soon as Miles dropped his Stetson onto it, served as a hatrack. The floor was planked with wood, but it was unfinished. Several knots in the wood had fallen out, leaving her to wonder what might crawl in through the holes at night.

The whole of the inside smelled of whatever was cooking on the stove. And of animal skins. And of male sweat.

It was no place for a woman.

What she felt must have shown in her eyes because Miles conceded, "It lacks a few amenities."

"A few?" She stared at the door leading to the other room. If things in the front room were this bad, she hesitated to think what she might find in the back. He had said there was a bedroom. Surely there was a bed. She would rather not think about the bed.

She crossed to the stove, located a potholder, and lifted the lid of the dutch oven. She found a spoon and stirred the contents of the pot. Beans. Chunks of meat in a sauce. Some kind of stew, then. She sniffed. Not bad, really.

"Are you hungry?" Miles asked.

"Actually, yes."

"So am I," he said. "Before we eat, I promised to show you the bedroom."

Verity swallowed hard. "The bedroom can wait, can't it?"

"I don't think so."

"Miles, I—"

He held out his hand. "Come with me, Verity."

She looked at his face, trying to gauge his intent. It was one thing to couple with him in the dark of night, when they didn't know if there would be a tomorrow. It was another thing entirely to consider lying naked with him in the bright light of day.

His gray eyes were inscrutable, his body taut. He held out his hand to her, as he would to a skittish mare, beguiling her to trust.

She glanced toward the front door of the cabin.

"There's nowhere to go, Verity."

She laid a hand against her chest, trying to control a heart that had begun to beat like a frantic bird's wings against her rib cage.

He took a step toward her.

She stood her ground. This was what she wanted. There was no reason to flee. But it was hard to resist the urge to run. The worst of it was, she didn't even know what she was running from. In Miles lay all her hopes of future happiness. But she was vulnerable. There were risks. He had not forgiven her for marrying Chester. He might never let himself fall in love with her again.

"Miles . . ." She stared at him, unable to move toward him or away. Before she could act, his lips came down hard on hers, stopping speech, stopping breath, stopping thought.

Oh, God, his mouth was wet and hot. His tongue came plundering, seeking secrets, demanding a response. Her body bowed against his, and she felt the hardness of muscle and sinew. Their bodies fitted together perfectly, as they had a lifetime ago.

Abruptly he released her and stood panting, eyes heavy-lidded, nostrils flared, body hard. Aching. He would be aching, she knew, because she ached herself.

He scooped her up, grunting when her weight put strain on his wounded arm, and carried her into the bedroom. It was a man's room, with a huge wardrobe and a dry sink and a ladderback chair. The immense four-poster bed was constructed of pine logs. But the exquisite patchwork quilt and lace-trimmed white pillowcases would only have been put there to please a woman.

He laid her on the coverlet and sat down beside her. She stared up at him as he gently spread her hair out on the pillow around her.

"I've dreamed about this moment," he said, his eyes searching hers. "Somehow it's hard to believe this is real."

"It's real." She smiled. "I have the aches and pains to prove it."

He brushed his thumb gently across her skin below the scab on her cheek. "I never considered what this place, this life, might do to you. The wildness of it. The hardness of it."

"It isn't what I would have chosen," she conceded. "But I'm not sorry to be here. I've been waiting as long as you have for this moment."

"You have?"

She caressed the scar where it slashed through his lip. "I used to dream of waking in your arms, of having you look at me with . . ." She cut herself off.

There was nothing remotely resembling love in his eyes as he looked down at her. Lust, yes. Love, no.

Could a love that had been smoldering, buried by ashes of misunderstanding for so many years, still be fanned into flame?

For a moment she thought he was going to act on the desire she saw flaring in his gray eyes. But he stood abruptly and said, "I've got some chores to do before supper."

"You're not going to . . . ?" She felt the heat all the way to her hairline as an amused grin flashed on his face.

"I'm tempted. But you can hardly keep your eyes open. Rest for a while. I'll see you at supper."

Then he was gone.

After supper, what then? she wanted to ask. But she knew the answer. He would join her in bed. And somehow they would have to pick up where they had left off twenty-two years ago.

Verity wasn't sure what had woken her, but as she listened, wind-driven dust and small bits of gravel *pinged* against the windowpane. An ominous sky, dark and brooding, filled the small, curtainless bedroom window. A jagged flash of lightning streaked down through the sky, followed instantly by a crash of thunder that made her curl into a protective ball.

It was hard to tell from the sky what time of day it was, but it felt too hot to be nightfall. Or morning, either. She felt disoriented because she had gone to bed in the afternoon. Was it possible she had slept the night through? Where was Miles?

She heard no human sounds in the house, only the eerie whistle of the wind through the eaves and the occasional rattle of the windowpanes.

A trickle of perspiration wormed its way down between her breasts. She brushed at a wisp of sweat-damp hair that was stuck to her cheek and kicked away the warm covers. As soon as she did, the cool draft seeping in through chinks in the log walls and up through the empty knotholes in the floor chilled her skin.

Which was when she realized she was wearing no more than her chemise and pantalets.

"Did you sleep well?"

She nearly came out of her skin. "Miles! You scared me half to death!"

He was sitting fully dressed in a ladderback chair in the shadowed corner near the head of the bed. As he rose and stalked toward her, she scrambled for the covers she had kicked away and clutched them against her.

"What are you doing here?" she demanded.

"Watching you sleep."

She felt flustered, at a disadvantage because he was dressed and she wasn't. A quick look revealed her corset, stockings, basque-waist, riding skirt, and jacket lying over the bedstead. She didn't remember disrobing. Her gaze shot to Miles's face. He answered the question before she asked.

"I undressed you."

"Why didn't you wake me?"

"You obviously needed the rest," he said.

"How long did I sleep?"

"All of yesterday. Most of today."

Her eyes narrowed as another thought occurred to her.

"Where did you sleep?"

"Beside you," he answered baldly.

She stared at the pillow beside hers that bore the clear indentation of someone's head.

Her gaze shot back to him. "I . . . You didn't . . ."

"I didn't," he said with a quirk of his lips. "But I wanted to very much."

"I'd like to get dressed."

He sat at the foot of the bed and crossed an ankle over his knee. "Go ahead."

She grimaced. This Miles was still too much a stranger for her to feel comfortable sharing such intimacies. "I'd like to be alone."

"I'd like to watch."

"You have no right—"

"You're my wife," he said quietly. "I have every right."

Verity realized he wasn't going to budge. But

she refused to let him make her feel embarrassed. For her age, she was very well preserved. And it wasn't as if he hadn't seen her—much more of her—undressed.

"Fine. Look all you want," she said, shoving the covers away and shivering as she set her bare foot on the rough floorboards.

He took her at her word, and she was aware of his gray eyes watching her intently as she slipped the corset over her head and tightened the strings behind her back. It wasn't an easy task without a maid, but she refused to ask him for help.

"I'll do it," he said.

He stepped behind her, and she could feel his warm, moist breath at her temple. Her heartbeat skittered, and her breath shortened.

"I don't need—"

"I'll do it."

She gasped as he tightened the corset another half inch and knotted the strings. His hands stayed at her narrowed waist a moment.

"Your waist is still small enough for my hands to nearly span it."

"Chester demanded that I keep my figure."

Miles tensed. "Is that why you never had another child?"

"No." She hesitated before admitting, "I desperately wanted more children."

"So why didn't you have more?"

She debated whether to tell him the truth. But it would serve no purpose to lie. "Chester never came to my bed after Rand was born."

His grasp tightened. "I'm sorry for you, Verity."

"I don't need or want your pity. I was glad he stayed away."

She let that admission hang between them, grateful when he didn't ask for further explanation.

"It isn't pity I'm feeling for you right now," he said, his lips pressed softly against her ear. "Far from it."

Miles was exercising every bit of self-control he had to keep himself from reaching for the two perfect mounds formed by her breasts when he had tightened the corset. He felt Verity quiver, heard her breathing falter. He let his hands slide upward until he was cupping soft flesh beneath a thin layer of muslin. His thumbs flicked across her nipples, which instantly pebbled.

"Don't."

"Why not? Why should we deny ourselves?"

"It's broad daylight."

"That never stopped us before."

The only time they had made love in the daylight was the very first time they had made love. It was hard to believe how long ago that had been. "You loved me then. And I loved you."

"I haven't forgotten, Verity. I haven't forgotten anything. But if you feel more comfortable waiting till dark . . ."

She nodded jerkily. "I would."

He released her and took a step back. It was a reprieve, not a pardon.

Verity edged away from Miles, grabbed her basque-waist, slipped it on and buttoned it to the throat, then stepped into the riding skirt and fastened it at her waist.

"Miles, is there any way I can get a message to Colonel Peters at the fort?"

"What sort of message?"

"About Rand and Freddy." She stopped dressing to focus her eyes on his. "I know you don't believe they're still alive, but if there's even the slightest chance . . ."

"There's paper and pen on the desk. Write your message. I'll have Frog deliver it this afternoon."

"Frog is back already?"

"He and Red turned up this morning."

"Did they see any sign of . . . of . . ."

"They didn't see any sign of the Sioux, or of Rand and Freddy. I'm sorry, Verity."

Her shoulders slumped. It was getting harder to hang on to hope. But Tom wasn't back yet. Maybe he would bring word of them.

When she sat down on the bed to slip on her stockings, Miles leaned back against the log wall, his arms and legs crossed in a nonchalant pose that she was distressed to see was only a pose. His jaw was rigid, his eyes heavy-lidded. She recognized the signs of arousal and hurried to finish and escape the room before he changed his mind about waiting.

The fire had already been started in the stove and, unless her nose deceived her, coffee was brewing. She hadn't a notion what to do to prepare a late afternoon breakfast. Where did one find the eggs, the kidneys, the bread with which to make toast?

Her stomach growled. She glanced over her shoulder at Miles, who was stretched out with his arms extended from the lintel above the bedroom doorway. Even at forty-three, he was an impressive-looking man. He had donned a new buckskin shirt that stretched across his broad chest. The fringed leggings showed off his flat stomach and muscular thighs. Their eyes met, and she felt the slow curl of desire in the pit of her belly.

"Are you hungry?" Miles asked.

It was plain from the way he said it that he didn't mean for food. "I'm starving," she said. Her answer was equally loaded with innuendo. "For breakfast," she added, in an attempt to curtail the growing aura of sensuality between them.

"Cookie came in early and fixed something for me. I think there's enough left for you."

"That was thoughtful of him." She lifted the lid on several pots. Beef and beans. Again. And in the dutch oven, a sort of scone. "Is this all there is?"

"That's it. Unless you want to cook something else for yourself."

Since she had no idea how to cook and no intention of reminding Miles of that fact, Verity said, "I'll eat this."

He sat down across from her at the table and watched every bite into her mouth until her stomach was so upset she had to stop eating. She looked for a napkin but didn't see one, so she daintily licked her lips clean. When she looked up, Miles was staring at her.

She thought she must still have a spot of food somewhere because he reached across the table and brushed his thumb across her lower lip.

"Is there something . . . ?"

She looked up into his face and found his eyes focused on her mouth. Slowly, lazily, his thumb grazed the length of her dampened lower lip.

A frisson of awareness sizzled through her. "Please don't, Miles."

"Why not?"

"I want something more from you, with you, than physical satisfaction," she said.

His gaze hardened, his jaw tightened. "I can't ever feel for you again what I felt for you in the past," he said. "That love died, Verity. You killed it."

She winced in pain at his accusation. "Without love, what's left for us?" she asked.

"You'll have a home, a husband, children."

All she had ever wished for, all she had ever dreamed. Except her dream had included love.

"That's not enough, Miles. Not nearly enough."

He stood, his whole body vibrating with tension. "It's all I have to offer."

"I want more," she insisted.

But he didn't offer more.

She thought he would reach for her anyway, but some unseen tether held him back. Abruptly he turned on his heel, stalked out the front door, and slammed it hard enough behind him that one of the hinges broke. The door creaked back open and hung there lopsided.

The war was on. It was a battle for their future. And Verity didn't intend to lose.

She crossed to the makeshift desk and sat down to write her note to Colonel Peters, but her thoughts were on the battle soon to be waged.

Miles had made no effort to hide the fact he *wanted* her, but he was equally honest about the fact he didn't *love* her. Should she give herself to him and hope that sex would grow into love? If Chester's long string of mistresses was any guide, that way lay sorrow. But sex could also be a powerful expression of love. Should she deny herself and Miles that closeness?

A knock on the broken door distracted her. "Who is it?"

A bared head of gray hair appeared in the open doorway. "Frog, ma'am. Boss said you had a letter goin' to the fort."

"Come in, Frog."

The door scraped open across the floor, and he stepped inside, clutching a battered hat to his chest. He stayed near the door, obviously uncomfortable alone with her.

She finished her letter, sealed it, and handed it to him. "Please deliver this to Colonel Peters."

Frog nodded his head. "Yes, ma'am. I'll do that." He backed out of the room, dragging the door closed behind him.

She crossed to the trestle table and began gathering up the dishes. She might as well get started with the simple things first. Eventually she would learn how to do it all.

There was a pump and a sink near the stove, and she carried the dishes there to rinse them off. The pump screeched, but no water came out.

"You have to prime it first."

She whirled and saw Miles silhouetted in the doorway.

She wrinkled her nose. "I know that." She had seen Mrs. Peters do it. She found the can of water near the pump and dumped it in, then pushed the handle a couple more times. Water came gushing out, splattering her clothing, the sink and the dirty plates.

"I need some soap and a cloth, or something to wash the dishes with." She began looking for both in the sideboard and found neither.

"I'm out of soap, and you can wipe off the dishes with your hands."

She turned to him, frowning. "With my hands?"

He shrugged. "It's good enough for me."

"Well, I need soap. And I refuse to wipe off food with my fingers."

He tried to open the door to leave, swore when it tilted crazily toward him, caught it and said, "I'll have Frog get another hinge for this door, too." He stuck his head out the door and yelled, "Frog!"

A moment later she heard boots on the wooden porch.

"Get a hinge for this door from the sutler," Miles ordered.

"And some soap," Verity reminded him.

"And some soap," Miles repeated. "Have him put it on my bill."

"Sure, boss. What kind of soap?"

"For dishes." He paused a moment and said, "Better get some sweet-smelling stuff, too, if he's got any. Something a lady would use."

Frog's voice sounded even croakier. "Tark's gonna give me a hard time, I ask for somethin' like that."

"Tell him it's for my wife."

"Do I have to, boss?"

"I'd appreciate it, Frog," Verity said from a spot behind Miles's shoulder.

Frog's color heightened. "Yes, ma'am. It'll be a pleasure, ma'am."

A moment later Frog was gone.

"Thank you, Miles," Verity said, backing away from him as he turned toward her, his hand on the door holding it upright.

"Tark will give him a hard time."

"Maybe you should buy soap more often. Then it wouldn't be such a novelty."

Miles laughed. "Touché."

She realized he was going to leave again. "Miles?"

"What is it, Verity? I've got work to do."

"What am I supposed to do around here?" she asked.

"Whatever needs doing." He paused and said, "If you like, you can start by attending a funeral service with me."

"What?"

"For the man who was killed in the first Indian raid. And for Shorty. We're gathering at the cemetery this morning so I can say a few words over them."

"I see."

"You don't have to go."

"I'll come."

Miles held the door open so Verity could precede him. He walked beside her toward the small graveyard behind the house. She saw several primitive crosses and wondered who else was buried there. The men were already assembled, including Frog, who had delayed his trip to the fort long enough to be present at the service.

Verity stood beside Miles, aware that the seven cowboys were looking everywhere but at her.

When Miles took off his hat, the other men followed, clutching a variety of headgear against their chests or legs. "Lord," Miles began, "we'll miss having Pete around, but I expect he's up in heaven talking your ear off. Take good care of him. Shorty wasn't much for praying, but he lived by the Commandments. He was a good friend and a good man. Take care of him, too. Amen."

"Amen," the cowboys chorused.

"Day's wasting," Miles said.

The cowboys wandered off, leaving Miles and Verity alone with the new graves. It was frightening to think a man could live and die with only a brief eulogy to mark his passing. Shorty had died too young. And who was Pete? How old had he been? Had he come here with hopes and dreams as she had?

The ragged wound in the earth where Pete lay buried was marked with a crude wooden cross that had his name burned into it. No dates of birth or death. No words of love and regard. The ceremony for the two men had been so pitifully short, Verity wondered why they had bothered having it at all.

She knelt in the knee-high grass between the two graves and began crumbling the large clods of dirt, smoothing out the surfaces of the graves. It seemed sad that there was no one here who cared enough to do it.

"Who was Pete?" she asked Miles.

"He showed up a couple of weeks ago. I didn't ask him where he came from, and he didn't volunteer."

"So you didn't really know him."

"I've known a hundred like him." Miles knelt on one knee beside her and reached for a large clod of dirt, which he crushed in his fist. He let the dust sieve back through his fingers onto Shorty's grave.

"This place isn't anything like England. It's so . . . unforgiving," Verity said.

"It's what England was a thousand years ago. Out here a man is forced to find out what he's made of inside. You carve yourself a place and live one day at a time. You don't have time to think about whether you're happy or sad, you're too busy trying to survive."

Verity placed her hand in the one Miles held

outstretched to her and allowed him to help her to her feet. She left her hand in his as he walked her back to the house.

"If we live for today, does that mean we forget the past?" she asked as he shoved open the front door and ushered her inside. "Are you suggesting we pretend it never happened?"

"We put it away," he said, lifting the door and fitting it evenly into the frame. "And live for today."

She waited for him to finish, to turn and seek out her eyes, before she said, "All right, Miles. I can do that."

"Does that mean you're accepting the terms I offered?"

"It means I won't argue with you anymore about the subject."

She watched some emotion halfway between relief and triumph cross his face.

Before he could reach for his prize, someone pounded on the door twice, and it fell inward and hung precariously on the single hinge. Red stood there, chest heaving. "You better come quick, boss. There's trouble."

"We'll finish this later," Miles said.

As he followed Red out the door, Verity wondered what disaster had befallen them now. A thought struck her. Maybe someone had found Rand and Freddy! Her heart leapt with hope as she hurried through the open doorway after the two men.

11

"What's the problem, Red?" Miles said as he stepped onto the porch. The wind whipped at his Stetson, and he tugged it down to keep it from blowing away.

"Prairie fire, boss. Probably started by lightning. 'Bout five miles west of the house. Coming this way in a hurry."

Miles felt paralyzed. So far he had been able to keep his crippling fear of fire a secret, but his men would expect him to work beside them putting out this fire. If he wanted to keep their respect, he was going to have to do just that.

His stomach shifted. A wind-whipped fire could turn in an instant, and he knew the damage fire could do to human flesh. Despite the cooling breeze, perspiration dotted his brow and the area above his lip. Miles forced himself to give orders in a calm voice.

"Load a couple of plows onto a wagon and get shovels and blankets," he said. "Have everybody mount up. We'll do what we can to keep the fire away from the ranch buildings."

"I can help."

Miles turned to find Verity standing on the porch, her hands holding her wind-blown hair out of her face. He saw her suddenly as she would look with her hair singed to the scalp, her eyelashes gone, her skin charred black.

"You stay here," he said in a hard voice.

Her hands dropped to perch at her hips. "I'm your wife. I can help."

"You'd only be in the way."

"I'll follow after you if you try to leave me behind."

"Damn it, Verity, how did you get so willful?"

"I took a lesson from you."

She surprised a laugh out of him. Then he sobered. He knew the dangers involved. He doubted she did. At least if he had her with him, he could be sure she was out of the path of the fire. If it turned toward the house and they couldn't stop it, she might be in more danger here than if she came with them.

"All right, you can come," he said. "But if I give an order, obey it like your life depends on it, because it probably does. Understand?"

She nodded.

"Let's go saddle up." He headed for the barn, not waiting to see if she followed.

"I have no idea how to attach one of those Western saddles to a horse," she said as she hurried along beside him.

"Sully!" he shouted. "Throw some leather on Blackbeard for the lady."

"Right, boss."

"Go watch him," Miles ordered. "You might as well learn now as later."

Red had hitched a couple of mules to a wagon that was loaded with plow blades, shovels, blankets, and two barrels of water. Another brace of mules was tied behind the wagon. Minutes later, Cookie climbed up on the wagon bench. The rest mounted their horses, and they all headed off in the direction of the red glow that showed against the dark thunderclouds on the horizon.

They crested a rise, and the jagged orange streak of fire and the blackened earth it left in its wake became visible in the distance. It stretched as far as the eye could see in both directions.

"My God, Miles!" Verity cried. "How can you possibly hope to turn that fire?"

Miles fought back the nausea that roiled in his stomach. His fingers clenched the reins until they were white-knuckled. "We have to try," he said grimly. "You stay with the wagon. Be ready with water and an extra blanket if one of the men needs it."

Red unhitched the mules that had pulled the wagon and hitched them to one of the plows, while

Pickles hitched the other plow to the team of mules that had been tied on behind. The two men separated their teams, and each began to plow parallel furrows about seventy-five feet apart. As soon as they had enough earth turned, the rest of the men set fire to the grass between the two furrows to burn it off and create a firebreak.

They worked with shovels to widen the furrows and used blankets to control the fire within the man-made break. When the prairie fire reached the break, there would be nothing left to burn, and with any luck, it would die. Of course, that presumed the furrow was plowed wide enough that the gusting wind didn't whip the fire across it.

Miles stayed on horseback to allow him to move quickly between the working men and supervise the operation. Mobility was the only thing that kept his fear at bay. He told himself the fire couldn't get to him, that he could outrun it on horseback, if need be.

But he had heard enough stories of fleet-footed animals caught by a runaway prairie fire to know he was only kidding himself. He kept his bandanna across his nose and mouth to keep out the worst of the smoke, but tremors of fear raked his body every time he caught a whiff of burned flesh from rodents that couldn't escape the blaze.

It seemed impossible to Verity that Miles and his men could succeed in creating a wide enough firebreak before the flames reached them. Acrid smoke choked the air around her and made it hard to draw breath.

Sully had stayed with her at the wagon. The whites showed around his brown eyes, and his nostrils flared. Verity wondered what awful memories the fire must conjure for him.

"Sully?"

It took him a moment to focus on her. "Ma'am?"

"Will they be able to do it?"

"Don't know, ma'am."

She paced the length of the wagon and back in agitation. "I need to be doing something. I want to help them."

"Don't think that's a good idea, ma'am. The boss said stay here. You better do what he says. I . . ." He swallowed hard. "A fire . . . it can get outta control quicker'n that." He snapped two burn-scarred fingers.

"I'll keep that in mind."

When she took a determined step in the direction of the fire, Sully reached out a hand to stop her. As soon as she paused, his hand came away. "Did you want something else, Sully?"

"Take a good look at me, ma'am."

She met his eyes squarely and tried not to let her gaze stray beyond the normal skin on his face. She lost the battle, her eyes drawn against her will to the gruesome scars on the sides of his head where his ears used to be. She kept her face blank, but her stomach revolted at the sight of his deformity. He kept staring at her until her gaze dropped.

"You think twice before you go rushing off," he

said. "This is what fire can do. I know from the way folks try not to look at me that it ain't a pretty sight. It'd be a shame if anything like this happened to you." He ducked his head, his forefinger on the brim of his hat. "That's all I got to say, ma'am."

Verity had some idea what it must have cost the young man to share even that much of his feelings. His warning kept her where she was a little longer.

She watched the men widening the trench with shovels. She didn't have the strength to do what they were doing. But the fire curved in on one side where the men were burning it between the furrows, and several men batted at the flames with blankets to keep them from spreading too fast. She could certainly help do that.

She watched, fidgeting, frustrated, feeling useless, until finally she decided that no matter what the danger, she could no longer stand by doing nothing. She had spent a lifetime on the sidelines. Here, in this new land, she had a chance to help determine the course of events, rather than to wait for things to happen around her. It was a heady feeling. And one that gave her the impetus to act.

She grabbed a blanket from the back of the wagon and headed toward the firebreak.

"Ma'am!" Sully called after her.

"Don't worry about me. I'll be careful!" she shouted back over her shoulder.

It didn't take her long to realize why the men had pulled their bandannas up to cover their faces. The smoke was stifling. She reached into the pocket of her riding skirt for her lace-trimmed handkerchief, which she tied around her nose and mouth. Now she looked as much like a bandit as the rest of them. She aimed herself perpendicular to the plowed furrow and began beating at the fire along the short edge of the firebreak to put it out.

It seemed like they worked for hours, plowing, shoveling, and then beating back the flames on the grass burning between the furrows. Smoke made her eyes water. Soot gathered on her eyelashes, on her hands, her face, her hair, her clothes. Her arms and back and shoulders ached from the constant *slap, slap, slap* as she beat at the fire with the heavy wool blanket.

"What the hell do you think you're doing?"

Verity started as Miles suddenly appeared beside her on horseback. "I'm helping."

"You're quitting." He yanked the handkerchief down to expose her nose and mouth. Immediately she felt the effects of the smoke.

"You've done enough," he said. "Get back to the wagon."

"No one else is quitting."

Her blanket had lain too long in one spot, and the fire caught hold of it. Miles reached down and jerked it out of her hands and threw it aside before she could get burned.

"This isn't your fight," he snarled.

"It's my land as much as yours," she retorted. "That makes it my fight."

"Boss!" Red shouted. "The wind is picking up!"

Miles lifted his Stetson, shoved a sooty hand

through hair so dark the soot didn't show, and tugged the hat back down over his brow. "I'm coming!" He turned a fierce look on Verity.

"Get back to the wagon," he ordered.

"I'm going," she said. "But only to get another blanket."

She had marched two steps before Miles yanked her up into his lap and spurred his horse back to the wagon.

"Sully!" he barked.

"Yes, boss."

"I thought I told you to watch Mrs. Broderick."

Sully gulped. "I—"

"This time keep her here!" he said curtly as he let Verity drop. She staggered, then caught her balance and stood glaring at him.

"Miles!" Red shouted again.

"I'm coming!" he shouted back. He turned a fierce look back on Verity. "I find you in trouble again, I swear I'll let you burn!"

He turned and rode away without looking back.

"You look plumb wore out, ma'am," Sully said, handing Verity a dipperful of water.

"I am," Verity admitted with a wan smile. She greedily gulped the water, then wiped her mouth and cheeks with her sleeve. It came away black with soot. She walked around to the open bed of the wagon and grabbed another blanket.

"What are you doin', ma'am?" Sully asked.

"Don't worry about me, Sully."

"The boss said to keep you here."

"I don't think you'd use force on a lady, would you, Sully?"

Sully gulped. "No, ma'am."

She patted him on the shoulder. "Don't worry about Mr. Broderick. I'll take care of him. And don't worry about me. I promise to be careful."

She pulled up her handkerchief and headed for a spot where the wind had carried the fire over the break.

Miles stared grimly across the burning landscape. They were losing the battle. Gusts of wind carried glowing ashes high into the air, where they eddied gracefully toward the dry yellow grass on the other side of the blackened furrow. At the moment, there were few enough that his men could beat them out as soon as they landed.

But he wasn't sure, with the increasing wind, how long they could expect to beat the odds. He glanced at the sky, wondering whether they could hope for respite from above. The dark storm clouds held gallons of water. The question was whether the sky would open and let it fall in time.

He kneed his horse toward Red. Maybe it was time to admit defeat and get the hell out of here while they still could.

The scrape with Miles had sparked Verity's adrenaline. It gave her the energy to spread the wool blanket and begin the backbreaking labor of slapping at the crackling grass again. She kept her distance from the others so that Miles wouldn't notice her.

Verity never saw the fire sneak around behind

her, never realized she was beating herself into the center of a circle of flame. She was completely focused on the fire in front of her, too exhausted to lift her head to see what was happening around her.

"Verity!"

Slowly, painfully, she straightened when she heard Miles call her name. Damn. He had caught her again.

It took her only seconds to realize her peril and to panic. She was completely surrounded by fire. The heat was suddenly unbearable, and smoke burned her eyes and choked her throat.

"Miles! Miles, help me!"

Miles felt terror punch him in the gut. He had told her he would let her burn. How could he have said such a thing? How could he have tempted the fates like that?

"Don't move! Stay where you are!" He was afraid she would try to run through the fire, or leap it, and get caught by the blaze. The wind whipped the flames almost as high as her waist.

He grabbed a blanket out of Pickles's hands and another one from Cookie and headed his horse toward Verity on the run. He heard the men shouting and running behind him, but he feared they would all be too late.

When he reached the edge of the fire that surrounded Verity, he flung himself off his horse. And froze. The only way to get to her was to go through the fire himself. He could see her terrified face, hear her terrified screams. Yet he was unable to make his feet move. He brushed frantically at an ember that landed on his sleeve.

"Miles!" Verity shrieked. "Help me!"

Something broke loose inside him. A fear even greater that the fear of his own death or mutilation. The fear of losing Verity for a second, and final, time. She was everything he had ever wanted in this life. He could not live in a world without her.

He smelled scorched corduroy and knew it was only a matter of seconds before the fire reached Verity's stockings and then her flesh. He wrapped himself in one blanket and charged through the fire carrying the other. Charred grass crackled underfoot. The instant he reached Verity, he wrapped her in a blanket to protect her face and hair and picked her up to make the trip back through the fire.

The flames seemed higher, hotter. He took a deep breath, and his lungs protested the smoke. His eyebrows and eyelashes were already singed off.

"Hold on to me, Verity," he said.

He ran, screaming a savage cry of defiance as he charged the fire. Moments later they were safe, and a dozen hands were beating out the fire on his shirt and helping him lower Verity to the ground.

He sank to his knees beside her. "Verity?"

She didn't answer.

The adrenaline that had carried Miles into the fire was wearing off, and the knowledge of what he had done made him violently ill. He crawled a short distance away and vomited into the grass. Sully was at his shoulder a moment later, handing him a bandanna to wipe his mouth.

"Is she all right?" Miles rasped.

"Her legs are burned," Sully said.

"Oh, God, no." All Miles could think of was the pain Sully had endured, the weeks and months it had taken for him to heal.

"It's not bad," Sully said.

Miles stumbled to his feet and made his way back to where Verity lay. At least she was alive. At least they had a chance for a future together.

How could he have refused to forgive her for what had happened in the past? How could he have been so stupid, so stubborn, so blind to what was really important? *A life with her. A chance to grow old with her.* He would forgive her a thousand times for marrying Chester Talbot, if only she was all right.

Verity could hardly breathe, she was so smothered in blankets. She struggled to free her face. When she did, she found herself surrounded by a circle of worried white eyes in sooty faces.

Miles knelt beside her. "How are you?"

She wanted to say "I'm fine" but her lungs were choked with smoke. She writhed in breathless frustration as his hand skimmed intimately across her fanny and legs.

"Don't fight me," he snarled. "I'm trying to find out how badly you're burned."

She grabbed at his hand to stop its wandering. "I'm okay," she rasped.

He lifted her into his lap and held her close. "I'm going to take you home," he muttered. "The fire can burn up the whole damned county for all I care."

"Miles—" Rain fell in two giant drops on Verity's cheek and nose.

"I'll be damned," Pickles said.

A few drops quickly turned into a deluge, and they could hear the fire hissing around them as the cold water met the hot fire.

"Thank God," Sully muttered.

Miles held Verity tight.

"I can walk, Miles," she said.

"The hell you can." He picked her up and headed for the wagon. "Hitch up the mules to one of the wagons," he ordered Sully. "I'm going to take Mrs. Broderick back to the house." He turned to the men and said, "Stay here and make sure that fire goes out. Sully'll bring the wagon back for the equipment."

Miles pulled the handkerchief free of Verity's neck where it had fallen and used it to wipe the worst of the soot from her face. "You're damned lucky. You could have been burned to death."

"Would you have cared, Miles?"

He answered by kissing her.

Oh, yes. Yes, I would have cared, Miles thought, as his tongue drove deep in her mouth. *More than I should. More than it's safe to care.*

When Miles set Verity carefully on her feet beside the wagon, she examined the ragged remnants of scorched material. Her stockings had holes singed into them, revealing pinkened skin. She touched the flesh gently with her fingertips and gasped.

Miles could see the burns on the backs of Verity's legs better than she could. In one or two spots blisters had popped up. He shivered. It had been close. What if he hadn't gotten to her when he had? What if her hair had caught fire? What if the fire had swallowed her whole?

Miles helped Verity step up into the wagon seat and saw her quail as the scorched corduroy made contact with her blistered skin in several places. But she didn't make a sound of complaint.

His hands were trembling, he suddenly realized. He balled them into fists, but that didn't help. It was a delayed reaction, he realized, to the horror of what had almost happened.

He kept the team at a walk during the ride back to the house because anything more caused Verity too much pain. It was nearly dusk before they saw the outline of the ranch buildings.

"Who's that standing on the porch?" Verity asked. "I can't see them in the shadows."

"Good Lord. It's Tom. And there's a woman with him."

"That's Freddy!" Verity said, recognizing her green riding habit.

Rand wasn't with them.

"Sully, catch the reins." Miles threw the reins toward the boy in the back of the wagon as they reached the front of the house. He stepped over Verity and off the wagon, ready to help her down. She stood gingerly, and he saw from the way the blood drained from her face that the shock must have worn off. She was in a great deal more pain now than she had been when the burns were new. A quick glance revealed the blisters on the backs of her legs had grown larger.

"Lady Talbot! Lady Talbot!" Freddy cried as she raced toward Verity. "It's Rand . . . He . . . He . . ." She burst into tears as Verity's arms closed around her.

Miles met Verity's eyes and found them liquid with tears.

"He's dead," Verity said dully. "He's really dead."

Freddy jerked herself out of Verity's embrace. "Oh, no, ma'am. He's not! But his wound is infected and he has a fever and I don't know what to do to make him better."

What neither pain, nor fear, nor foreboding had accomplished, relief did.

Verity fainted dead away.

12

Miles laid Verity carefully on his bed beside the fevered young man who was already occupying it, then eased her onto her stomach to keep her blistered calves from coming into contact with the bedding.

The white-faced young lady who had followed him inside hovered anxiously nearby.

"Fred—Lady Winnifred?" Miles said.

She nodded jerkily. "Who are you?"

"Miles Broderick. I'm . . . a friend of Lady Talbot's."

"Tom—Mr. Grimes said the two of you got married," Freddy countered, eyeing him curiously.

Miles flushed, caught in the lie. "We did."

"I can hardly believe it. Why—"

"I'm sure Verity can explain everything to you later. Right now I need to tend to her burns."

Freddy looked anxiously at Verity's unconscious form. "Will Lady Tal—Mrs. Broderick—be all right?"

"We've been fighting a brush fire all day. She's just exhausted, and she has some burns on her legs."

"They look painful," Freddy said, moving aside the charred corduroy and exposing Verity's ruined stockings and the blistered skin above her half-boots.

"I've got a salve I can put on them that should make her feel better and help her heal."

"Can you help Rand, too?" Freddy asked.

For the first time, Miles took a good look at Verity's son. He was a handsome young man who—

The hair stood up on Miles's arms. His gaze shot from Verity to Rand. From her blond hair lying on one pillow . . . to his black hair on the other. The bottom fell out of his stomach.

Miles bit back a gasp.

"Is something wrong?" Freddy asked.

"That's Verity's son?" Miles queried in a cautious voice.

"Yes, sir. That's Rushland."

Miles tensed. "What color are his eyes?"

"Why, they're gray, sir. Why do you ask?"

Miles stared at the young man and felt a shock of recognition. It was like looking at himself as a younger man.

No! It can't be. She would have told me. She never would have married Talbot if she had been pregnant with my child.

But the irrefutable evidence that this was not—could not possibly be—Chester Talbot's son lay there on the bed in front of him. He felt dizzy.

He had a son. He and Verity had a son.

Unless she had lain with some other man after her marriage to Chester. Not probable, knowing her—and Chester. But possible.

"How old is Rushland?" Miles asked.

"Twenty-one. He'll be twenty-two next month."

Oh, God. He had been born within a year of Verity's marriage. Rand had to be his son! He catalogued the young man's features. The nose was the same as his own, and the chin. The black hair, of course. And Rand's eyes were gray . . . like his own.

Verity, what happened? Why didn't you tell me I had a son? Why did you keep him from me?

Why hadn't he gone back to England? Why hadn't his parents told him about Rand in one of their infrequent letters? They must have seen the boy. They must have guessed.

Chester must have known, too.

That realization froze Miles where he stood.

He understood so much now. Why Chester had not come to Verity's bed after Rand was born. Why she had sent her son away to school at so young an age. Why she had told him he would like Rand, because Rand was nothing like Chester. Of course not. Rand was not Chester's son.

Miles examined the terrible wound on his son's shoulder and the four distinct claw marks on his belly. He had come impossibly close to losing a son he had never known he had.

"How long has he been unconscious?" he asked Freddy.

"Most of the day. For a long time his wound wouldn't stop bleeding." She swallowed hard. "He's been feverish, too, but surely now that he's in a warm bed and can have good food and hot tea, he'll get well, won't he?"

If the wound doesn't get infected, Miles thought. *If he hasn't lost too much blood. If the fever doesn't get worse.* "I'm sure he'll be fine," he reassured her.

"I'm so glad you got back when you did," Freddy said. Words tumbled out of her mouth, falling over themselves in a rush to be said. "I was a little concerned when we arrived, because the house seemed abandoned. But Tom—Mr. Grimes said from the look of things you would be back soon. And here you are.

"Mr. Grimes tended Rushland's wounds along the trail. He said it would be better to leave them open to the air now that's he's in bed than to bind them. Do you think he's right?"

"Tom knows as much as any man I've met about doctoring," Miles said. "I'll get the salve for Verity's burns."

The instant he shut the bedroom door behind him, Miles leaned back against the log wall, closed his eyes, and took a deep breath. His son was here, in the next room. And for the moment, alive. Miles felt as though he had been kicked in the groin—

breathless, the pain so bad it threatened to double him over.

All the years lost that I can never get back. The chance to be a father to my son stolen from me. Damn you, Verity!

But he had a son! Rand was here in his house. In his bedroom.

He grinned, then forced the giddy look from his face. Randal Talbot wasn't out of the woods yet. He had better not celebrate his good fortune until he was certain it wasn't going to be ripped from his grasp.

Miles was less willing to examine his feelings toward Verity at this moment, because they were so violent. She must have known she was pregnant with his child when she married Chester. Rand's existence made mincemeat of her claim that she had been blackmailed into marriage. He couldn't imagine her letting herself get forced into marriage with a man who wasn't the father of her child.

Why had she done it? Probably because she was pregnant and had to get married right away and really was horrified at the thought of facing him across the breakfast table for the rest of her life.

How gullible he had been to believe her lies! He felt betrayed all over again.

Miles shuddered as he imagined what Chester must have done to her when he discovered her deception. He worried about what harmful things Chester might have said . . . might have done . . . to his son—his enemy's son—over the years.

Miles was not immune to the irony of the fact

that in ruining Chester Talbot, he had left his own son destitute.

He wondered if Verity had ever told Rand the truth. He wondered if his son had loved another father in his place. He wondered if Chester had taught Randal Talbot to hate Miles Broderick.

Maybe Rand won't want anything to do with you when he finds out who you are.

That was a possibility he had to consider. It terrified him to think his son might not even give him a chance to be his father.

Miles shoved himself away from the wall and headed for the sideboard. While he was rooting around for the tin of bear grease he planned to use on Verity, he remembered Tom. He owed the man a great debt of gratitude.

"Hey, Tom," he called through the still-slack front door to the porch, where Tom was waiting to talk to him, to tell him what had happened. "Come on in here, and tell me how you ended up rescuing these two kids."

Tom eased into the house and stood with his thumbs hooked in his belt. "I got a good look at the boy," he said with a smirk. "Is he yours?"

Miles halted in place. "Is the resemblance that obvious?"

"It wasn't at first. Then I put two and two together. I mean, how you knew the lady a long time ago, and how quick the two of you got hitched. The more I looked at the kid, the more I saw you. Is he your son?" Tom repeated.

"I don't know. And I'd appreciate it if you'd

keep your guesses to yourself. I have to work this out in my own good time."

Tom cocked his hip. "Whatever you say, boss."

"You don't look any the worse for wear. What happened to you? You just disappeared."

"Those Sioux led me one helluva chase. The two I was after got away, but they led me right to your son and the girl. Sorry," he said when Miles frowned. "The *kid* and the girl."

Miles found the bear grease he had been hunting. "I have to tend to Mrs. Broderick's burns right now, but I'd like to hear the rest of the story later."

"Sure, boss."

Miles paused with his hand on the bedroom door and turned to glance over his shoulder. "I owe you, Tom. I won't forget it."

Tom shrugged. "All in a day's work."

"Speaking of work, I'd appreciate it if you'd go with Sully and help the boys load up all that equipment we used to fight the fire."

"Sure, boss. I'll talk to you later."

Freddy had apparently been busy while Miles was gone, carefully removing Verity's half-boots and charred stockings and shifting her skirt upward to expose the burned areas on her legs. She started when Miles reappeared in the doorway. "You can't come in here while Lady Talbot is undressed."

"She's Mrs. Broderick now," Miles reminded her gently.

"Oh." Freddy put a hand to her head. "So much has happened . . . I'll leave her to your care."

Freddy retreated to the other side of the bed, smoothed a stray lock of hair from Rand's forehead, and settled on the edge of the ladderback chair in the corner with her hand over his.

Miles forced back the wave of nausea that rolled in his stomach when he saw the blisters on Verity's legs. It reminded him too much of Sully. He sat beside her and gently began to smooth on the bear grease unguent.

"Can you tell me how Rushland got the claw marks on his belly?" Miles said, needing conversation to distract him from the sight before him.

"He was attacked by a bear. A *huge* one." Freddy brushed at the lock of hair that had fallen back onto Rand's forehead. "He was willing to sacrifice his life to save mine. He . . ." She swallowed hard. "He loves me, you see."

Miles glanced at Freddy. She looked more guilty than happy about the situation. "How did you two escape this huge bear?"

"Rand sent me up a tree so I would be safe, while he led the bear away from me. He managed to squeeze himself under a rotting log, but I could see the bear was going to dig him out. So . . . so I climbed down from the tree—"

Miles stopped what he was doing to look at her incredulously. "You what?"

"I climbed down from the tree and—"

"What did you think you were going to accomplish besides getting yourself killed, too?" Miles asked.

"I didn't think," she said pertly, "I only knew I

had to do something. I couldn't sit by and watch Rushland be killed for me when I don't even—I had to do something."

"What did you do?" Miles asked, intrigued.

"I yelled at the bear."

Miles rolled his eyes. "Lord save us from the stupidity of greenhorns. What did the bear do?"

Her jaw jutted pugnaciously. "He came after me."

"I guess he would," Miles said. A grin slipped free.

"It wasn't funny," Freddy said. "In fact, I was terrified. I ran as fast as I could, but the bear kept getting closer and closer. I heard Rushland shouting at me—"

"He had crawled out of his hole?"

She nodded vigorously. "I was afraid the bear had mauled him terribly, but those four claw marks are the worst that happened. Of course I didn't know that at the time. Rand threw a rock at the bear, trying to distract him. But . . . the bear kept coming after me."

She shuddered. Her eyes glazed, and she seemed to be reliving the incident. "I couldn't catch my breath. I was so scared, and I had run so far. The bear was growling and making awful noises. I tripped and fell. I . . . I could smell him, he was so close." She shook herself free of the memory.

"It's strange what you think of at a time like that." She shot him a mischievous look from beneath lowered lashes. "I imagined my parents having to explain my demise. They would never live down the infamy. *The Duke and Duchess of Worth announce that their daughter, Lady Winnifred Worth, was eaten by a bear . . .*"

Miles chuckled, and she joined him.

Her laughter stopped, and she was reliving the incident again. "I remember screaming for Rand . . ."

Miles knew Freddy was temporarily unaware of him, because she was using the familiar name, rather than the formal one.

"I remember Rand calling my name . . ."

The story stopped, and Miles glanced up at her, wondering what had caused the interruption. She was quivering. Her lips were pinched.

"The bear . . . the bear . . . knocked me down." Her eyes closed, she swallowed, and when she opened her eyes, she had returned to the present. "Then we heard the shots. It was Mr. Grimes, you see, chasing two Indians on horseback. The Indians never even slowed down, but Rand waved at Mr. Grimes, and he rescued us.

"He bandaged Rand's shoulder where the Indians had shot him—it had started to bleed again—and helped us find our horses. Then he led us safely back here to your ranch.

"And that's another thing," Freddy said, her brow furrowing. "Mr. Grimes said this is the Muleshoe Ranch. Are there two of them? Muleshoe ranches, I mean. Because I understood Rushland's mother owned the Muleshoe Ranch, but Mr. Grimes said you've been living here for years!"

"I promise there's an explanation for everything. I think it might be better to wait and let Verity tell you all about it," Miles said, using her incapacitation to postpone the inevitable. "Why don't you get yourself something to eat and drink," he suggested. "I'll look after these two and call you if there's any change."

For a moment he thought she might take him up on the offer, but she shook her head. "No, Rushland may wake up and need me."

Her mention of Rand caused his glance to shift to the other side of the bed. Miles shuddered to think what might have happened to the two young people if Tom hadn't come along when he had. It might have been a long time before they found Rand and Freddy's bodies, or rather, whatever the scavengers had left of them.

Verity had better not try to keep him from claiming his son. The fates had given him a second chance to be Rand's father. He damn sure wasn't going to waste it.

He had nearly finished spreading the unguent on Verity's legs, but he must have pressed a little too hard in his agitation, because she groaned.

"Have you decided to join us again?" he said silkily as her eyes blinked against the light. He clenched his teeth on the question he was dying to ask.

Why didn't you tell me about my son?

Verity felt like she was swimming upward from a deep pool of water toward the light. When she blinked her eyes open the first thing she saw was Miles's face.

"How do you feel?" he asked.

She felt confused, uncertain where she was. Then it all came back to her. She grabbed Miles's arm, her nails biting into his skin. "Rand?" she said in a choked voice. "Rand?"

"Is lying right beside you," he replied in a cool voice.

She turned her head, saw her son, and shoved the back of her hand against her mouth to stifle a sob of joy. She tried turning onto her side toward him, but cried out when the blisters on her legs touched the cotton bedsheets.

"You need to be careful," Miles warned. "The backs of your legs are burned worse than we thought."

Verity wasn't concerned about herself. Her only goal was to get herself turned around so she could see her son. "Please, help me, Miles."

He carefully turned her over to face Rand and sat behind her to support her back as she reached out to trace Rand's upper chest near the spot where the bullet had left so much damage.

Verity realized, suddenly, that Miles hadn't mentioned a word about Rand having black hair. Surely he had noticed. Surely he suspected the truth. But with Freddy in the room, she didn't dare bring up the subject.

She shot Miles a look over her shoulder, but his eyes gave nothing away. She turned her attention back to Rand.

"The bullet wound looks bad," she said, her stomach curling as she felt Rand's pain deep inside herself. "Are those *claw* marks?" she whispered, her hand sliding down to his belly.

"Rand and Freddy had a run-in with a bear—"

She gasped.

"But they came out of it just fine."

Verity saw Freddy sitting beside the bed next to Rand and reached out to clasp her hand. "Oh, Freddy. You're both safe and alive! I can hardly believe it. How did you escape from the Sioux?"

"An Indian woman helped us get away. Hawk's wife, actually."

"Why would she do that?" Miles asked.

"She . . . uh . . . wanted Hawk all to herself. You see, he wanted to make me his wife, too."

"Good God!" Miles exclaimed.

"It's all over now," Verity said. "We're all together again. That's what's important." Her brow furrowed as she surveyed Rand's wounds. "Rand is going to be all right, isn't he, Miles?"

"He's lost a lot of blood, and he's got a fever. But there's no infection yet. With rest, with time, there's a good chance he'll pull through."

"But?" Verity asked, hearing the hesitation in his voice.

"But the wound could turn putrid. Or, if he's too weak from loss of blood, he may not be able to fight off the fever, and that could kill him."

"You're saying he's not out of danger yet?"

"Not yet."

She slumped back against him. "I think I'd like to lie down again."

Miles helped Verity to lie down, plumping the pillow under her head. He settled himself at the foot of the bed, his arms crossed, his back against the bedpost, one hip on the mattress, one foot on the ground. "Rest," he said. "Don't worry about Rand. I'll keep an eye on him for you."

She wondered if there was some meaning hidden in his offer. *Do you know Rand is your son? Is that why you're willing to watch over him? I can't believe you haven't noticed the resemblance. Why haven't you said something?*

"Lady Winnifred, maybe you'd like to go outside and get a breath of fresh air," Miles suggested.

"I don't—"

"You don't want to make yourself sick," Verity said. "Rand will need you when he regains consciousness."

"I guess I could use a breath of air," she said as she rose from her chair.

Neither Miles nor Verity said a word until the door closed with a resounding *click* behind her.

"Is Rand my son?"

Even though Verity had fully expected the question, her heart skipped a beat.

"Is he?" Miles demanded, his voice slicing through the air between them. "Answer me, damn it!"

"Yes! Yes, he's your son."

Miles gave a strangled cry of anguish. His head

dropped back against the bedpost, and he covered his eyes with his arm.

"I didn't know," she said, struggling to sit up, pleading for understanding. "I didn't know I was pregnant when I married him."

His hand came away from his face, and she was frightened by the mask of rage that confronted her. "How could you not know?"

"I thought my courses were late because I was so unhappy, because—"

He snorted rudely, cutting her off. "Don't bother lying, *Verity*."

"You have to believe me, Miles."

"Why didn't you ever send word to me? Why didn't you find a way to let me know? All these years when I could have known him . . . Wasted!"

"Why didn't you contact me?" she retorted. "I didn't even know if you were alive, at first. You simply disappeared. Chester had threatened to repudiate Rand if I told you about him. Our son would have been a bastard. Rand was innocent. He didn't deserve to suffer."

"So you let my enemy claim my son as his own?"

"What else was I supposed to do?" she cried.

"Divorce him."

She gritted her teeth in an attempt to still her trembling chin. "You know I couldn't do that. If I had divorced Chester, the courts would have let him keep Rand. I was the only one standing between our son and Chester's hatred for you."

Miles ran an angry hand through his hair, leaving it standing on end. "Does Rand know about me?"

She hesitated a moment before replying, "No."

Miles turned his face away from her and groaned like an animal in pain. "Did he love Chester?" he gritted out.

"Don't torture yourself, Miles."

"Answer the question!"

"What do you want me to say? He believed Chester was his father. He wanted Chester's love." Her lips twisted bitterly. "He never got it." She saw Miles's glistening eyes through a mist of her own tears. "What's going to happen now?"

"What do you mean?"

"Are you going to tell Rand you're his father?"

"He has a right to know who his real father is. And what kind of woman his mother is."

Verity's face blanched. "Bear in mind—if you decide to blacken my name—that Rand loves me. He won't thank you for it."

"I'll take my chances."

"At least give him time to get well before you tell him. Please, Miles."

"I'll wait, Verity. But I'm the one who's going to tell him. You're not to say a word to him about any of this."

"Can I be there when you tell him?"

"I don't know. I'll have to think about it."

"There's another thing you should consider, Miles."

"What?"

"Rand is going to be suspicious of the circumstances surrounding our marriage. He knows I had a deed to this ranch. And he'll find out you've been in possession for quite a while. He'll wonder why I would marry a stranger the same day I met him—the same day he disappeared. What are we going to tell him?"

Miles stared at her. "You've never told him a word about me? About loving me, lying with me, before you married Chester Talbot?"

Verity heard the underlying pain that caused the sarcasm. She shook her head and whispered, "I couldn't."

"Tell him whatever you want," Miles said brusquely. "Make up something. You're good at it."

He didn't wait to hear her retort. He was gone from the room before she could even think of one.

13

Miles shook Verity awake. "Rand's fever is worse. Unless we can get it down, he's going to die."

"Tell me what to do."

Miles wasn't sure what he had expected—that Verity might fall into a swoon or shriek and tear at her hair—but he was frankly surprised by her calm, rational response.

He had spent an uncomfortable night sitting in the ladderback chair beside Rand, his legs stretched out in front of him, his ankles resting on the foot of the bed. He had listened to the house creak and settle as the wind blew through the eaves and swirled up from the knotholes in the wooden floor. The past few difficult days had taken their toll, and he had fallen asleep. He had woken only when the pink light of dawn seeped through his eyelids.

He felt guilty for not keeping a closer watch on his son. Regrets weren't going to help now, just fast, efficient action.

"You can help me sponge him down," Miles said. "Maybe we can cool him off that way." It was a remedy for fever that had worked in the past.

Verity eased her legs over the edge of the bed, but even that small movement caused her to hiss with pain. She was stripped to her chemise and pantalets and had nothing else to put on.

"Do you have a shirt I can use to cover myself?" she asked.

Miles got a worn chambray shirt from his wardrobe and watched while she put it on and buttoned it. It irked him that as angry as he was with her, his body still responded to the feminine swell of her breasts beneath the masculine material.

"Are you sure you ought to be out of bed?" he said. "Can you even walk?"

"I'll crawl, if I have to, but I'm getting out of this bed."

Miles helped Verity onto her feet, being careful to keep her legs from brushing against the sheets. "Is that better?"

She tested her weight on her legs. "Yes. Thanks."

Miles picked up a kerosene lantern from a table beside the bed and led the way into the other room. The added light woke Freddy, who had gone to sleep on a pallet Miles had rigged for her in front of the fireplace. He had been lucky to get her to lie down at all. She had wanted to stand vigil over Rand with him. She was still completely dressed in her rumpled green riding habit. Her only concession had been to remove her calfskin boots.

It dawned on him that if Rand survived, he would marry this woman. Freddy would become his daughter-in-law. One look at her hands, and he knew she hadn't done a lick of work in her lifetime. As the daughter of a duke, she had most certainly been pampered, most likely spoiled rotten. Her behavior in the incident with the bear proved she didn't have a particle of sense.

But he couldn't deny her beauty. He had seen how Tom was smitten with her. That tumbled mane of auburn hair, her astonishing, long-lashed green eyes and pouty-looking, bowed lips, all set in a porcelain, heart-shaped face, would turn any man's head for a second look. But beauty didn't count for much in a land like this.

The fact she had sat for hours by Rand's side and stared at the ugly, oozing wound on his shoulder without fleeing or fainting dead away showed a stronger stomach than he had thought any gently bred English lady possessed.

The fact Freddy had climbed down from the safety of a tree in an attempt to rescue Rand spoke of extraordinary courage. It wasn't a bad trait for a man to look for in the mother of his sons. Unless you considered the impossible odds she had faced. That made her behavior reckless, perhaps even stupid.

He wondered if there was any more to Lady

Winnifred Worth than surface beauty and a strong stomach and a penchant for danger. Had his son sought out a woman of substance for his wife? Or had he merely chosen for beauty and rank and fortune?

He decided to reserve judgment on the girl. In a land like this, there were plenty of opportunities to test a person's mettle. The weak ones didn't survive. The cowardly ones ran. Only the strongest, the sturdiest, the bravest stayed to carve a life in the wilderness.

Freddy raised herself on one elbow. "Is Rand all right?"

"His fever's worse," Miles answered. "We're going to sponge him with cool water to try to bring it down."

Freddy shoved the quilt out of her way and began drawing on her boots. "What can I do to help?"

Verity's heart went out to the young woman sitting on a makeshift pallet on the hard floor. She had also been observing Freddy, whose face was half hidden in shadows, half lit by the soft pink light of dawn. She saw someone who, three mornings ago, had been a naive seventeen-year-old, cosseted and protected from such vulgar horrors as a man's naked chest.

The Freddy who scrambled to her feet and stood waiting for a word from her had serious green eyes that had aged a lifetime in a few days. It seemed ridiculous to treat her like the child-woman she had been before she set out on this journey.

"Get another cloth and a bowl of water. You can work on Rand's shoulders and chest, while I do his legs." Verity primed the pump and ice-cold water began gushing into the tin bowl she had set in the sink.

"What do you want me to do?" Miles said.

"You can refill our bowls, so we're always using cool water."

Verity was already heading back to the bedroom when she realized she needed more light. "Miles? The lantern."

He lit the lamp on the kitchen table to provide light in the main room until the sun was fully up, then led the way back to the bedroom. He set the lantern back on the table beside Rand, so Verity and Freddy would be able to see what they were doing.

Before they let Freddy into the bedroom, Miles and Verity stripped Rand completely and rearranged the sheet over him so his chest and legs were exposed, but he was still decently covered.

"You can come in now, Freddy," Verity called when they were done.

Miles and Verity exchanged a poignant look as Freddy's eyes sought out Rand.

Will she be able to stay the distance? Miles wondered.

Is she going to break Rand's heart? Verity wondered.

Freddy crossed to Verity's side, took the cloth Verity handed to her, dipped it in the cold water, and wrung it out. Her hands were trembling as she brushed the cloth across Rand's shoulder.

Miles and Verity caught each other's eyes again. She had passed the first test. There would be others. All they could do was wait and see. There was no more time for thinking, for worrying, for wondering. They were too busy ministering to Rand.

Verity stood at the foot of the bed and began the endless chore of sponging Rand's fiery skin with cool water, repeating the process again and again. It wasn't long before the mattress beneath him was soaked. She and Miles decided the wet mattress couldn't hurt because the dampness beneath Rand also helped cool his flesh.

None of them was sure of the efficacy of the treatment. Rand became restless, struggling against the hands that attended him.

"Rand," Verity said. "Please, be still. You're going to be all right. Everything will be all right."

He quieted for a while, but moments later cried, "Freddy! Freddy!"

Freddy dropped the cloth she held and reached for Rand's flailing hands. "I'm here, Rand. I'm right here."

"Dead," he muttered. Tears leaked from his closed eyes. "Bear . . . too late."

Freddy turned stricken eyes to Verity. "He seems to think the bear killed me. He doesn't remember we were rescued. He's suffering, Lady Talbot. What can I do?"

Verity didn't correct the girl's mode of address. Her marriage to Miles seemed to have happened in another lifetime. She met Miles's eyes as he entered the room with another bowl of water.

"He's rambling, muttering nonsense. He doesn't seem to remember he and Freddy were saved from the bear," she told him.

"It's the fever," Miles said. "Keep talking to him, Freddy. Perhaps your voice will soothe him."

Freddy edged onto the bed and took one of Rand's hands in both of her own. "I'm here, Rand. We're both safe. The bear ran away. The shots scared him away. Don't you remember?"

"Freddy," he moaned.

"I'm safe, Rand. I'm alive."

Freddy turned beseeching eyes first to Verity and then to Miles. "He's still crying."

"Keep talking," Miles ordered. "Just keep talking." He had taken Freddy's job sponging off Rand's shoulders and chest. Rand's hallucinations meant the fever was worse. Miles's heart jumped to his throat and hammered there.

Don't die, he pleaded. *I want to get to know you. I want a chance to be your father.*

Freddy bent close to Rand's ear to speak in whispers that couldn't be heard by Miles and Verity. "It's been quite an adventure, hasn't it, Rand? Who would ever have thought we would be captured by Indians? Or chased by a bear? My friends won't believe me when I tell them everything that's happened. Neither will my parents.

"They must be terribly worried about me, Rand. I'm going to have to write them soon and tell them I'm well. They'll be surprised that we're not married. I've been thinking about what you said, Rand. Not that I think anyone in England would ever hear the story of what happened to us, but . . . I have . . . feelings for you I don't quite understand . . ."

She talked to him for hours, while his parents kept applying the cooling water to his skin. At last he seemed more quiet. She kept murmuring to him, begging him to open his eyes, to please wake up.

Freddy gave a small cry of surprise when Rand's eyes actually opened. She held her breath as they closed, then blinked open again. "Rand?"

He turned his head to look at her. His eyes seemed unfocused at first. "Freddy?" he rasped.

She jumped to her feet, startled by the sound of his voice. "Lady Talbot! Mr. Broderick! Rand's awake. He knows me!"

Rand looked around him, obviously confused and disoriented. "Where am I?" He tried weakly, futilely, to rearrange the sheet to cover himself better. "Get out!" he said to Freddy. "Mother, get her out!"

"But, Rand—" Freddy protested.

Verity put an arm around Freddy's shoulders and began ushering her from the room. "I think we should leave Rand alone for a little while."

"But, Rand—" Freddy cried beseechingly.

"Get out!" he shouted. It came out as more of a croak.

Freddy hadn't shed a tear through all that had

happened, but a sob, part relief, part confusion, part fatigue, broke free.

"Go ahead and cry, Freddy," Verity said as she closed the bedroom door behind them and headed to the closest chairs at the kitchen table. "I feel like having a good cry myself."

Rand was irritated and irritable. He was still trying to cover his nakedness, but his hands wouldn't obey his commands. He had woken to find himself lying in bed stark naked in a room populated by his fiancée and his mother and a stranger. When the stranger began to help him with the sheets, he muttered, "I can do it myself."

"Another day, maybe. Right now you're weak as a two-day-old kitten. Lie back, and let me do it."

Rand let his hands collapse at his sides and stared balefully at the man who straightened the sheet to cover him from toes to chest.

"Where am I?" he asked, his voice hoarse from disuse.

"The Muleshoe Ranch."

His brow furrowed. "My mother's place."

"Mine," Miles said in a soft voice.

The grooves in Rand's forehead deepened. "Grimes said the Muleshoe already belonged to somebody else. I was sure he had to be wrong."

"It's a long story. Are you sure you want to hear it now?"

"I need to know what's going on," Rand said.

"The man who sold Chester Talbot this land sold it to me first. Your mother's title to the Muleshoe was never valid."

A myriad of chaotic emotions churned through Rand. Distress, disappointment, disgust. He stared at the man across from him, realizing who he must be, knowing the answer to the question he was about to ask, but needing to hear it spoken aloud. "Who are you?"

"Miles Broderick. I'm . . . an acquaintance of your mother's."

"Grimes said you married my mother." It was an accusation.

"I did."

"Why?"

After a short hesitation he said, "Because the ranch your mother came here to claim, the Muleshoe, belongs to me. She needed a place to live. I wanted a wife." He lifted a shoulder in what started as a shrug but ended before it was complete. "So we got married."

Rand's lips pressed flat. His expression turned ugly. "In other words, you blackmailed her into marrying you."

"She could have refused."

Tension simmered between them.

I know who you are, Rand thought. But he didn't say the words. Couldn't say them. His father —Chester Talbot, he corrected himself—had told him everything on his deathbed.

"You already know you're not my son," Chester had rasped past the death rattle in his chest.

"Yes, I know," Rand had said, his heart in his eyes, a lump in his throat. Chester had told him that much of the truth three years before. He was there to hear the rest of it. "What is my father's name, sir?" he had asked.

"Miles Broderick is the blackguard who raped your mother and abandoned her. Miles Broderick, Viscount Linden, is your father."

Chester had warned him not to confront his mother. "She will lie to you, as she did to me. For your own good, of course. She will not want to take the risk that Broderick may kill you in a duel. He is the villain in all of this. I have always hated him. It will be up to you—if he ever sets foot in London again—to avenge your mother's honor."

It had been awful to know who has father was, to realize he came from such bad blood, and to still feel curious about the man. One of the reasons Rand had been so glad to come to Wyoming was because he had learned his father was here, and he had wanted to find him and punish him for all the hurt and harm he had caused.

Miles Broderick had proved himself the villain Talbot had named him. Hadn't Broderick forced his mother into marriage? Hadn't he somehow stolen the Muleshoe Ranch, which should have been his mother's home, away from her? As soon as he was well enough, Rand decided, he would take the steps necessary to carry out the duty laid on him by a dying man.

He would have to avenge his mother's honor. He would have to kill Miles Broderick.

Another thought rose, one he found both alarming and intriguing. *Does Broderick intend to claim me as his son?* His face set grimly. *Miles*

Broderick will rue the day he tries to be my father. I don't have a father. I am that ugly name I was taunted with as a child, that I fought with my fists to deny. I am the bastard they accused me of being.

His eyes fell closed, and he sighed in exhaustion. Moments later, he was asleep.

Miles checked to make sure Rand was merely sleeping and that the fever had not returned, but his son was breathing deeply, evenly, and without difficulty. Miles laid his hand on Rand's forehead. His skin felt normal, cool in comparison to the previous fiery heat during the worst of the fever.

A sick feeling of dread churned Miles's stomach. He had felt the animosity rolling off his son in waves. It was a fair guess that Randal Talbot hated his guts. What had Chester told him? What had he done to poison his son's mind against him?

You won't win, Chester. He's my son. I'll find a way to reach him. I'll find a way to undo the damage you've done.

A swell of aching tenderness rose within him as he gazed at his son. Here was flesh of his flesh, blood of his blood. Was it too late to be a part of his son's life? Would Rand, when he knew the truth about his birth—that his parents had been desperately in love with each other when he was conceived—still feel enmity toward Miles for what had been the tragic folly of a young couple in love? Would Rand understand why Miles had ruined Chester? Would he blame Miles for the theft of his inheritance?

Miles realized he was going to have to make some decisions, and soon, about whether—and what—to tell Rand about himself.

"Is he asleep?"

Miles glanced up and saw Verity in the doorway. "Yes. The fever's broken."

"Freddy is settled again. The poor girl was exhausted." She put her hands to the small of her back and arched in the age-old way a woman does when she has labored long and hard.

"You look exhausted, too."

Verity sat on the edge of the bed, but Miles couldn't make himself go to her even though he could see the difficulty she was having. She eased back, trying to keep her knees bent so her burned calves wouldn't come in contact with anything.

When she cried out with pain, Miles could keep his distance no longer. She wasn't the only one to blame for the tragedy that had occurred. He had to accept at least some of the responsibility. Now that his initial shock and anger had passed, he realized it was her fear of just such a virulent response from him that had kept her from telling him sooner that Rand was his son—even though she must have known he would figure out the truth the instant he laid eyes on him.

"Sit down, Miles," she said, patting the bed beside her.

He sat down uncomfortably in the small space.

"Did you talk with Rand?"

"Yes."

"What did he say?"

"Rand doesn't approve of our marriage."

"That was to be expected," she said.

He felt an ache in his throat. "He hates me, Verity. Chester must have said something, lied to him about me."

"I was afraid of that," she murmured. She put a hand on his arm. "All Rand has to do is spend time with you, and he'll see what a good man you are, Miles."

He shook his head. "It can't be that easy."

"It can. You're both a great deal alike," she said. "Stubborn, headstrong. But fair."

He took the kiss without asking, needing it, needing hope. She gave him the comfort he sought. Her hand slid into the hair at his nape.

He raised himself enough to look into her eyes and spoke quietly to avoid waking Rand. "Do you remember how it was between us the first time, Verity?" he whispered. "Do you remember the day we made our son?"

How could she ever forget? Verity thought. She stared into his gray eyes, remembering.

It was summertime, and oh, so unbearably hot. Dark, dangerous thunderclouds had threatened. She had slipped away to the pond at the edge of her father's estate, taken off her shoes and stockings, and stuck her toes into the icy water. Even then, a trickle of perspiration had wiggled its way down her back beneath her sky blue merino gown.

Miles had appeared on horseback looking like a centaur, he was so finely made and so much a part of the animal. He had flashed a confident grin—he had been so charming in those days—and asked, "May I join you?"

He hadn't waited for her answer. He had already known what it would be. They were young and foolish and in love.

Verity closed her eyes to force the memories away. "Don't make me remember, Miles."

"It was a sweet time, wasn't it? Sometimes I hardly believe it myself. I was Rand's age." He turned his head so he could see his son. "We were such babies. If you had a chance to change the past, would you have denied me, Verity?"

"That isn't a fair question."

"I suppose not. But I'm asking it anyway."

She met his gaze steadily. "No, Miles. I wouldn't change a thing. I loved you so very much. I've never been as happy before or since. I wouldn't give up that joy."

"I wish I had known about Rand. I would have done things differently."

"Would you have come back?"

"It's easy now to say I would have. But I'm not sure."

"Why not?"

"You could have fallen in love with Talbot. I wouldn't have been able to bear seeing that. It was easier not to know. I stayed away, I never asked, so I wouldn't have to know."

"Why didn't you ever marry?"

"I never loved another woman." He didn't explain that since she had taken his heart, he'd had nothing left to give another woman. That would have sounded too self-serving—or too pitifully sad. Unfortunately, it was the truth.

Her lips pressed the pulse beneath his ear. "It was probably better you didn't return," she whispered. "I was never very good at resisting temptation."

"Could I have tempted you?"

"There were nights when the memories of the two of us together haunted me."

She remembered the cool grass beneath her buttocks. Being naked beneath the brooding sky. She remembered the feel of his silky hair against her throat, and the wetness, the hotness of his mouth on her breasts.

She remembered the sharp pain of losing her virginity, the way Miles's hard body had filled her, stretched her, thrust within her. She remembered the feel of his sweat-slick shoulders beneath her fingertips, the wet curls at his nape. The musky smell of sex.

And the rain, first in sprinkles, then pelting harder and harder against their naked bodies. Washing away the blood and the guilt and leaving them fresh and clean and new. She even remembered the laughter as they donned their soggy clothing in a redeeming ray of sunlight, kissing and touching each step of the way.

The afternoon of her deflowering remained such a vivid recollection, it might have happened yesterday.

"Yes, Miles," she whispered, raising herself

enough to touch her lips to his. "You could have tempted me."

He buried his face in the niche between her neck and shoulder. "We were fools."

"It's never foolish to love. Perhaps we were guilty of poor judgment. I don't know." She sighed and soothed herself and him by caressing him, running her fingers through his hair and clasping him close. "It would be nice to have a crystal ball, to be able to see into the future. Perhaps if we knew what was coming, life would be too terrifying to live. I've learned to face each day, one at a time, and survive it the best way I can."

"Thank you for my son, Verity."

She felt her throat clog. "You're welcome, Miles."

He raised his head and looked into her eyes. "Where do we go from here?"

"That's up to you, Miles."

"Shall we start all over? Shall I woo you and win you again?"

He already had her heart. He always had. Didn't he realize that? "Why now, Miles?"

"I think that would be obvious."

"Rand." She bit back the disappointment she felt. She should have known. He wasn't really interested in winning her love. He wanted his son's favor. And he wasn't above using her to get it.

"I want my son to get to know me, Verity. I want to be his father. Or at least try. That will be easier if you and I are friends."

"We were never friends, Miles. Only lovers."

"Are you refusing my offer?" he asked.

"To be your friend? Or to be your lover?"

Miles's eyes narrowed, and a muscle in his jaw worked. "Why are you making this so difficult?"

"I have the most to lose in this arrangement."

"Meaning Rand? You've had him for twenty-one years, Verity. Don't you think it's time I had a chance to be involved in his life? We could be a family if you'd cooperate."

"Rand is a grown man, not a child. He's ready to start a family of his own. It's too late for what you want."

"No, it's not," he said stubbornly. "Rand could still use some fatherly advice. This is a different land, with different customs. I could be a help to him."

"You don't need me in order to do that for him." She wanted Miles to come up with a different reason to pursue a relationship with her, something more personal. And he was resisting.

"What do you want from me, Verity?"

"Nothing you seem willing to give," she said bleakly.

"So we leave it like this? You on one side of the fence, and me on the other?"

She could tell he was angry from the tension in his body. His voice gave away his frustration.

"I'm willing to live here with you as amicably as possible. You're welcome to establish a relationship—of whatever kind—with Rand. But leave me out of it."

"Fair enough," he said, rising from the bed.

She edged over onto her side, turning her back on him, feeling the hopelessness of the situation. Only it wasn't quite hopeless. He had gotten past the revelation that he had a son, and he was still talking to her. Maybe she should have cooperated more with him. Maybe she should have given him what he wanted.

She felt him lay a quilt over her shoulder. "Go to sleep, Verity," he said. "You have another challenging day to survive tomorrow."

"Miles—"

He cut her off as he shut the bedroom door behind him.

14

Verity's burns healed quickly. Within ten days, new skin had begun to replace what had been burned by the fire. By the end of two weeks, she was able to sleep comfortably in any position. The day came shortly thereafter when she woke up and realized she felt well enough to get up and get dressed. But she had absolutely nothing to wear.

"I've been thinking about that problem," Miles said. "And I've come up with a solution. I'll be right back." The twinkle in his eyes should have given her some warning.

She discovered what he found so amusing when he returned to the room and presented her with long johns, a gray wool shirt, a pair of denim jeans, a belt, socks and cowboy boots, all cheerfully donated by his cowhands.

"You expect me to wear men's trousers?" Verity asked.

"You'll be riding astride from now on," he said. "Until I have time to take you to Cheyenne to shop for a new wardrobe, this will have to do. I've already given Freddy a similar outfit."

Over the weeks Verity and Rand had been recuperating, Miles had cajoled Freddy into calling him by his first name. She had insisted he call her Freddy in return. Because Freddy felt awkward calling Verity "Mrs. Broderick," and "Lady Talbot" was no longer correct, and "Lady Linden" was absurd under the circumstances, Verity had asked if Freddy didn't think she could just call Verity by her name, too.

Freddy agreed, and that put everyone on a first-name basis. Or almost everyone. Rand refused to call Miles anything but "sir." His continuing formality pointed up the awkwardness of strangers forced to live together in a too-small space.

Freddy appeared in the doorway wearing jeans, a plaid shirt, and her leather half-boots. She held out an imaginary skirt and mimed a curtsy. "Good morning, Verity." Her impish grin was broad enough to make her eyes crinkle at the sides. "These trousers are really quite comfortable. I don't know why I didn't try something like this sooner."

"What would your parents say?" Verity asked, dismayed at how precisely the jeans outlined the young woman's figure.

"They'd be appalled," Freddy said. "Which I admit contributes to my affection for the fashion." Freddy did a complete turn to show off her rear end in the form-fitting pants.

"You look marvelous to me," Rand said from his side of the bed. His grin was just short of leering.

"They're positively indecent," Verity muttered.

"And wonderfully comfortable and eminently practical," Freddy said. "Which is probably why men have always worn them," she said, crossing the room and settling herself on the mattress beside Rand.

Rand winced as he propped himself up on his elbows, but it was evidence of how much healing had occurred in his wounded shoulder that he could manage the feat at all. "My only reservation is the reaction you'll get from the cowhands."

"My men won't say or do anything to embarrass either woman," Miles said. "A lady's treated with respect out here."

Verity arched a brow. "Even if she isn't dressed like a lady?"

"Even if she's buck naked or branded. No man would lay a hand on a respectable woman in the West unless he wanted every other man within a hundred miles to come after him with a rope."

"That makes me feel much better," Verity said wryly.

"Will you wear the trousers, or not?"

"I don't seem to have much choice," Verity conceded.

It didn't take a day for Verity to concur with

Freddy's assessment of trousers. They were comfortable and practical. They also attracted a lot of male attention.

Freddy was naturally flirtatious and used to being fawned over by the young bucks of the *ton,* and she quickly became a favorite of the cowboys. But Verity wondered how far the rugged ranch hands could be teased before one of them crossed the line. She kept a constant eye on Freddy, fearing the worst. But it never materialized.

While he was recuperating, Rand stayed in the bedroom with his mother. Miles retreated to the bunkhouse at night. Freddy slept near the fireplace on a Missouri featherbed—which of course involved no feathers at all, but was merely a mattress filled with straw ticking over a wooden frame that Sully had knocked together for her.

It was late September before Rand's shoulder was well enough for him to take up residence in the bunkhouse, at which time Miles was able to resume sleeping in his own bed. The day Rand moved out of the bedroom and Miles moved back in, the two men circled around each other like two dogs around the same bone.

Rand didn't trust Miles with his mother.

Miles wasn't about to give Verity up, even to please his son.

They had spoken little to each other over the past month and their relationship had turned as cool as the late September weather. Two sets of hackles rose as Miles dropped his shaving kit onto the four-poster bed while Rand gathered up his beaver brush and razor from the dry sink and put it in a bag to take with him to the bunkhouse.

"Stop it, both of you," Verity said. She put herself between them, turning first to Rand. "Miles is my husband. This is where he belongs." And then to Miles, "He's my son, Miles. He only wants to protect me."

"From me?" Miles snarled.

"From you," Rand retorted.

Verity saw the anger and pain in Miles's eyes at this show of mistrust from his son. It was a far cry from the friendship Miles had hoped for. Maybe Miles ought to bite the bullet and confess to Rand that he was his father, Verity thought. She didn't know why he was procrastinating. Rand was no less distant or hostile toward Miles now than he had been a month ago.

"Look, Rand—" Miles began.

Rand picked up the small bundle of belongings he planned to take with him to the bunkhouse and headed for the bedroom door. "I don't care to listen to anything you have to say, sir."

Miles snagged him by the arm as he passed by. "You're going to get some advice, anyway. If you're smart, you'll heed it."

The two men, both with the same dark hair, both tall and lean, stood glaring at each other with equally stormy gray eyes. Tension bristled between them.

Verity held her breath as Miles spoke.

"Keep your eyes open and your mouth shut in

the bunkhouse. Let everybody else do the talking. You just listen."

"Is that all, sir?"

Miles nodded curtly.

Rand jerked himself free and left the room without another word.

Miles huffed out an angry breath. "Damn that boy of yours, Verity! He's as stubborn—"

"As you are?" she finished for him.

"I was never that bad, was I?"

"Worse," she said with a smile. She crossed to him, slipped her arm through his, and raised herself on tiptoe to kiss his lips. "Give him time, Miles. He's had to adjust to so much in the past year. Please, give him some time."

Miles stared bleakly out the bedroom window. He watched Rand kick viciously at a stone as he stalked toward the bunkhouse. He wished he could spare his son the pranks he knew would be played on him as part of his initiation by the cowboys whose ranks he was joining in the bunkhouse. But if Rand was going to become one of the men—and perhaps, eventually, their boss—he would have to prove himself to them. There was nothing Miles could do to ease his way.

Besides, if his son couldn't handle the hard cowboy life, it was better to find out now. Miles would be sorry to see Rand fail, but the West was no place for a man without courage—or the sense of humor that helped make it possible to endure a life of such constant adversity. It took grit, guts, and gumption to handle the kind of deadly "jokes" cowboys played on one another. But for men who often had to rely on each other in life-and-death situations, it was important to test the limits—to find the razor's edge—of a new man. His son was about to endure that trial by fire.

Rand simmered with anger. He resented having to listen to Miles Broderick spout advice. He had conceded that the move to the bunkhouse was the most practical solution to a crowded situation. Truthfully, he had been looking forward to living in the midst of real live cowboys, who were objects of great mystery and compelling interest to him.

But he didn't need anyone to tell him how to comport himself with strangers. He had been sent away to boarding school at an age when he was among the smallest of the boys there. He had learned early how to survive as an outsider in alien surroundings.

When Rand stepped through the bunkhouse door, he found the reality of cowboy living fell somewhat short of the myth. The smell of the place was enough to gag him. Licorice, of all things, from scented chewing tobacco that had missed the brass spittoon in the corner and landed on the floor. Coal oil and smoke from the tin lamps. Tobacco. Manure that had clung to boots and then dried and dropped off onto the floor. The rank smell of unwashed bodies.

"Guess you got tired of ridin' the bed wagon," Frog said in welcome. "Pick any bunk ain't got a blanket on it."

Since there was only one stacked bunkbed without a blanket on it, the advice was obviously given tongue-in-cheek. It was Rand's first, relatively harmless, experience with the Western sense of humor. He ended up on a top bunk above a man called Chip, at the opposite end of the room from the stove. He imagined it got cold this far from the fire in winter.

He saw something tacked to the wall at the head of his bed and looked closer in an attempt to figure out what it was. It looked amazingly like a human ear.

"What is that?" he asked Chip.

"Last man had your bed didn't listen when he was spoke to. We put his ear up there to help him out."

Rand's eyes got huge as he looked at the shriveled human ear. If that was really what it was.

He glanced suspiciously, surreptitiously, at the six other cowboys in the bunkhouse, all of whom must have heard what Chip had told him, but each of whom had busied himself with something so it appeared he was paying no attention. Rand's eyes stopped on a man who had no ears. He swallowed hard. Then the cowboy turned and Rand saw the awful scars that explained what had caused his abnormality.

Maybe the tacked-up ear was real and maybe it wasn't. But he decided he ought to take Miles's warning about keeping his mouth shut and listening a little more seriously.

Rand noticed, once he started looking, that

each of the cowboys seemed to have some sort of flaw that set him apart. He rubbed the four stripes on his stomach. Since his episode with the bear, he fit right in. He decided to make up his bunk and get some sleep and began unrolling the mattress over the wooden bunk frame.

"You got any pants rats, be sure to kill 'em 'fore you throw 'em on the floor," Frog said.

"What?"

"Ten-cent fine every time you throw a grayback on the floor without pinchin' it dead first," Sully explained.

Pants rats? Graybacks? Rand had no idea what they were talking about, but he didn't want to show his ignorance. He watched Frog scratch, reach inside his long red underwear and retrieve a bug, pinch it, and drop it over the edge of the bed. *Good God! Lice!*

Rand felt like blurting that he didn't have lice, but that might have insinuated that he was somehow different or better than the others, who all apparently accepted the warning as appropriate to a newcomer. He kept his mouth shut. This daunting experience was not dissimilar from his first days at Oxford, when upperclassmen at Trinity College had intimidated the new arrivals, frightening them with rules and regulations and customs that they would invariably violate—only to be castigated severely for their failings. Rand wondered what form of punishment these roughened outcasts would exact from him.

He dragged off his Hessians and removed his

kerseymere trousers and the navy blue wool shirt Miles had loaned him before sliding onto the mattress and spreading a blanket over himself. Then he turned on his side and surveyed the inhabitants of the bunkhouse.

Tom and Cookie sat at a table near the fire playing with a greasy deck of cards, while Sully lay on his bunk reading a well-thumbed volume of Robert Burns's poetry. Chip was playing dominoes. Frog was picking lice from his clothing.

Pickles was spitting tobacco juice at a brass spittoon ten feet from the bed, missing about a third of the time. Red was shaving his head in front of a cracked mirror with the largest, sharpest knife Rand had ever seen.

He must have been more tired than he thought, because the next thing he knew Cookie was banging a pot and shouting "Rise and shine!"

He bolted upright but realized immediately it was still pitch black outside. There was, however, plenty of light from a lantern hanging on the wall nearby to see the snake, its head raised and its tail viciously rattling, coiled at the foot of his bed.

He sat paralyzed, staring at the rattler—which was probably what saved him from being bitten. He swallowed hard. Beads of perspiration formed on his forehead and above his lip. His tongue slipped out to catch a salty drop and the snake weaved and rattled threateningly.

His brain was racing, looking for a way to escape the situation without getting bitten by the snake, which was obviously poisonous, or resorting to the humiliating alternative of begging the men to rescue him. Outside his range of sight—and a safe distance from the snake—he could hear the cowboys slapping their sides with laughter. Some joke! He was liable to end up dead.

On another level he knew this was a test, like the time Dickie Featherstone had held him out his third-story bedroom window at Trinity by his ankles, threatening to let him go unless he pleaded for mercy. The problem was, if you begged for mercy they let you back in, but they never let you forget it. He had dared Dickie to drop him and had actually kicked one foot free before Dickie got scared he was really going to fall and pulled him back in. They had been fast friends ever since.

Rand's hands had reflexively clutched the blanket, and he realized suddenly how he could escape his peril. With a quick flick of his wrists he snapped the blanket, sending the snake flying into the midst of the laughing cowboys. They yelped in surprise and scurried in all directions. A second later Rand landed feet first on the floor, grabbed the gun from a holster hanging from an upper bunk, and shot the head off the snake just as it coiled to strike at Red.

The gunshot was deafening in the small room. It took a moment for the commotion to cease and for everyone to realize that no one was hurt and the snake was dead.

Rand settled Tom's gun back in its holster, walked calmly over to the snake, and picked it up by the tail to admire it. The diamond pattern was actually quite beautiful. "I've been wondering where you fellows got the snakeskins for those fancy hatbands. Thanks for finding one for me."

The cowboys stood for a moment slack-jawed before Frog slapped his knee and said, "Guess he got us, boys."

Red slapped Rand on the back. "Shoulda seen the look on your face when you saw that snake. Thought I was gonna die laughing!"

"I just thought I was going to die," Rand admitted with a crooked grin.

The cowboys guffawed again.

Rand held the five-foot-long headless snake out in front of him with forefinger and thumb. "Anybody have any idea how to separate the skin from the snake?"

Red took the snake from him and pulled out his knife. "Here, I'll do it for you."

Rand was still shaking, but none of the cowboys seemed to hold that against him. Only Tom still kept his distance.

"I hope you don't mind that I borrowed your gun," Rand said.

"Just don't make a habit of it," Tom replied. "How did you know I keep a bullet chambered?"

"I didn't."

"Damned lucky shot," Tom said.

Rand didn't contradict him. Better they should think him a lucky shot than find out how good he really was and challenge him to some hair-brained shooting contest like Harry Frazier had done. "Yes, really lucky," he murmured.

But luck had nothing to do with it. Most of his friends had spent time every year at the family hunting box in the country shooting whatever game was in season. Since Rand had always preferred to be anywhere but where his father—Chester Talbot—was, he had accepted every invitation he got—and become an excellent shot.

He accepted the snakeskin from Red, found a place to lay it where he wouldn't have to look at it again anytime soon, and went back to bed.

The next morning, Miles joined Rand at the trestle table in the bunkhouse where the men ate their morning and evening meals and asked, "How was your first night in the ram's pasture?"

Everyone stopped, spoons and cups poised, while the cowboys waited for Rand's answer.

Rand was still trying to understand what Miles meant by *ram's pasture.* When he figured it out, he grinned. That exactly described the atmosphere he had found in the bunkhouse—men with not much more on their minds than females, eating, and butting heads.

"The bed was fine," Rand said at last. "I slept like a log."

The men resumed shifting in their seats, forks clattered, and cups were set down. The green pea hadn't done badly.

Miles slanted Rand a measuring glance. "You sure there were no problems? Thought I heard a shot about two o'clock this morning."

Silence descended around the table once again.

"Oh, that was just me killing a snake for my

new hatband. Cookie woke me up and Frog pointed it out and Tom loaned me his gun and Red was kind enough to skin it out for me. Real nice bunch of fellows you have working here, sir."

The men exchanged sideways looks and knowing nods. Rand had passed another test. A cowboy never complained. He kept his trouble to himself.

"How about some Arbuckles to go with your biscuits and whistleberries, Randy?" Cookie said.

As simply as that, Rand had a nickname. It was another sign of his acceptance by the cowboys.

Rand didn't have a chance to answer before Cookie poured him a cup of something thick and black and ladled a spoon of something else into a bowl in front of him. He watched Cookie fill the other men's cups from the same speckled blue pot. He lifted his cup, sniffed, then took a swallow.

Arbuckles turned out to be coffee, thick as tar and twice as disgusting. It woke him up and caused him to want to empty his bowels, which was, he supposed, the purpose of it. Whistleberries—he chuckled when he thought about it—were beans.

That was how Rand began his apprenticeship as a cowboy. He was tested again and often during the next few days, in ways that were equally dangerous. It was Tom's idea to rimfire a green bronc and put Rand on it. It was Sully who actually found the cocklebur and put it under the saddle blanket before he pulled the cinch tight on the half-broken mustang.

The instant Rand's weight pressed the spiny bur

into the mustang's back, the animal bucked high and came down stiff-legged. Rand landed face first in the dust of the corral. It was a wonder he didn't break his neck. In fact, he reinjured his shoulder. He ignored the pain and got back onto his feet.

The cowboys sitting around the corral fence, which included Miles, watched to see whether Rand would lose his temper or, even worse, refuse to get back on.

Rand did neither. He took one look at the white-eyed animal with its ears laid back and said, "I think this poor fellow probably has a bellyache from having the cinch too tight. Let me loosen it up a little and give it another try."

Of course, when he loosened the cinch and rearranged the saddle on the blanket he found the prickly bur that had caused the problem. "Why, look here," he said as though amazed at what he'd found—though he wasn't amazed at all, because Archie McMahon had pulled the same trick on him when he was ten. "A bur must have got caught in the blanket."

He pulled it free, flicked it over his shoulder, retightened the cinch, and remounted the bronc. It was a diabolical creature, stiff-rumped and vicious, and Rand landed twice more in the dust before he finally rode the mean out of him.

It was soon clear Rand had once again earned the cowboys' respect, if not their actual admiration. He caught Miles looking at him with approval, but he turned his back on his father when he started toward him. He didn't need or want Miles Broderick's approbation.

But he didn't particularly want to kill him anymore, either.

Rand had been well enough for at least a week to challenge Broderick to a duel and avenge his mother's honor. But, Rand was neither stupid nor blind, and it hadn't taken him long to realize his mother was in love with the man. During the long hours they had spent confined in bed recuperating, she had several times sung Broderick's praises, until Rand had been forced to pretend sleep to shut her up.

And he was not unaware of the special effort his father was making to befriend him.

Miles had taken him on a tour of the ranch, pointing out landmarks and explaining how Rand could always find his way back to the bunkhouse if he was careful to look over his shoulder at where he had come from every so often to make note of the terrain.

Rand had listened, saying nothing, using as his excuse for his silence the fact that Broderick had told him to keep his eyes open and his mouth shut. But he was not immune to the fact this was his father. He saw himself reflected back in Miles's familiar gray eyes.

He felt Broderick's frustration . . . and his pain.

"You're handling yourself well with the men," Miles had said.

Rand had felt an odd clutch at the compliment,

the first one he'd had from his father. It was more than he had ever gotten from Chester Talbot.

"Thank you, sir," he had replied.

"I'm going deer hunting later in the week. Would you like to come?"

More than anything, Rand had wanted to accept that invitation from his father. But he didn't want to get to know or like Miles Broderick any better. Not if he might have to kill him.

"No, thank you, sir," he had answered.

Miles had tried to hide his disappointment, but Rand had seen it and felt bad for the man.

That was when he had made up his mind to confront Broderick and ask for his version of the story Talbot had told him. It had been on the tip of his tongue to ask his father what had really happened between him and his mother when Red had caught up to them. The cowboy had come to tell Miles about some fence that was down. All three had gone to repair it. The opportunity to ask questions and get answers had passed.

Rand had remained in a sort of limbo, unwilling to ask for the truth, afraid of what he would hear, unwilling to challenge Miles Broderick to a duel because, honestly, it wasn't only for his mother's sake anymore that he didn't want to see the man dead.

While Rand spent his days learning the ropes as a cowboy, Freddy was learning the distaff side of life on a working ranch. And avoiding Rand whenever she could.

Rand had raised the subject of marriage within a day of his fever breaking, but Freddy had insisted they wait to discuss it until he was completely recovered from his wounds. He had tried to raise it again the day he moved into the bunkhouse, and every day since, but she refused to agree with him that they should make the trip to Fort Laramie to get married by the chaplain.

"I'm not ready yet," she had protested.

"You can't put it off forever, Freddy."

"I need time, Rand."

"For what?" he asked. "I love you, Freddy. I want to make you my wife."

Freddy had felt like crying, his voice was so gentle, his kiss so fleeting and tender. She had been on the verge of agreeing to wed him when he made the mistake of saying "I won't take no for an answer, Freddy. You have no choice in this."

If only he hadn't said it quite like that. She was pretty certain she was falling in love with Rand—if she wasn't in love already. But she would never, could never, be happy married to a man who gave her ultimatums and expected her to obey them. And she wanted to make sure Rand understood that before she tied herself to him.

"You can't make me marry you, Rand," she said.

His jaw set. "I will if I have to, Freddy."

"Just try," she threatened. "And see what happens!"

She had stomped off, and they had been at loggerheads ever since. She had punished Rand by flirting outrageously with the ranch hands. She focused on Tom, who seemed the most powerful and dangerous—and therefore the most attractive—because he walked around wearing a gun on his hip.

She saw Rand sitting on the corral, and he gestured for her to come over to him. Instead, she turned her back to him and, hips sashaying in her form-fitting trousers, headed into the barn, knowing full well that Rand knew that Tom was working there. Once inside, however, she didn't seek out Tom. Instead, she sat down on a loose stack of hay with her legs tucked under her and began playing with a batch of four-week-old kittens.

She wasn't really surprised when Tom sat down cross-legged beside her. At least two of the kittens quickly climbed onto his trouser legs.

Freddy held a ginger kitten against her cheek. "They're absolutely adorable, don't you think?"

"So are you," Tom said.

Freddy was used to flattery and accepted it as her due. She batted her eyelashes at Tom, as she would have at one of the English lords who had surrounded her at many a *ton* ball and said, "I'm not half as soft as they are."

"Let me see." Tom reached out and caressed her cheek. Freddy drew back, startled. No *ton* gentleman had ever dared so much.

"You're much softer than the cat, *niña,*" Tom said.

She managed a laugh, still certain she could handle the mild flirtation, and not a little flattered that an older man—Tom had to be at least ten years Rand's senior—could find her attractive. Of course, she thought, refusing to let conceit take root, it was easy to be the center of attention when you were the only unattached female around.

She didn't count Verity because Miles had already claimed her. She hadn't sorted out their relationship just yet, but she had figured out from things she heard them discuss that they must have known each other very well sometime in the past.

While she was somewhat thrilled by Tom's praise, she was able to put it in perspective. "Thank you, Mr. Grimes," she said primly. "Try to imagine me with ears and whiskers, and you'll see the kitten does a better job of looking cute."

Tom smiled. "You're clever, too. I like that."

The compliment appealed more than it should have. Intelligence wasn't much prized in an Englishwoman. Females were valued more for their bloodlines and their ability to breed an heir. Unknowingly, Tom Grimes had hit upon the perfect appeal to her vanity. She was willing to let him tell her more about how wonderful and intelligent she was. She was thinking it was too bad Rand couldn't be hearing all this. Then he might realize she could make up her own mind about what she wanted to do with her life.

"What else do you like about me?" she asked.

He laughed. "That you're daring, maybe even reckless."

She frowned. That didn't sound like much of a compliment for an English lady. But, she conceded, it also hit close to the truth. Her indulgent parents had perhaps allowed her to act in too forward a manner much too often.

One of the kittens had climbed onto her thigh, and Freddy hissed as its claws dug in.

Tom reached out to free the kitten from the denim. However, when the cat was free, his hand remained.

"Please take your hand off me," Freddy said in a firm, quiet voice.

His hand tightened on her thigh.

Freddy clambered to her feet. "I think I'll go back to the house now."

Tom rose at the same time, caught her wrist, and swung her into his embrace. She doubled up her arms between them, but he held her firmly against him. With only denim to separate them, she could feel the blunt ridge of hardness against her belly. It frightened her more than she wanted him to know. It seemed she had completely underestimated the uncivilized nature of this place.

She met Tom's gaze and said, "If I scream, every man on this ranch will come running." As threats went, it seemed powerful enough.

He remained undaunted. "Scream. I'll say you saw a rat and came running to me. What else could I do but offer you comfort?"

Her eyes narrowed. "Rushland will kill you."

He laughed aloud. "That tenderfoot? I'd put a bullet between his eyes before he got within ten feet of me."

Freddy felt a chill slide down her spine. One look at the merciless eyes in Tom's handsome face convinced her he wasn't just talking. He would do it. "Miles will—"

"The Old Man is too busy with his own pretty lady to bother about you and me. How about a kiss?"

"No!" She turned her head, and his lips landed on her cheek. She shoved hard against him with her fists, twisting her head first one way and then the other to avoid his kisses. "Let me go!"

She didn't scream, because she believed his threat. Rand wouldn't have a chance against him.

"Let her go."

Tom released her and took a step back. "This is none of your business, green pea," he said with a malicious smile.

Freddy was at first relieved that Rand had come, then terrified at what might happen. "Be careful, Rand," she warned. "Mr. Grimes threatened to shoot you!"

"Go back to the house, Freddy," Rand said.

"But, Rand—"

"Do what I say!"

"You can't order me around," she answered sharply, frightened and alarmed by the deadly menace in Rand's gray eyes and the killing light in Tom's. "I'll go where I like, when I like. And I plan to stay right here."

Tom laughed. "If that was my filly, she'd go where she was reined."

"I don't belong to anyone," Freddy retorted. "Nobody has the right to tell me what I can and can't do." That right was inviolable. Fighting for it was what had gotten her into this mess in the first place.

"Hear that, green pea?" Tom said. "The little lady gave you your marching orders. Now skedaddle back to the ram pasture like a good little boy."

"I have no intention of going anywhere before I teach you a lesson in manners." Rand lifted his fists in a boxing stance.

Tom bent over and hooted with laughter. "If that isn't the damnedest thing I've ever seen. A flat-heeled gunsel all puffed up like a banty rooster."

Tom pulled his gun from the holster so fast Freddy didn't see him do it. The lethal revolver was suddenly in his hand, pointed at Rand.

"I'm telling you to butt out," Tom said in a brittle voice.

Rand paled, but he didn't move a step in any direction. "If you're going to shoot, shoot. Otherwise, put that thing away and defend yourself."

"Why, you—"

The sound of another gun being cocked froze Tom in place.

"Put the gun down, Tom," Miles said.

All three of them turned to the door of the barn where Miles stood with his Colt Peacemaker aimed at Tom's heart. Verity's frightened face showed beyond his shoulder.

"I said put the gun down."

Tom slowly lowered his gun to the barn's dirt floor.

"Kick it toward me."

Tom did as he was ordered.

Miles leaned down to pick up the gun without taking his eyes off Tom and tucked it in his belt. Then he returned his gun to his holster. "If you two have some business to settle, you can do it now."

"Miles—"

"Shut up, Verity," Miles said.

"Rand—"

"Be still, Freddy," Rand said.

"Step back and give them room to fight, Freddy," Miles said.

Freddy backed her way across the straw-strewn floor to join Verity, who put an arm around her shoulder. It was questionable which of the two women was supporting whom. Freddy had a heightened awareness of her surroundings. The stench of manure, the incessant buzz of the flies, sunlight streaming in mottled golden shafts through cracks in the slatted wall, the stomp of a horse in one of the stalls.

"All right, Tom. You wanted to fight," Miles said. "Here's your chance."

Something malevolent flickered in Tom's dark eyes. Then he charged, butting his head into Rand's stomach and knocking him backward into the dirt, sending his hat flying.

Nothing could have made Freddy leave, and yet it was difficult to watch the pounding Rand took in the first minutes of the fight. He was no match for the wily older man, who had apparently won his share of barnyard brawls.

Freddy wasn't sure how the other cowhands found out about the fight, but they filtered in through the door and stood watching as the two men locked in mortal combat. No one lifted a finger to help. No one—not even Miles—attempted to stop the fight.

Rand's lip was cut and bleeding. One eye was swollen nearly shut. He seemed to be favoring his wounded shoulder.

Freddy felt her heart racing, felt the blood pounding in her temples. She felt sick inside that she might have been even the least bit responsible for provoking the fight. She was afraid for Rand. And for herself.

What if Tom won the fight and claimed her as his prize? What if Rand won and refused to have anything more to do with her?

Of the two alternatives, she found the latter more terrifying, because she had realized as she watched blood drip from Rand's bruised and battered—and much beloved—face that she would die if he walked out of her life. The next time Rand asked her to marry him—and surely he would ask again—she was going to say yes.

15

Rand was losing the fight. His head ached, and his eyesight was blurred. He could barely keep his fists up to protect his face from the beating Tom was giving him. He had considered himself a good boxer at the club in London where he practiced, but he hadn't counted on having dirt thrown in his eyes to blind him or on being kicked in the groin. This wasn't two gentlemen enjoying a bout of fisticuffs. It was a war for survival.

Rand was too battered to feel humiliated, too tired to feel defeated. His body keep saying *Give up!* His mind kept answering *Never!*

Then he saw an opening. Tom had gotten too confident, had lowered his guard. Rand swung for Tom's chin with his right fist and connected with a loud *crack*. Tom reeled and shook his head. Rand followed with a left and felt his knuckles split as he caught Tom squarely in the nose.

Blood gushed. Tom howled and grabbed his broken nose.

Rand punched him twice—right, left—in the belly, and Tom fell to his knees. Rand lifted his right one more time for a roundhouse to the temple that knocked Tom unconscious.

Rand stood there, his knuckles bruised and bleeding, his left eye swollen nearly shut, his body aching from a dozen blows, and wondered why he did not feel triumphant. He looked around the barn, searching for Freddy, his glance passing each of the cowboys gathered there. He saw neither condemnation nor admiration in their eyes, merely acceptance. It made him feel good in a way that applause or cheers in Gentleman John's Boxing Saloon in London never had or could.

When he finally found Freddy in the crowd, he saw she was in tears.

"Don't cry, sweetheart," he said, opening his arms to her. She ran to him, and he grunted painfully as she collided with his battered body.

"Oh, Rand, I'm so sorry. I never thought—I didn't know—" She lifted her hand to his face, but never touched the bleeding skin. "Look at your poor face. And your eye! Does it hurt?"

The question was so ridiculous it made him want to smile. Which was a mistake, because that *did* hurt. He carefully dabbed at the blood on his split lip. "Are you all right?" he asked.

"He only—" Freddy looked around at the circle

of grim faces, remembered how Miles had described the fate of any man in the West who touched an unwilling woman, and revised what she was going to say. Rand had beaten Tom senseless. She didn't want to see any more blood shed. "He didn't hurt me. I'm fine."

Cookie had filled a pail with water from the horse trough outside the barn and dumped it on Tom to wake him up.

Tom sat up sputtering, groaned, and crossed his arms over his belly.

"Because you saved Rand and Freddy's lives, I'm willing to forego hanging you," Miles said. "But I want you off Muleshoe range before sundown. Cookie will have your wages ready when you ask for them."

Cookie extended a hand to help Tom to his feet. "Come on, Tom. Time to hit the trail."

Rand set Freddy behind him as Tom shot her a look of utter hatred.

"What about my gun?" Tom said.

Miles took it from his belt, emptied the cartridges into his palm, and handed the gun to Tom. "Good-bye, Tom."

"She wanted it," Tom said angrily.

Rand didn't think he had the energy to lift his arm, but his fist connected with Tom's mouth before the man knew what had hit him, and he landed on the ground again. Rand stood over the bleeding carcass and said through tight jaws, "Apologize to the lady."

"Go to hell!"

Rand grabbed Tom by his shirt, yanked him to his feet, and drew back his fist.

"I'm sorry!" Tom yelped. "Damn it to hell! Let me go!" He jerked himself free.

Rand let him go, because it was all he could do to stay on his feet. He watched as Tom's glance skipped from one to another of the men for any sign that they supported him, but they all had faces of stone. He had stepped over the boundary of accepted behavior and made himself an outlaw in their eyes.

In silence Tom crossed to the tack room, collected his saddle, bridle, and blanket, then headed out to the corral to retrieve his horse.

"Rand?"

Rand looked down. The hand Freddy had around his waist also held his hat. She was lifting his arm over her shoulder to help support him.

"Let's get him into the house," Verity said, coming to support Rand's other side.

"You men have work to do," Miles said. "Get to it."

The cowboys disappeared.

Miles followed the two women as they bear-led Rand into the house. If he hadn't been constrained by the eyes of the cowboys he knew were on them, he would have picked Rand up and carried him. He thought he might have to, after all, the way Rand was weaving as he walked.

The women settled Rand in a chair at the kitchen table and hurried to collect the things they would need to clean up his face and hands.

"That cut on your cheek may need stitches," Verity said.

"Put a plaster on it, Mother. It'll be fine."

"Do you have anything I could use, Miles?" Verity asked.

Miles opened the top drawer of the sideboard, where he kept medicines and bandages in the niche beside the spoons and held up a sticking plaster. "Will this do?"

"I suppose it will have to, if Rand won't agree to stitches." Verity manipulated the cut on Rand's cheek to close the gap and applied the bandage.

"Ow, Mother."

"Don't be a baby, Rand. If you insist on fighting, you have to suffer the consequences."

Miles chuckled. "If I knew two pretty ladies were going to fuss over me, I think I might be able to rustle up some fisticuffs."

"Don't you dare!" Verity warned.

Rand hissed as Freddy dipped his entire right hand into a bowl of water. "That hurts!"

"What do you expect?" Freddy said with asperity. "I don't see a single knuckle that isn't torn and bleeding."

Miles recommended a slab of raw meat for Rand's black eye, but Rand said he would rather put up with the swelling than go to so much fuss.

"If it's all the same to everybody, I'd like to lie down somewhere for a while. I feel a little woozy."

Miles tipped Rand's chin up to look into his eyes. "You seeing double?"

"No. I'm just a little dizzy."

"Is there something wrong with him?" Verity asked Miles.

"Aside from all the cuts and bruises, not a thing," Miles replied. "He'll be fine."

Rand rose and headed for the door.

"Where do you think you're going?" Verity asked, hands on hips.

"To the bunkhouse to lie down."

Verity pointed to the bedroom door. "You'll lie down right here where I can keep an eye on you."

"Mother—"

"Miles, tell him not to argue with me," Verity said.

"Don't argue with your mother, Rand. Besides, you'd lose face with the hands if they caught you lying down in the middle of the day—even after a licking like the one you just took."

"You're kidding," Rand said.

Miles shook his head. "Afraid not. There's no mollycoddling here."

"Mollycoddling?" Verity said. "He's just been beaten within an inch of his life!"

Miles turned to her, his face somber, his piercing gray eyes hooded. "If you two women weren't here, I'd have cleaned him up and sent him back out to work the rest of the day."

"What kind of place is this?" Verity asked, shaking her head in disbelief.

"Unforgiving. Unrelenting. A man here doesn't get second chances."

"All the more reason Rand should take time to recover from this awful brawl."

Miles shrugged. "I won't argue the matter."

Rand picked up his new Western hat with its snakeskin band—it had simply appeared on his bunk one morning—and gingerly set it on his head. "Guess I'll be getting back to work."

"Suit yourself," Miles said. But he was thinking his son had sand. He wondered whether Rand had inherited any of his grit and gumption from his father, or whether it was the way Verity had raised Rand that had given him such strong character. Likely the latter, for which, he supposed, he ought to thank her sometime.

"Rand, you can't do this," Verity protested.

"Please don't worry, Mother. I'll be fine."

Freddy bit her lip but said nothing.

"What? No complaints? No criticism?" Rand chided her, slipping a torn knuckle under her chin and forcing her to look him in the eye.

"You heard what Miles said. The other men expect you back at work."

He caressed her chin between his finger and thumb. "Thanks, Freddy," he murmured.

"For what?"

"For having confidence in me."

"I'd feel better if you'd let me come along, Rand. I promise I won't get in the way."

"What about it, sir? Can Freddy come along and help mend fence?"

"I don't see why not," Miles said. "It might be useful to have someone around if you keel over."

"Let's go," Rand said, ushering Freddy out

ahead of him. "I'll bring her back for supper," he promised.

The instant the front door closed behind them, Verity whirled on Miles. "I can't believe what I just saw. He has no business walking around injured like that!"

"You've raised him to be a fine, strong young man, Verity. Now let him act like one."

"He should be in bed."

"If he wants to be boss of the Muleshoe someday, he's doing exactly what he should be doing."

"What's so important about impressing a bunch of misfits in strange hats and cowboy boots?" Verity ranted.

Miles eyes turned flinty. "He isn't doing it to prove anything to them. He's doing it to prove something to himself."

"Exactly what is he proving?"

"That he can keep going when he doesn't think he can. That nothing can beat him down. That his body is only a vessel, and his mind can make it work far beyond what it should be able to endure."

"You sound like you're speaking from experience."

"I am."

"It seems your lessons were harder than mine."

His lip curled. "I doubt that. Different, perhaps."

"I don't want to lose him, Miles."

"Neither do I, Verity." *Not now. Not yet. Not ever in my lifetime.*

He watched her deep-blue eyes turn liquid, then

brim with tears. He opened his arms, and she stepped into them. He had missed having her there. She had only come to him for comfort, but she had come to him.

And then she whispered, "Make love to me, Miles."

His heart thudded. He didn't say a word, afraid he would say the wrong thing. He simply picked her up in his arms and carried her into the bedroom, closing the door behind them with his foot.

He sat her on the bed and stood before her to undress. He unknotted his bandanna and let it drop, then started unbuttoning his shirt. He yanked it down off his shoulders, then pulled his long john shirt up over his head.

She stood and took the two steps that brought her close enough to touch. Her fingertips roamed through the dark hair on his chest, then slid around him to caress the awful scars on his back. "Turn around, Miles."

"Verity—"

"I want to see. Turn around."

Miles felt as though someone were tightening a band around his chest, making it impossible to breathe, but he did as she bid him. He had seen the scars himself only once, nineteen years ago, by holding his shaving mirror up before an oval dressing mirror in a room in the Menger Hotel in San Antonio. The sight had made him gag.

He flinched as her fingers traced several of the dozens of lash marks left by the cat-o'-nine-tails. Then he felt her lips against his flesh.

When he allowed himself to breathe again, his exhale become a groan.

"Miles."

She touched his arm, urging him to turn around again to face her and when he didn't, moved around to stand in front of him. She braced her hands on his forearms and stood on tiptoe to kiss the scar at the edge of his mouth.

That bit of tenderness broke the bounds of restraint that had held him still for her examination. His arms circled her and pulled her tight against him. His palms cupped her buttocks in the worn denim, rubbing her belly against his hardened shaft. His mouth captured hers and, with a groan of yearning and satisfaction, he thrust his tongue into her mouth in an imitation of their bodies being joined.

"I want you," he said urgently against her lips. "I need you." *It isn't safe to love her.*

"Yes, Miles. Yes." *To anything. To everything.*

He lifted her into his arms and laid her on the bed.

Verity never took her eyes off Miles as he unbuttoned her buttons, one at a time. She would have been just as happy if he had ripped the shirt off her, but he removed it slowly and carefully, briefly caressing her stomach, her shoulders, her back, until she was trembling when he was done.

He untied her chemise and drew it over her head, dipping his mouth to capture one of her nipples while her hands were caught overhead in the garment. Once she was free, her fingers tunneled into his hair, and she lay back on the bed, holding his mouth against her breast, where he suckled until her body arched upward. His hand cupped her through her jeans, his thumb seeking out the bud of her desire.

She groaned, a guttural sound of unbearable pleasure. "Miles, please," she begged. For release. For satisfaction. For the chance to give back to him the joy he brought to her.

Her hands roamed his chest and shoulders and slid down his back, until the belt around his jeans stopped her journey. She quickly found the buckle and removed it, then resumed her journey of exploration.

Miles stripped Verity bare, the patience somehow dissipating the more of her flesh he touched, the more of it he saw, and then he stripped himself. He found the marks on her belly where the skin had stretched to accommodate his son and kissed them reverently, wishing he had possessed the right to hold her when their child was growing inside her.

He postponed the moment when they would be joined, not wanting the touching, the tasting, the tantalizing to end. He spread her golden halo of hair across his pillow. He lifted handfuls of it to his nose to smell the scent of it and pressed it against his cheeks to feel its silky texture.

"Tell me your secrets, Verity. Fill me full of you. Make me drunk with the scent of you."

You know them all, she started to say. Only there was a hope she had . . . a secret she could not be sure of yet . . . something wonderful if it was true . . . A new life was growing inside her.

Verity laughed, a bubbling sound that filled them both full of hope and happiness—however fleeting it might be.

Miles was lying beside her, his hands caressing her. She provocatively spread her legs and returned his invitation. "Come here, Miles. Fill me full of you. Make me drunk with the scent of you."

He never took his eyes off her as he mounted her, pressing into her slowly.

Verity grasped his forearms, and her eyes slid closed as he pushed himself inside her to the hilt. "Oh, Miles," she breathed on a sigh of exquisite pleasure. "How very good it feels to have you inside me."

He captured her mouth with his and let his tongue stroke inside. She groaned and arched beneath him as his body mimicked his tongue.

Miles fought his body's urge to reach the pinnacle of satisfaction he knew would mean the end of their lovemaking, while his hands, his mouth, his body worshiped her.

Finally, he gave in to the urge to spill his seed within her, his heart pounding, his breathing ragged, his body slick with sweat. A guttural sound, the savage groan of primitive man in the grip of animal passion, rose from his throat at the moment of climax.

It was sweet, oh, so sweet, to hear an answering

cry of satisfaction as her body tightened around him, shuddering in an ecstasy as she found a pinnacle of pleasure to equal his own.

"I'm heavy," he said, starting to slide off her.

"No, please. Don't move just yet."

"Mother, I'm—" Rand stood paralyzed in the bedroom doorway.

Miles said something succinct as he grabbed for a sheet to cover Verity from Rand's shocked gaze. "Don't you know enough to knock on a closed door?" he said in a harsh voice.

"I d-didn't expect—" Rand stuttered.

"Rand, we—" Verity began.

"I can see what's going on, Mother," Rand snapped.

Miles could see Verity was distraught. "Get out!" he snarled at Rand. "We'll join you in a minute."

Miles tried to pull Verity into his embrace, to comfort her, but she scurried away from him. "Verity—"

"Don't say anything, Miles. Please." She thrust a hand through her hair in agitation, shoving it away from her face, then reached for her long johns and began shoving her feet into them.

"We did nothing wrong." Miles protested. "We're married, for Christ's sake! We—" He could not say they loved each other. But what they had done had felt very much like love, even if neither of them was willing to label it that. "Rand has to accept the fact that we're married."

"He was so shocked. The look on his face—"

Miles felt the heat on his neck. "Damn it, Verity! If he had knocked first, he wouldn't have been embarrassed!"

She was already dressed. He was still standing there stark naked.

"You might want to put on some clothes and join us," she snapped. "Obviously, something has happened that Rand thought was important enough to make him burst into the room without knocking."

Miles had forgotten about that. He dragged his jeans on, buttoned them up and followed her, bare-footed and bare-chested, into the main room.

When Verity opened the bedroom door, she found Rand pacing restlessly in front of the fireplace. He stopped abruptly, flushed, and lowered his eyes.

Verity's cheeks felt hot, and she knew her color was high. She opened her mouth to speak and couldn't think of a thing to say.

"I'm sorry for barging in like that, Mother," Rand said, still refusing to look at her. "I thought you might know where Miles was."

An awkward pause ensued. She had known exactly where he was . . . naked in bed with her.

"You found me," Miles said flatly. "What the hell was so important it couldn't wait?"

Rand's eyes narrowed, and a muscle jerked in his jaw. "I need your help, sir."

"For what? Spit it out!"

"Freddy's been kidnapped."

"God*damn* those troublemaking Sioux!" Miles spat.

"It wasn't Hawk," Rand said. "It was Tom."

16

Miles suddenly noticed the new cut under Rand's eye and the shirttail where he had wiped off the worst of the blood. He reached out to check the wound, but Rand stepped out of his reach.

"What happened?" Miles asked.

"Freddy and I were working in the south pasture stringing barbed wire when Tom showed up out of nowhere. I didn't have time to reach for my rifle before he had a gun on me.

"He swore he'd shoot me dead if I got in his way. I would have resisted, but I was afraid Freddy might end up catching a stray bullet." He gestured toward the cut. "Tom used his gun barrel to do this, then hit me on the back of the head and knocked me out.

"I don't think I was out very long. I figured together we'd have a better chance of catching up to him before anything happened to Freddy. That's why I was in such a damned hurry to find you," he finished, his voice rife with hostility and tinged with sarcasm.

Miles was already heading to the bedroom to finish dressing. He talked loud enough to be heard in the other room. "Could you tell which way Tom was headed?"

"South. Ow, Mother, leave me alone," Rand protested as Verity checked the goose egg behind his ear.

"Maybe Tom has friends in Cheyenne he thinks will help him hide her," Miles reasoned aloud from the bedroom. "We've got to catch him before he gets there."

"I'm going with you," Verity said, starting to pack a bag with food—salted pork, dried beans, flour, and canned peaches—for the three of them.

"You'd only be in the way," Miles said from the bedroom doorway, where he stood tucking in his shirt and stomping his feet into the cowboy boots he wore in colder weather.

"You can't leave me here to wonder what's happening," she said. "I'd go mad. Besides, I don't trust the two of you alone together."

"Mother—"

"Don't argue with her, Rand. You won't change her mind," Miles said.

Rand shot him a virulent look. "Don't tell me how to speak to my mother. Who do you think you are—"

"That's enough, Rand," Verity interrupted. "I'm

going. That's final. The sooner we leave, the sooner we'll find Freddy."

"You'll both have to borrow coats from the men," Miles said. "And bring along wool blankets to roll up with your ground cloths behind the saddle."

"What for?" Rand said. "It's warm outside."

"It's also the end of September. We could get a snowstorm this afternoon and be plowing through six-foot drifts tomorrow. You don't travel out here without planning for the worst."

Miles debated whether to bring some of his men along. He decided against it for several reasons. First, he wasn't sure he could control them when they caught up to Tom, and he didn't want to be part of a lynch mob. Second, he wanted the time alone with Rand. Third, he didn't believe it was necessary. He was certain that two against one was sufficient odds to defeat Tom Grimes. A man who would kidnap a woman—and pistol-whip an unarmed man who had defeated him in a fair fight—was a coward at heart.

He would order his men to stay behind, and they would heed him because he was the boss. A man who rode for the brand did what he was told, whether he liked it or not. It was one more part of the unwritten code that ordered life in a land where there was no civil law, no authority other than the boss, for miles in any direction.

Once they were on their way, Rand rode ahead of Miles and his mother, nursing his anger and hiding his fear. He wondered if there was anything he could have done to prevent Freddy's abduction. It was his fault for paying so much attention to her and not enough to what was happening around him.

It had been hard not to watch her when she bent over in those skin-hugging jeans. Hard not to notice how the sun caught in her auburn curls and gave them the sheen of russet leaves in an English autumn. Difficult even to breathe when she slipped open a button and waved the two halves of her shirt, trying to catch the breeze and cool her milk-white skin.

Was it any wonder he had set the wire cutters aside and reached out to cup her chin in his hand? Any wonder he had watched in fascination while those vivid green eyes of hers turned heavy-lidded as they gazed up at him. Any wonder he had been utterly lost as his lips gently touched hers.

Gently, because he had a cut at the right corner of his mouth. She had drawn back hesitantly, looked at his mouth, then caressed the hurt with her tongue. When she slipped her tongue into his mouth, his body had hardened instantly and completely.

He had ached to pull her close but resisted the urge. "Freddy," he murmured. "Freddy, love."

"Yes, Rand," she said. "What is it?" She looked up at him with liquid eyes, pools of emerald green that drew him into their depths. Surely that was love he saw.

"Freddy, let me hold you close, please," he begged.

Her lids lowered to hide her eyes, but she took a step closer. His arms curled around her, slowly, carefully, for his own battered body's sake as well as in consideration for the tenderness of hers.

He felt the pebbled tips of her breasts against his chest, and he knew. She wanted him as much as he wanted her. It surprised him, and he realized it probably embarrassed her. That was why she hadn't been able to meet his gaze. That was why her eyes were lowered even now.

He tipped her chin up. "Look at me, Freddy." He wanted to see the truth. He wanted to see the desire in her eyes. And the love.

Her green eyes flashed at him almost defiantly.

It was there. The passion. The need to equal his. Lips that were full and ready for his kisses. But the love? He wasn't sure. He couldn't be sure.

"I'm a sorry sight for those beautiful eyes, love," he murmured against her lips.

"The bruises will fade, Rand," she said, grazing his face with her fingertips. "The cuts will heal." She smiled, and the warmth spread to those green pools. "You'll have quite a roguish scar on your cheek, I'm afraid."

"As long as you don't mind, Freddy."

"I don't mind."

He widened his stance, put his hands firmly on her waist, and pulled her into the cradle of his thighs. He would never have dared such a familiarity if he had thought there was any chance they would not become man and wife. But that issue had been settled in his mind on the night they had spent alone together in the Indian camp. She belonged to him. And he belonged to her.

She caught her breath and stared up at him, her eyes luminous.

He slid his hands around to her back, lowered them to her buttocks, and pulled her tight against him, so she could feel his arousal. He waited for the fear to rise on her face, or any sign of rejection. He saw nothing but excitement, anticipation, and trust. That caused a momentary qualm. She was putting her welfare in his hands. It was his duty to care for her. Because he had worn the label of bastard, he knew the consequences for a child born out of wedlock.

But it was hard to let her go.

"Feel how much I need you, Freddy," he murmured against her temple. "How much I want you."

"I want you, too, Rand," she admitted in a small voice. "But—"

"But we aren't married yet," he said with a resigned sigh and a rueful smile. "Let's go to Fort Laramie, Freddy. We could be married today."

"I love you, Rand. Truly, I do."

He cut her off with a quick, hard kiss.

She broke away and put her palms flat against his chest. "I planned to say yes if you asked me again to marry you, but I've been thinking about it ever since. I'm not sure it's what I should do. It wouldn't be very fair to you."

Rand forced himself to hear the entire message. *She loved him. But she didn't think she should marry him.* That was not a yes, unless one wished to delude oneself, which he did not.

He gripped her shoulders to keep her from escaping him. "If you love me, why shouldn't you marry me?" he asked.

"I'm not the kind of wife you need," she said miserably. "You need someone who can work by your side, who can help you build a new life here. I'm not that person. I'm spoiled and willful and obstinate." She held out her soft, lovely hands, without a blister or a callus on them. "I won't be any help at all. In fact, I'll just c-cause a lot of t-trouble." She said the last almost as a wail.

He stared at her stunned for a moment and broke out laughing. "Do you really believe all that rubbish?"

"It isn't rubbish!" Her eyes flashed at him with something very like the spoiled willfulness she had just ascribed to herself. "I'm trying to do something unselfish for once in my life," she said. "I'm thinking of your happiness when I say I would be a bad bargain as a wife."

"I'll be the judge of that."

She proved her obstinacy by replying, "No, you won't. I think I know myself better than you do."

Rand frowned at her, perplexed. "Let me see if I understand you correctly. You won't marry me because you don't have calluses on your hands?"

She flushed a ruddy color that wasn't entirely unbecoming. "Don't make fun of me, Rand. Not when this is so hard for me."

"I only want to understand what's going on

here. You love me enough to give me up to some other—much better—woman?"

Her eyes brimmed with tears. "Oh, yes. That much."

He felt a thickness in his throat, a swelling of emotion, that was foreign to him. She was very young. And very naive. And he loved her very, very much. "Oh, sweetheart. Don't you see? If I love you . . . and you love me . . . nothing else matters."

"Oh, Rand," she cried. "You just don't understand."

"I'm trying very hard, sweetheart. Can you help me?"

But he had never heard her explanation. Tom had appeared and cut short their conversation.

Perhaps she didn't love him after all, Rand thought. Maybe she had been looking for a way to ease their separation. Maybe he should have taken her word for it that she was the wrong woman for him. The devil of it was, a perfect woman wouldn't have suited him at all. He was too far from perfect himself.

He would find her, and he would make her explain herself. And he would kill Tom Grimes for daring to lay hands on her again.

With Rand ahead of them leading the way, Miles and Verity were left alone with a great deal of silence between them.

"I haven't been having much luck making friends with my son," Miles said at last. "I realize now I should have told him everything as soon as he was well enough to listen. Maybe if he knew all the forces that were against us all those years ago, he could understand why I brought you here and accept our marriage."

Verity glanced sideways at Miles, who was staring straight ahead at Rand. "The question is, when he knows everything, will he blame me for it?"

"He has no right to condemn you."

She smiled sadly. "I was the one responsible for keeping him in the dark about his real father."

"He can handle the truth, Verity."

"What is the truth?"

"We were star-crossed lovers. We should have spent our lives together. But circumstances . . . the fates . . ."

"And Chester Talbot . . ."

"And Chester Talbot," he repeated in a quiet voice, "kept us apart."

"Oh, Miles. It sounds impossibly romantic. And so very tragic. Is that really what happened to us?"

He sought out her eyes. "We've found each other at last."

"But we lost love somewhere along the way."

Verity had thought, if she let herself think about it at all, that Miles would tell Rand everything the instant they stopped for the night. She hoped Rand would realize Miles was no dragon that needed to be slain. The monster was already dead.

But they didn't stop that first night, not until the small hours of the morning. They were all so tired they rolled up in their blankets and were asleep almost instantly. When they awoke, they ate some canned peaches, but Rand was too impatient to cook a hot meal, and Verity wasn't about to let him go off ahead of them alone.

Miles and Rand discussed the best course of action and followed it through the next day. Verity saw that, whether the two men realized it or not, they were forming a bond on this journey that would stand them in good stead when the truth was told. She also realized that Miles had no intention of saddling Rand with any more problems until Freddy had been rescued. His son's needs took precedence over his own.

When they found the camp where Tom had spent the night, they knew they were on the right trail. But it appeared he hadn't taken any more of a leisurely rest than they had. There were no ashes from a fire, only a large area where the grass had been pressed down by two bodies lying close together.

Verity saw how Rand's mouth tightened and noticed the narrowing of Miles's eyes. She could read what they were thinking on their faces. Had Tom taken the time to ravish Freddy? Or had the fear of imminent pursuit kept him from taking what he wanted before he was completely safe? They wouldn't know the answer until they caught up to him.

They continued south for another day and another night before the trail disappeared.

Rand was off his horse and down on one knee, trying to figure out what had happened. "Buffalo came through here after them," he said when Miles joined him.

"We can take the chance they're still headed south and keep going. Likely the sign'll show up again," Miles said, searching for movement on the southern horizon.

"I think he might have changed his mind about going to Cheyenne," Rand said.

"What makes you say that?"

"Freddy will convince Tom that he's a dead man the instant he shows up in a crowd with her. She's got a sharp tongue and a brain, and she's not averse to using either."

"He could have gagged her," Miles said.

"I'd like to see him try."

Miles knew Rand had to make himself believe Freddy was unhurt, or he wouldn't be able to function. Privately, he was less optimistic about finding Freddy untouched. There had been signs of a struggle in the grass where Tom and Freddy had spent the night. He wondered whether it made sense to prepare Rand for what he would probably find or keep his thoughts to himself.

"When I find him, I'm going to kill him," Rand said.

Miles realized then that Rand knew the truth. Whether he could deal with it when he caught up to Tom was another matter. "Just don't make the mistake of underestimating him."

Rand glared at him, clearly agitated at this setback, frustrated by their lack of success in finding Tom, and in a killing rage over what he believed had happened to Freddy. "I don't need any advice from you!" he snapped.

"I'm your fa—" Miles snapped right back. He cut himself off, but he could see it was too late. Rand realized what he had almost said.

"My *father?* Is that what you were going to say?"

The blood drained from Miles's face at the look of revulsion on Rand's.

"Chester Talbot told me the truth before he died. I know you raped my mother. I know I'm your bastard son."

"There was no rape," Miles said. "But yes, you are my son." He was relieved to say the words at last. But there was no joy in them. Chester had sown seeds of deceit that had grown into full-blown hatred in his son.

Then, because the dam had finally been broken, Rand's questions came gushing out. "Why didn't you marry my mother when she found herself pregnant with me?"

"There were reasons—"

"I can't believe a pregnant woman would refuse to marry the father of her child," Rand snarled. "Not if she lay willingly with you, as you claim."

"I didn't know about you," Miles snarled back. "She never told me!"

"Why not?"

"You'll have to ask her that."

They glared at one another, chests heaving, fists bunched, neck hairs on end.

"I've done fine without a father so far," Rand said. "I don't need you."

Miles felt as though he had been stabbed in the heart. "Please, Rand, if you'll only let me explain—"

"No," Rand said. "I've heard enough." He turned and strode toward his horse.

"Wait!" Miles had to grab Rand's arm to stop him. "Wait, damn it!"

"Let me go."

"Which way are you headed now?"

For a moment it seemed Rand wouldn't answer. Then he said, "I'm going north."

"There's nothing up north but Fort Laramie. Tom wouldn't go there."

"There are reservation Indians, hangers-on, living in tipis near the fort. I heard the men talking in the bunkhouse. Tom has relationships with a few of the squaws. I figure he'll try to hide out with one of them."

"All right. We'll ride north again."

Verity was waiting anxiously with the horses when Miles walked back to her. "I could see you arguing with Rand. Did you tell him everything?"

"He had already heard everything from Chester. Only Chester had his own version of the truth—a little parting gift of malice before he died. He told Rand I raped you and then abandoned you."

"Oh, Miles, no!"

"He hates me, Verity," he said bleakly.

"How . . . how does he feel about me?"

Miles rubbed irritably at the days-old beard

that shadowed his face. "I don't know. I had to tell him you never gave me a chance to marry you. That you never told me you were pregnant. He asked why you hid your pregnancy from me. I told him he'd have to ask you that himself."

Verity's face paled. Her world was shifting off its axis, and soon nothing would ever be the same again. She was trying to regain her balance, looking for a haven where she would be safe when things turned topsy-turvy. But it was difficult to anticipate the consequences of the looming disaster.

"Where is Rand going now?"

"Rand thinks Tom is going to hide out with the reservation Sioux camped near the fort. He's heading north again."

"What if we can't find Tom's trail?" Verity asked.

"Let's not worry about that until it happens," Miles replied.

The three of them rode north, their third day and night on the trail. They managed to avoid talking to each other. The questions about the future that funneled through all their minds remained unasked and unanswered.

The morning of the fourth day dawned cloudy and cold.

Verity felt a deepening sense of despair, which she knew Rand and Miles shared. After four miserable days on the trail, they were right back where they had started, not fifteen miles from the ranch.

By noon, the temperature had dropped fifty degrees. It began to snow. It was hard to keep the horses headed into the frigid wind when their inclination was to turn their tails to it.

The two men tied their bandannas around their hats to hold them on, donned their wool coats, and turned up the collars to keep the whirling snow off their necks. Verity did the best she could to stay warm, but her fingers froze in her thin leather gloves, and her feet felt like blocks of ice. It wasn't long before her teeth were chattering, and her lips were blue.

The snow fell in large, thick flakes. The horses began floundering in knee-deep drifts. It was difficult to tell which direction they were going. All landmarks were fast disappearing beneath a blanket of white.

Miles kneed his horse to catch up with Rand, who had relentlessly ridden ahead of them the entire journey.

"I'm going to take your mother home," Miles said. "I suggest you come with us."

"What about Freddy?" Rand asked.

Miles saw the fear deep in Rand's eyes and knew there was no comfort he could give. "If Tom's smart, he'll head back to the ranch. At least he has a chance with us. Winter here kills without mercy, without discriminating between good and evil."

Rand shook his head. "I have to keep going. What if Tom leaves her out here somewhere all alone? I can't stop until I find her."

"Likely Tom's snug inside a warm tipi along

with Freddy. You're the one who'll end up freezing to death."

"I don't want to live without her."

Miles heard the vehemence in his son's voice. And the resolution. He couldn't—or rather, wouldn't—force Rand to return to the ranch with him. But he doubted his son, the English tenderfoot, had the knowledge it would take to survive this kind of cold out in the open.

"I don't want us to part like this with things unsettled between us," Miles said.

"What else is there to say?" Rand asked bitterly.

"I loved your mother," Miles said. "We were engaged to be married when you were conceived."

"Do you love her now?" Rand challenged. "Is that why you brought her here? Is that why you married her?"

"No," Miles conceded. "I brought her here to punish her for marrying Chester Talbot instead of me. I never knew about you—never guessed I had a son—until I laid eyes on you."

"That's hard to believe."

"He's telling the truth," Verity said, reining her horse up beside Miles. "I was the one who lied to you, Rand. Or, rather, I withheld the truth."

Miles saw the struggle on Rand's face. His next words seemed torn from him. "Why, Mother? All those years of whispers behind my back. All the teasing and the taunts. Why couldn't you have told me the truth?"

Her eyes were full of shared pain. "Chester Talbot threatened to repudiate you if I ever revealed the truth. He's the villain in this piece—if you must have one. He and Miles were mortal enemies. Chester killed your uncle, Gregory, and he threatened to kill your father if I didn't break my engagement to Miles and marry him. Even so, I didn't know about you until after the vows were said."

"Talbot always knew the truth about who I was?" Rand asked.

"Your hair is black, Rand. Like your father's," she said simply. "Yes. Talbot knew from the first."

"That's why he kept himself from me?"

"Yes. And why he lied to you on his deathbed. He hated Miles. He had since they were boys."

Rand's gaze shifted from one parent to the other, as though to discern the truth from their faces, assimilating everything he had been told, evaluating it. It was clear he hadn't yet swallowed everything they had fed him. Much of it was still stuck in his throat.

"Rand—" Verity began.

"Don't say another word, Mother. I've heard quite enough." Rand kicked his horse and headed him north into the sleeting wind.

Verity sat paralyzed on her horse, unable to believe her son could speak so sharply to her.

"Wait here," Miles said. "I'll be right back." He quickly caught up with Rand. He reached over to catch Rand's reins and draw his horse to an abrupt halt. "There was no need to hurt your mother like that."

"She hurt me," Rand replied.

"Not intentionally. You must know that."

"I don't know anything for sure right now."

"I meant it when I said I'm returning to the ranch," Miles said. "I won't take a chance with your mother's life."

"I'm going on," Rand replied.

Miles didn't know what he could say to stop Rand from taking a course he thought would only result in his son's death. He grabbed at his Stetson when a gust of wind threatened to whip it off his head. The storm was worsening. "You know, Rand, Freddy may already be dead."

Rand turned glittering, savage gray eyes on him. "Don't say it! Don't even think it!"

"That doesn't keep it from being true."

"I would know if she were dead." Rand pounded a fist against his heart. "I would feel it here."

Rand didn't say more, but he had bared quite enough of his soul. Miles knew what his son hadn't said. *She's the other half of me. That's how I would know.* Miles glanced over his shoulder at Verity, shivering, teeth chattering with the cold. And knew what his decision had to be. He could not save them both—the woman who was the other half of him, the son he barely knew. He would have to choose.

"I'm taking Verity home," he repeated for the last time. "I think you should come with us."

"I can't."

Miles offered his hand and waited to see if Rand would take it.

He didn't.

Miles withdrew his hand and tugged his hat down once more. "Take care of yourself. A word of advice. Don't fall asleep. If you think you can't go any farther, stay close to your horse, use his body heat to stay warm. If he freezes up, wrap yourself in your ground sheet and your blanket and cover yourself with snow. It'll keep you warm.

"If you survive the storm, keep heading north until you reach the Platte. The Sioux will be camped somewhere along the river. I won't look for you—I won't tell your mother to look for you—before the snow thaws. That could be a couple of weeks . . . or a couple of months.

"If we don't see you before Christmas, I promise I'll hunt for you—for what's left of you—in the spring and see you get a decent burial."

For a moment he thought Rand would change his mind, that he would see the sense of returning to the ranch to wait out the storm. His son was made of sterner stuff. He stood his ground.

"Good luck, Rand. And good-bye. You'd better get going. Your mother's likely to set up a howl when she finds out you're not going back with us."

Miles had already turned his horse's tail to the wind when Rand called out to him.

"Miles!"

He looked back over his shoulder.

"Take care of her for me."

Miles felt the lump in his throat and swallowed it down. "I will."

He kneed his horse back to where Verity waited for him. "We're heading back to the ranch."

"Thank God. I'm half frozen. Tom will find a place for him and Freddy to get out of the storm, won't he?"

"If he doesn't, there's nothing we can do to save them. We'll be lucky to save ourselves."

Miles headed northeast, so Verity wouldn't realize they weren't following Rand, using the rapidly disappearing shape of the landscape to guide him home.

Verity kicked her horse and followed after him. She kept her eyes focused on the wind-swept tail of the horse in front of her, which was about as far as she could see in the blowing snow. She was muffled to the ears in her scarf, her shoulders hunched down deep in her coat, so numbed with cold that she never realized they had left Rand behind.

17

Rand knew the bitter taste of failure. His father had been right. He was no match for a Wyoming blizzard. There was little chance he would be rescuing Freddy; he would be lucky to escape with his life.

His horse had stumbled into a prairie dog hole hidden by a drift and sprained a hock. He had unsaddled and unbridled the animal and left it to fend for itself. He had taken what supplies there were, tied them in a pack on his back, grabbed the rifle from the boot on the saddle, and kept walking into the wind. Rand figured that had to be north, but he had no way of knowing for sure.

He had spent the day traveling, squinting against blowing, blinding snow, but he didn't think he had gone very far. Even where it hadn't drifted, the snow was thigh-deep now. It was hard to hold on to his optimism through the day as the wind rose higher, the snow layered deeper, and the temperature plummeted. The snow had stopped falling, but the wind never died, and the sun never came out. Gray clouds hovered, waiting to drop enough snow to bury him once and for all.

He had never felt such cold in his life. He could barely bend his fingers, and his feet felt too heavy to lift. Soon he would no longer be able to walk. Miles had warned him not to sleep, but he was so tired, he didn't know how long he could keep going.

Then he saw them. Except, where he had expected to find two figures, he found three.

Rand shook his head, thinking perhaps the cold had affected his vision, or maybe he was only wishing the figures there, because he wanted so badly to catch up to Freddy. He looked again. And saw three again.

Because of the way they were bundled up, he couldn't tell who they were. Maybe it wasn't Tom and Freddy, after all. Maybe it was three completely different people.

He started to shout and wave his hands to attract their attention. He didn't know what stopped him, but suddenly he knew it was the wrong thing to do. Maybe those were Sioux.

Better to find out who they were before he identified himself. He had to get closer. But there was no way to hide himself in the snow. He would simply have to hope they didn't look in his direction.

Finally, he was close enough to make out faces.

His heart skipped a beat. He felt a surge of triumph. It was Freddy and Tom. His gut tightened as he identified the third person. Hawk.

Rand could see Tom was holding a gun on the Sioux, who stood about five feet away from him. The snow around the Indian was stained a vivid red. It appeared Tom had shot Hawk. But Rand couldn't see enough of the Indian's body beneath his shaggy buffalo robe to know how bad the wound was. The Indian held his hands away from his body, and it was plain he had no weapon.

Rand watched Tom raise his gun and aim it at the Indian's belly and realized all at once that he was going to murder the man in cold blood.

Rand struggled to his feet, rifle in hand, and yelled as loud as he could, "Tom! Tom!"

The crisp, cold air carried his cry to the threesome. Tom turned to look, and the Indian made a run for it. He didn't get far before Tom turned his revolver back on him again. Tom was going to shoot Hawk in the back!

Everything seemed to happen in the flicker of an eye.

When Rand heard Tom fire, he felt as though he had been shot himself. It was cold-blooded murder!

Then he realized Tom's shot hadn't killed the Sioux. Hawk had grabbed his side and was still running—staggering, actually—away.

To his horror, Rand saw Freddy grab Tom's wrist and struggle to wrest the gun from him. In his mind's eye he saw the revolver accidentally discharging, killing Freddy. He had to save Freddy. He had to kill Tom.

At Birdie Arthur's hunting lodge in York Rand had snuffed twenty candles at twenty paces after drinking an entire bottle of brandy. He ought to be able to hit a target as large as Tom when he was stone-cold sober. But he had never pointed a gun at another human being, and he found it difficult to hold the rifle steady. His hands were shaking too much.

A blast of wind sent snow swirling into his eyes. He swiped at his eyelashes to brush away the flakes that had caught there, blinding him. When he looked again, Tom was raising his gun to hit Freddy with it.

Rand held his breath and squeezed the trigger slowly, easily. He heard the deafening report in his ear . . . and watched Tom fall.

He ran then, as fast as his frozen feet could carry him through the heavy snow, toward the brutal tableau before him. When he arrived at the scene, Freddy was kneeling beside Tom.

"Hold it right there!" she called to him. She rose and faced him, Tom's revolver in her hand—aimed at him! She was wrapped up in a blanket so that all he could see were eyebrows white with frost and a nose as red as a berry. She couldn't keep the revolver level in front of her, even with both hands.

"Freddy, it's me." He yanked his woolen scarf away from his nose and mouth, where he had wrapped it to keep the wind from biting at him.

"Rand?" She dropped the gun and lunged

toward him through the snow. "Rand! Oh, God, Rand!"

He opened his arms, and she fell into them sobbing. He closed his arms around her. The days and nights without food or sleep, the hours spent fighting the bitter cold, all seemed worthwhile. He was holding her, and she was blessedly, beautifully alive.

Abruptly he caught her shoulders and pushed her away so he could look at her face, into her eyes. He pulled the blanket askew so he could see her better. "Are you all right? Are you hurt?"

"I'm fine," she said. But she wouldn't meet his gaze. She kept her chin tucked close to her chest.

"Did Tom—"

"He's dead," she said. "Tom is dead." She looked up at him at last. Her skin was bleached of color. Her lips had thinned to a narrow line. Her eyes possessed a melancholy that made him want to howl with agony.

Tom had hurt her. He had hurt her.

That was as close as Rand could come to making himself accept what must have happened. Maybe it hadn't. Maybe the worst hadn't happened.

"Did he— Did Tom—" He couldn't get the words out.

Her face crumpled, like dead leaves thrown on a fire. "Oh, Rand," she sobbed. "Oh, Rand."

He gathered her in his embrace and held her close, felt her quivering, shaking, and knew it wasn't from the cold. He wanted to shake Tom

Grimes like a terrier shakes a rat. He wanted the man alive again so he could strangle him with his bare hands. He wanted to castrate him and watch his lifeblood ebb away. There was no punishment terrible enough for a man who had stolen a young woman's innocence and replaced it with ugliness.

Freddy has been brutalized.

As horrible as that sounded, it was yet another euphemism. Rand made himself think it.

Freddy has been raped.

His body shuddered with the force of what he was feeling. He did what primitive man must have done a million years ago when he felt battered by merciless fates. He raised his face to the leaden sky, opened his mouth, and let forth a ululating wail of anguish, a cry of helpless rage.

The wind swept it up and carried it away and left them cold and alone in the quiet that followed.

A sudden gust of frigid wind snatched at Rand's hat, reminding him where he was. Night was falling. The end of day had snuck up on them, and Rand was faced with the awesome knowledge that he had found Freddy but was in no position to rescue her. He had no idea where they were, they had no shelter, and with the coming of night, the temperatures were likely to drop far below zero. They would probably freeze to death during the long hours of darkness.

But he refused to concede defeat.

"Freddy," he said. "We have to get on the horses and get moving."

"What about Hawk?" she asked, glancing toward where the Indian had finally fallen in the snow. "Is he dead?"

"I don't know."

Rand was learning fast in this brutal land. He had killed a man for the first time. He had seen the haunted eyes of the woman he loved and known a rage he had never imagined himself capable of feeling. And he had realized he couldn't leave a man—even an Indian who had caused them endless trouble in their lives—to die in the cold.

"I'll see if he's still alive," he said. "You wait here."

"Rand, I—"

"Freddy, don't argue with me," he snapped. "I'm not sure how dangerous he is, and I don't want you getting hurt."

She stood, head down, hands clasped in front of her and said, "Yes, Rand."

It was then he realized what Tom had really stolen when he had taken her virginity. Her confidence. Her spirit. He had mangled the complex and delicate nature that made her the person she was. Rand wanted the old Freddy back. He wanted her to fight him. He wanted her to demand her own way.

He stood watching her for a moment, but she made no move to contradict him again. He left her and walked to where the Sioux had fallen in the snow.

Rand had Tom's revolver in his hand when he

slowly turned Hawk over. The Indian's eyes were open and wary.

"How bad are you hit?" Rand asked.

"Bad enough," Hawk answered.

"I'd help you if I could," Rand said as he knelt beside the Indian. "But I don't know a thing about doctoring, and I haven't the vaguest idea which way to go to find someone who does." He helped Hawk sit up, but it was plain the Indian was sorely wounded.

"Perhaps we may help each other," Hawk said.

"How's that?"

"If you will bring me my horse, I will lead you to my village."

Rand's eyes narrowed. "I won't be made your prisoner again."

"I owe my life to you," Hawk said. "That is a debt I would not dishonor."

"Meaning what?"

"You will be my guest so long as you wish it."

"What about the woman?" Rand asked, unwilling to trust the Indian.

"The woman is mine."

Rand pressed the revolver to Hawk's chest and cocked it. "Not if I kill you first."

Hawk's dark eyes remained steady on his. "Then you will both die in this storm."

Rand knew he was right, but even that fate might be preferable to what Hawk intended for Freddy. "The woman is mine," he said. "I want that understood before any of us moves an inch from here." He would rather kill Freddy himself, or die with her in the cold, than give her to another man to be brutalized.

Hawk stared at him for another moment before he said, "Perhaps we should let the woman choose between us."

Of course Freddy would choose him. But if Hawk needed to hear the words to end this farce, he was willing to let Freddy speak them. "Freddy. Will you come over here?"

Rand uncocked the revolver but kept it in his hand.

Freddy had spent the past few minutes alone wondering whether Rand had done her a favor by saving her life. Tom had promised to kill her long before they reached civilization. It would have been a blessing, she decided. She felt used. Dirty. Guilty. Even though she was the victim. She could never become anyone's wife now. She was no longer worthy of the honor.

Besides, no man would want her. She had seen the revulsion in Rand's eyes when he looked at her. And the pity. Nor could she face her parents again. Or anyone she knew. She wanted to hide somewhere. Even better, she wanted time to go backward so she could obey her parents. She had been wrong to fight against them. She had wanted adventure. She had never dreamed it would all turn out like this.

"Freddy?" Rand called for the second time.

She crossed obediently to Rand and stood beside him.

"Is this your man?" Hawk asked Freddy.

Oh, she had wanted him to be. She loved him so much—had only just realized how much. But she could never marry him now. Her body had been despoiled. And she could never bear to have another man do that horrible thing to her. Not even Rand. She could not be any man's wife.

When she didn't speak, Rand answered for her.

"Yes," he said irritably, "she's mine."

"No," Freddy countered in a hushed, unFreddylike voice. "I don't belong to anyone."

It was something she had said many times before, but Rand had never heard it said like this—woefully, sadly, not the least bit defiantly. He felt like crying.

"Do you wish to be this man's woman?" Hawk asked.

Freddy glanced quickly at Rand and lowered her eyes again. "No."

"She has spoken," Hawk said.

"What the hell is going on here, Freddy?"

Freddy could see Rand was furious. She should have been frightened. But how could mere anger frighten her when she had lived through much worse? "I'm sorry, Rand."

For not fighting harder when he tore my clothes off. For fighting to live when he threatened to strangle me. I should have let him kill me. But I didn't want to die. I was so afraid to die! So I clawed his face and made him mad, and instead of killing me he kept me alive and did awful, terrible things to me.

"Since she does not claim you, I will take her," Hawk said.

Freddy only belatedly realized the situation she had created. "Rand?" She looked at him with terrified eyes.

"I don't give a damn what she said," Rand snarled. "She's mine. You can't have her." He cocked the gun and pressed the icy barrel against Hawk's temple.

"Rand, don't!" Freddy cried.

Hawk didn't move a muscle.

"I'll kill you before I'll let you have her," Rand said.

"Then we will all die."

Rand swore low and viciously. But he didn't remove the gun.

"Very well," Hawk conceded. "You will be free to go whenever you wish."

Rand pondered that for a moment. He didn't trust Hawk not to try and claim Freddy once they were in the village and surrounded by Sioux, but there were more options that could be pursued if they were alive, than if they were dead. "She stays with me in the village," Rand said.

Hawk nodded.

"And you'll guarantee our safety from the other Indians?"

"You will be safe as my guest," Hawk promised.

Rand had no other choice but to accept Hawk at his word. He uncocked the gun. "All right," he said. "Let's go. Can you get up by yourself?" he asked Hawk. "Or do you need help?"

Hawk tried to get up, but hadn't the strength. Rand didn't ask again, simply reached down and helped the Indian to his feet. The Sioux tried to take a step by himself, stumbled, and would have fallen except Rand caught him. He put Hawk's arm around his shoulder to support him. "Bring Hawk's horse, Freddy," he ordered.

"I don't want to go, Rand." She would rather he left her there to die. She suspected it wouldn't take long to freeze to death. If she turned chicken-hearted, if the fear of death rose to make her struggle once more to survive, it would be too late once Rand and Hawk were gone to do anything to save herself.

"Damn it, Freddy," Rand bellowed. "This is no time to act like a spoiled brat. Get the bloody horses, now!"

Freddy headed for the horses, but she walked. She was in no hurry. Living wasn't the great prize Rand apparently thought it was. She wouldn't thank him for making her go on when she wanted life to stop here.

She led Hawk's horse to where Rand stood supporting the Sioux. Rand helped Hawk onto his pony, then helped Freddy mount and took Tom's horse for himself.

"We'll follow you," Rand said.

Hawk grunted and headed his horse into the wind.

They were riding north again.

Verity had never been so enraged in her life. It had taken them half a day to reach the Muleshoe. She hadn't realized until they dismounted from their horses at the ranch and she looked around for Rand that he wasn't with them. It was only then Miles admitted that Rand had decided to continue searching for Freddy.

She paced, prowling the too-small cabin like a she-wolf in a cage. "How could you! You knew I wouldn't have come back if Rand wasn't coming, too! How could you leave my son behind to die!"

"He's a man, with a mind of his own. He knew the danger. He made his choice, and I respected it. I understand what you're feeling, Verity. He's my son, too."

She hissed in a sharp breath. Her eyes glowed with fury. "No. No, he's not yours. Not in any way except that you planted the seed. You were never there when he was a baby who needed coddling, or a youth who needed comfort for a skinned knee, or a young man who ached with hurt because the other boys taunted him about his—"

She cut herself off.

"Taunted him about what?"

She turned her back, heading for the bedroom, but Miles caught her arm and swung her around to face him.

"Taunted him about what?"

"About you," she snarled.

He was so shocked he let her go. "What?"

"Oh, not you, precisely," she said, shoving a hand through her hair and making pins fall helter-skelter. She began pacing again, back and forth, back and forth, as though she could find some escape from the nightmares of the past, the pain of the present. But there was no escape.

She stopped abruptly and rubbed the heels of her hands against her eyes. "I don't know how many fights Rand fought. I only saw the results. He would arrive home for holidays with black eyes, cut lips, bruised jaws. And always some rousing tale of why he had fought the battle. And I believed him." She rubbed her forehead. "I think I must not have wanted to know the truth, so I didn't press him for it.

"The fights stopped after a while, I think because the word had spread that Rand was the very devil with his fists. But as he got older, things weren't settled with fists any longer. Three years ago he threw down a glove to a young man who impugned my honor and challenged him to a duel."

"Good God."

"Of course the young man's mother came to me and begged me to get my son to apologize and release her son from the obligation. Naturally, Rand should be the one to back down, because everyone knew he wasn't Chester's son. Everyone knew he was another man's bastard.

"You may imagine my shock." She smiled bitterly. "I had imagined myself so clever to have hidden the truth. And all the time everyone had been snickering behind my back."

"What did you tell her?" Miles asked.

"I told her that if Rand had issued the challenge, he must have believed the insult. I was full of pride in my son for defending me, and I sent the woman from my house in righteous indignation."

She turned to Miles. "You see, I was sure no one could really know the truth. Who was there to tell? You were gone to America. I had said a word to no one. And Chester, why he had the most to lose from such a rumor. He never would have confirmed it. I felt justified in denying the story, certain I could never be proven wrong.

"But I spent the rest of the morning remembering all the times Rand had fought over the years. And wondering how such a rumor could have gained such credence.

"And I remembered all the times Chester had sat in the library with an empty bottle of port at his elbow, ranting at me for giving him another man's son for his heir.

"And I knew. He must have done the same thing once upon a time . . . perhaps even more than once . . . at his club. The men who heard him must have gone home to their wives with the story. Children must have heard their parents discussing it at the supper table. That explained why Rand had been in so many fights as a boy. And I knew I had to stop him from fighting that duel."

She paused and looked Miles in the eye. "I didn't believe my honor was worth my son's life." She smiled ruefully. "Of course, I had missed the point entirely, which Rand was quick to inform me when I confronted him."

"You tried to stop the duel?"

She nodded. "I pointed out to Rand that the rumor had no power to hurt me. Do you know what he said? 'It hurts me, Mother.'

"I realized then he was fighting for his honor, as well as mine. If he was not acknowledged as Randal Talbot, what right did he have to become the Earl of Rushland?"

"Did he fight the duel?"

She shook her head. "I asked him to do one thing for me before he proceeded further with his plans. I asked him to speak with his father—with Chester—about the subject."

"Why would you do something like that when you believed Chester was guilty of starting the rumor in the first place?"

Her face was ashen as she admitted, "I thought Chester would lie."

"Oh, no."

Her eyes brimmed with tears. "He told Rand the truth. Oh, not the name of his father. He refused to give Rand even that much of you. But he took great relish in divulging to me that he had told my son I was a slut and a whore and that I had tricked him into marriage while I was carrying another man's brat."

Miles started toward her, but she stopped him with an outstretched palm. "Please, don't touch me, or I won't be able to finish. And I want to finish this."

Miles stood frozen like a marble statue, his face implacable. "Go on, then. Tell me the rest."

"When Rand came out of the library, I knew something had gone awfully, terribly wrong. He looked at me with . . . It wasn't loathing, although after the garbled truth his father had told him, it should have been. Perhaps disappointment. And of course, disillusionment. I was not as perfect as he had always given me credit for being.

"He said, 'I will apologize to Griffith Wilkerson at my earliest opportunity, madam.' And he left the house."

"So there was no duel," Miles said, "because he apologized for throwing down the glove, thereby admitting to the world—to all of London society—that he was a bastard, after all."

"Yes. And he has never once, in the years since, mentioned the subject to me again, not even to ask your name. Until today."

"Bloody hell!" Miles shoved all ten fingers through his hair. "What a mess we've made of it, Verity."

"I can't argue with you about that. All I'm concerned about now is getting him back alive."

"There's nothing we can do until this storm ends. We can go after him then, if that's what you really want. But he's not a boy any longer, he's a man. He deserves the chance to be treated like one."

Verity moaned. "He's a babe in the woods in a place like this."

Miles thought of the incidents with the rattlesnake and the bucking bronc when the Muleshoe cowboys had tested Rand's mettle. And all the fights he had endured as a boy. And the twisted lies about Verity he had heard from Chester years ago and accepted. His son could handle adversity better than most men he knew.

"We have to trust Rand to come back when he's ready—when he's found Freddy, or given up trying."

"What if he's lying somewhere hurt?"

"If he is, he'll be dead long before we can get to him," Miles said, giving her the brutal, unvarnished truth.

"I'll never forgive you if he dies."

Miles's jaw tightened. "I made a choice, Verity. I couldn't save you and Rand both. I chose you."

He was telling her she was everything to him. But she was so distraught she didn't hear what he was saying.

"Rand is my whole life."

What about me, Verity? Where do I fit in?

"You should stop worrying so much about your son and start thinking more about what you want for yourself," Miles said.

"I wouldn't know how to put my needs first."

"Then don't you think it's about time you gave it a try?"

Before she could move, before she could anticipate what he had in mind, he picked her up in his arms, and headed for the bedroom door.

18

Willow awoke when a blast of cold air hit her. She rose instantly at the sight of Hawk in the arms of the white man she had helped escape barely a moon ago. Her glance flickered beyond him. Her heart sank to her toes. Somehow Hawk had found the woman and brought her back.

"Lay Hawk down here," Willow said, pointing Rand to the sleeping pallet she had just left. She didn't ask how badly Hawk was hurt. She would know in a moment when she examined him. But it must be serious. Otherwise, Hawk would never have allowed the white man to carry him like a child.

"Your wound has healed?" she asked Rand as she began to undress Hawk.

He rolled his shoulder gingerly. "It's fine," he said. "You did a good job."

"What are you doing here?" she asked.

"We're only seeking shelter from the storm," Rand said. "Then we'll be on our way."

"The woman is mine," Hawk said in Sioux. "Do not let her leave, no matter what he says."

While she tended Hawk, Willow instructed Rand, "You must take off your outer clothing and sit near the fire. Not too close," she warned. "It will do harm to warm up too quickly."

She eyed the white woman. Even with a nose as bright as a chokecherry, she was very beautiful. And a threat to Willow's peace and happiness. Hawk had been furious when he returned to find the white woman gone. Willow had told him he did not need another wife. And she had promised to kill the next white woman he brought back with him to the village.

He had scoffed at her and said he would do as he pleased. He had promised to find the white woman and return with her.

He had kept his promise.

She intended to keep hers.

With the many medicines Willow had at hand, there were ways the white woman could die that none would know of her part in it. Except Hawk. She would tell him what she had done, so he would never bring another woman to take this one's place after she was gone.

She would prepare a sleeping draught, she decided, one that was strong enough to keep the white woman from ever waking again.

* * *

At first Freddy tried to resist Rand's efforts to free her from the several wool blankets she had been using in lieu of a real coat. "I'm cold, Rand. I need these blankets to stay warm."

"You heard Willow," Rand said. "You'll warm up faster without them. Come on, sit here by the fire—not too close—and get warm."

Freddy couldn't believe how good the heat felt. She held out her hands in front of it. First the palms, then the knuckles. She inched her toes toward the circle of rocks that rimmed the fire and gave off heat of their own. It wasn't until she began to warm up that her teeth started to chatter.

"I never realized a person could get so cold." She had only been making conversation, but she saw Rand responding to what he must have thought was a complaint by wrapping one of the wool blankets back around her. She tried not to flinch when he touched her, but couldn't help herself. She knew he wanted to put his arm around her, but she did nothing to encourage him. Then she caught sight of his hands. He quickly tucked them into the waist of his trousers.

"Let me see your hands," she said.

"I'm fine, Freddy."

"Let me see them," she insisted.

He held them out to her.

"Oh, Rand." She reached out, as though to touch him, but pulled her hand back before she made contact. It was infuriating to feel so . . . frightened . . . when she knew Rand would never hurt her. She simply couldn't bear to touch—or be touched by—another human being right now.

"Your hands are frostbitten," she said at last.

"A little."

It was more than a little, Rand conceded. He had given Freddy his gloves to help keep her hands warm, and alternated the hand he used to hold the reins, putting it inside his coat pocket to warm it. Both hands had gradually gotten colder and colder. From the look of them, he could expect to be plagued by chilblains in the future.

At least they had a future.

But he was worried by Freddy's behavior. He was trying to understand and accept her sudden aversion to being touched by him. But it made him feel like a villain, and he knew he wasn't. He felt sure that if she would only let him hold her—gently—in his arms, they would both feel better. But he didn't know the words to persuade her fear away, so touching her right now was out of the question.

His eyes strayed to the other couple in the tipi.

Rand made it a point not to watch what Willow was doing to Hawk. He had endured the same surgery himself recently enough to empathize with the pain he knew was involved. Hawk had to be in terrible agony as Willow dug out the bullets, but he never made a sound.

At last Willow left Hawk's side and joined them by the fire.

She heated water and threw a mixture of herbs into it. Rand thought it was some potion for

Hawk's injuries until she poured out a small amount and offered it to Freddy.

"This will bring you comfort," she said.

"What is it?" Freddy asked.

"Something to warm you inside and out. Drink," she said, urging Freddy to take a swallow.

Freddy took a sip, murmured at the sweet taste, and said, "Here, Rand, you should drink some of this, too."

Willow took the cup from Freddy to hand it across the fire to the Rand, but she tripped and it spilled before it got to him. "I will make more," she said.

Willow put more water on the fire and settled beside them to wait for it to boil.

"How is Hawk?" Rand asked.

"Neither bullet hit more than flesh. I have removed them. He is strong. He will be well again."

"We owe him our lives," Rand said.

"I do not understand," Willow said, holding a handful of herbs over the water on the fire. "Did you come with him willingly, then? Are you not captives?"

Rand shook his head. "No. We're guests."

She raised a skeptical brow. "Hawk said this?"

Rand threw another piece of kindling onto the fire, giving him time to find an honest response. "I am his guest. The white woman belongs to me. And she's leaving with me," he added, eyeing Hawk on the other side of the tipi.

"Ah." It was plain from the simple sound that she recognized the distinction he had made. She withdrew the handful of herbs and emptied them back into a leather pouch.

"Aren't you going to make more tea?" Freddy asked.

"These herbs are no longer fresh," Willow said. "I will get others."

She suited word to deed and prepared another brew that wasn't as sweet as the first, Freddy said, but which Rand agreed warmed his insides as much as the fire warmed his skin. "I will keep Hawk with me in this tipi," Willow said after they had each finished a cup of the reviving brew. "You two may stay the night in the tipi where Hawk left you before. It is not far. I will take you there."

Rand exchanged a look with Freddy. She didn't want to go back out into the cold any more than he did. But the lure of privacy was powerful. "I'll wrap you up in a blanket and carry you," he promised her before she could open her mouth to protest.

"Your shoulder is bothering you," Freddy said. "I can walk on my own."

And she did, keeping her distance from Rand as Willow led them to the tipi that had been their prison.

"I will light a fire," Willow said.

Rand would have protested except, to be honest, neither he nor Freddy was in any condition to do it for themselves. Willow stayed long enough to show them a kettle they could use to melt snow for warm water and left more herbs for tea.

"You would be wise to wrap yourselves together in a buffalo robe to share the heat of your bodies,"

Willow said. "I will come when it is daylight, to see if there is anything you need."

A flurry of cold and snow whirled through the tipi. Then she was gone.

Freddy eyed Rand askance once they were alone together.

"Why are you looking at me like that?" Rand asked.

"Like what?"

"I'm not going to hurt you, Freddy," Rand said in a quiet voice.

"I won't lie next to you, Rand, even if we would be warmer because of it. I won't!" Freddy said. "I can't!"

Rand reached out to her, and she jerked away from him. He felt the pain of her rejection, and told himself that any woman who had been through what she had endured was bound to be a little anxious about being touched by a man—any man.

But he was the man who loved her. He wasn't going to hurt her. He only wanted to hold her. To help her.

"Freddy, let me hold you," he said. "I promise I won't do anything else."

Freddy stared at Rand with eyes that were ages older than they had been a week ago. "Please, Rand, if you care at all for me you'll leave me alone. I feel . . ."

She couldn't say *dirty* aloud. It revealed too much that she didn't want him to know. About how she felt. About what had been done to her. "I don't want to be touched. I couldn't stand it."

"All right, Freddy. I'll lie on the other side of the fire from you. I'll take the blankets. You can have the buffalo robe."

"You're sure you won't be cold?"

He would be cold. But he wasn't going to force her to do what was obviously so distasteful for her. "I'll be fine."

They bundled up as best they could on opposite sides of the fire. Their thoughts ran on similar planes, but were nothing alike.

I have to be patient with her, Rand thought. *It'll take time for her to get over what happened.* Of course she was feeling low now. But he knew, for a certainty, that his Freddy would come bouncing back.

Freddy was nowhere near so sanguine about the situation. She would never get over what had happened to her. The devastation was irreversible. There was no recapturing virginity once it was gone. There was no reclaiming innocence once it had been taken.

I'll never let another man touch me so long as I live, she thought. Her chest felt like someone was sitting on her, holding her down.

"I want to go home, Rand," she whispered into the flame-licked shadows.

"We will, Freddy. Soon."

"I mean to England."

"If you want to go back, I'll find a way to get us there."

"Alone, Rand. I want to go back alone."

He pushed himself up onto his elbow and strained his wounded shoulder. "Damn and blast!" It wasn't the shoulder that made him swear. It was the futility he felt. They should have been married by now. She should have been his wife. There should have been no question of her returning to England, with or without him. They were right back where they had started months ago. She was as elusive, as unattainable, as she had ever been.

But he was responsible for her happiness now in a way he had not been before. He had to make her see that running away wouldn't solve anything. It hadn't made his problems go away. It wouldn't end hers.

Freddy heard Rand swearing and pushed herself upright. "Is something wrong?"

"I hurt my shoulder again."

Four days ago, a lifetime ago, she would have crossed the small distance between them to see if she could help him. But she didn't want to touch him, because he might think he could touch her in return. "Is it all right now?"

He sighed. "We have to talk about this, Freddy."

"My mind is made up. You can't change it."

"Not about England, Freddy. About . . . about what happened with Tom."

"No."

"I don't think any less of you, if that's what you've been thinking. I—"

"Stop!" She pressed her hands against her ears

and closed her eyes to shut him out completely. "I'm not listening."

"I know you can hear me, Freddy."

She rolled over and turned her back to him, curling herself in a protective ball. "I won't listen! Blah! Blah! Blah! I'm not listening!"

"Bloody hell, Freddy! You have to listen to me!" He leapt up and covered the distance between them in two strides, jerking her onto her feet. She made a small, whimpering sound and dropped into a crouch, her shoulders hunched against his touch.

He half expected her to start screaming and was relieved when she didn't. He tried to lift her up, but she resisted, remaining curled into herself in a way that shut him out. He didn't want to force her any further, so he knelt beside her and did his talking to the back of her head. At least her hands weren't over her ears. She was using them to hug herself.

"I love you, Freddy. There's nothing on this earth that could stop me from loving you. Don't you see? Nothing else matters. We'll forget any of this ever happened and—"

She laughed, a spine-chilling sound. "Forget! Maybe you can forget. I can't!"

He touched her shoulder, and she yanked herself free with a strength that surprised. She rose to face him, her green eyes glittering eerily in the light from the fire. "Would you like to know what he made me do? Let me tell you. Let me describe it for you. Perhaps that will make you see why I can never *forget* any of it."

Her eyes were wild, frightening.

"Freddy, please—" he pleaded.

But she wasn't with him anymore. She had retreated to wherever it was that fiend Tom had taken her, reliving the horror, the awfulness of it all. Her mouth moved, but no sound came out. Just whimpers. Pitiful crying noises.

"Freddy, stop it. Do you hear me? Stop it!" He lurched to his feet and grabbed her shoulders, shaking her once, twice, until her eyes cleared of their tortured look and focused on him again.

"Rand?" She looked at his hands on her arms and shuddered.

He released her instantly and took a step backward. "I'm sorry, Freddy. I won't touch you again. And I'll take you home to England, if that's what you want."

He paused and said, "Or you can go back alone. I . . . I won't ask you to talk about what happened ever again. It's a closed book." A horrifying tale that would be remembered and perhaps relived for the rest of her life, he feared.

"Lie down and get some sleep," he urged her. "I promise you we'll head back to the ranch as soon as the snow melts."

"It must melt soon, Rand, don't you think? It's only September. That's awfully early for snow, isn't it?"

"It would be in England," he said. "But this is a strange place, Freddy, with its own set of rules."

"Surely the sun will come out and melt the snow away tomorrow. Don't you think?"

He said what he knew she wanted to hear. "You're probably right, Freddy. It's an unseasonable storm. The sun will have to come out and melt the snow soon. Very soon."

None of them could have predicted the cold was there to stay, or that it would snow on and off for the next two weeks. None of them could have known the wind would blow for another week after that, until the landscape had brown, barren patches of naked earth and drifts elsewhere looming twelve feet high.

Travel in such weather was impossible.

Then winter was upon them in earnest, and there was no letup in the bitter cold, which kept the snow from melting even when the sun finally did come out again.

None of which mattered to Hawk, whose wounds had putrefied, or Willow, who spent those weeks keeping him alive one day at a time. Until, at last, the fever eased and the awful redness around his wounds turned a healthier pink and healing began in earnest.

Willow gave their two "guests" little enough of her attention but made sure they had food and knew to stay out of the way of everyone in the village until Hawk could confirm to the others what status they held.

"I have told them you are Hawk's guest and that the woman belongs to you," she told Rand. "But that does not mean someone will not take offense if you offer insult. And Hawk is not well enough to protect you should a quarrel occur."

"We'll keep out of everyone's way," Rand assured her. "Is there anything we can do to help?"

"There is hunting to be done," she said. "But I do not expect you will be much help with that."

"I'm a pretty fair shot."

She shrugged. "Crooked Knee is Hawk's uncle. Go and see if he will take you with him. I do not think you should go alone." It was because she thought he would get lost, but she did not want to insult him by telling him so to his face.

"Just point him out to me," Rand said.

Rand had gone to Crooked Knee, but the elder Sioux had refused to have anything to do with him. Rand realized he was lucky he was a "guest" and not a "captive," or the situation might have gotten sticky. It was plain the Sioux would have delighted in putting a period to his existence.

Rand had gone out on his own, making note of the landmarks before—and behind—him, as Miles had taught him in the little time they had spent together at the ranch. He could easily have shot several rabbits, but he remembered how much Freddy dreaded the thought of eating them. So he stayed out in the cold until he found a lone deer, and brought it home over his horse's back.

Willow had been surprised and pleased with the meat for her cooking pot. But Freddy hadn't even been aware of his effort. She had retreated into a world of her own. A world that shut him out.

During those early days and weeks they spent

in the Indian camp, Rand kept his distance from her as she had asked. It was difficult not to reach out to her, she was so obviously suffering. But he was afraid of making things worse for her if he forced her into any sort of intimacy, even something as simple as a hug of reassurance that he was there for her, that he still loved her, that she would never be less in his eyes because of what had happened to her. He did not pressure her in any way to accept his touch.

Until the day came when he had no other choice.

19

Hawk had apparently changed his mind. He wanted Freddy after all.

They had been in the Indian village nearly six weeks, during which time Rand had begun to feel safe. He knew Hawk watched Freddy, but then, her striking red hair made her an object of curiosity to all the Indians. Rand hunted and gave what he killed to Willow to cook for them, while Freddy carried water and collected firewood and did other necessary chores. But otherwise, he and Freddy kept strictly to themselves.

Over the past few days, the weather had continually warmed. Nearly all the snow had melted. Rand had figured if it continued mild like this another day, he and Freddy might risk a run for the ranch. It had never crossed his mind that Hawk might decide to lay claim to Freddy at this late date.

Hawk had summoned him, but instead of waiting inside the tipi for him, the Sioux had been standing outside in the cold, wrapped in an immense buffalo robe. Rand had realized why the instant Hawk began to speak. It wasn't a social call.

He wanted Freddy. And none of Rand's arguments against it were having any sway.

"She said she did not wish to be your woman," Hawk reminded him.

"And I told you she's mine," Rand replied. "You promised we would be free to go whenever we wished."

"I said *you* would be free to go."

"You understood my demands when I let you live."

"I never agreed to them," Hawk said.

Rand was furious at Hawk's treachery. "You said she could stay with me."

"I have not broken my word."

"You can't have her," Rand said, his gray eyes turning cold. "I'll kill you first."

Hawk's black eyes stared back at him, unfeeling, undaunted. "You may kill me, but you will never live to reach the edge of the village. And the woman's fate will be sealed. You are in no position to make threats."

"She's mine. You can't take her from me."

Willow, who was standing at a cooking fire nearby, said in a quiet voice to Hawk, "If the woman is this man's wife, she cannot be yours."

"But the woman is not his wife," Hawk retorted.

Rand immediately realized the weapon Willow had given him—and why she had done it. She wanted Hawk to herself. Obviously, if he married Freddy, it would solve both their problems.

He got a sick feeling in his gut when he thought of how Freddy was going to react to the idea of getting married. His teeth clenched. She would go through with it when she understood the alternative. "Is there some ceremony we need to perform to get married?" he asked.

Hawk remained mute.

Rand turned to Willow. "What do I have to do to make Freddy my wife?"

Willow explained the simple ceremony while Hawk stared at her grim-lipped.

"That's all?" Rand said. It didn't seem like enough.

"That is all," Willow confirmed.

Hawk was plainly disgusted at being outmaneuvered, but since he hadn't repudiated Rand's status as guest, there was little he could do to stop Rand from proceeding.

"We will come when the sun sets to witness your claim on the white woman," Hawk said through tight jaws.

Rand realized Hawk was planning to see with his own eyes that the door was well and truly closed on any claim he might have to Freddy. There would be no pretending. They were going to have to go through with the Indian ceremony.

Not that Rand thought it would have much validity outside the confines of the Indian village, but he realized, as he walked slowly back toward the tipi he and Freddy shared, that it might be the lever he needed to force Freddy out of the shell into which she had retreated. He wanted her to feel alive again. Even if it was only to fight him over an Indian marriage ceremony. When all was said and done, the ceremony would be performed. Neither of them had any choice about that.

He wasn't sure when he made the decision that he was going to make love to her. But the thought was firmly fixed in his mind. He felt certain that if he didn't claim Freddy here and now, when they returned to civilization she would slip away from him. Here she could not escape him. Here, he could help her heal her wounds and become whole again.

It nearly broke his heart to see her scramble away from the doorway when he entered the tipi. "It's me," he said to calm her agitation.

"You were gone a long time."

"Hawk wanted to talk to me. There's going to be a Indian ceremony this evening, and we've been invited."

"What kind of ceremony?"

"It's a wedding, actually."

"What do we have to do?"

"Nothing, really. Just show up."

Her eyes narrowed suspiciously. "Who's getting married?"

"We are."

She stared at him open-mouthed. "But you said it's an Indian ceremony."

He settled himself in front of the fire cross-legged, because he knew he was less intimidating to Freddy sitting down. "If I don't make you my wife, Hawk plans to make you his," he said. "Take your choice."

She sank down onto the buffalo robe across the fire from him. "But I don't want to marry anybody. Not that an Indian ceremony is real . . . I mean . . . it wouldn't be valid."

He caught her frantic glance and held it. "It's real, Freddy, as long as we're here in this village. And there's no telling how long we'll be here. It could be months."

She was fidgeting with her hair, pulling it forward over her shoulders to play with the ends, then throwing it out of her way again. "All right, I'll go through with the ceremony. But that's all, Rand."

She darted a glance at him to see if he had gotten the message. He had. She wasn't just scared of the sexual act, she was terrified of it. He resisted the urge to try to comfort her. She didn't want him near her.

He was convinced there was no easy way for her to overcome her repugnance for the sexual act. But it was something she had to do if she was ever going to achieve any sort of normalcy in her life. He would be as gentle and understanding as it was possible to be, but he was going to consummate their marriage.

* * *

"Willow has offered to loan you a ceremonial Indian dress."

"I don't need a dress."

That sounded more like his Freddy. Argumentative. Opinionated. "No, you don't need one. But you'll look very pretty in one. Would you wear it for me? I'm only going to get married once, and I'd like my bride to be beautiful so I'll be the envy of all the other fellows."

He could see she was tempted to smile, and her lips actually curled up on the sides.

"You're impossible, Rand."

"I don't try to be."

Then the smile was gone and her heart was in her eyes and she was looking at him. "This isn't how I imagined it, Rand. Whenever I thought of getting married I imagined St. George's Cathedral with all my friends there admiring me in a lovely satin gown. My hair would be in ringlets and I would wear just a touch of rouge that would make me feel decadent and put roses in my cheeks.

"It isn't going to be like that, is it?" she said wistfully.

"No, Freddy. We won't be among friends. But the sky can be our cathedral. And you'll be wearing a dress the likes of which London society has never seen, something so unique our grandchildren will be telling stories about it for generations to come. And you won't need a touch of rouge, because the icy cold will put roses in your cheeks."

It would turn her nose into a berry, too, but he

wasn't going to tell her that and spoil the lovely picture he had painted. Because she was smiling now with her mouth, if not her eyes, and he could tell she saw the whimsy of the wedding he had described.

They were interrupted when Willow entered the hide doorway and stood waiting to be noticed. She was holding a beautiful white buckskin dress, decorated with colorful beads and porcupine quills, over her arm.

"I'll leave so you can get dressed," he said to Freddy. "I'll be back in a little while to get you."

Her eyes pleaded with him, *Isn't there a way out of this?*

But there was nothing he could do. Her safety depended on this marriage. He wouldn't risk losing her to Hawk when he could end the danger by marrying her.

As he left the tipi, he realized he needed some time alone to think. The tipis were spaced about twenty feet apart in a long line on both sides of a small creek to give them easy access to water and privacy. He turned his back on the creek and headed out onto the open prairie.

Freddy wasn't the only one terrified of the night to come. Rand was not inexperienced in bedding a woman. He had mounted his first mistress when he was eighteen, and in the three years since, he had learned a great deal about pleasuring a woman's body and taking pleasure from it.

But he had never before broached a frightened woman, certainly not one who had previously been brutalized by a man. He had no idea whether Freddy had been injured in the attack by Tom, but he had to assume that whatever damage had been done had healed, because she had made no complaint and was physically able to do the chores Willow had given her.

Rand felt the sweat break out on his forehead. When the time came, it was going to take every ounce of courage he had to consummate his marriage.

"You are a fortunate woman," Willow said, "to have such a good hunter for your husband. You will always have meat in your pot and skins for clothing."

"I don't know how to cook. And I'm not much of a seamstress," Freddy snapped.

"If you stay among us, I will teach you what you need to know," Willow said.

"I'm not staying, so there's no need to waste your time," Freddy retorted.

The Indian woman had behaved so placidly in the past that Freddy hadn't realized Willow had a temper—until she felt the brunt of it.

"I will leave you, since you do not wish my company."

Willow was halfway to the entrance of the tipi before Freddy's conscience smote her.

"Wait!" she cried. "I'm sorry. It's just that I'm so very frightened. I don't want to be married. I don't want to have a husband."

Willow turned and came hurrying back to her.

She caught Freddy's hands in hers, and Freddy found herself looking into eyes that were surprisingly comforting.

"No woman is ready the first time," she told Freddy. "But I can see your man cares for you. He will not hurt you."

"But—" Freddy found herself unable to confess what had happened with Tom.

"Come," Willow said, leading her out of the tipi. "I can hear from the shouts of the others that your husband is waiting outside for you. Everything will come right. Tomorrow you will chide yourself for being so foolish."

Anything was possible, Freddy supposed. If she survived the night.

The ceremony itself was simple.

She and Rand stood before their tipi, with the entire village ranged around them. Rand took her hand in his and turned to the crowd of strange faces.

"I take this woman for my wife," he said.

Willow had explained the Indian ceremony to her, and those were the only words that had to be spoken to bind them.

But Rand lifted her chin so their eyes met and added, "I love you, Freddy. I'll do everything in my power to make you happy. And I promise to honor and cherish you all the days of my life."

Tears welled in her eyes, blurring his beloved face. She knew Rand was waiting for her to make a similar pledge. But she couldn't. Not after what had happened. She swallowed over the painful knot in her throat. "I . . . I'm sorry, Rand."

She saw the disappointment in his eyes, but was helpless to ease it.

Her heart began to beat frantically when Rand picked her up in his arms and headed into the tipi. Behind them she heard the raucous shouts of the Sioux.

The ceremony was complete.

"Put me down, Rand," she insisted as soon as the hide covering had closed behind them.

He set her on her feet but didn't release her. She could feel the heat of his hands at her waist. His face was pale almost to whiteness and his expression somber. She had never seen him look so serious. She realized his hands were trembling when he reached for hers. She would have pulled away, but the momentary panic in his eyes made her hold still for him. His flesh was warm. His touch was gentle.

"I have something I want to say, Freddy."

"What is it, Rand?" she said in a whisper.

"I want to love you, Freddy. I want us to have a wedding night."

"No, Rand—please don't do this. I can't! Don't you understand?" Then she was crying in earnest.

His arms slid around her.

At first she struggled against him, but his embrace, though loose, was inexorable, and at last she stood quiet in his arms, her body quivering. His arms closed tighter around her, and she felt the warmth of him, the safety of his embrace.

She reached for him with a cry of anguish and sorrow. "This isn't the way it was supposed to be," she said, sobbing. "Not like this, Rand. Not like this!"

"Shh. Shh, my darling, my love."

She didn't realize what he was doing until it was done. He had released the ties at the shoulders of the exquisite Indian dress, and the creamy soft buckskin was sliding away, leaving her skin bare.

"Rand, no!"

"Shh. Shh," he soothed again. "I'm your husband. I love you. I would never hurt you."

He was undressing himself one-handed, keeping the other around her to keep her from fleeing. Although, now that she was naked, where could she possibly have run?

Then he was naked, too.

She turned her head away, refusing to look.

He put his hand under her chin and forced her eyes upward. "Look at me, Freddy. Look into my eyes. What do you see?"

Love. Tenderness. But nothing that suggested he intended to stop what he was about to do.

"I'm scared. I'm so scared."

His smile was crooked, self-deprecating. "So am I, dearest. So am I."

"You, Rand?"

"Of course. The fellow is the one who has to do everything right, you know. And I want to do everything exactly right," he said in a fierce voice. "I want you to think only of me, Freddy. Only of me."

His hands surrounded her, and he pulled her

close. She gasped as their bodies met, and she felt the heat and the hardness of him. This was not at all like what had happened with Tom. He had torn her clothes half off and then thrust himself inside her. It had been nothing like this. Nothing at all.

Rand's lips sought hers, and before she could think to refuse him their mouths were joined. This was also different. There was no hurt, no grinding of teeth, no pain.

His lips were utterly soft. His tongue probed her mouth seeking admittance, and she granted it to him. She was surprised into a moan by the pleasure he brought.

One of his hands slid down to her buttocks to keep her in the cradle of his thighs, while the other cupped her breast and held it for his mouth.

Ah! She ached. Desire spiraled downward and curled in her belly, and she arched toward him.

He groaned, an animal sound that frightened her. She drew away, and he crooned to her, calling her back. He wanted her. He needed her.

A knot inside her began to loosen. The tender bud of femininity that had been crushed began to flower once more. She could feel desire for Rand. She could be a woman for him.

His mouth caressed her. His hands adored her. His body worshiped her. Until her knees buckled, and she could no longer stand upright on her own.

He laid her down and lowered himself onto her.

And it all came back to her. It wasn't Rand, it was Tom, and he was forcing himself on her and she was trying to resist. But he was too big, and she couldn't push him away.

"No! Don't! Please don't hurt me. Please!" Terror made her breathless. Panic made her heart pound in her chest. She clawed and kicked and bucked beneath him, but he didn't let her go.

He didn't hurt her, either.

"It's all right, darling. It's me. It's Rand. I love you, sweetheart. Please, Please, don't be frightened."

She managed to focus on his face and saw the tears in his eyes. There were scratches on his cheek. His jaw was taut, his body equally tense. But there was no mercy in those gray orbs. He might not want to do what he was about to do, but he was going to do it.

She forced herself to relax. She widened her legs beneath him and said in a harsh voice, "Just do it. Get it over with. I won't fight you anymore."

"It's not that easy, love," he said.

"I give you permission. Do it."

"I'm afraid I . . . ah . . . can't right now."

It took her a moment to figure out what he meant. When she did, she turned her head to the side so he wouldn't see her despair. She had unmanned her husband on their wedding day. He could not feel enough desire for her to broach her. She caught her lower lip in her teeth to keep an agonized groan from escaping, but she failed, as she had failed as a woman and as a wife.

"You can let me up now," she said.

"We're not finished here yet."

She felt his lips against her throat. And the tiny spiral of pleasure that followed as he kissed his way to her ear and downward toward her breasts.

"Rand," she murmured. "Rand, what are you doing?"

"I'm making love to you, Freddy. The way a woman should be loved on her wedding day."

The lump was back in her throat. "Why don't you let me go, Rand?"

"I can't Freddy. It's not just your happiness I'd be giving up, it's mine. Please. Look at me. Let me love you."

She kept her eyes on his, said his name over and over to remind herself it was him. And the feelings came. Feelings she had never imagined. With his mouth, his lips, his tongue, and his teeth, he worshiped her body. And asked nothing in return.

She reached tentatively for his shoulder and felt him tense as her fingers touched his flesh. Muscle and sinew, and beneath it, bone. She let her fingertips wander into the damp curls at his nape. Down his back. Then around to the hard muscles of his abdomen and the crisp black curls on his chest.

"God, Freddy, when you touch me—"

She jerked her hand away, horrified that she had done something wrong.

He caught her hand and pulled it back against his chest. "You didn't let me finish, sweetheart. It feels good, Freddy. I love it when you put your hands on me."

He showed her how to touch him and touched

her in return. It was a gentle exploration of each other's bodies.

But he had not forgotten his intention. She knew it when his hand slipped between her thighs.

She froze and gasped as he slid a finger inside her. She had expected it to hurt, but she was wet and it glided easily into the passage. He kissed her again, his tongue thrusting in tandem with his finger inside her. She felt her body arch instinctively toward his hand as he withdrew his finger from inside her.

"I think it's best if we do this together," he said in a quiet voice.

She gritted her teeth and steeled herself for his intrusion. Instead, he took her hand and led it down to touch what had so frightened her. "No, Rand!"

"It's a part of me, Freddy, that wants to be inside of you. You can decide how much and how fast."

She tried to draw her hand away again, but he held her firmly against him. It took a few moments for her to feel the heat of him, and the softness of his skin, and the hardness of his shaft.

"You're too big," she whispered.

"I promise you I'm not," he said with a small smile. "But we'll go as slow as you want."

He helped her place the soft tip of him at the entrance to her body and pushed just a little with his hips. "Does that hurt?"

She could tell from the strain in his voice that this was as difficult for him as it was for her.

Which kept the panic at bay long enough for her to consider what he had said. "No. No, it doesn't hurt. Yet." But she knew it would soon. She gritted her teeth. Because she loved him, because he wanted this so badly, she was willing to bear the pain for him.

He pressed farther into her and paused. When she made no objection, he spread her legs farther apart with his knees and pushed onward.

"I think it hurts," she said, grasping his arms tightly and gritting her teeth.

He started to slide out of her, but to her surprise, her body arched upward, to take more of him. Her eyes flashed open, and she stared up at him.

He was searching her face. "Are you sure it hurts?"

"You're . . . I'm . . ." She groaned as he slid into her all the way.

"I'm inside you, Freddy," he murmured in her ear. "Oh, God, Freddy, it's wonderful."

She felt like crying, because it *was* wonderful. She bit her lower lip and arched upward to meet his slow thrusts. Once. Twice. Thrice.

His hands slipped under her buttocks to support her, and he began moving steadily within her. Their bodies were slick with sweat, their lungs laboring to keep them alive.

Then he was arching upward and backward with a look on his face that was almost pain as he spilled his seed within her. She felt her body tightening around him, convulsing with pleasure. She followed him over the precipice into an oblivion of joy.

They were still wrapped in each other's arms minutes later when they heard horses thundering by the tipi. Rand jerked himself from Freddy's embrace, yanked on his trousers, and shoved past the flapped doorway to see what was going on.

"What is it, Rand?" Freddy asked, hastily wrapping her nakedness in the buffalo hide. "What's happening?"

Rand frowned. "Hawk and about a dozen braves are riding out of camp. It looks like they're going on another raid."

20

Verity lifted a heavy cast-iron dutch oven from the heat and set it in the center of the four-hole stove to cool. Her scones—she had learned to call them biscuits—were done. She lifted the lid and peeked inside. Lightly browned and fluffy. She allowed herself a smile. During the past six weeks, Viscountess Linden had turned into a damned fine cook.

Verity crossed and stood looking out the front window at the pink and purple dawn. She hoped it portended more of the warm spell they'd been having. Every day during the past week, the temperature had risen a little more. The snow was gone from the prairie, leaving behind a sea of dead yellow stalks. If Rand was stranded somewhere, he might be able to take advantage of this break in the freezing temperatures to make his way home. If there was a God, and if he was merciful, Rand would bring Freddy with him.

But it was hard to keep on hoping.

When Verity had first sent a letter to Colonel Peters asking him to keep an eye out for any sign of Rand and Freddy, he had responded by dispatching word to the reservation Sioux that he would pay for any information as to the whereabouts of the couple. When Rand and Freddy had showed up safe and sound at the ranch, Verity had informed Colonel Peters, and the colonel had relayed a message to the Sioux that the missing white folk had been found.

Apparently, some of the Sioux had not gotten the second message, because two weeks after Rand had disappeared in the snowstorm one had shown up at the fort with Rand's horse, demanding payment for information concerning the location where he had discovered the animal.

The Indian said that when he caught the mustang it bore no saddle or bridle, but he knew it belonged to a white man because of the horseshoe brand on it. There was no way of knowing whether the Sioux was telling the truth, but the horse had a sprained right hock that suggested Rand might have unsaddled the animal himself because it was too injured to be ridden.

Despite the freezing weather, Miles had gone with the Sioux to the spot where he said he found the horse. But Miles had seen no sign of Rand, dead or alive.

Miles had not given her a chance to dwell on

Rand's and Freddy's fates. He had kept her busy with endless household chores in the daytime. And he had claimed her body in bed at night. Verity blushed as she remembered the animal sounds she had uttered as he made love to her the evening just past.

As though her thoughts had conjured him, Miles came up behind her and slipped his arms around her. His palms came to rest possessively on her belly. "Good morning," he murmured, nuzzling her nape. She laid her hands over his, leaned back against him, and smiled.

She knew for certain now that she was going to have another child. Miles would have another chance to be a father. She was going to tell him so today.

"How are you?" he asked.

She had been plagued by morning sickness for a week. That was how she had known for sure she was pregnant. She had told Miles it must have been something she ate—her first attempt at ham and lentil soup—to give herself a little more time to accept the idea before she told him about it. But he had given her the perfect opportunity to speak, and she wasn't about to pass it up.

"Actually, Miles, I'm pregnant."

It was so quiet you could hear daylight coming.

"Miles?"

His palms gently circled her abdomen through her jeans, feeling for changes in her shape. It was too soon for him to find any.

"Are you sure?" he asked.

"As sure as a woman can be."

His hands slid up to her waist, and his arms tightened around her. He said quietly, "I can hardly believe it."

She wanted him to turn her around. She wanted to see his face, to know what he was feeling. He kept himself hidden from her, forcing her to ask, "Are you happy, Miles?"

She felt a shudder roll through him.

"I never thought . . . I never planned . . ." He sucked in a breath of air and huffed it out again.

"Miles—"

Suddenly he was whirling her around, hugging her, pressing kisses on her eyes and nose and mouth. He lifted her high and swung her around. The boyish grin on his face brought a smile to hers.

"God, Verity! A baby!"

"Set me down, Miles," she said with a laugh. "You're going to make me sick."

Immediately he was all concern. She landed on her feet, and his hands cradled her belly as he asked, "Are you all right? Did I hurt the baby?"

"We're both fine."

"How long— I mean, when—"

"You're going to become a father for the second time in May." Too late she realized she should have phrased it differently.

Miles plowed all ten fingers through his hair, then turned his back on her and stood, hands limp at his sides, staring out across the prairie. His jubilation had ended as quickly as it had begun.

She knew he was thinking of his first child, the son who, even if he returned alive, might still be lost to him. Knew he was lamenting what had been snatched from his grasp. Wishing things had been different. Wondering what would have happened, if only . . .

She stood at his shoulder and said, "This could be a new beginning for us, Miles. We could do everything right this time. We could love each other freely and take joy in the birth of our child."

"I don't know, Verity," he said with a sigh. "What if something goes wrong again?"

"Something probably will," she said. "It always does."

He slanted his head to look at her, a wry smile distorting the scar at the corner of his mouth. "And you still want to try?"

"I'd rather try and fail than never try at all," she said. "I love you, Miles."

She had said the words before, but he had not believed her. She waited to see if he would accept them now.

He turned and took her hands in his. His thumbs caressed her knuckles, and she realized her hands now resembled Mrs. Peters's. They were red and rough from the harsh soap Frog had brought for her to use on the dishes and callused from churning butter and sweeping floors and scrubbing laundry. She started to withdraw them, but Miles tightened his grasp.

She looked up and met his gray-eyed gaze and knew he did not mind.

"They're good, strong, hard-working hands," he said. "The hands of a rancher's wife."

"Oh, Miles." She knew then it would be all right. He would let himself forget the past. He would let himself love the child to come. And he would let himself love her again. One day she would hear the words "I love you" on his lips and know he meant them from the heart.

In fact, it might happen sooner than she had dared to hope, if the torment on his face was any sign of the struggle going on inside him to tear down a lifetime of walls and let her in.

"Verity, I—"

The door burst open with such force that the second hinge, the one that had not been replaced, broke from the strain. Verity opened her mouth to make a sound of disgust and froze when she realized who stood in the doorway.

"Rand! Rand!" She jerked her hands free and raced toward him. He caught her, and she hugged him tight around the waist. Tears blurred her eyes and a swell of feeling choked off speech.

It wasn't until she heard Miles speak that she realized Freddy was right behind Rand. She shoved herself away from Rand and searched Freddy's face for signs of distress as a result of her kidnapping. Freddy's teeth clamped her lower lip, and her eyes lowered protectively from Verity's regard. Freddy's gaze flickered to Rand for . . . for reassurance, Verity realized. Something awful *had* happened to Freddy, but Rand had somehow made it all right. It was Verity's acceptance of her dishonored state that Freddy doubted.

Oh, dear child, how could you think I would hold you to blame? I, who have been brutalized by a monster, would never think less of you for being a victim, as well. Verity opened her arms and enfolded the young woman in a circle of warmth and welcome.

She angled her head to Rand and asked, "Where have you been? How did you get here?"

"We've been living at Hawk's camp," Rand said.

"What in heaven's name—"

"It's a long story, Mother," Rand interrupted. "And we don't have much time. Hawk is on his way here with a raiding party. We followed him from the village. He's camped not far from here. I think he's planning to attack at daybreak."

The sun inched beyond the horizon, and a shaft of sunlight struck Verity in the face. She exchanged a panicked look with Miles.

"How many men does Hawk have with him?" Miles asked Rand.

"At least a dozen, sir," Rand said.

"I'll go alert the men. You barricade the windows here in the house. And do something with this goddamned door," Miles said, kicking it savagely as he stalked outside.

They set frantically to work. Once the windows were shuttered, the only view of the outside was through the gun holes that had been cut at various points along the log wall when the house was built. Rand rolled a nearly full flour barrel close to the door for use in blocking it as soon as Miles was back inside.

But, the attack came before he returned to the house.

"You can't lock Miles out!" Verity cried when Rand started to roll the barrel into place.

"We can't wait for him, Mother," Rand said. "We need to make sure the door is going to stay closed so we can concentrate on defending ourselves."

He dropped the barrel into place and accepted the Winchester Freddy handed him from where it had been racked over the mantel. "You two cover the bedroom window," Rand said. "I'll watch the front."

It was plain neither woman wanted to let him out of her sight, but Rand gave them both a severe look and ordered, "Go!"

They went.

Rand hoped all Hawk wanted was a few more cattle. But he knew from stories he had heard in the village that Hawk had recently attacked a ranch somewhere in the area and burned it to the ground, merely for the hate he bore the white man.

Though he hadn't let the women see it, he was worried about Miles. He fully expected him to try to make it back to the house, but there was an awful lot of open ground to be covered between here and the bunkhouse. Miles would make an easy target for the Sioux.

Rand had spent a lot of time thinking about his father over the past six weeks. The whole story had spilled out to Freddy on the nightlong race to get back to the Muleshoe before Hawk. Freddy had interrupted frequently in typical Freddy fashion to ask questions, forcing him to put into words all the things he had been thinking about Miles Broderick.

"Do you like him, Rand?" Freddy had asked.

"It's hard not to like him."

"Do you want him to be your father?"

"I don't think I have any experience with the sort of father Miles Broderick would be."

"What do you mean?"

"He's so helpful . . . so interested . . . so . . ."

"Fatherly?"

"Is that what fathers are supposed to be like? Mine never was."

"Talbot, you mean?"

"Yes. Talbot."

"Why not give Miles a chance, Rand?"

"I suppose I should," he had said at last. He hadn't admitted his reservations to her. *What if he disappoints me? What if he doesn't live up to all my expectations?*

In the end, all Rand had determined for sure was that he wanted to get to know Miles Broderick better. That wasn't going to happen if the fool man managed to get himself killed in the next few minutes.

Rand kept a sharp eye out for movement through the gun hole closest to the front door. Sure enough, he caught sight of Miles edging his way along the log wall of the bunkhouse, getting ready to brave the run across the open field that separated the ram pasture from the house.

"Go back inside," Rand muttered. "I can take care of the women. Stay where you are."

But he knew if it had been him, he would have come. He realized he hadn't expected any less of Miles. That, he supposed, was the big difference between the man who actually was his father and the man who had let himself be called by that name from the time Rand was born. Broderick never thought of himself first. Talbot always had.

Rand eyed the flour barrel and realized he had better move it out of the way. His father was going to be in a hell of a hurry by the time he hit the front door.

As he heaved the barrel out of the way, Rand heard a Sioux war cry and the sound of galloping hooves. He hurried back to the gun hole to see what was happening.

His father was halfway to the house, running at full tilt, Colt in hand, when a lasso settled around his shoulders and jerked him violently to the ground. The gun flew out of his hand as he was dragged away in a rising cloud of dust.

Rand raced for the door and swore when it stuck in the frame. He pounded it with his fist to unjam it, then dragged it open.

"Rand, is something going on in there?" his mother called.

"Everything's fine, Mother," he called as he raced out the front door. "Stay where you are."

Rand didn't take aim, just swung the rifle up as he ran down the porch steps and fired. The shot missed, but it scared off Hawk, who let go of the rope, kicked his pony into a gallop, and disappeared behind the barn.

Rand didn't bother shooting again, although he could hear other weapons being fired at the escaping Sioux. His entire attention was focused on his father. Miles had been dragged some distance, and Rand wasn't sure how badly he was hurt.

He sank down on one knee, just as Miles rolled over and shoved himself up on his hands. Rand loosened the lasso and pulled it up and off.

"Hold on to me, Father," he said. He slid his arm around the injured man, hauled him to his feet, and headed back toward the house at a shambling run.

He was aware of Miles eyeing him the whole, impossibly long distance to the front door.

Why did I call him Father?

He hadn't planned to say it. It had just come out. Was it because he had always dreamed of having such a father? Was it because in the heat of the moment he had spoken what he yearned for in his heart?

They stumbled up the porch steps and inside the house under the covering fire of the men in the bunkhouse. Rand settled his father on a chair at the table and hurried back to replace the door in its frame and roll the flour barrel back into place. He had just pivoted back around when screams and gunshots erupted in the bedroom.

Both men headed for the closed bedroom door on the run.

Freddy had dreaded facing Miles and Verity after the ordeal she had been through. Rand had convinced her that neither of them would do or say anything to make her feel uncomfortable.

"Mother loves you, Freddy. And she knows I love you. She'll welcome you back with open arms."

He had been blessedly right. Freddy had felt a great weight drop from her shoulders when Verity had hugged her. What guilt and shame was left, she could carry with Rand's help.

She and Verity had each claimed one of the gun holes on either side of the bedroom window. Freddy had a Winchester rifle. Verity had Miles's Colt .45.

"Do you see anything?" Freddy asked.

"Nothing's moving over here," Verity replied.

"Do you think anyone in London would believe me if I told them about this?" Freddy said with a whimsical smile.

Verity looked at Freddy standing there in jeans, holding a rifle aimed out a hole in a log wall at savages on the other side and laughed. "No. They'd think you were making it up."

Both women sobered as their eyes met and held.

What was happening now was all too real. What had happened to Freddy had been real, too.

"Do you want to talk about it?" Verity asked.

Freddy's breath shuddered out. "I'm not sure I can."

Both women froze at the sounds of commotion in the next room. Their eyes focused on the closed bedroom door.

"Rand, is something going on in there?" Verity called.

"Everything's fine, Mother. Stay where you are," Rand called back.

Verity stared at the door a moment longer, but when there was no further disturbance, she turned her attention back to Freddy.

"What have you and Rand been doing all these weeks?"

"Rand spent the time hunting . . . I gathered wood and carried water . . . And we got married."

"You *what*?"

The waggish smile that curled Freddy's lips was a mere shadow of her former mischievous grin, Verity thought, but it was a start.

"Of course, it was only an Indian ceremony," Freddy said. "But Rand says we'll be seeing the chaplain at Fort Laramie the first chance we get."

"I'm so happy for you, Freddy," Verity said. "And for Rand. He's lucky to have you."

"How can you say that," Freddy whispered, "after . . . ?"

Verity dropped the Colt on the foot of the bed as she crossed to put her arms around Freddy. "A beastly act performed upon you can't take away who you are inside," she said.

Freddy shivered. "Rand said the same thing. But I feel . . . I feel . . ."

"Unclean?" she supplied.

Freddy nodded.

Verity stepped back arm's length to look into Freddy's eyes. "I don't know what comfort I can give. I—"

A fifty-pound barrel of horseshoe nails came crashing through the shuttered window, spraying nails everywhere when it broke apart on landing and leaving a gaping sunlit hole through which two ferocious, war-painted Indians could clearly be seen.

Both women screamed.

For a panicked instant, Verity forgot what she had done with her gun. The Indians were already climbing inside the hole they had created by the time she remembered where it was.

"Freddy, get away from the window!" she shrieked as she raced for the bed.

Freddy had already begun to level the Winchester at the first Indian coming through the ragged opening. Before she could gather the nerve to fire, he grabbed the end of the barrel and shoved it upward. When she pulled the trigger, the shot blasted harmlessly into the ceiling.

By then, Verity had the Colt in hand, but the second Indian was upon her. He grabbed her wrist to wrench the weapon from her and the gun went off, wounding him in the stomach. He lurched but didn't fall.

Then all hell broke loose.

The two men charged through the bedroom door like avenging angels, faces contorted in masks of rage and retribution. The Indians tried to disengage to meet this new foe, but seeing reinforcements, the women harried their attackers as best they could.

Miles leveled the mortally wounded Indian with one powerful blow of his fist.

The other Indian had managed to wrest the rifle from Freddy's hands. When he turned to fire at Rand, Freddy gave a fearsome shriek and threw her shoulder into his body, knocking his aim askew.

The bullet landed with a *thunk* in the wall beyond Rand's head.

The Indian dropped the rifle, which was useless in close combat, to grab a knife from the sheath at his waist, while Rand closed the distance between them.

Using his own rifle as a defense against the Indian's first deadly swipes, Rand saw an opening and slammed the butt of his Winchester hard up under the Indian's chin, sending him flying head over heels backward through the hole in the wall.

The Sioux scrambled to his feet and ran for safety around the corner of the house. Rand started out through the window after him, but Freddy grabbed his arm.

"No, Rand. Let him go. Please."

Rand ushered Freddy and Verity to the relative safety to be found in the front of the house. Miles followed as soon as he made sure the dying Indian had no weapon, closing the bedroom door behind him.

Verity could see through the gun hole nearest the front door that the Sioux were retreating, sprinting to safety on horseback amid a hail of bullets from Miles's men stationed in the bunkhouse and the barn. As she watched, the Indian she had left wounded in the bedroom, who had seemed on the verge of death, came into view perched precariously on his mount, racing to catch up with the others.

In the distance, she saw that several other Sioux had stampeded the cattle.

"They're taking our cattle, Miles!" she cried.

The look on his face was bitter, angry. "They'll keep them running until they're scattered all over hell and gone," he said. "It'll take us a month to round them all up again. At least, all of them we're going to find. Hawk will cut out a herd for himself, just like he did last time."

Verity didn't suggest going after the Sioux. A few cattle weren't worth putting Miles and Rand in danger. She held her breath waiting to see whether the idea would occur to Miles.

It did.

"Could you find Hawk's village again?" Miles asked Rand as the two men rolled the flour barrel away from the door and yanked it ajar.

"Probably," Rand answered, as all four of them flooded out onto the porch.

"I'll get the men," Miles said, heading down the

porch steps. "This time Hawk isn't going to get away."

"Miles, let them go," Verity pleaded.

"This has to be done, Verity," he said, not even turning around, his voice implacable.

"Father," Rand said.

Verity watched the word stop Miles in his tracks. He pivoted to face Rand, one foot on the bottom step, one on the ground.

"Let him go, Father. Hawk saved our lives. Not willingly, but Freddy and I would have died in the blizzard if he hadn't helped us. We've been guests in his village. I've met a great many of the people who live there. I don't want to kill them."

"So we let him get away with this?" Miles asked. "He'll be back, you know."

"We'll be ready for him," Rand said.

In that one sentence Rand had revealed his intention to stay at the Muleshoe, to be a son to his father. Verity felt her heart leap with gladness. She saw the fierce light of joy in Miles's eyes.

"Son, I—" Miles's voice cracked, and he cleared his throat. "We'll need to get started on a place for you and Freddy," he said.

Freddy came up beside Rand and laced her arm through his. "What do we need to do first?"

"First," Verity said, eyeing the front door hanging cattywampus, "somebody needs to fix all the holes in this house, or we're going to end up with drifts to the ceiling the next time it snows."

"Yes, dear," Miles said with a grin. "Anything else?"

"Well, now that you mention it, I think there's something else you should tell Rand."

Miles looked at her quizzically. She saw the moment he realized she was talking about the baby. He walked up the steps onto the porch, held out his arms, and closed them around her as she stepped into his embrace. They turned together to face Rand and Freddy.

"Mother?" Rand asked, his expression worried.

Miles cleared his throat again. "Your mother and I have an announcement to make."

"What is it?" Freddy asked, now as anxious as Rand.

"I . . . we . . ." Miles looked at her helplessly.

She realized suddenly what held him mute. He had just made peace with Rand. Would this news cause a rift between them again? But it had to be said. It wasn't something she could hide for very long. And better now than later, when Rand might think another secret had purposely been kept from him.

Verity turned to her son and said, "You're going to have a brother or sister, Rand. I'm expecting a child in the spring."

Rand stood thunderstruck for an instant. He thrust a hand through his hair in a way that reminded her of Miles. Then his glance slid to Miles and a smile teased his lips. "Are you sure you can handle two of us at one time, Father?"

Verity felt the tension ease in Miles's body.

He chuckled and said, "Believe me, son, I'm sure willing to give it a try."

"Well," Freddy said, "wait until Mother and Father hear about this!"

"I don't know, Freddy," Rand said with a grin. "I don't think this holds a candle to the story about the bear."

"Personally, if you're looking to provide exciting dinner conversation in London, I think my rescue of your mother in the buffalo stampede deserves some consideration," Miles said.

Rand and Freddy laughed.

Verity looked around her and found she had everything a woman could want. A home—full of holes though it might be—a family—growing larger every day—and a husband who loved her—though he had never said the words.

She knew she would hear them someday. All she had to do was keep loving him until that day came.

Epilogue

Wyoming Territory 1876

She could hear him pacing in the other room, his booted feet echoing on the hollow floorboards. When he reached the log wall, he pivoted and marched back the other direction.

She gripped the bedsheets as another pain racked her belly.

Verity, Lady Broderick, Viscountess Linden, writhed as she labored to expel the child, biting back the scream that sought voice because she didn't want to worry the child's father.

"Please let me call him, Verity," Freddy said. "Miles should be here at your side."

She wanted him there, desperately. But Miles had tried to sit with her earlier and had turned so completely white when he saw the pain she was in that she had thought he was going to faint. But it had been wonderful grasping his hand as the pains clawed periodically at her belly, feeling his strong fingers massaging the continuous ache in her lower back.

Before she could call him, the pain passed, as many others had since she had woken that morning. They were not so bad yet that she could not last a little longer without him.

Sunlight streamed through the bedroom windows, lighting the corners, chasing the shadows away. Freddy turned down the kerosene lamp before heading into the kitchen for more hot water.

Then Miles was there, standing in the doorway.

"Are you all right?" he asked. "Freddy said you were between pains."

Which was why he had felt it safe to come in, she thought with an inward smile. She patted the bed beside her. "Come sit here, Miles."

He came and sat. "How much longer is this going to take?"

She did smile then. "Babies have their own schedules to keep."

"I didn't know it would hurt you this much," he admitted with a guilty look. "I had no idea."

"The pain is a small price to pay for the joy to come." Verity gripped his hand and groaned. She tried to keep her face bland, not to let the pain show. If the agony on his face was any indication, she wasn't doing very well.

"Freddy!" Miles shouted. "Freddy, get in here!"

Rand appeared in the doorway. "Freddy went outside—to the necessary. Is there anything I can do?"

Verity watched the two men eye each other helplessly and felt the urge to laugh. She gasped instead when she felt the urge to push. She was shocked, because it had been so little time since the pains had started. This labor wasn't at all like the one before. There should be more pains. It should take longer.

"The baby's coming!" she said, surprised and a little frightened by the speed of events.

"Oh, my God!" Miles said. "Go get Freddy!" he ordered Rand.

Verity met Miles's panicked glance and said, "Please don't worry. Everything will be all right." She wasn't really sure of that anymore. Maybe she should have gone to the fort two weeks ago, as Miles had asked her to do.

"Damn you, Verity! You need a woman at a time like this who knows what to do. I don't know how I let you talk me into waiting for the labor to start before sending for Mrs. Peters. I should have known she wouldn't get back here in time."

At least they were assured Mrs. Peters's journey wouldn't be held up by the threat of an Indian attack. The Sioux were no longer a danger this far south. They had all headed north to join with others of their kind who were intent on resisting the white man's encroachment on their land. An army led by General Custer was searching for them even now.

Hawk had not raided the Muleshoe for more than a month. Verity and Miles had speculated that he had retreated north with the other bands of Sioux.

"Didn't want to . . . be away from you so . . . long at the fort," she said between panting gasps. "Besides . . . I've been through this . . . before."

In anticipation of just such an emergency as this, she had explained to Freddy everything that needed to be done. Freddy had been more than willing to help with the birthing. Miles had joked that he would probably be more help than Freddy, because he had delivered his fair share of calves and colts over the years.

Now, Verity realized, his boast was going to be put to the test. "Miles," she said. She didn't have to say the rest. He knew he was going to have to deliver their child.

He looked at her with something close to resignation, his face serious, his eyes anxious, his mouth pressed flat with fear. He glanced one last time at the doorway for help. No one was there. He moved aside the sheet that covered her.

"I can see the baby's head!"

Verity grunted with effort as her abdominal muscles clamped down, forcing the child out. There was no breath for speech, no time to tell Miles what to do.

She felt the child slip from her body along with the last of the pain and heard Miles make an exclamation of surprise and delight.

She lifted herself on her elbows and looked between her upraised knees at the grinning man supporting a tiny, slippery baby in his large hands.

"We have a daughter, Verity."

Verity felt her nose sting, felt her chin quiver, felt tears of joy well in her eyes.

Rand and Freddy appeared breathless at the door and stood frozen in a tableau of disbelief at the sight of Miles with a baby in his hands.

Tears glistened in Miles's eyes as he said, "You have a sister, Rand."

Several things happened quickly after that.

Rand and Freddy ran to get more hot water and cloths to clean the baby and Verity.

Miles laid the baby down on the bed near Verity's hips to wait for the expulsion of the afterbirth and to cut the cord. When that was done, he wrapped the placenta in the newspaper that had been laid under her and put it aside on the floor. He swaddled the babe in a cloth that had been laid nearby for that purpose and carried the child to the head of the bed to lay her in Verity's arms.

She unwrapped the cloth and looked at her daughter.

She had black hair. Like her father.

Miles sat beside her. "She's so unbelievably small," he said, touching the tips of the baby's fingers and noting the tiny fingernails. Five tiny fingers closed immediately around his forefinger. He tried to pull away, but his daughter hung on tight. "And so strong," he marveled.

"What shall we name her?" Verity asked. The

first time Miles had been given no say. She wanted him to have it now.

"She's your daughter, too," Miles said. "What name would you like?"

"Whatever name you choose," she told him with a smile.

He smiled back. "Then I'd like to name her after my mother, Margaret Caroline Broderick. We can call her Maggie, or Meg, if you like."

"Hello, Meg," Verity crooned to her daughter.

"I love you, Verity."

Verity looked up slowly from her daughter's face into the face of her child's father. It was the first time Miles had said the words aloud. She hardly believed she had heard them. "Would you mind repeating that?"

His lips curved. "I love you. I have for quite some time, you know."

"I know," she answered with a cheeky grin. "I've just been waiting an awful long time to hear you say it."

He chuckled and leaned forward to press a gentle kiss on her mouth. "I appreciate your patience. I won't make you wait so long to hear it again."

"Right now would be nice."

"I love you, Verity."

"I love you, too, Miles."

Rand and Freddy reappeared at the bedroom door. Rand had his arm around Freddy's shoulder.

"We have something we'd like to tell you," Rand said.

Miles and Verity looked at him in expectation.

Rand and Freddy exchanged a loving glance before Rand turned back to them and said, "You're going to be grandparents. Freddy's expecting a baby!"

"Oh, Rand! Oh, Freddy, that's wonderful!" Verity said.

"Isn't it wonderful, Miles?"

She laughed when she saw the expression on his face.

"I can hardly wait," he said. "We get to go through all of this again in a few months!"

Incredibly, unbelievably—and to his utter delight—he was right. Pamela Juliet Talbot made her appearance three weeks early. Grandfather Broderick delivered the baby.

LETTER TO READERS

Dear Readers,

Hi! Some of you have written to me asking about books for which the working titles have changed. If you're hunting for *Daisy and the Duke,* that book was retitled *The Inheritance* and is available from your local bookstore. If you're looking for *Lord of the Plains,* you have it in your hands.

For those of you who have enjoyed my bestselling Hawk's Way series, I've written a compelling, full-length contemporary novel titled *I Promise* that is scheduled for publication by Avon Books in August 1996. Ask your bookseller for the exact date it will be available.

As always, I appreciate hearing your opinions and find inspiration from your questions, comments, and suggestions.

Please write to me at P.O. Box 8531, Pembroke Pines, FL 33084 and enclose a self-addressed, stamped envelope so I can reply. I personally read and answer my mail, though as some of you know, a reply might be delayed if I have a writing deadline.

Happy Trails,

Joan Johnston

December 1995

ACROSS A MOONLIT SEA
Marsha Canham

Bestselling author Marsha Canham, winner of the *Romantic Times* Lifetime Achievement Award, has won national acclaim for her novels of breathless romance and exhilarating adventure. Now her magnificent new work sets sail on the high seas, where pirates rule and the fires of love and war rage on and on. . . .

Once you've read her, you'll understand why people call her books

"Extraordinary . . ."—*Romantic Times*

"Engrossing . . ."—Nan Ryan

"First-rate . . ."—Elaine Coffman

"Exciting . . ."—*Affaire de Coeur*

The following is an excerpt from *Across a Moonlit Sea*, coming from Dell in February 1996.

CHAPTER ONE

She emerged from the receding bank of mist like a ghost ship. The air was dead calm, the water smooth as glass. The lines of her rigging were frosted with dew and glistened with a million pinpricks of light as the first rays of the morning sun found her. She had originally carried four masts, but the mizzen and fore were badly damaged, the latter cracked off halfway up the stem and folded over on itself, suspended in a harness formed of its own ratlines. What few scraps of canvas she carried were reefed, as if she knew she was going nowhere fast. The huge mainsail hung limp, half of it in tatters, the rest valiantly patched wherever it was possible and bolstered by a new array of lines and cleats to give it some hope of catching any breeze that might whuff by. There was more damage scarring her rails and hull, and she was listing heavily to starboard, weary with the weight of all that hope.

Captain Jonas Spence frowned through the thick wire fuzz of his eyebrows. "I see no lanterns. No signs of life on any of her decks."

His second-in-command, Spit McCutcheon, duplicated the frown but he was not looking so much at the silent galleon as he was the dense gray wall of fog behind her.

"There could be a dozen ships out there, lyin' in wait, an' we'd not know it," he muttered through the wide gaps of his front teeth. " 'Tis just the kind o' trap a bloody-minded Spaniard would set. Use one of our own as bait to lure us in, then"—he leaned over the rail and spat a wad of phlegm into the water twenty feet below—"pepper us like a slab o' hot mutton."

Spence's frown deepened, the lines becoming crevices in a face already as weathered and hardened as granite. He was a tall bull of a man, as broad across the beam as his ship, as bald as the pickled gull's eggs he ate by the crockful. "Mutton?" He glared at McCutcheon. "Did ye have to say mutton, ye flat-nosed bastard? Now I'll be havin' the taste of it in my throat the whole blessed day long." Spence snorted again and raised his hand to his eyes, shielding them against the molten silver glare of what little dull light did manage to break through the dissipating clouds. He took a slow, careful sweep along the half of the horizon that was clear, halting when he came upon the ghostly galleon and the gray miasma of mist behind it.

"We'll send the jolly across," he decided. "If there are a dozen papist bastards out there, they'll be goin' nowhere, either, in this cursed calm. An' if she's genuine, there might be souls aboard who need our aid. Helmsman! Ye'd best haul us in. Keep a square or two aloft for steerage in case a wind does come along."

The *Egret* was armed, as any reasonably minded merchant trader should be, and had seen her fair share of fighting, mostly against Spanish and Portuguese privateers who objected to Spence's interference in their trade monopolies. But as any Englishman knew, a man was only as good as the ship he sailed. Both the Spanish and the Portugee had clung to the centuries-old design of square-rigged masts, which meant they could only sail where the wind took them. English vessels were fore-and-aft rigged on all but the main square sail, adding maneuverability in the yards that allowed them to sail circles around more cumbersome galleons, who could only watch and grow dizzy.

The wounded galleon before them was definitely English in design and flew the cross of St. George on what was left of its topmast, though it was as tattered and charred as her other pennants.

"Below Aulde George, there," Spence said, narrowing his amber eyes to bring the topmast into better focus. "Do ye recognize the pennon?"

"Crimson on black. A stag, or a goat, I make it." McCutcheon shook his head. "The crest is not familiar to me."

"Aye, well, it *feels* like it should be familiar. At any rate, she's no simple merchant wandered too far from home. She's showin' ten bloody demicannon an' fourteen culverins in her main battery as well as falconets and perriers fore an' aft."

"Mayhap she'll have shot to spare an a tun or two o' powder if her magazine is not underwater." McCutcheon's graveled voice did not betray too much optimism. "Or if she did not use it all gettin' herself in such a condition."

"Well, we've no choice but to take a look. An' no harm in passin' by the armory on the way."

"Aye," Spit grumbled, and passed the order over his shoulder. "Cutlasses an' pistols, ten shots apiece. Lewis, Gabinet, Brockman, Hubbard, Mawhinney—" He paused in naming the best musketmen on board and his wizened gaze settled on one particularly expectant face.

The amber eyes of the captain, which more often than not twinkled with mischief and good humor, had not retained their joviality in his offspring. Solemn and serious most times, Beau Spence's eyes were large and fiercely proud and more often than not brought to mind a tigress stalking its prey. Beau's hair shone with hints of red in the brightest of sunlight, and then only on the rare occasions she left it unplaited. Most times she kept the rich auburn braid bound as tightly as her doublet, which, though considerably smaller in size than any other garment on board, did a fair job in flattening and smoothing any distractions that might lure a lecherous eye from his work. Moreover, being the only woman on board a ship full of lusty-minded men, she had shown no hesitation or lack of skill in using the razor-sharp dagger she wore strapped about her waist, or—as one poor gelded bastard had discovered—the wickedly thin stiletto she kept sheathed in the cuff of her boot.

There had been some who had balked at the notion of a woman joining the crew of the *Egret*—what soundly superstitious sailor would not? But she knew every plank, spar, and cleat on board. She worked as hard as any of them and ofttimes harder than most, if only to prove she was deserving of their respect. Seven voyages ranging from six months to a year's duration had more than proven it. She was a dead shot with a pistol and could hold her own with a cutlass against men twice her size. And even if the tiger eyes had not been focused intently on Spit McCutcheon, almost daring him to pass her by, he probably would have called her name.

"Aye, Beau. Fetch yourself a cutlass an' join the party. Have Roald break out some pipes o' water as well; no tellin' what we might find over yonder."

As the jolly boat came within hailing distance of the unknown ship, the crew's attention was fixed steadfastly on the looming hull. There were still no signs of movement on board, no glimpse of a curious head, no ominous creak of a falconet swiveling on its iron cradle to take aim on the advancing boatmen. There was only the soft rush of water sliding under the keel of the jolly boat, and the faint clinking of two small iron rings that dangled from a broken spar high above the deck.

"Ahoy there! Anyone aboard?"

Spence's booming voice sounded unnaturally loud as it rolled across the gap and echoed off the hull of the wreck.

Spence signaled the oarsmen to bring them up to the gangway ladder. He was first up the steps, with the grizzled, bone-thin McCutcheon a beat behind. Beau was next to last and made the climb with no difficulty in spite of the perilous tilt of the hull.

The sight awaiting them at the top caused them all to stop in a group inside the gangway hatch. The deck was a wasteland of debris. Planking was torn and blackened from fire, ropes and rigging lines snaked haphazardly across the ruin; the forecastle structure was gone completely, leaving only a gaping black hole in the deck. Barrels and buckets were upturned or on their sides, smashed timbers lay strewn over hatchways, and torn sheets of canvas sail hung limply from the spars overhead.

A ferocious battle had indeed been waged, not too recently to judge by the lack of staining from blood and ash. But recently enough to retain the stench of charred wood and decaying bodies.

"Ahoy!" Spence shouted again. "Be there anyone on board alive enough to hear the sound o' my voice? If so, sally forth an' show yerselves without fear o' harm, for we fly the cross o' St. George an' serve Her Most Royal Majesty, Elizabeth of England."

Something—a boot scraping on wood or a piece of debris carelessly unsettled—startled every pair of eyes in the direction of the bulkhead below the mangled remains of the forecastle. A man emerged from the shadows of the hatchway, too tall to do so without ducking his head. His shirt was torn and filthy, the lacing long gone to some other use so that the edges of cloth hung open to his waist. Both sleeves were gone, baring arms that were carved from slabs of rock-hard muscle, bulging with more than enough power to steady two fully primed and cocked arquebuses on the group at the rail.

He stood with his long legs braced wide apart as if balancing himself against heavily rolling seas. His eyes were piercing even at that distance, so pale a blue as to be almost silver. His hair fell in thick black waves to frame a squared jaw and a wide pillar of a neck, both blunted under a heavy growth of coarse gunmetal stubble. From the deep V of his opened shirt, a similarly dark forest of hairs gleamed smooth and silky beneath the linen.

Yet, as formidable as he succeeded in appearing, his skin had an unhealthy waxen cast beneath the bronze tan. His lips were cracked from lack of water, the whites of his eyes were shot with bright red veins. Despite the bulk of muscle that shaped him, his cheeks betrayed a hint of gauntness suggesting he had gone even longer without food than water.

"Who are you?" he rasped. "What ship?"

Spence lifted a hand to signal his men to caution as he took a wary step forward. "My name is Jonas Spence. My ship is the *Egret.* We hail from Plymouth, our home port, an' have been in the Caribbee these past eight months seeking honest trade."

"An honest English merchantman? I count five guns in your starboard battery."

"Aye, an' I count two dozen in yer main, another half score in yer bow an' stern for chasers. Nor have I heard a name for you or yer ship, though I see by yer flags we both claim loyalty to England's queen."

The silver eyes flared with an unaccountable fury for

a moment before he answered. "My faith in a man's loyalty is not as secure as it may have been a month ago, Captain Spence. You will forgive me if I feel a need to err in favor of caution."

"Ye're alone here?" Spence asked, scanning the deserted deck.

"If I were, I would have gone mad long before now." He lowered the snouts of both muskets, obviously a signal to the rest of his men, who began stepping forward out of hatchways and from behind piles of debris.

"Your ship, Captain Spence. She looks to be sound and steady. A welcome sight, you may believe."

Spence swelled his chest. "Aye, she's a sound beauty, all right. Eight months we've been at sea an' only hauled over once for a scrapin'."

"You met with no trouble from the Spaniards?"

"We looked for none. As I said, we're honest merchants goin' about honest business. Honest enough to share our names as well as our water," he added, glancing pointedly at the shadowy figure against the bulkhead.

"You are absolutely right, Captain Spence," said the blond man, standing next to the giant who now hastily stepped forward into the sunlight. "We have been unconscionably rude." He thrust out his hand. "My name is Pitt. Geoffrey Pitt. Honored to make your acquaintance. And you truly do have to forgive Captain Dante his manners, not that he ever had any great excess to boast in the first place."

"Dante?" Spence's fiery eyebrows speared together over the bridge of his nose. "Not . . . *Simon* Dante?"

Geoffrey Pitt attempted to look surprised. "You have heard the name before?"

"Heard the name?" Spit McCutcheon echoed the question with a slackened jaw. "Christ Jesus on a stick . . . is there a warm-blooded man on either side o' the Ocean Sea who has not heard the name o' Simon Dante?

As a fact, where we just come from down in the Caribbee, we were told half the bloody Spanish fleet were out scourin' the Indies for him—that's why we were able to slip in an' out again without drawin' too much notice."

"Well, as you can see," Pitt acknowledged with a little too much strain behind his smile, "they found us."

Spence turned on the stump of his wooden heel, his eyes widened out of their creases as he surveyed the wreckage strewn about them. "Then this ship—this is the *Virago?*"

A second spin had Spence staring up the topmast at the ragged flags that still hung limp against a windless sky.

"It wasn't a stag or a goat, ye block-brain," he hissed at McCutcheon. " 'Twas a wolfhound. A crimson wolfhound an' a blue fleur-de-lis on a black field: the arms o' Simon Dante, Comte de Tourville."

Even Beau was markedly impressed as she stared, along with the other members of their boarding party, at the saturnine features of Dante de Tourville. The Spanish called him Pirata Lobo—the Pirate Wolf—because of his cunning and prowess at stalking and cutting the richest ships out of the plate fleet. The English called him a rake and a hero, often whispering his name louder than those who sailed in the company of the vaunted sea hawks Sir Francis Drake, John Hawkyns, and Martin Frobisher. It was also rumored that while the queen called him "that bloody Frenchman" in public, in the privacy of her chambers she called him something very different indeed. A genuine titled nobleman, he was French by birth, half English by blood, and reputed to be all larceny by nature.

Suddenly, the *Virago* gave a deep-bellied groan and took a noticeable swoop to starboard. Something in her holds must have given way, for there was the sound of cracking timbers and water rushing through a breach in the hull, and she took a moment to steady herself as her weight settled again.

"Ye can't be thinkin' ye can keep her afloat much longer? The first ripe gust o' wind will push her over." Captain Spence said, sympathetically.

"Hopefully, we can buy a little time."

"Are your holds—full or empty? I only ask in order to determine if your ship can bear any more weight. Several tons worth, to be exact."

Spence's startled gaze went from Pitt to Dante.

Dante ignored the Captain's surprise. "Have you a winch and cables on board?"

"Oh, aye. Aye," Spence said, striving to suppress his excitement. "Cables thick as my arm an' a winch stout enough to lift a brace of oxen."

Visions of crates full of gold and silver bars sent a visceral thrill through the members of the boarding party, for surely the grateful Frenchman would offer to compensate Spence for his troubles. As spry as she was and as bold a captain they had at the helm, the *Egret* had been plagued with nothing but foul luck on this voyage. Two months into the venture a storm had forced them into Tortuga, where most of their trade goods had been confiscated by greedy port officials. They had some barrels of rum and bales of spices, but it would barely bring enough in Plymouth to cover the cost of the expedition.

Spence's thoughts had taken a similar turn and were abuzz with so many possibilities, he almost did not hear what Dante said next.

"It isn't gold we'll be transferring, Captain Spence. It's guns."

"Eh? *Guns,* did ye say?"

Dante nodded. "A commodity far more valuable than gold these days and as you have already noted, we have a pretty arsenal on board the *Virago*. I may be able to do nothing to save my ship, but I sure as hell can save the guns to use again another day. These demicannon fire thirty pounds four hundred yards, with enough power behind them to blast any ship clear out of the water."

"Any ship except the one that found you," Beau remarked under her breath. Spit glared at her again, but he was too late.

The startlingly piercing eyes located the source of the whispered sarcasm and Beau felt the tiny hairs across the back of her neck ripple to attention. He walked toward her, pushing past the coughing McCutcheon, whose attempt to camouflage what she had said went for naught.

He came right up and stood in front of her, close enough for the menacing heat that radiated off the masses of muscle and brawn to have melted any man's courage.

"Did you say something to me, boy?"

The gunmetal jaw was level with the top of Beau's head and she had to square her shoulders and tilt her chin up to meet him squarely in the eye. It was a gesture her father knew all too well and she thought she heard him groan but she could not be certain; the blood was suddenly pounding in her ears, too loudly for her to hear anything but the sound of her own heartbeat.

This close, she could not help but be awed by the sheer size and presence of the silvery-eyed sea hawk. His legs were long and thick with muscle, barely contained by the filthy woolen hose; his waist was lean, his belly—where it showed through the carelessly open V of his shirt—was flat and hard as a board. Chest and arms would have flattered a gladiator, with power flexing through every sweat-sheened sinew. His neck was a solid pillar, the jaw blunted somewhat under several weeks' worth of bearding, but as imposing as the man himself, with a deep cleft shadowing the center point of his chin. His lashes were absurdly long for a man, black as ink, framing eyes that burned with equal measures of contempt and arrogance. Beau could feel herself tensing, her blood humming as it did in the hot, still moments before battle. She suspected he was singling her out for a reason, being the smallest and slightest among the boarding party, wanting to establish his superiority from the outset.

"In the first place, I am not your boy," she said evenly. "And what I said was, your invaluable guns did not appear to be all that effective against the Spaniards who found you."

If it was possible for him to become any angrier, he did, and Beau would have reason later to remember the chilling fury that turned his eyes from silvery gray to a clear, crystalline blue. For the moment, however, all she could see were exploding starbursts. His hand had come up with the speed of a striking cobra, grabbing her under the chin and lifting, squeezing so tightly, the air was instantly and painfully cut off from her lungs. Only the tips of her toes touched the decking as he brought his face near enough to hers, she could feel the heat of his breath scorching her cheeks.

"For your information, *boy,* it was six ships, not one, that found us. We sank four on the spot and sent the other two limping off to perdition, *more* than *likely*"—he gave her two violent shakes to emphasize his words—"to sink before the night was out."

Beau's hands clawed at the vise clamped around her throat, but it was like trying to pry away bars of steel. She could barely see through the blackness clouding her eyes, could not think for the pain. She tried reaching for one of the guns at her waist, but the attempt was knocked aside. She tried kicking and scuffing him with her bootheels, but he parried her efforts with ridiculous ease, causing Spence to throw up his hands with a roar.

"Aye, that's enough!" he shouted. "Leave go of her, ye blackhearted bastard. *Leave go of her, do ye hear me!"*

Geoffrey Pitt reacted first. He whirled and looked closely at Beau's red and swollen face, then at the front of her doublet where the strain of her frantic efforts to free herself had resulted in the prominent outline of breasts.

"Simon! Simon, for Christ's sakes—it's a woman!"

Dante's eyes screwed down to slits. The veins in his temples and throat were throbbing, the ones in the back of his hand and forearm stood out like blue snakes. He blinked to clear the sweat from his eyes and found himself looking down into a face that was too smooth and flawless to ever know the need for a barber's skills, into hot amber eyes that were blazing with outrage and indignation, but were, beneath the feathery lashes, a woman's eyes.

"What the hell—"

"Beau! Beau, are ye all right, lass?" Spence shoved past the Cimaroon and crouched awkwardly on one knee. "Slow an' deep. Breathe slow an' deep."

Beau clutched his arm for support and dragged at gulps of air. After a minute she glared up and found Dante de Tourville.

"You . . . son of a . . . *bitch,"* she gasped. "You . . . *sonofabitch!"*

"Aye," Spence grunted. "Ye're all right."

He pushed to his feet again and glowered at the Frenchman. "It might be she has a sharp tongue in her head at times an' ought not have questioned yer courage so . . . bluntly. But ye had no call to choke her either."

"The captain isn't quite himself—" Pitt began.

"I need no one to make excuses for me," Dante snapped, rounding on his own man. "Nor does the situation warrant one. She spoke out of turn. Maybe she will think twice before doing so again—to me, anyway. In the meantime, Mr. Pitt, we don't have much time. I want as many guns transferred to the *Egret* as we can manage."

"Hold up there," Spence snarled. "She's still my ship an' I've not agreed to take any o' yer bloody guns on board yet."

"You don't have a choice, Captain Spence. And I don't have the time to argue."

"Ye'll damn well make time, by God, or ye'll be arguin' with this!" Spence stepped back and drew his cutlass.

"I had hoped it would not come to this, Captain," Dante said grimly. "I had hoped you would not force me to take command of your ship."

"Command o' my ship?" A thin red trickle of blood ran down Spence's throat and began soaking into his collar, but the sheer audacity of de Tourville's statement caused the leathery face to break out in a wide, disbelieving grin. "There are near a hundred fully armed men on board the *Egret.* Are ye plannin' to force them as well?"

"I won't have to if they see their captain cooperating."

"Faugh!" Spence snorted disdainfully. "That'll be a cold bloody day in hell! Ye can slit my throat three ways to Sunday an' I'll not give the order to hoist a single sail."

While every man within earshot held his breath and waited, Dante stared at Spence, at the wide slick of blood that streaked his throat and spread across his collar. Something in the fierce, burning topaz of the captain's eyes made Dante look down to where Beau was still crouched on the deck. He took a casual step toward her and used the barrel of his musket to lift her chin, and there was no mistaking the similarity in the bright, hot sparks of amber that flared up at him. His own gaze narrowed in speculation as he glanced back at Spence.

"Such rare coloring," he mused. "Unlikely there should be such an exact match within a thousand miles . . . unless the two were related somehow. She appears to be too young and fresh for a sister. A daughter, perhaps? One with a long, shapely throat more than suitable for slitting in order to ease you of some of your stubbornness."

Spence stiffened perceptibly. But instead of bowing to the implied threat, he allowed a wide, somewhat contemptuous grin to settle across his face as he folded his arms across his barrel chest.

"A clever deduction, Cap'n Dante. And, aye, Beau's my daughter. The sweet fruit o' my loins. Mayhap that's why *she* doesn't take any kinder to threats than I do."

Dante met the long lashed amber eyes again and almost smiled with the rush of promissory menace that flowed through his veins. Carefully, he set the musket aside, and carefully, he curled his hands into fists by his sides.

Spence cleared his throat. "The way I see it, Cap'n, ye've another six, maybe eight hours, topmost, before yer ship goes belly down. If I were you, I'd start talkin' fast. Ye talk *bold* enough, there's a certainty, but if ye want our help, ye'll have to convince me there's a fine enough reason for givin' it."

Simon Dante searched the captain's weathered features with eyes that had lost none of their cold intensity. "I'm genuinely sorry, Captain. If I had an hour to spare, I might be able to convince you we aren't demented fools, but as you already determined, time is of the essence. You say you want a fine enough reason to order your men to help us?" He reached around to the small of his back and, quicker than she could react to avoid it, held a pistol out at arm's length, pressing the nose flush against Beau's temple. "Will this do?"

IN THE WAKE OF THE WIND
Katherine Kingsley

From the writer *Romantic Times* calls "A miracle worker, a writer who understands the map of the human heart," comes an enchanting story of fate and desire and the many pitfalls along the path to true love.

Praise for Katherine Kingsley

Winner of a *Romantic Times* Career Achievement Award for Historical Adventure

"Irresistible . . ."—Mary Jo Putney

"Unique . . . elegant . . . sensitive."
—Connie Rinehold

"If you haven't discovered Katherine Kingsley, you don't know what you're missing. She's a writer who never disappoints."—Lindsay Chase

The following is an excerpt from IN THE WAKE OF THE WIND, coming to a bookstore near you in March 1996.

CHAPTER TWO

Serafina took one last look around the crumbling castle that had served as home for the last eleven years. She was going to miss Clwydd acutely. She remembered the day she'd arrived, numb with grief over her father's death and the strain of the funeral, feeling like a duck out of water, stripped of the only home she'd ever known, reeling from the shock of having been turned out of Bowhill by her detestable cousin and his mother without one kind word.

The memory still hurt after all this time, and Serafina winced as humiliation came rushing back in full force. She didn't really know why she was thinking about that awful day now, except that she felt an immense gratitude to Aunt Elspeth for having taken her in, for having made her welcome in her castle on a cliff when Serafina had nowhere else to turn until her marriage to Aiden.

" 'Ere, come along now, Miss Serafina," Tinkerby said from behind her, startling her out of her thoughts. "Time's awasting, and your auntie's loaded up that blasted bird. You know he won't keep his beak shut for more than two minutes, and I'm not inclined to stand about getting my eardrums broken."

Serafina turned and gave him a fond smile. "Coming, Tinkerby. I was just saying my good-byes."

"Aye, well good-bye is the best thing I can think of your saying to this drafty old pile of mortar. I daresay it'll be missing you a good deal more than you'll be missing it. And your husband-to-be is waiting too." He winked. "Won't have him saying that I held up your nuptials, not when he's so anxious to have you at his side, if you know what I mean."

Serafina blushed; she wasn't exactly sure what Tinkerby meant, but she knew she needed to be better prepared than she was. She hadn't been able to get another word out of Elspeth on the subject and she was no closer to discovering the mystery.

"You see, Tinkerby?" she said, gently teasing. "You thought I was making everything up about my destiny with Aiden and it all happened just as it was supposed to."

"I still think that part about destiny is a lot o' nonsense," Tinkerby said. "But I'm prepared to admit I was wrong about his lordship. Mind you, I wasn't to know he was in the Americas all that time. Hard to marry you when he was an ocean away, I'll give you that."

"Thank you," Serafina said, kissing his cheek. "Oh, Tinkerby, I don't think I've been so excited in my entire life!"

She sobered, longing to ask Tinkerby the question that had been uppermost on her mind the last few days, ever since she'd learned that Aiden had summoned her. "Do you think . . ." she said, hesitating. "Oh, Tinkerby, how do you think he'll find me? Do you think he'll find my face displeasing?"

Tinkerby chuckled. "I'm sure I can't speak for his lordship, Miss Serafina, but you put me in mind of your mother when she first came to Bowhill, that you do. Why do you ask?"

"Because everyone said I was such an ugly child," Serafina blurted out. "I think I've improved a little, but my eyes are still a funny color and the bridge of my nose is too wide and my mouth is too full and—and my front tooth is crooked." She regarded him gravely.

"I don't see a thing wrong with your eyes, your nose, your mouth, or that tooth, for that matter. It's hardly crooked at all to my way of looking, just a little bit off perfect. You should have seen my wife—now there was a mouthful of teeth. Stuck right out they did, but I didn't love her any less for that."

"Oh," Serafina said with acute disappointment, seeing what Tinkerby was gently trying to tell her. "I suppose he'll find me too skinny as well. I never have been able to put flesh on my bones."

"As for that," Tinkerby said, standing back and regarding her with an assessing gaze, "I'd say you were a slight thing, but not sickening for it, and that's what matters. Don't you worry, missie. You may not be a beauty like one of those statues I once saw in Kensington Gardens, but you have character and that's what counts."

"I suppose you're right," Serafina said with a sigh. "I'll do my best with what I have and hope Aiden won't be too terribly disappointed."

The journey to Rutland stretched interminably. Elspeth insisted on stopping every afternoon for a three-hour-nap, which she enjoyed stretched out in the back of the carriage, snoring peacefully. Even on the fourth afternoon as they neared their final destination of Townsend, Elspeth insisted on stopping, despite Serafina's desperation to continue. She watched with helpless frustration as her impossible aunt pulled the curtains across the window. Aiden was five miles away at the most, no distance at all, a mere heartbeat after eleven years of interminable waiting, and her aunt insisted on snoring away three hours of precious time. Serafina wanted to scream.

"Go on then, missie, have yourself a nice walk in the woods," Tinkerby said soothingly. "You know there's no changing that one's mind once she's set it. You've a lifetime ahead with his lordship and a few hours isn't going to make any difference."

Serafina shot him one last resentful glare, then took off at a fast pace through the forest that bordered the post road, determined not to let her vexation get the worst of her, not an easy task.

She wandered for some time through dappled thickets, steadily following the elusive sound of water and finally found its source. A bright, bubbling stream ran along one side of a clearing, wending its way over a bed of rock and climbing around and over fallen wood. Damp moss padded the edge of the slight embankment, and Serafina fell to her knees and drank deeply of the cold water, first remembering to thank the goddess for providing her with refreshment.

When she'd finished, she sat up and stripped off her shoes and stockings, then pulled her skirts up around her knees, paddling her feet in the stream with contentment as she wove a chain from the wildflowers she'd picked along the way. She placed the wreath on her head, humming a little song.

Then, since she had nothing better to do for the next two hours, Serafina curled up on her side, resting her head against her arm, and let the warm sun carry her off into sleep.

Soon. So soon now, and she'd be in Aiden's arms . . .

Aiden had spent ten aggravating days chasing down first the archbishop of Canterbury to obtain the blasted special license, and then chasing down various creditors and bank managers to determine the exact severity of his father's financial crisis. It had not been a rewarding period of time. And now bloody Miss Serafina Segrave was about to arrive to bail his father out and seal Aiden's miserable fate.

He stormed down the stairs and through the hall, intending to ride into the village and get himself thoroughly drunk. And then his sister's voice rang out from the open doors of the drawing room.

"Aiden? Aiden, where are you going?" she called in alarm.

"Out," he said shortly.

"But they'll be here at any time," Charlotte said, dropping her embroidery into her lap, her face pulled into a worried frown as she took in his appearance.

"Precisely."

"Oh, Aiden, do be reasonable," she said in a cajoling tone, wheeling her chair forward. "You're not even dressed for dinner yet, and you can't come in smelling of horses. What will Miss Segrave think?"

"I don't give a damn what Miss Segrave thinks, or what her aunt thinks, or what you think for that matter, Charlotte. I'm going out, and you can all consider yourself fortunate if I find my way back by tomorrow morning. I've been busy trying to save our communal skin," Aiden said tightly. "And since the only way to do that is to slip my head into the noose Father's arranged for me, I'm damned if I'm going to hang myself a minute sooner than I have to. You and Father can look after dear Miss Segrave and her aunt perfectly adequately."

"But Aiden . . . you can't leave me alone with them. What am I to say? How am I to explain your absence?"

"Look, Lottie," he said, deliberately softening his tone at her wounded expression, "I'm sorry. I'm in a particularly foul mood, which is one of the reasons I'm vacating the premises for tonight. I'll try my best to be on better behavior tomorrow, but you know how I feel about this impending marriage and the parties involved in perpetrating it on me."

He crossed over to her chair and took her hand, dropping an affectionate kiss on her hair. "And I realize I'm being a selfish bastard in behaving as if I'm the only one who's going to suffer because of this marriage," he said, giving her fingers a squeeze. "But never fear. If Miss Segrave thinks she's going to take over Townsend lock, stock, and barrel, she has another think coming, and I'll be the first to set her straight."

Aiden saddled his horse himself, since the one groom left to them was busy with other duties. He was glad that at least his father hadn't sold off Aladdin along with everything else. God, he found it depressing to see what had become of Townsend in the three years he'd been away, evidence of neglect everywhere.

He turned toward the west and kicked Aladdin into a fast canter, choosing to head cross-country rather than take the road, mainly because he didn't want to risk being spotted by Miss Segrave and her approaching entourage.

The sunlight had softened into gold as late afternoon approached, and Aiden cut across Townsend's meadows, slowing Aladdin's gait to a walk as they approached Rockingham Forest.

Here the sunlight dimmed and diffused into patches, lending a sense of timelessness, and he breathed deeply, drinking in the familiar tang of new leaf and brush, the rich loam of earth, his ear attuned to the gentle call of birds hidden in the trees, the babble of the stream that ran as a tributary from the river.

He steadily followed the bank, the surest guide through the forest to the path leading to the village. It was easy enough to become lost in the vast sprawl of wood where not too many ventured, other than the occasional poacher.

Aladdin suddenly snorted and shied and Aiden came back to reality with a jerk, bringing the gelding back under control with his legs and a gentle restraining pull on the bit. He looked around to see what had startled Aladdin and nearly unseated himself.

Just off to the left of the stream lay a body. A woman's body, curled onto its side, the face down, a mass of dark hair tangled around one arm, a bedraggled wreath of flowers on her head. Her feet were bare, her skirt hitched up about her knees. She made no movement.

"Sweet Christ," he whispered in real alarm and brought Aladdin to an abrupt halt, quickly dismounting. He approached the body with trepidation, hoping against hope that he hadn't stumbled across the scene of a murder.

He knelt and reached out one tentative hand, gingerly touching a shoulder, expecting it to be stiff and cold. The next thing he knew the body heaved itself up to a sitting position with a very lifelike squeak and he found himself looking into a pair of wide, startled eyes the most extraordinary shade of light green, surrounded by a thick fringe of dark lashes.

He stared, for once in his life speechless.

She stared back, her rosy mouth slightly open, her small high breasts rising and falling in a rapid rhythm, but other than her initial squeak she made no sound, just gazed at him with those arresting eyes. Aiden vaguely registered the impression that she was one of the most enchanting creatures he'd ever seen.

"I—I beg your pardon for disturbing you," he stammered. "I thought you were dead, you see."

She blinked, looking exactly like an owl startled out

of its sleep. "You thought I was dead?" she said, cocking her head to one side. "What an extraordinary idea."

"Yes, I know," he said, thinking that her voice sounded like liquid music. "I see that now, but one doesn't usually trip across sleeping maidens in the middle of the woods." He glanced around. "Especially sleeping maidens with no visible chaperones."

"What do I need a chaperone for?" she asked, as if he had just posed the silliest question on earth.

"To protect you from men like myself," he said, unable to resist a wolfish grin. "I'm precisely the sort of rogue they're designed to guard you against."

She regarded him with open curiosity. "Ah," she said after a moment of examining him as if he were an interesting scientific specimen. "I've always wondered what a rogue looked like."

"I hope I don't come as a disappointment," he said with amusement, still half convinced she was a fairy, even though the worn, muddied state of her dress indicated she was simply a girl from the village. Still, she was utterly captivating and refreshingly unsophisticated. He didn't think—no, he was certain—that he'd never met anyone like her in his life.

"Well . . . I haven't anyone to compare you to, but I don't find you disappointing at all," she said, chewing on her lip thoughtfully. "You're very handsome. Am I supposed to be afraid of you?"

"Probably," he said, thoroughly gratified and entertaining the most roguishly impure thoughts. "Are you?"

"I'm terribly sorry, but I'm not," she said apologetically. "I know that rogues are supposed to ravish young women, but I don't think you'd be interested in ravishing me."

"Why not?" he asked.

"Because you don't love me," she said perfectly calmly. "Surely you don't ravish people you don't love?"

Aiden smothered a laugh. "You really are an innocent, my dear. What makes you think love has anything to do with it?" he asked, unable to resist pursuing this extraordinary line of conversation.

"But of course it has," she said in astonishment. "I can't imagine it would be very interesting any other way, and why else would it be called lovemaking? To be truthful, though," she said with a little sigh, "nobody's ever told me much of anything when it comes to the subject, and I confess I long to know."

"Do you feel your education has been neglected?" he said, not entirely believing his ears.

She regarded him gravely. "I'm not sure. After all, it seems as if it must be such a natural process that one ought to be able to work it out without instruction. It's just the details that trouble me, you see, and I haven't anyone to ask." She looked at him with a little gleam of curiosity. "I don't suppose . . . no. That probably wouldn't be proper."

"Decidedly not proper, but I wouldn't let that trouble you." Aiden ran his hand over his chin, desperately trying to keep a straight face.

"Well, I suppose we'll never see each other again, so it doesn't really matter," she said with a decisive nod.

"Exactly." Aiden sat down and stretched out his legs, crossing them at the ankles, and leaned his weight back on his hands. "Er, are you planning on being ravished at some point in the future? Perhaps you have a rendezvous in mind that leads you to this line of inquiry?"

"Oh, yes!" she said brightly. "How did you know?"

"Just a lucky guess," he replied. "In that case, maybe I could give you one or two helpful pointers."

"Well . . . I would like to know if lovemaking is a pleasant experience." She regarded him expectantly.

"Hmm. I would have to say very pleasant," Aiden said, his eyes dancing with suppressed hilarity.

"As nice as kissing?" she asked earnestly, looking as if she found kissing the most marvelous thing in the world.

"Decidedly better than kissing." His gaze dropped to her rosy lips again and lingered there, mentally tracing their outline, wondering what it would be like to feel them beneath his own.

"Oh, how wonderful," she said with satisfaction. "That is exactly what I was hoping for. Umm—can you tell me what actually happens? When one seals a vow in the flesh, I mean?"

Aiden bit the tip of his thumb, stifling a surge of laughter. "I—I suppose the best way to put it is that a man and a woman become very close, as close as it's physically possible to be."

"But *how?*" she asked, her face a delicious riot of confusion.

"Well . . . they go into each other's arms," he said, trying to find words that wouldn't shock her. "And they kiss and caress, and then, when both are feeling completely delighted with each other, the man joins his body with the woman's."

"How does he do that?" she demanded insistently.

"Hmm," Aiden said. "Let's see. You know, of course, that men are built in a different fashion to women?"

"Yes, of course," she said impatiently.

"Good. Because the man takes that part of himself that makes him male and he places it in that part of herself that makes her female. Do you understand?"

She raised her eyes to his after a minute. "I think so. Do they take their clothes off?" she asked, her brow puckered. "I can't see how else they might do this thing."

Aiden wasn't sure he could take much more of her questioning without losing his self-possession. "Generally speaking they do, unless they're in a terrible hurry. But it's the sort of thing you want to take your clothes off for."

"Oh. Like bathing," she said, her face lighting up.

"As far as I'm concerned, it's much more fun than bathing," he replied, his lips quivering. "The only thing I must caution you about is the possibility of conceiving a child," he added. "You do understand this is often the result of lovemaking?"

"Of course I do," she said indignantly. "Isn't that the whole point?"

Aiden stared at her, nonplussed. "My dear girl, with that attitude I think you might seriously consider the option of marrying this gentleman. Unless, of course, he is already married."

She stared back at him, her mouth half open, and then she suddenly burst into peals of laughter. "Oh! You are funning with me. I'm sorry—I don't go out much in the world, so it is not always easy for me to tell."

"The truth of the matter is that I'm about to be married. And if you bring the notion of love into it, I think I might well strangle you."

She clasped her hands in her lap. "Oh . . . I see," she said, lowering her gaze. "If that's how you feel about marriage, I don't see why you're being married at all."

Aiden threw away the piece of grass in disgust. "I gave my word to my family, and that's that. So I'm to be tied to a harridan—an ugly harridan on top of it—for the rest of my days." He dug his fingertips into the earth as if he could ground himself against the fresh rush of anger that surged through him. "As God is my witness, I'll do my duty, but I'll despise the witch until the last minute she draws breath. And believe me, that can't be soon enough."

She stood then, surprisingly tall and so slender that he knew he could span her waist with his hands. And wanted to. But he managed to keep his hands to himself as he rose to face her. The top of her head came to his shoulder, and he looked down at her. "Are you going now?" he asked, infinitely sorry at the prospect.

"Yes, I must leave," she said. "I truly am sorry for your predicament, and even sorrier that you hold such a pessimistic attitude. But as foolish as it sounds, I wish you all happiness despite it." She held out her hand, her palm sideways as if she were a man.

He took it gently and turned it over, feeling the fragility of her bones, yet the strength in her grip as her fingers clasped his. "Thank you," he said quietly. "It's a hopeless wish at best, but appreciated."

And then, in one of the more misguided moments of his life, he pulled her to him and kissed her exactly as he'd wanted to from the moment he'd first looked into her eyes.

She didn't pull away at first, probably from sheer surprise, and he had the satisfaction of feeling her parted lips soft and warm under his, her breath mingling with his own, her mouth warm and receptive before she came to her senses and wrenched herself out of his grip.

"You really *are* a rogue," she said furiously, rubbing her hand over her mouth as if she could wipe away his touch. "I'm beginning to think you deserve everything coming to you." Her entire body trembled with indignation.

"I'm sorry," he said, not really meaning it. That kiss, as brief as it had been, was the sweetest he'd ever experienced. "I didn't mean to do that."

"Oh yes, you did," she said, her eyes sparking with anger. "It didn't happen just by accident, did it? And if you ever try such a thing again, I—I'll have my husband call you out, and you'll be very sorry." She picked up her shoes and stockings and marched off, her head held high, her back straight.

Aiden watched her disappear into the forest, her

stride long and graceful, putting him in mind of an enraged nymph. An inexplicable longing burned in his chest. He felt as if life itself had just walked out of his grasp.

ALWAYS YOU
by Jill Gregory

Praise for Jill Gregory's previous books:

"Utterly magical"
Romantic Times

"Great from start to finish"
"Spectacular writing"
Rendezvous

"As good as they get"
Affaire de Coeur

Jill Gregory has written five wonderful historical romances for Dell. Her sixth is coming your way in April 1996. In *Always You,* Jill's most beguiling love story yet, a woman is saved from marrying the wrong man by a man who seems right—in all the wrong ways! Jill writes western historical romances that are truly memorable. Wrap yourself up in the magic created by this winner of the *Romantic Times* Career Achievement Award.

Rawhide, Wyoming

He'd never stalked a woman before.

He didn't much like it. But there was no other way.

As the tall, quiet stranger sat with his hat pulled low over his eyes and his long legs stretched out beneath a small square table in the Ginger Horse Saloon, he drank whiskey and let the talk swirl around him, talk as thick and heavy as the tobacco smoke that drifted over the baize-topped gaming tables and the gleaming mahogany bar.

The place was like many others he had passed through in Arizona, New Mexico, Nevada. Flocked red-velvet wallpaper, brass chandeliers. A big, crowded room teeming with cowboys and ranchers and townsmen. There were some gamblers and a half dozen red-lipped women in cheap, gaudy dresses and strong perfume—heady, floral fragrances that vied for attention with the odors of tobacco, whiskey, and sweat. A piano player pounded at the keys of the instrument in the corner; coins clinked; boots scraped against the floor.

A typical place, the stranger thought, *full of colors, sounds, smells.*

And talk.

Talk about Melora Deane.

She was the belle of the town, maybe even the belle of the territory, from the sound of it. Daughter of rancher Craig Deane of the Weeping Willow Ranch, one of the largest spreads around.

He finished his whiskey, ordered another, and listened some more.

Almost everyone in the Ginger Horse had something to say about her. The men talked openly, admiringly. They said she was a handful. A beauty. They said she was every inch her father's daughter.

And they said she was getting married tomorrow to Wyatt Holden.

The stranger was the only one who knew she wasn't.

Because tomorrow this time Melora Deane would have vanished. And the stranger in the gray shirt and sleek black pants, with the silver-handled gun belt slung low on his hips and the dark blue neckerchief loosely knotted at his throat, was the only one who would know what had become of her.

* * *

Weeping Willow Ranch

Melora Deane hunched her tired shoulders over her father's desk and frowned down at the sea of payroll ledgers before her.

A cold, hard lump of rage rose in her throat. "Those damned rustlers! I'd like to string up every single one of them single-handedly!"

She brushed back several loose strands of dark gold hair that had escaped from her ponytail and forced herself to read the figures over again. Maybe there was a mistake.

There wasn't. Melora closed her eyes, the lump in her throat tightening into a thick knot.

Outside the window a meadowlark sang, a beloved, familiar song she'd heard all of her life. The sound was both lovely and painful, ripping through her heart. She took a deep breath and compressed her lips, thinking of the vast, beautiful Wyoming rangeland that stretched for miles in every direction, of the cattle grazing freely across the rolling Deane property.

Anger flooded her.

She and her sister, Jinx, were rooted here, to every

inch of grassland and foothill that encompassed the Weeping Willow. It was their home, their birthright. And they were in danger of losing it forever.

First we lost Pop. Now we're in danger of losing the ranch. I won't—can't—let it happen.

She dropped her head and scrubbed her knuckles across her wet eyes. *Don't cry—think!* she told herself furiously. But it was hard to hold back the tears. She loved the Weeping Willow with every fiber of her being, and so did Jinx. It was their legacy from Pop, it represented everything he had built, everything he had been, but now the rustlers who had murdered him were destroying the ranch too.

And so far she hadn't found a way to stop them.

"For a girl who's getting married tomorrow, you're working much too hard." Aggie Kerns scolded her from the study doorway.

Melora glanced up, then shook her head at the slim, tiny woman who had taken care of her and her sister since their mother died eight years ago. Nearly sixty, with small shell-blue eyes and gray curls that sprang out all over her head, Aggie was a reassuring presence, firm and practical and loving. She possessed a brisk manner and a warm heart, and she was wonderful with Jinx. Especially lately, since their father's death.

"Don't lecture me, Aggie." Melora grimaced. "I just have to go over another set of books—"

"No, you don't, Mel. Not tonight. Why, tomorrow this time you'll be on your honeymoon, and you haven't even done all your packing yet, I'll wager." As the girl conceded this with a guilty shrug, Aggie sighed. "Just as I thought. Now listen to me, honey. You let Wyatt take over all these financial matters for you after you're married. See if he can't sort things out. My word, you've done enough worrying about stock and rustlers and expenses to last you a lifetime."

"We'll see." Melora opened the center drawer and replaced the ledger books. "I don't want the Weeping Willow to be a burden to him, Aggie. It's my responsibility. But at the very least," she added as Aggie opened her mouth to argue, "I'll get his advice."

Wyatt had already offered to go over all the books with a fine-tooth comb for her, to turn his considerable business acumen to the task of straightening out the affairs of the Weeping Willow Ranch. He had even offered to invest money in more stock and to hire on more hands so that the range could be patrolled at night. *He's wonderful,* she thought, her heart fluttering as she pictured the lankily handsome black-haired man she was going to marry in only a few hours.

But Wyatt had all his town businesses to look after, and his own neighboring ranch, the Diamond X, which he'd inherited four months ago from his uncle. *Keeping the Weeping Willow solvent is my job,* Melora told herself. She just had to figure out a way to do it.

But Aggie was right about one thing. The mounting debts would have to wait until after her honeymoon. First things first. She was just rising from her chair to go upstairs and pack when she heard the clatter of approaching hoofbeats.

"Goodness, who can that be?" Aggie demanded.

It was Melora who strode to the study window and saw the tall gray-hatted rider approaching, handling the splendid black stallion with the confident ease of a man long accustomed to being in control. At the sight of him, a smile, the one that had won Melora Deane countless hearts, sparkled across her face.

"It's Wyatt," she exclaimed, and shot out the door like a firecracker.

Tall, dark, roguishly handsome Wyatt Holden was everything Melora had ever wished for. As he dismounted and swept Melora into his arms, she felt completely happy.

"Let's take a walk," Wyatt said, after thoroughly kissing her. "I've brought you a present."

"Give it to me right now, Wyatt. You know I can't bear to wait for anything!"

He chuckled, drawing her along with him into the grove of cottonwoods beyond the corrals. "After tomorrow, honey, neither of us will have to wait for anything," he said in a deep, low tone.

Melora grinned, and a faint blush stained her cheeks. She knew what Wyatt was referring to. Anticipation tingled through her, with only a little bit of anxiety thrown in. *Married!* she thought in wonder, studying Wyatt's smooth profile as hand in hand they strolled beneath the cottonwoods. *Tomorrow night this handsome man with the charming drawl and the adorable dimples will be my husband.*

She'd known him only a few months, but it was all the time she needed. Wyatt had arrived in Rawhide after his uncle Jed Holden, the Deanes' neighbor, had succumbed to pneumonia and left the Diamond X ranch to him. From the moment Melora set eyes on him at the May Day town dance, she'd known that he was different from all the other men who'd pursued her. Those others, both at school in Boston and here in Wyoming, had been boys. Wyatt Holden was a man. A self-assured, intelligent, sophisticated man, who didn't fawn over her or show off in front of her or drive her loco trying to steal a kiss. That wasn't his style.

He had quickly become one of Rawhide's leading citizens, respected even by her father's friends, the older, established ranchers in the valley. He had investments all over the West, he'd told her, a fleet of fishing boats in San Francisco, a freight company in Kansas, and a saloon in Nevada. He'd already bought a livery stable in

Rawhide and was considering taking over the Paradise Saloon as well.

"I'm investing my future in Rawhide," he'd explained the night he proposed. "Because I love you." He'd gone down on one knee in the ranch house parlor, gripped both her hands in his, and urged her to share that future with him.

Now the future was about to begin. *At last,* she thought, thinking with shivery anticipation of the extravagant pink satin nightdress she had splurged on from Lacy's catalog, which she intended to wear tomorrow night. She imagined herself gliding toward Wyatt in that lovely, floating confection, pictured the way his eyes would light as he studied her. He would sweep her into his arms. And they would kiss—a long, dreamy kiss. And then he would untie the silk ribbons holding the bodice together and . . .

Her thoughts broke off abruptly as Wyatt halted beside a fallen log. "Have a seat right here, Melora. And close your eyes. Now, give me your hand."

Into her outstretched palm he placed a small box wrapped with a yellow velvet bow.

At the sight of it Melora's gold-flecked brown eyes shone with anticipation. As she lifted the lid, she caught her breath, and her mouth formed a perfect O. "Wyatt, it's lovely!" she gasped, carefully lifting out the exquisite pearl cameo nestled inside. Its thin gold chain glistened in the fading light. "I've never seen anything half as beautiful."

"I have." Wyatt tipped her chin up and gazed down at her, his expression so intent she felt her pulse begin to race. "Every time I look at you, Melora, I see the most beautiful treasure on earth."

Was there ever a sweeter, more wonderful man? Melora flushed with pleasure as he fastened the clasp for her. His touch was warm, sure, and gentle. She imagined those sure hands touching her tomorrow night in their hotel suite. Imagined them undressing her. And a warmth spread through her, filling her with anticipation.

Wyatt's smile was full and satisfied as he studied the cameo circling her throat. Pleasure gleamed in his piercing, deep blue eyes. "There now. It's not half as pretty as you are, honey, but as a little prewedding token of my affection, it'll do. Are you excited for tomorrow? All packed for the honeymoon, I hope."

"Actually, I have a little more to do. I've been working on the payroll . . . oh, let's not talk about it."

He sat down beside her on the log. His dark eyebrows drew together as he smoothed back a strand of her pale, silken hair that had fallen over one eye. "I hate to see you tiring yourself out and worrying endlessly about the ranch. After the wedding I'm going to take over for you."

"I can't ask that of you. The Weeping Willow's debts are my responsibility—" she began, but Wyatt cut her off, frowning, placing a finger against her lips.

"And you're my responsibility, Melora. Don't you trust me to straighten out your affairs?"

"Of course, I do!" Distressed at this very notion, Melora threw her arms around his neck. "It's not that at all! Wyatt, I just hate to bother you with my problems." She searched his face anxiously. "You've had your own share of troubles to deal with; the rustlers have been stealing from the Diamond X as well. And you have all your other businesses to keep track of."

Wyatt paid no heed at all to the squirrels chasing one another through the brush or to the purple darkness gathering around them. His vivid blue eyes fixed themselves upon her intently, and his voice was low and strong. "There's nothing more important to me than your happiness, Melora. Nothing. And I know you won't be happy if you lose the Weeping Willow. Believe me, honey, I'll do everything in my power to help save it for you."

Gratitude swelled within her. For so long she'd wrestled alone with the burden of keeping the ranch going. It still took some getting used to, the notion that she was going to have a husband who wanted to help her, a man whom she could depend on to stand by her and Jinx. Relief, gratitude, and love poured through her as she tightened her arms around Wyatt's neck and kissed him.

"Thank you, Wyatt. I promise not to dump all my problems in your lap, but I would appreciate some help. Some advice . . ."

"Whatever I can do." His lips nuzzled hers, warmly, excitingly. "We'll tackle all these problems right after the honeymoon. In the meantime," he told her, tracing a finger across her delicate jaw, "I don't want Mrs. Wyatt Holden worrying her head over matters that her husband can attend to."

It was so like Wyatt to want to shield her from any problem, any worry. As he drew her close, Melora reflected on how lucky she was to have found a man who was so perfect. Really, she decided as he kissed her again, Wyatt was almost too good to be true. . . .

She was in a happy daze by the time he left, and she floated upstairs to her pretty rose-papered room. *Tomorrow night, tomorrow night, I'll be a bride, tomorrow night.* The refrain ran through her mind all during her bath. She was humming as she patted herself dry with a towel, slipped into a gossamer white cotton nightdress, and began to brush her hair. She dipped and whirled before the mirror, admiring the delicate cameo still clasped about her throat and studying the way the low-cut nightdress clung to her curves. This was the last night she would sleep alone—the very last night. After this she and Wyatt would make love every single night, they would wake up in each other's arms, kissing, touching. . . .

She twirled toward the closet where her hatboxes were stacked, her heart light. She never saw the man who glided like a dark ghost through her open window; she didn't hear even a footfall until it was too late. . . .

CAPTIVE
by Joan Johnston

Praise for Joan Johnston's previous books:

"Fabulous . . . Powerful . . . Moving"
Romantic Times

"Tremendous . . . First rate . . . Highly recommended . . . Unforgettable"
Affaire de Coeur

"Sparkling characters . . . Dynamic dialogue . . . Delicious!"
Rendezvous

Joan Johnston, whose six previous Dell historical romances have won raves, returns in May 1996 with *Captive,* her seventh historical romance from Dell. It's set in Regency England, but it's not the usual game of mannered morality—especially with an American heroine who's got her work cut out for her trying to tame the beast that is her ward! Charlotte Edgerton and the Earl of Denbigh have more in common than the relation who left them to each other, but neither the southern belle nor the society gentleman can see beyond the other's unreasonableness until a moment of truth —and passion—opens their eyes.

Joan Johnston is a winner of the *Romantic Times* Best Western Author of the Year Award. Here's a taste of what's to come. Don't miss the rest of the fun!

How dare the Earl of Denbigh confine her! Charlotte had every intention of roaming the boundaries of the earl's estate whenever she pleased. Denbigh had no right to hold her captive in her room. She would never make the promises he was demanding in exchange for her freedom. Dress like a *lady*. Act like a *lady*. Talk like a *lady*. She would dress and act and talk just as she always had, and be damned to him.

She wasn't an English lady; she was an American. The guardian who had been appointed—mistakenly—in her father's will was wrong to try to force her into a mold she didn't fit. Like squeezing her feet into dainty satin slippers when leather riding boots would fit so much better. She liked wearing trousers. She liked riding astride. She liked saying exactly what was on her mind.

And what was wrong with the way she was? It had been fine for dear Papa. Oh, how she missed him! If only he had not taken ill and died. The earl wanted to change her only so he could marry her off and be rid of the onerous duty her father had laid upon him. He had no interest in "a spoiled chit of seventeen."

Charlotte didn't want to change. She didn't want to be married to some stuffy old English lord. She was going to plead one last time with Denbigh to spare her such a fate. If he refused to listen . . . she would simply have to run away.

Charlotte shoved open the door to the earl's study without knocking, intending to confront him—and gasped.

He sat on the edge of a claw-footed sofa, his dark head pressed against a reclining woman's naked bosom.

She stood frozen, her eyes riveted to the sight of his mouth releasing a damp rosy crest. "Milord," she whispered.

He rose like a hungry lion above its feast, his mane wild, his eyes feral, then viciously angry as they focused on her.

"Out!" he rasped. "Get out!"

She backed away, then turned and ran. But not back to her room, where he had ordered her to stay. Instead she headed out the front door—where she was forbidden to go—slamming the heavy portal defiantly behind her.